## *Savage Surrender*

Yasmin allowed the slave to massage the sweet-smelling cream into her sex as Rianna looked on, colouring with embarrassment. Yasmin lifted her hips and urged the slave's hand against her until she gave in to her climax. Determinedly Rianna concentrated on washing herself, pushing away the helping hands of the other slaves. Yasmin, pink-faced and happy, smiled at Rianna. 'Your upbringing has clearly denied you much pleasure,' she said.

'Life here is very different,' Rianna replied, wondering what other humiliations were in store for her.

# Savage Surrender

## DEANNA ASHFORD

BLACK
*lace*

Black Lace novels are sexual fantasies.
In real life, make sure you practise safe sex.

First published in 1998 by
Black Lace
332 Ladbroke Grove
London W10 5AH

Typeset by SetSystems Ltd, Saffron Walden, Essex
Printed and bound by Mackays of Chatham PLC

ISBN 0 352 33253 0

# Chapter One

*A* shaft of sunlight broke through the clouds, stream-ing in through the large, arched window at the far end of the great hall of the castle of Nort, home of Gerek, Protector of Harn. Golden rays pierced the gloomy interior, focusing on the raised dais in the centre of the great hall where a man and woman were standing.

'It is not possible,' Gerek, Protector of Harn said with controlled fury. 'I've told you that any number of times before.'

'So you have.' Rianna glared at her father, her green eyes full of defiance. 'But I refuse to accept that a woman cannot be named Protector of Harn. It is my birthright. I am your only child, yet you intend to name my spineless cousin, Otis, as your heir.'

'Because I have no other choice,' Gerek replied in frus-tration, high colour staining his weather-beaten cheeks. 'The law clearly states that the Protector must be a man.'

'Huh! Otis is no man,' Rianna sneered. 'He's a coward and a fool. Harn will not be safe in his hands.'

'Otis will be well advised by those that surround him. I have made sure of that.'

'But I would make a far better Protector.'

'Maybe so, Rianna,' Gerek agreed. 'But the law clearly states a woman cannot succeed.'

1

'Then change it!' she challenged.

Gerek sank on to his ornately carved throne. 'Nothing is that simple. Even if I wanted it, the people would never accept such a change. Centuries of tradition cannot be ignored. Here in Harn, men are warriors and masters, while women are homemakers and bearers of children.'

'But my mother was a warrior,' Rianna stormed, frustrated by his old-fashioned rigidity.

'And I respected Kitara's right to be a warrior – it was part of her heritage. But you are not your mother and you must defer to my wishes.'

'If only mother were still alive,' Rianna said sadly. 'She would make you see that I am right.'

'I would give everything I own to see your mother just once again. Nine years have passed since her death, but I still miss her.' Gerek's expression softened. 'You are so like her, my child.'

Rianna was the most beautiful woman in his kingdom. She was tall, almost as tall as Gerek, with long shapely limbs, and skin as pale and flawless as alabaster. Her large, green eyes dominated her heart-shaped face, their shimmering depths as beguiling as the deepest of forest pools. Long, luxuriant curls of a glorious golden-red framed her face, enhancing her delicate beauty. Rianna's striking looks turned the heads and stirred the loins of every man that laid eyes on her.

'Mother would never have made me marry a man I've never even met.'

'Your mother was well aware of the responsibilities that come with our position, Rianna. This alliance will ensure peace between Harn and Percheron. Your future husband is no ordinary man. Lord Sarin rules a land four times the size of Harn. He has a wealth and power I can never aspire to. Most women would be happy to be betrothed to him.'

Rianna proudly raised her head. 'But I am not most women. Only devotion to you and my loyalty to my country will send me to Percheron, nothing else.'

She had always known that her marriage would be

arranged, but expected to be allowed some choice in the matter of her future husband. That was before Lord Sarin had invaded a number of small principalities on the western borders of Percheron and Harn. If it had not been for her hasty betrothal, Harn might well have suffered a similar fate. Gerek's army could never withstand the military might of Percheron, and her marriage had been arranged many months ago. But the arrival yesterday of Chancellor Lesand, the personal representative of Lord Sarin, made her uncomfortably aware of what the future now held for her.

'I wish I could let you choose you own husband, Rianna. But I am sure you will grow fond of Sarin. Perhaps even one day you will come to love him as much as I loved your mother.' Gerek rose to his feet and moved to take Rianna in his arms, but she backed away from him.

'No, Father. Tender words of encouragement will not make me change my mind.'

'Neither will your protestations alter my position on this matter,' Gerek said harshly. 'In order to ensure the future safety of Harn, the marriage must go ahead. The final details will be settled and the marriage contract will be signed this very evening. In the circumstances, I suggest that you order the maidservants to begin packing. Chancellor Lesand wishes to depart before the end of the week.'

'Rianna! I have been looking for you,' Veba scolded, rising from her seat in the window embrasure just outside her charge's room. 'Where have you been?'

'In the stables,' Rianna replied. 'I was seeing to Freya. Joab, one of the stable-boys, says that she is off her food.' The pretty white mare had been a recent gift from her father, and Rianna loved her dearly. 'You worry too much, Veba.'

'Worry? Why not?' Veba seemed agitated. 'Look at the state of you, child. Your dress is filthy and your hair is a mess.'

3

'No matter, the gown is old.' Rianna glanced down; the hem of her dress was damp and muddied. 'I shall not be taking this garment with me. Father has provided me with many new gowns, and together with the ones –'

'Hush,' Veba interrupted. 'You should not tarry here. The Chancellor is waiting in your chamber.'

'In my chamber? For what reason?' Rianna frowned. 'Is that not a little improper?'

'It appears that a short ceremony has to be performed before the marriage contract can be signed,' Veba explained. 'Chancellor Lesand wishes no delay. He intends to carry out the ceremony as soon as possible.'

Rianna was bewildered. No mention had been made of any ceremony during all the discussions with the Chancellor and her father. 'Very well,' she said with an irritated sigh. Beckoning Veba to accompany her, Rianna pulled open the heavy oak door and stepped inside her room.

The stone walls of Rianna's chamber were hung with brightly coloured tapestries depicting the many flowers and animals of Harn. A number of large, cream sheepskins were sewn together to cover the cold stone flags. To the right, in an alcove set apart from the rest of the room, was a wooden four-poster bed, hung with lavish curtains of lemon brocade. There was little other furniture, only a couple of chairs and three carved oak chests which held most of Rianna's clothes.

'Lady Rianna,' greeted Chancellor Lesand as he rose with graceful elegance from the chair in front of the window. 'You have returned. I was becoming a little concerned.'

'I was not aware you were waiting for me, Chancellor. After talking to my father, I visited the stables. I am sorry if I kept you waiting longer than necessary.'

'It is I who should apologise,' Lesand smiled cautiously. 'I am intruding on your privacy, my lady.'

Rianna stifled her irritation at the intrusion. 'No matter, Chancellor. I understand you wish to perform some kind of ceremony?'

4

'Indeed,' he nodded gravely. 'It is a necessary pre-requisite to the marriage contract.'

'It is odd the matter was not mentioned to me before.' Rianna was very aware of the tangled state of her hair and shabbiness of her dress. Lesand had never seen her so ill-attired.

The Chancellor, as usual, looked immaculate in a long, blue velvet robe embroidered with gold. Although well past fifty, he was still an attractive man. Tall and slender, with a narrow face and rather prominent nose, he had the olive skin and dark hair that appeared prevalent among the men of Percheron. The soldiers who accompanied Lesand were all clean shaven, but he had a small, distinguished-looking, goatee beard.

Rianna found Lesand fascinating and so very different from all the other men she knew. Gerek and his courtiers never wore such elaborate garments or paid so much attention to their appearance, and the warriors of Harn did not pomade their hair or manicure their nails.

The Chancellor looked uneasy, perhaps even embarrassed. 'A regretful oversight, I assure you. The ceremony is necessary to the wedding contract.' He cleared his throat. 'The prospective bride must be examined to ensure she has no unsightly scars or defects. Also it is necessary to confirm that she has not been defiled by another man. Above all else, Sarin's bride must be a virgin.'

Rianna paled. 'Does my father know of these requirements?'

'He does,' Veba confirmed, moving to her side and gently taking hold of her arm. 'My child, most noblemen expect a virgin bride. It is not unusual for them to ask for it to be physically proven.'

'That is so,' Lesand added gravely.

The information did not make Rianna feel any better, but she knew she would have to submit to this indignity. Her father would never forgive her if she refused the examination; it was even likely he would insist it was carried out forcibly.

5

'And who will conduct this ceremony?' she asked, doing her best to hide her discomfort.

'I will,' Lesand acknowledged, inclining his head.

'You!' Rianna exclaimed, her eyes opening wide in surprise.

'Yes. The examination must be carried out by one of Lord Sarin's most trusted servants. Therefore, he has assigned me to the task.'

'But I thought only a woman . . .?'

'In the circumstances that is not possible,' Lesand replied with polite regret. 'I assure you my lady, it will pain me as much as it does you.'

'Then I have no choice?' Rianna's voice shook with emotion.

'Come, my sweet.' Veba tenderly led Rianna towards the bed as she whispered, 'You are the daughter of the Protector. You must submit to this examination with royal dignity.'

There was nothing dignified about this, Rianna thought heatedly.

While the Chancellor turned diplomatically towards the window to afford Rianna some privacy, Veba began to unlace the back of her gown. Once Rianna was naked, Veba helped her to lie down on the bed, then covered her with a white linen sheet.

'Courage,' Veba whispered. 'Bear your discomfort in silence. Most noble ladies have to endure this.'

'But not at the hands of a man, usually it is a midwife,' Rianna muttered.

Veba said nothing more, just walked over to the Chancellor and advised him that her mistress was ready. Ordering the nurse to stay by the window, Lesand stepped over to the bed, pointedly ignoring Rianna's expression of unease.

'I have told your maid she may remain as long as she does not interfere with my task,' Lesand said in a soft reassuring tone. 'Now please turn on to your stomach.'

Rianna rolled over, keeping a tight hold on the sheet. But there was little point in her display of modesty, for as soon as she was settled, Lesand pulled the sheet down to her feet, exposing the whole of her body to his view. She stiffened, pressing her face into her pillow. Her hands clenched at her sides. The Chancellor was examining her, looking for disfiguring blemishes or scars. The room was quite chilly, but Rianna felt hot with shame and embarrassment. She began to wish her body was less than perfect, that she had a birthmark or terrible scar. Then Lord Sarin would refuse to wed her and she could remain in Harn forever.

'You are beautiful, Lady Rianna.' He touched her back, running his fingers down the length of her spine until he reached the crack of her bottom. 'Your skin is as soft as the petal of a rose. My master will be well pleased with his bride.'

So far Rianna had managed to retain her composure. However, she could not hold back her gasp of horror as he pulled her buttocks apart, exposing her tiny nether mouth. The terrible intimacy made her want to shrink away from him, beg him to stop. She clenched her teeth, forcing herself to remain motionless while he stroked the small, puckered entrance to her anus. But then he pressed against the ring of flesh as if intending to force his finger inside. 'No,' Rianna gasped.

'Do not concern yourself,' Lesand said coolly. 'I have seen enough.' He removed his hands from her body. 'Now, please turn over so that I can complete my task.'

Reluctantly, Rianna rolled on to her back, knowing that her breasts and sex were now exposed to his view. She half-closed her eyes, peeping at him through her long lashes, while a crimson flush of humiliation stained her cheeks.

Lesand leant forward, touching her lightly on the shoulder. His fingers slid caressingly over her creamy skin. Moulding his palms to her contours, he cupped her breasts and squeezed her tender flesh. The feel of his cool hands was not entirely unpleasant, and when he touched her nipples, rubbing them with his fingertips

7

and plucking at the tiny nubs, they began to harden, growing into sensitive peaks.

'Your body was made for love,' he said huskily.

Rianna did not reply; she was too intent on steeling herself as his hands moved lower. He stroked her belly and ran his fingers through the red-gold curls at her pubis. Rianna swallowed, her mouth suddenly dry. Oddly enough the caressing touch had become almost pleasurable. She felt a sudden desire to relax completely, let her legs fall open and give herself up to the strange languor that was overtaking her limbs.

She gave a soft involuntary sigh as Lesand's hands slipped between her thighs. He cupped her sex, pressing against her vulva with the palm of his hand. Rianna's sex was hot, her pouting, pink lips swollen. He slid one finger into the warm moist opening, and stroked the soft inner flesh. As Lesand began to explore her secret valley, the heat of her embarrassment was replaced by another, more fiery warmth, deep within her belly. Gradually the compelling motion of his fingers became more and more enticing.

Rianna clenched her hands at her sides feeling confused by the amazing sensations that were building inside her. She no longer knew for certain if she wanted Chancellor Lesand to finish or continue.

'Part your legs wide, then bend your knees and lift your hips towards me,' he commanded.

Modesty overcame her again. She forced her limbs to move, her legs trembling as she did as she was ordered. The most secret parts of herself were being revealed to a virtual stranger. An unfamiliar moisture filled her sex and she prayed that Chancellor Lesand would not detect her body's strange response to his touch.

'Don't be afraid, this will not hurt.' Lesand took a small porcelain jar from his pocket and dipped his finger in the sweet smelling oil contained within the pot.

Rianna tensed, biting her lip as she watched Lesand lean forward. He carefully peeled apart her swollen sex lips to inspect the deep pink flesh within. Moving his fingers along the valley he anointed it with the aromatic oil. The viscous liquid coated her secret flesh, polishing it to perfection. His oiled fingers delicately brushed the tip of her clitoris, the touch as gentle as a butterfly's wing. The sensation was exquisite, and sent a thousand bowstrings reverberating through her body. Rianna shivered and unconsciously pushed her hips up towards him.

She heard Lesand make a sound from deep in his throat as his fingers circled the delicate bud. He stroked the tiny nubbin, then squeezed it gently and she jerked her legs in surprise. Why did she gain such immense pleasure when he touched that one small portion of her body? An unfamiliar, aching tightness was growing inside her that begged for release.

Suddenly, to her consternation, Lesand's attention moved away from the bud. She wanted to cry out and beg him to continue touching the tender spot, as the tiny, throbbing nubbin wept for his touch. Determinedly she held back her moan of disappointment and stayed silent, cursing her body's lewd immodesty.

She had known all along why Lesand was examining her, but she still tensed in surprise when he began to massage the tight ring of flesh that protected her womanly sheath. It gradually began to soften and relax, enabling him to slide two fingers deep inside her.

Soon his searching fingers discovered the fine membrane of her virginity. 'You are fortunate that the proof of your chastity is intact, my lady,' he said with a faint smile. 'I hear that you are a great horsewoman. Exercise can often damage such a fragile barrier of flesh.'

Rianna expected him to withdraw his fingers from her at once, but they lingered inside her, gently stroking the velvety walls. She shuddered, relishing the unexpected enjoyment the intimate caresses were invoking deep within her feminine parts. Her inner flesh rippled with excited pleasure, and of their own accord, her hips began to move in an accompanying rhythm. The stretching and stroking sensations were leading her upwards towards the brink of something wonderful and unknown. Just as she was about to reach the summit, Lesand gently eased his fingers from her body, leaving her moist, throbbing and wanting. He looked down at her, a calm, unreadable expression on his face. Rianna blushed and clamped her legs together, feeling confused by her unbidden response and inwardly bewailing her unseemly behaviour.

'I regret I had to be so intrusive,' Lesand said apologetically. Pressing her legs down on the bed, he covered her trembling body with the sheet. 'Lord Sarin ordered me to gauge your sensitivity to matters of a sensual nature. Being a man of Epicurean tastes, he wishes to be assured that his bride will be a willing partner in the pleasures of the flesh.'

'Maybe so, Chancellor,' she said in an icy tone, her mind in total turmoil. 'But now this is at an end, I would be obliged if you would depart. I wish to be alone.'

Gerek strode into his bedchamber. Sunlight streamed in through the two, deep-set window alcoves, one each side of the large fireplace, the hearth of which was empty as the spring weather was uncommonly mild. Dominating the room was a large four-poster bed, with thick, red velvet bed curtains that could be tightly drawn in the chill of winter. A matching red velvet spread covered the bed, and thrown across the top was a skin of creamy white fur. No one Gerek knew had ever laid eyes on such a pelt. Kitara had purchased it from a travelling merchant who claimed it came from a rare white bear that only lived in the frozen wastes of the far north, well beyond the borders of Harn. Other skins, mostly wolf or brown bear, were scattered upon the floor, almost totally concealing the cold stone slabs.

Gerek shrugged off his leather jerkin, dropped it on the floor and sat down on the bed. He had never met Sarin, but knew him to be a firm, sometimes brutal monarch, who ruled Percheron with an iron hand. However, he was also a patron of the arts, and worshipped beauty above all else. Gerek was certain that Rianna's loveliness would win his heart and perhaps in time Rianna would come to care for Sarin.

He wondered if Kitara would have agreed with his decision. Would she have been prepared to sacrifice her daughter for the good of Harn? Even now, after all these years, he still missed Kitara. He only had to close his eyes to conjure up a vision of her wondrous beauty. Her musky feminine scent had driven him wild with desire every time he had been close to her. After her loss he'd spent many hours just lying on his bed, holding her garments close, comforted by the lingering smell of her. But that sweet scent had long since faded from her belongings.

A vision of Kitara in all her naked glory filled his mind; long firm limbs, sleek hips, and a waist so narrow he could span it with his hands. Her breasts had been perfection itself, full and uptilted, tipped by dark brown nipples that begged for the touch of his lips.

Gerek sat down on his bed, his mind consumed by thoughts of Kitara. He would have given everything he possessed to once again touch the soft curve of her belly and the sun-kissed red fleece of her sex. His fingers ached to explore the secret pink crevices between her shapely thighs, to feel the moist welcoming warmth as he plunged his manhood into her again and again, while she begged him to move harder and faster.

He groaned softly as the familiar heat of desire flooded his belly, forcing blood into his groin and filling his flesh until it expanded and grew firmer. His penis began to throb insistently, pressing against the constricting leather of his breeches. Gerek savoured the pleasure ache of his arousal, enmeshed in dreams of his lost love.

His private thoughts were interrupted by a cautious knock on his door.

'Enter,' he growled, irritated by the intrusion.

'My lord,' said a nervous-looking page as he entered the room. 'Chancellor Lesand bade me bring you this.' The page moved cautiously towards the bed. He was carrying a large pewter tray on which reposed a heavy green bottle and a silver goblet. 'Wine from Lord Sarin's vineyard.'

'Pour me some.' This was a rare treat for Gerek; usually he drank ale or mead, both of which were produced locally. There were no vineyards in Harn, as the weather was too inclement, so wine was uncommonly expensive and only drunk on special occasions.

He watched the page place the tray on a carved oak table and carefully pour a generous measure of wine into the goblet. 'Bring it here,' Gerek ordered.

'My lord.' The page carried the goblet over to the bed, his hand shaking slightly as he handed it to Gerek.

Gerek took a large gulp of the rich red wine, feeling its smooth warmth slide down to his stomach. It tasted good, of warm sunshine and ripe summer fruit. 'A fine wine. Send my thanks to the Chancellor. Your name, boy?'

'Adan, my lord,' the page stuttered.

'Adan, I wish you to seek out the maidservant known as Jenna. It is likely you will find her in the sewing room at this time of the day. Bid her come to me.'

'Yes, my lord,' Adan replied.

'And hurry, boy,' Gerek growled.

After Adan departed, Gerek drained the goblet in a few gulps and let it drop to the floor. Of all the castle maidservants who regularly shared his bed, Jenna was his favourite. She wasn't exceptionally beautiful or fine of figure, but she had a wild uninhibited approach to lovemaking that pleased Gerek. The other maidservants just lay there and let him do what he wanted. Jenna, on the other hand, took the initiative and guided his pleasure to even greater heights.

The wine increased the fire in his loins, and Gerek shifted position, easing the tight leather of his breeches away from his swollen shaft. Doubtless Jenna would not take long in coming to him, as she was always ready and eager for sex whatever time of day or night he sent for her.

He listened to the familiar sounds drifting in through

the open windows; the idle chatter of servants, the clatter of horses' hooves on the cobblestones, and the distant clash of metal upon metal as his men-at-arms practised their swordplay. Life in Harn was good, he reflected. He had a comfortable home, food in his belly, servants to do his bidding, and a number of willing wenches to share his bed.

Moments later, Jenna entered the room breathless from running, her cheeks flushed, her hair awry.

'Protector,' she smiled. 'You sent for me?'

'I have need of you.' Gerek hoped Jenna's passions would help him forget his concerns for Rianna's future. It mattered not how bad he felt, he told himself, her fate was set and there was nothing he could do to change it. 'Come here and take off my boots,' he ordered.

Jenna stepped forward, and knelt to ease off Gerek's long leather boots. The first slid off easily, but the other proved more difficult. She turned her back to him, knelt astride his lower leg and closed her sturdy thighs. Gerek braced his bare foot against one cheek of her round bottom, while she pulled at the heel of the boot. The boot seemed reluctant to forsake Gerek's leg, but eventually it came off, leaving his foot still between her thighs. With a husky laugh he pressed it upwards, trying to rub her crotch through the thick worsted of her skirt.

'What is your desire now, lord?' she asked as she rose to face him.

'Need you ask?' He grinned wickedly. 'Remove your dress.'

Jenna's work-roughened fingers reached for the small bone buttons at the front of her blue wool gown. Usually she took her time, unfastening them slowly and seductively in order to heighten his arousal. Today, she seemed eager to be rid of the garment. She pulled her bodice apart, ripping the buttons from their fabric loops, heedless of the damage to her gown.

Jenna never bothered with undergarments, and her large breasts spilt temptingly from the opening. They jiggled slightly as she unfastened the rest of the buttons to reveal her softly curving stomach. Thick curly brown hair, even darker than the hair on her head, covered her mound. It brushed the juncture of her thighs, which she kept firmly pressed together. Gerek knew what delights she was concealing; her secret flesh was rosy and inviting, the colour deepening when she was fully aroused.

The other maidservants smelt of soap and little else. Jenna, however, always smelt of spring flowers and fragrant herbs. Many times she had fed him some strange concoction brewed from herbs to help enhance their lovemaking. Jenna's mother was a midwife and healer, as her mother before her had been, but Jenna's interest in herbs extended no further than their use in prolonging pleasure. Once, she had rubbed a handful of strange leaves all over his penis. The skin had stung and his shaft had become so hard it had felt as it might burst. It had remained erect for hours and hours, and they had made love all night.

Jenna let her dress drop to the floor and slipped off her sandals. Her breasts were full and pear-shaped, the tips drawn out somewhat and ending in large reddish nipples, surrounded by aureoles of a deeper reddish brown.

'Loosen your hair,' Gerek said hungrily, as the fire in his loins increased.

She lifted her hands to unpin her long hair. As she strained her arms upwards, her breasts were raised high on her ribcage, making them appear even fuller and more rounded than usual. The skin tightened and her nipples swelled provocatively, turning into two firm cones, begging to be touched.

The small dark tufts of hair in her armpits were revealed, and Gerek recalled how Lesand had told him that, in Percheron, women believed such hair unattractive and removed it from their bodies. He wondered what Jenna would looked like totally denuded. When she opened her legs, the swollen pink lips of her sex would be easily visible; such a sight he would find immensely arousing.

Hairpins scattered across the floor as Jenna shook her head and her long hair cascaded down over her shoulders and back. Strands of hair fell over her breasts, almost covering them, apart from two hard nubbins peeping enticingly through the brown curls.

Gerek went to unfasten the ties that held his white linen shirt together. 'No, lord. Let me attend to that.' Leaning forward Jenna pushed his hands away.

Letting his arms fall limply to his sides, Gerek watched Jenna undo the knotted fastenings. Her hair fell forward, sweetly scented strands brushing his cheeks, while her voluptuous breasts jiggled enticingly in front of his eyes. He could not resist touching one, cupping the generous globe in his palm and feeling its weight. He squeezed the soft flesh, hearing her indrawn hiss of pleasure as he began to knead it gently.

Gerek's hands were toughened by many years of training with the sword, axe and bow. The tips of his fingers were now as hard as old leather. He rubbed the pad of his thumb over her nipple, grazing the sensitive nub which grew in size, jutting out obscenely. He milked the tiny teat, rolling it between his fingers. Jenna quivered with pleasure and gave a breathy moan. Straining his head forward, Gerek went to pull the nipple into his mouth.

'Not yet,' Jenna implored. 'Let me undress you first, my lord.' She pressed her palm down hard on the mound at his groin.

'Hurry!' he groaned as his pleasure ache increased. His cock throbbed excitedly, the swollen end pulsing, but it could grow no bigger, confined as it was by the tight leather.

Smiling, Jenna removed her hand. 'Not too quickly,' she whispered huskily.

She eased off his linen shirt to reveal his broad, well-muscled chest. His skin was deeply tanned and marked by scars from wounds received in battle. A thick mat of crisp brown curls covered his chest, descending in an arrow towards his flat belly. Sinking to her knees, she

15

ran her hands through the springy hair, caressing the raised ridges of his many scars. His iron-hard stomach was banded by a wide leather belt. Jenna fumbled with the ornate silver buckle, struggling to unfasten it, but her eyes kept straying to the swollen mound of his sex where the soft brown leather of his breeches was stretched drum-tight over the engorged flesh.

Gerek groaned, his senses aroused to fever pitch. The musky scent of desire seeped from Jenna's body, and he could hardly bear to wait a moment longer; his sex screamed out for the touch of her lips and fingers.

'I can see your need is urgent.' Jenna unfastened the buckle, letting the belt drop to his sides, then she tugged at the laces of his breeches. The thin cords became tangled as she tried to unfasten them. She cursed under her breath and pulled harder, snapping one of the cords in her eagerness to release Gerek's phallus from its confinement.

At last the laces gave way, allowing her to pull his breeches apart. Gerek's engorged cock reared out of the opening. The stem was rigid, the bulb at the top hard and a dark purplish red, while a tiny bead of moisture dangled like an enticing dewdrop from the narrow mouth at its tip.

'Pleasure me, now,' Gerek demanded.

Jenna licked her lips, pleased with his swift arousal. Almost three weeks had passed since he had last sent for her, and she'd begun to think he was tiring of her company. She comforted herself with the thought that he had sent for no other maidservant and slept alone, eventually convincing herself that his lack of desire was only caused by his concern over the imminent marriage of the Lady Rianna.

'Yes, lord,' she said softly, as Gerek raised his arms above his head. The muscles in his chest stretched, his belly tightened, and his penis jutted upwards even higher.

The sight of him dressed only in the form-fitting

leather breeches with his sex exposed was powerfully erotic, adding an extra facet to Jenna's pleasure. Trembling in her eagerness, she jerked his breeches apart even more, pulling the tight leather away from the base of his cock. It reared from its bed of pubic hair, which was much thicker and coarser than that on his chest. Gently she eased his soft seed sac from its hiding place. Every month that he bedded her, she hoped that one of his seeds would take root within her body and grow into the son Gerek had always desired, but her prayers had remained unanswered.

Placing her hands on his thighs, Jenna pushed his legs apart as wide as they would comfortably stretch and stepped between them. She leant her head forward, allowing her long hair to fall across his chest and belly, so that with every movement of her head the soft strands would tantalisingly stroke his flesh.

First, she just touched the rigid shaft, gauging his readiness for fulfilment. The skin was tight, but not as yet taut as it could be. When it was fully engorged the surface was stretched so hard that the skin turned smooth and shiny. Curving her hand around the base, just above the root, she began to pump up and down, moving only half a finger length at first, not wanting to bring him to a climax too swiftly. With slow precision she slid her hand higher, until she was milking the shaft in a smooth erotic rhythm.

Gerek's eyes closed, and his mouth parted in a series of breathy moans. He rolled his head from side to side. 'Yes, oh, yes,' he groaned.

His penis grew iron-hard, while the tiny bead of moisture at its mouth elongated and increased in size. Eventually it became too heavy to remain where it was, and rolled slowly down the side of the head. Jenna stopped it with her finger, rubbing the salty moisture all over the domed tip.

Gerek shuddered, his stomach muscles trembling. 'Pump harder,' he grunted through gritted teeth, pushing his hips up towards Jenna. 'My need is great. I have denied my body for too long.'

'For far too long,' Jenna replied huskily.

Lifting the seed sac, she gently stroked the velvety skin. The sac had increased in size, the balls it contained hardening into two firm stones. Employing just the tip of her tongue she licked his sex head. When it was shiny with her saliva she pursed her lips and slid them smoothly over the glans. She began to suck, pulling at the inflamed flesh, running her tongue around the rim until she heard him groan softly again.

With one hand she pumped the shaft, while the other stroked the root of his sex, the bag of his testicles, and the tender ridge of skin just behind it. She slid her lips further down the stem, taking more and more of it into her mouth, until the head of his cock hit the back of her throat.

Gerek stretched his body, arching his back and pushing his hip upwards, trying to force all of the stem into her mouth. Jenna accommodated as much of his shaft as she could, while she squeezed her thighs together. The heat of her own desire was throbbing richly inside her sex. She was still savouring the sensation when she felt Gerek's organ pulse and his muscles tense. She acted swiftly. Pulling his penis from her mouth, she placed her thumb on one side of the rim of his cock head and two fingers the other side, then she pressed them hard together for a few seconds.

'What!' Gerek gasped, opening his eyes.

Jenna knew his urge to ejaculate had vanished. Almost simultaneously his erection began to subside. Grey eyes, which had been glazed with pleasure, hardened in fury. 'Forgive me, lord. You will recover in a moment,' Jenna said, scared by his sudden anger. 'I just wanted to extend your pleasure, and prevent you from finishing too swiftly.'

'Wench, you forget yourself,' he growled. But he made no attempt to push her away as she ran her fingers over his gradually softening organ. Jenna took that as a sign he was willing to overlook her audacious actions and wanted her to continue.

'Let me show you,' she whispered, touching the wrinkled skin of his shaft with the tip of her tongue. She began to lick its entire length, employing long leisurely strokes, while her hands caressed his chest and played with his nipples, squeezing and pinching the tender buds.

Jenna's moist warm tongue lapping at his penis, and the growing ache in his nipples soon served to excite Gerek and revive his arousal. He drew in his breath. 'Do not presume to do such a thing again without my permission,' he warned, but it was obvious that his anger was slipping away as his desire began to grow once more.

His cock, glistening with her saliva, stirred. Life flooded back into Gerek's flaccid flesh. The shaft began to harden, slowly growing rigid again. Jenna pressed gentle kisses on the stem, watching the skin gradually stretch into tautness, and the bulb swell until it was firm and shiny. His cock reared into the air, straight and proud, whereupon Jenna began to smack it around the root using just the pads of her fingers. The colour of the stem deepened to a rich red, while the plum turned a darker purple. With each rhythmic smack, it jerked in unison, the skin stretching back so tight that it looked ready to burst.

Gerek's muscles were hard and knotted, the tendons in his neck stood out, and sweat beaded his brow. He groaned imploringly, making Jenna shiver with pleasure, the heat in her belly growing stronger and stronger. Her only desire now was to be impaled on his thick shaft of flesh and to feel its thrusting deep inside her vagina. Moisture seeped hungrily from her sex, contributing to the increasing stickiness between her legs.

'Let me feel you inside me,' she begged. 'It has been so long since I have been filled with your manhood. My body aches for the joy of it.'

19

'Wilful whore,' Gerek said harshly as he pulled her towards him, lifting her body atop his.

Jenna eased her hips downwards until the tip of Gerek's penis slid into the opening of her honey pot. She then slowly sheathed herself on his sex, pushing down until he filled her completely and the head of his cock nudged the neck of her womb. Jenna sighed contentedly as his body stretched and filled her secret flesh.

The wooden frame of the bed creaked as Jenna lifted her hips until almost the entire length of his slick shaft was revealed, then she plunged her body down again, grinding her pelvis against his.

Gerek groaned and dug his fingers harder into the soft flesh of Jenna's waist as he felt her vagina tighten. She began to wildly pump herself up and down on his phallus in a frenzied dance of seduction. Soon her face was flushed, and her body wet with perspiration. At each thrust, she rotated her hips and arched her back. Gerek found the contrast in pressure highly erotic as his cock followed the movements of her silken sheath.

The musky odour of her pleasure filled Gerek's nostrils. He inhaled the sharp scent, his fingers straying towards the crack in her bottom. With each welcoming movement he pulled the fleshy globes further apart, the rough pads of his fingertips grazing her sensitive inner flesh.

Jenna's excitement increased. Her body jerked, and her breasts bounced up and down in front of his eyes. Juices flowed from her vagina, generously coating Gerek's phallus, and contributing to the soft sucking sounds of flesh upon flesh. She ground her pelvis against Gerek's, lifting herself to repeat the frenzied movement again and again.

Lost in his own haze of pleasure, Gerek was barely aware that his thumbs were pulling at the ring of skin that guarded Jenna's bottom mouth. The tip of one ragged nail scraped the sensitive barrier, making Jenna gasp with wanton bliss. Her vagina throbbed, milking

Gerek's engorged shaft. He lost control completely, his cock pulsing as the seed surged from his body. Pleasure came to them both in wave upon wave, taking them over the summit and into the chasm of ecstasy.

Rianna lay on her back, looking up at the sky. When she was younger she had spent hours staring at the clouds, seeing in them the shapes of dragons and other mythical creatures. But she was in no mood for such flights of fancy today.

After Lesand left, she had not allowed herself to spend time wallowing in misery. Instead, she'd changed into the breeches and jerkin she always wore for riding, and run straight to the stables where Joab had Freya waiting for her. She had ridden to this clearing in the woods at the base of the hill on which the castle of Nort stood. Just behind her was a small wooden hut which her father had built with his own hands. Gerek and Kitara had come here when they wanted to get away from the pressure of royal life. Now it was derelict and abandoned, and only Rianna came to this secret place.

Masses of bluebells carpeted the leafy glade, filling the air with the smell of spring. Rianna sighed – she would miss the contrasting seasons they had in Harn. Percheron lay in the far south and it was warm all the year round.

When she first met Chancellor Lesand, he had told her of the luxurious life that awaited her in Percheron. The castle of Nort was tiny compared to Lord Sarin's marble palace, with its miles of corridors and hundreds of elaborately decorated, high-ceilinged rooms.

And what of her bridegroom, Lord Sarin? She reached into the pocket of her jerkin to pull out the miniature Chancellor Lesand had given her. It was oval in shape, a little bigger than a hen's egg, and surrounded by a gold frame studded with precious stones. She stared at the portrait, trying to seek out the true measure of her future husband. He was undeniably handsome, with striking, rather angular features, olive skin, jet black hair, and dark piercing eyes. There was a coldness to the set of his thin-lipped mouth that she found oddly compelling, but also a little unnerving. Soon she would share a bed with this man, and be obliged to submit to his sexual demands.

Yesterday, Veba, her elderly nurse, had spoken at some length about the duties of a wife. Rianna had listened carefully, finding it strange that Veba had mentioned nothing about the physical side of marriage. Rianna was not a total innocent, she had watched stallions mate with mares. It had always seemed reasonable to conclude that a coupling between a man and a woman was much the same – a hasty, rather uncomfortable event that had to be endured. But since the humiliating examination by Chancellor Lesand, Rianna had been forced to reassess her opinions. When Lesand touched her secret feminine parts, Rianna had found the experience surprisingly pleasurable. The contact aroused strange desires and filled her head with visions she did not yet understand. She found herself looking at Joab in a different light when she spoke to him in the stables a short while ago. Never before had she realised how attractive he was, how broad his shoulders were, and how tightly his breeches clung to his sturdy thighs. She noticed that the bulge at his crotch was enticingly large, and for a moment she paused to wonder what he would look like unclothed.

Even riding here on Freya felt different. The smooth movements of the mare, and the feel of the hard saddle pressing against her sex had rekindled the strange heat in her groin. Perhaps lovemaking with her husband would turn out to be a most pleasurable experience.

Rianna shivered and turned on to her stomach, still staring at the portrait of Sarin. Her breasts felt fuller and heavier than before, and she was left wanting, craving the feel of hard male hands caressing her body. She wished she was more knowledgeable about what went on in the marriage bed. If only her mother was here to advise her, life would be so much simpler and far less daunting.

# Chapter Two

*L*eaving the noise and warmth of the great hall behind him, Gerek stepped into the wide, rather chilly, passage that led to his private quarters. He was angry; the evening meal had been an uncomfortable experience, mainly because Rianna had barely spoken and had totally ignored Chancellor Lesand.

As soon as the meal ended, Rianna excused herself, claiming she was weary and intended to retire to her bed. Once she had departed, Gerek apologised profusely for his daughter's unseemly behaviour. However, Chancellor Lesand insisted the apology was unnecessary, saying he could understand that Lady Rianna was upset and embarrassed by the undignified examination she had been forced to endure. Nevertheless, that did not make Gerek feel any better; in many ways Rianna was far too wilful for her own good.

The corridor bore left, following the line of the castle walls. One of the wall lanterns lighting the way had gone out, leaving the corridor just ahead of Gerek in almost total darkness. He frowned, irritated by the servants' neglect; one man was assigned just to keep the corridor lanterns alight.

Suddenly he saw a movement in the shadows. His hand flew to his dagger. 'Who goes there?' he asked harshly.

'It is I.' A figure stepped from the darkness.

'Jenna!' Gerek exclaimed. 'What are you doing here? You should be with the Lady Rianna, helping her prepare for her journey to Percheron.'

'She dismissed me. The noble lady has no more need of my services this evening.'

Jenna moved closer to Gerek. Her face looked pale in the flickering light of the distant lanterns. She was wearing a dark, hooded cloak. Gerek frowned; it was odd to see her dressed in such a manner. Only in the depths of winter was it necessary to wear such garments indoors. It was a chilly night, but not that cold.

'Then you best retire to your bed with the other maidservants,' Gerek said curtly. 'I am in no mood for company tonight.'

'Perchance you are in the mood for this!' She pulled apart her cloak, beneath which she was totally naked.

'Ye gods!' Gerek exclaimed.

'Do you not like what you see?' Jenna asked, letting the cloak fall to the stone-flagged floor.

Gerek stared at Jenna in astonishment as she ran her hands over her lush curves, lewdly outlining her breasts before trailing her fingers downwards to stroke the soft brown curls at her pubis. 'You forget yourself, wench.'

Gerek disapproved of her forward behaviour, yet he could not tear his gaze from her body. His belly tightened as he admired her pale body, the most intimate parts of it half-hidden by dark beguiling shadows of the night.

'Forget myself,' Jenna repeated. Smiling, she lifted her hands to cup her full breasts, holding them out to him. The nipples were firm, teased to a point by the chill night air. 'Do you not find the sight of these pleasurable?'

Gerek didn't know whether to admonish her or throw her to the floor and take her with unbridled lust. Her actions tonight reminded him of Kitara. In times long past, when he and his wife had met in some secluded area of the castle, they had often taken the opportunity to slake their desire for each other, their coupling made even more exciting because a servant or man-at-arms could come upon them at any moment.

'What foolishness is this?' he asked, his voice husky with restrained passion.

'Foolish I may be, lord.' She gave a soft laugh. 'But you still desire me, and I you.' Opening her thighs, she boldly stroked her sex. 'See how moist my pudenda is already. I long to feel your magnificent cock thrusting deep inside me.'

Gerek grabbed hold of her and pushed her against the stone wall of the corridor. 'I am the master here,' he growled. 'I decide when and where I take you.'

'Then decide,' she challenged with surprising boldness. Pressing her hand on the fustian covering his groin, she felt the hardness of the engorged rod that lay against his belly. 'Whatever you say, you cannot deny that you want me.'

'My anger is aroused, not my lust,' he grated.

'They seem much the same to me.' She grasped him harder, moving the rough fabric so that it grazed his sensitive male flesh.

Gerek groaned, and grabbed hold of her breasts, roughly massaging the creamy globes. She gasped with painful pleasure as he cruelly squeezed her nipples.

'Take me,' she pleaded.

Gerek cursed under his breath, staring at her with cold dark eyes. 'You try my patience, Jenna.'

'Do anything you want to me, master.' She winced but did not complain as he pinched her nipples even harder.

'Anything?' He slapped the undersides of her breasts. 'Even chastise you?'

'If you desire it.' He slapped her breasts again and she shivered, revelling in the spiked pleasure.

Gerek knew that he should tell her to be gone, order her back to the maids' quarters, but his desire was aroused. His penis throbbed, jumping in anticipation as he envisaged taking her here and now. The fiery heat in his loins would not be easily extinguished. If he dismissed her now he would not rest easy tonight.

He pressed his body hard against hers. The metal studs of his doublet scratched her breasts, and the rough stones of the wall dug into her naked back. Gerek ground his engorged groin against her belly, forcing her buttock cheeks apart, allowing the rough stone wall to chafe her sensitive inner flesh. Jenna appeared to welcome the discomfort as she squirmed excitedly against Gerek.

'My body burns for you, Protector,' she moaned.

A pool of oily lust speared Gerek's belly. 'Greedy whore,' he muttered.

Capturing her mouth, he kissed her with desperate urgency, and boldly, she responded. Their tongues entwined and began to move in an erotic dance of mutual passion.

Pulling back a little, Gerek slid his hand between their bodies, seeking the fastening of his breeches. His cock was iron hard, and in his eagerness he snapped the cords holding the fustian together. The fabric parted and his engorged penis reared out of the opening.

'Never have I seen one so huge,' she whispered hungrily.

'Are you well versed in such matters?' Gerek grated. The stones of the wall grazed the back of his hands as he cupped her buttocks and parted her fleshy globes. Roughly, he pressed his index finger against her nether mouth, invading the ring of tight muscle.

'Oh, yes.' Jenna shivered. 'Push it deeper,' she begged.

As he pushed his finger deeper inside her, she grabbed hold of his member, curving her fingers around the rigid shaft. 'Wanton bitch,' he grunted.

She gave a soft laugh, and rubbed her hand up and down Gerek's cock, until he felt as if it might explode. Unable to wait any longer, he eased his finger from her anus. Planting his feet slightly apart, he braced himself. Then, with his large hands cupping her buttocks, he lifted her.

The head of his erect phallus beat urgently against the brown thatch of her maidenhair. Grabbing hold of his shoulders, Jenna lifted herself just a fraction higher and his penis slipped easily between her thighs. Gerek dug his fingers into her buttocks, as he jerked his pelvis forward, entering her with one deft stroke. She twined her legs around his hips, eager to increase the depth of his penetration. Immediately he thrust harder, jamming his pelvis against hers until his cock head nudged the neck of her womb.

Jenna's hot moist flesh clung to his shaft, desperate to suck the very life essence from Gerek's body as he thrust into her again and again. She gasped with pleasure as his movements became fiercer. Gerek pushed her back hard against the stone wall, his weight driving almost all the breath from her body. Overcome by her mounting bliss, she was oblivious to the cold air brushing her flesh and the sharp stones digging into her skin.

With one final thrust Gerek climaxed, the pulsing pleasure draining him completely. The strong sensations died away, leaving him weak and near helpless. He leant limply against her, his legs trembling slightly.

'Lord,' she whispered. 'Did I please you?'

Gerek did not reply. Straightening, he took a deep breath, then lowered her to the floor. 'Be off to your quarters, wench.'

'But, my lord . . .' Jenna put her hand on his arm. 'I am not yet finished. A few moments more of your attention is all I need.'

Roughly, Gerek pushed her away, and began to ease his flaccid penis back into his breeches. 'That is not my concern. I took you for my pleasure, not yours.'

Jenna touched her hot, swollen sex. 'Please,' she whimpered. 'Do not dismiss me like this. My body screams for the touch of your hand.'

'Then that will be the punishment I promised you, Jenna,' he replied coldly.

Tears of frustration filled her eyes. 'I know I was wrong, but I only wanted to please you, lord. Don't leave me unfulfilled.'

'If you are that desperate, then I suggest you go to the guard room. Tell them I sent you. Any one of my men-at-arms will be happy to pleasure you until you beg for mercy.' Gerek said cruelly, wanting to impress upon Jenna that she should never act in so forward a manner again. Turning away from her, he strode along the corridor towards his private quarters.

'This journey seems endless,' Rianna grumbled as she stared out of the window of her conveyance. All she could see was mile upon mile of flat uninteresting grassland stretched out either side of the road.

They'd left the castle of Nort almost five days ago, and for the last two days they'd been traversing the southern plains of Harn, which were virtually uninhabited as the soil was unsuitable for cultivating crops.

To ensure Rianna's comfort on the long journey to Percheron, Lord Sarin had arranged for a special conveyance to be constructed. A tiny house had been built atop a flat bedded wagon, containing both travelling and sleeping quarters for his bride. The house was a little cramped but luxuriously appointed, with a bed for Rianna, a folding bed for her maid, and padded benches to sit upon while on the road.

'We have many days of travel ahead of us, my lady,' Jenna said in a suspiciously sulky tone.

Veba had fallen ill just before their departure and was deemed too unwell to travel. Gerek had asked Jenna to travel in Veba's place. In the normal course of events Jenna would have been honoured to become the Lady Rianna's personal maid, but she had made it clear she had no wish to leave Gerek. Angered by her pleading words, Gerek had bluntly ordered Jenna to accompany Rianna, insisting that there was no one else he could trust to care for his daughter.

'Far too many, Jenna.' Rianna peered out of the window, curious to know why her conveyance had come to an unexpected halt. 'I wonder why we've stopped. It is too early for the noonday meal.'

'Doubtless we'll be moving again soon,' Jenna replied distractedly.

'I will have no more of this.' Jumping to her feet, Rianna moved to the rear of their wagon. 'I will ride for a while. It will be good to have some fresh air, as I am unused to being so confined.'

Pushing open the door, Rianna sprang on to the rough road, which was little more than a track of hard-packed earth. She soon spied the reason for their unexpected stop: behind her conveyance was a wagon piled high with baggage; some of the contents had worked loose, and servants were clustered around the wagon trying to secure the load.

'My lady, is something amiss?' A sallow-faced youth, one of the servants from Percheron assigned to wait upon her, approached and bowed respectfully.

'Have my horse saddled. I wish to ride for a while.'

'Chancellor Lesand has not issued orders allowing you to ride, Lady Rianna. It would be safer for you to remain inside your wagon,' the youth stuttered.

Rianna frowned and tapped her foot impatiently. 'Do you dare to question my orders?'

'No, my lady.' He bowed again and added ingratiatingly, 'I will have your horse saddled immediately.'

As he left to do her bidding, Rianna took a deep breath and looked around her. The day was warm, with a slight breeze moving the sweet-scented air. The grass was a lush green, spreading as far as she could see, but in the far distance she could see a range of mountains, their high peaks reaching up to the clear blue sky.

She thought of her father, as she had often these past few days. She missed him desperately. Her unhappy musings were interrupted by a familiar whinny. Glancing in the direction of the sound, she saw the servant leading Freya towards her. The mare seemed restive; she had not been ridden since the day before they had left the Castle of Nort. Freya wore one of Rianna's favourite gifts from Sarin, a saddle and reins of tooled red leather, liberally decorated with gold.

'It appears we are both impatient for our freedom.'

Rianna patted the mare's nose. 'A long gallop will do us both good.'

She sprang lithely into the saddle, arranging her skirts so that her legs were discreetly covered down to her lower calves, exposing only her long, beige suede boots. Rianna had decided not to wear breeches, thinking the Chancellor might disapprove of such immodest garments.

Spurring Freya forward, she guided her on to the grassy plain and urged her into a canter. The mare needed no prompting as her nostrils caught the smell of freedom. They galloped across the flat plain towards the distant mountains, warm air caressing Rianna's face. The ribbon holding her hair loosened and her long locks streamed out behind her. She laughed joyously, feeling free and exhilarated, the throbbing of Freya's hooves reverberating comfortingly in her ears.

When she had ridden some distance, she slowed her mount and glanced back at the caravan, knowing it would be unwise to stray too far from the protection of her military escort. A mounted man-at-arms, wearing the Chancellor's black and red livery, had followed her, but he was discreetly keeping his distance to ensure her privacy. Rianna was not surprised, knowing the Chancellor would never have allowed her to ride alone. There was little chance of bandits in this barren area, but there could be dangerous wild animals such as bears or wolves.

Ignoring her unwanted escort, she urged Freya into a canter again. However, the ground became rougher, scattered with many large stones. Fearing for her palfrey's well-being, Rianna turned and rode back towards the caravan. The long line of wagons had begun to move again and Rianna decided to ride alongside them.

Over the last couple of days a number of merchants had joined the caravan, feeling safer to travel to Percheron under the protection of Chancellor Lesand's soldiers. There were now at least six new wagons within the train, but there was also an unfamiliar and very odd looking conveyance at the rear which Rianna had not noticed before. It appeared to be a heavy metal cage bolted on to a flat bedded wagon. Mounted men-at-arms, wearing a distinctive gold and black livery, surrounded the wagon. Rianna's curiosity was aroused. She wondered if they were transporting some rare beast back to Lord Sarin's private menagerie. But judging by the thickness of the bars, the creature had no chance of escape, and there was little need for it to be so heavily guarded.

She guided Freya forward until she was close enough to see what was inside the cage. To her disappointment she saw nothing but a pile of straw. However, a most unpleasant odour wafted towards her and she wrinkled her nose in disgust.

'My lady . . .' The soldier, who had been following her, manoeuvred his mount forward to ride beside her. 'It is not safe here. It would be best for you to ride at the front with Chancellor Lesand.'

'First tell me what kind of savage beast is in that cage.'

He gave a gruff laugh. 'Savage maybe, my lady, but no beast. It is a man – a prisoner.'

'What prisoner could deserve such barbaric treatment?'

The smell was stronger now. A stomach-churning mixture of sweat, stale urine and excrement.

'He deserves nothing better,' the soldier said dismissively. 'The more he suffers the happier I will be.' There was pure hatred reflected in his tone.

'Have you no compassion?' She saw the straw move. A grubby arm became visible, the wrist heavily manacled and chained.

'Not for him,' he sneered.

Rianna wondered what terrible crime the man had committed. Her father was a hard man at times, but even he would not have imprisoned someone in such foul conditions. Angered and disgusted by the prisoner's predicament she decided to raise the subject with Chan-

31

cellor Lesand. Spurring her mount forward she rode to the front of the caravan.

Chancellor Lesand, riding a beautiful honey-coloured horse with a cream mane and tail, was heading the caravan accompanied by his captain of the guard, Feroc.

'Lady Rianna, it is good to see you.' Lesand smiled warmly. 'The ride has put a welcome colour in your cheeks.'

'Indeed it has,' she agreed, slowing Freya's pace so that she could ride beside him. 'But the malodorous smell has turned my stomach.'

'Smell?' Lesand enquired, raising his finely arched eyebrows. 'To what are you referring, my lady?'

'The prisoner in the cage at the rear. No one, however wicked, should be confined in such dirty conditions.'

'It is not your concern,' he said curtly, his charming manner dissolving in a moment. His expression hardened. 'Just content yourself with the knowledge that the captive deserves no better.'

'What is his crime?'

At first Chancellor Lesand did not answer. However, after a long uncomfortable pause he replied. 'The prisoner led an unsuccessful revolt against his sovereign, Lord Sarin. Many soldiers were killed in the battles. When it was clear he had lost he fled, intending to take refuge in the eastern kingdoms and seek their aid in raising another army to fight Lord Sarin. But we captured him before he could cross the border.'

'But is it necessary for him to be chained and caged?'

'Since then he has twice attempted to escape, so total confinement is very necessary. Lord Sarin has issued orders that the prisoner be taken in chains to Percheron in order to answer for his crimes.'

'Surely the cage can be cleaned, and the prisoner allowed to wash himself. The smell, I assure you, is quite disgusting,' she said with a determined tilt to her chin.

'I cannot agree to even that,' Lesand said stonily, his mouth set in a thin line.

'Then I fear it will prove impossible for me to continue

32

my journey. The wind has turned, and the smell enters my conveyance, making me feel most unwell.'

'I am sorry, my lady,' he muttered.

'Yes. I shall insist on stopping to rest. It may even become necessary for me to return home.' She stared at him with calm determination, wondering if he would be willing to give in to her demands.

'You appear most resolute.' He smiled tightly.

'Compassion fuels my resolve.'

'I would venture to suggest that you try to quell such conduct in future, my lady. Lord Sarin does not welcome such forward behaviour from the ladies of his court. His decisions are never questioned – and his will is absolute.' Lesand awkwardly cleared his throat. 'However, at present, I am prepared to make concessions, purely to ensure your continued comfort and well-being. I have no wish for the prisoner to fall ill and die; Lord Sarin would never forgive me.'

'So you will agree to my demands?'

He nodded gravely. 'Indeed I will.'

'I am obliged to you,' she said with a sweet smile.

By mid-afternoon the caravan had left Harn and entered the northern reaches of Percheron. Rianna was at last in the land of her betrothed. Now she felt there was no turning back. The flat, barren plains had been replaced by gently undulating countryside, thick with brightly coloured wild flowers. Here in Percheron, even the sky seemed a more vivid shade of blue.

They stopped close to a lake surrounded by trees. It was late afternoon, and all the travellers were pleased to have a few extra hours of rest and relaxation. Normally, they did not break their journey until dusk was falling.

Chancellor Lesand had promised Rianna that the prisoner would be allowed to cleanse himself, and that the cage would be scrubbed out with hot water and strong vinegar to kill the terrible odours. Rianna was determined to ensure he kept that promise, so she decided to check on the captive's situation herself.

Leaving Jenna to her own devices, Rianna walked through the trees to the edge of the lake. The water looked cool and inviting, prompting Rianna to cast off her clothes and plunge into the blue-green depths. However, she had other matters to attend to at present. Lifting the skirts of her green silk gown, she made her way through the trees.

Lesand had told her that the soldiers escorting the prisoner were members of Lord Sarin's personal guard. They were camped in a clearing a short walk from the rest of the caravan. Rianna cautiously approached the camp site, taking advantage of the shelter provided by the trees and bushes. She stopped behind a leafy bush covered in glossy green leaves and trumpet-shaped pink flowers, and peered surreptitiously into the clearing.

The door of the prisoner's cage was wide open and the foul-smelling straw was being raked out to be burnt. But where was the captive? She looked around. There were a number of soldiers waist deep in the lake laughing and splashing each other, while two soldiers stood apart from the others, in slightly deeper water, each holding the end of a heavy chain. A head broke the smooth surface of the water between them. The prisoner stood up, water streaming from his body, and shook his head, causing his long hair to flap wetly around his face.

Rianna could hardly believe her eyes. She had expected a pathetic malnourished creature, not this magnificent male. He was taller, far taller than any man of Harn, and broad-shouldered, with the finely-honed physique of a warrior. Every inch of his golden-skinned body was covered by hard muscle. He was strikingly handsome with the features of a true nobleman; his nose was straight, flaring slightly at the nostrils, his mouth wide and full-lipped. She wasn't close enough to make out the colour of his eyes, but they were an attractive almond shape which added to the piquancy of his good looks. His long hair was at present darkened by the water, but she guessed when dry it would be a pale golden-blond.

Impatiently, the two soldiers tugged at the captive's chains which were attached to heavy manacles on his wrists. It was clear the prisoner's ablutions were at an end. He waded from the lake, following the soldiers towards the bank.

As the prisoner slowly emerged from the water, a sudden heat scorched Rianna's cheeks. His escorts wore black woollen breeches, now dripping wet, but the captive was totally naked. She had never seen an unclothed man before, and could not tear her gaze from his superb body. The rippling muscles of his chest were covered by a sprinkling of golden hair, descending like an arrow towards his flat stomach, and leading her eyes downwards to his groin. The hair grew much thicker around his male parts, placing emphasis on the loose sac of flesh fronted by a thick phallus, the skin of which was a few shades darker than that on his body.

She watched his limp manhood sway enticingly as he strode forward, and her knees began to feel weak. Forcing her gaze away from his male organs, she re-examined the rest of his body. Droplets of water lay on his chest, gleaming damply in the late afternoon sunshine. There were a number of large bruises marring his smooth flesh, and two half-healed wounds, both red and inflamed. One cut deeply across his left upper chest and shoulder, the other extended from his groin to lower thigh. If left unattended, Rianna feared they would putrefy and spread poison through his magnificent body. She decided to ask the Chancellor for his permission to tend the captive's wounds. The Chancellor would surely agree, as he wanted this man alive and fit enough to face Lord Sarin's punishment.

The soldiers escorting the captive found amusement in tugging roughly on his chains. Once, he stumbled and almost fell, but regained his balance, moving with far more grace and dignity than the soldiers, whose sodden breeches clung unflatteringly to their scrawny legs. The prisoner was led towards two trees placed about ten paces apart, and stationed between them. The soldiers attached the chains leading from his wrist manacles to the trees at about shoulder height and pulled them tight. The captive's arms were jerked apart, allowing him to move no more than a pace forwards or backwards.

Leaving the prisoner, the soldiers moved away to dry themselves and dress. Soon the sun would set. It was becoming steadily cooler as the afternoon heat diminished. A light breeze sprung up, wafting lazily through the trees to brush the captive's damp flesh. He shivered slightly, but there was no sign of discomfort or concern on his face, his expression calm and aloof.

The other soldier moved from the water. As they dressed, two of their companions, who'd not bothered to bathe, approached the captive. They began taunting him, but he ignored their shouts and raucous laughter, staring stoically ahead.

Frustrated by his lack of response, the soldiers began to poke and prod the prisoner.

One jabbed his stomach, while the other tugged at his pubic hair. At last the prisoner reacted, and snarling angrily, he leapt at them. His chains prevented him from touching the soldiers, but they still jumped fearfully back, far out of his reach. They stared at him nervously as he strained against his constricting chains. Even in his fury he was beautiful, thought Rianna. Each twist and turn emphasised the perfect lines of his muscles, the magnificence of his male physique.

An ugly, thickset man, wearing only a piece of cloth wrapped around his waist, secretly approached the prisoner from behind, and grabbed hold of his hair. The prisoner was clearly the stronger of the two but, taken by surprise, he was unable to prevent his head being jerked brutally back, thrusting his hips and sexual organs into prominence.

The other soldiers crowded forwards, joining their two comrades, cheering loudly as the thickset man ran a meaty hand over the prisoner's chest, pinching his copper-coloured nipples until they hardened and deepened in colour. The captive struggled fruitlessly, his face contorting in disgust as the meaty hand moved lower. It closed around his penis, jerking it upright. A few well-placed pumping strokes caused the organ to stiffen. The prisoner's cheeks reddened in shame, and for a moment he closed his eyes, unwilling to witness the spectators' lewd amusement.

'So much for pride, barbarian,' the thickset man sneered as he let go of the captive and stepped back a pace.

The prisoner's tense mouth softened with relief, but it was clear his humiliation was not at an end. Urged on by shouts of encouragement from the crowd, the thickset man grinned, and ducked under the taut chain stretching towards the left tree trunk. Then he moved to stand in front of the captive.

'My pride has nothing to do with this,' the prisoner replied in a voice choked with fury.

'It is said that pride goes before a fall, barbarian. You have fallen far for a noble lord, haven't you?' the soldier jeered. Chuckling menacingly, he unfastened the cloth around his waist and let it drop to the ground. His stubby penis was dark red and partially erect. He curved his hand around the base of the organ and crudely pumped it up and down until it stiffened and grew hard.

The prisoner looked at him with disdainful disgust, then pointedly turned his head away to stare calmly into the distance.

'Look at me,' the thickset man growled. 'See what is in store for you.' The prisoner did not respond, and his tormentor tensed in fury. 'By the gods, you *will* look at me.'

He reached forward and cruelly pinched the captive's penis. The prisoner didn't even wince, although it must have been painful. Rianna clenched at the silk skirt of her gown, crumpling the fine fabric in her hands as she waited to see what would next befall the helpless captive.

'Pray tell me, what is there to look at?' the handsome

warrior asked caustically. 'Only a pathetic creature, clumsily attempting to pleasure himself.'

'Then I order *you* to pleasure me.' The soldier gave a leering grin. 'The men will loosen your chains. Then you will fall to your knees and take me in your mouth. Refuse and you'll be punished.'

'Why should I refuse?' The prisoner smiled contemptuously. 'Your paltry cock will be easy enough to sever with one quick snap of my teeth.'

A red flush of humiliation flooded the soldier's cheeks. 'Better still, I'll have you chained down, your buttocks spread wide. I'll plunder your arsehole until you beg for mercy.'

'Do it, Rorg!' the watching soldiers shouted excitedly.

Rianna was horrified. Surely they wouldn't stoop to such degradation, but she feared it was possible, judging by the ugly mood of the crowd. Her palms felt sweaty, her knees weak. She was appalled, but there was another much darker emotion lurking deep in the pit of her belly which urged her to stay and witness what would happen next.

'In no time at all you'll come to enjoy such sweet agony,' Rorg taunted, placing his hands on his hips and pushing his pelvis forward to emphasise his stubby penis. It stuck out from his body almost at right angles, twitching obscenely as he took a swaggering step forward.

'Try it,' the prisoner growled half under his breath.

Rorg was so intent on entertaining his watching colleagues that he forgot just how close he was to the captive. He failed to see the prisoner lunge forward, straining each muscle and sinew to its fullest extent as he lifted his leg and kicked Rorg hard in the groin.

Rorg made a high-pitched squeal like a stuck pig, the sound immediately silencing the raucous shouts of the crowd. Then he crumpled to the ground, clutching vainly at his wounded sex. He lay at the prisoner's feet, moaning and twitching pathetically.

The prisoner grinned challengingly at his audience,

but his satisfaction was to be short-lived. A number of soldiers surged forward, two dragging Rorg away, while the others grabbed the prisoner and rained down blows on his helpless body. Being totally outnumbered, he made no attempt to resist, perhaps resigned to his ignominious fate.

'Stop!' an authoritative voice commanded. 'That's enough. Do you want to anger your sovereign lord?' A man with a long, ugly scar down one side of his face, wearing the uniform of a sergeant, stepped forward and threw a pile of chains at the prisoner's feet. 'Confine him properly this time.'

Immediately the soldiers did as ordered, clamping the manacles around the prisoner's ankles, then attaching the chains to the base of the trees, forcing his legs wide apart like his arms. He was now entirely at their mercy. Rianna shivered as a soldier stepped forward and placed a whip, made of thin strips of plaited leather, in the sergeant's hand.

'Rorg was one of my best men.' The sergeant tapped the whip menacingly on the palm of his hand.

'If he was one of your best, then I pity you,' the captive said defiantly. 'Any one of my soldiers was worth ten of him.'

'But you still lost the battle,' the sergeant sneered.

'There will be many more.'

'Not for you, slave.'

'I am no slave, I am Tarn of Kabra. Sarin may take my freedom, even my life, but I will never be his slave.'

'It is *Lord* Sarin to you,' the sergeant jeered. 'And do not try to deceive yourself, Tarn, you are his slave.'

'I have never bent my knee to him and I never will.'

Rianna admired the prisoner's brave defiance. Kabra, a land to the east of Percheron, had been conquered by Lord Sarin many years ago. Obviously Tarn was a nobleman of Kabra who had urged his people to rebel. Rianna began to feel even more sympathy and pity for Tarn, as members of the nobility captured in battle were usually treated with respect.

'Your foolish pride will be your downfall, slave. You must be punished for your insolence.' The sergeant tapped Tarn's phallus with the handle of the whip. 'A measure of pain, carefully applied, can stir the senses even of the most determined.'

'Do your worst, I'll welcome the agony. It will remind me that the soldiers of Percheron are cowardly scum,' Tarn said with bravado. 'Beat me senseless, kill me, I care not.'

'I'll not give you the pleasure of dying. My aim is purely to humiliate, to help you understand what it feels like to be a lowly slave. Today you will take the first step towards total and absolute submission.'

Even from this distance, Rianna thought she detected a faint quiver at the corner of Tarn's mouth. She knew that a true warrior would not welcome enslavement; far better to die a glorious death in battle.

'If I were not chained I would crush you with my bare hands,' Tarn replied defiantly.

The sergeant laughed and took a step closer to Tarn, watching his chest rise and fall, his breathing a shade faster than normal. 'Admit how scared you really are. Tell me, what does it feel like to be so totally helpless?'

He grabbed hold of Tarn's scrotum, cupping it roughly, before slowly squeezing it until a flash of pain crossed the prisoner's features. Satisfied by Tarn's first real sign of discomfort, he curved his thick fingers around the captive's phallus and pumped it vigorously.

Tarn's expression remained calm, but his body tensed, his powerful thighs trembling slightly. Even in his stoic dignity, his inner shame was a tangible entity. However hard he tried, Tarn could not blot out the lewd shouts of encouragement from the watching soldiers. Neither could he prevent his body from automatically reacting to the unwanted touch. His dignity and self-respect were slowly and surely being dragged away from him.

He tensed, clearly trying to control his body's responses, but his resistance was useless. The rough stimulation was causing his phallus to harden, the skin on his cock rolling back to reveal the moist, purple glans. Rianna could not tear her eyes from the rigid stem crowned by the swollen bulb.

A faint shiver passed over the firm muscles of Tarn's stomach, revealing his inner humiliation, as the sergeant stepped back and grinned with cruel satisfaction.

'You'll learn, slave,' he growled, ducking between the chains to move behind the prisoner. 'You no longer have any rights over your own body. You do whatever you are ordered. That includes offering your arse if you are told to.'

Grabbing hold of Tarn's buttocks, he pulled them roughly apart. Tarn winced as the sergeant touched the tender flesh ring surrounding his small nether mouth, then rudely probed the tight opening. Despite the chill of approaching night, sweat beaded Tarn's brow. He jerked and clenched his teeth as the stubby finger penetrated his anus, grazing the tender interior.

'You're tight, but you'll soon become accustomed,' the sergeant growled, slapping Tarn on the rump as he thrust his finger deeper into the virginal opening. 'When I move my finger thus, the sensation becomes almost pleasurable. I wager that in no time at all you'll be begging me for more.'

'Never,' Tarn hissed, despair fleetingly distorting his handsome features.

'You know Lord Sarin only too well. He'll soon find a way to destroy your wild spirit. Try to envisage what punishments he has in store for you, traitor.'

Stepping back a pace, the sergeant cracked his whip. There was a roar of approval from the crowd which made Rianna shiver apprehensively. The mood of the men was ugly, and she dare not move from her hiding place and go for help. She wasn't even certain that Chancellor Lesand would put a stop to Tarn's punishment. He had displayed no sympathy for the captive.

Tarn's cheeks were flushed with humiliation. His full mouth quivered, then hardened determinedly as he readied himself for the first cruel sting of the lash.

Rianna waited, riotously disturbing thoughts crowding her mind, unfamiliar notions that bespoke a darkness in her soul that she had never known existed. She was filled with the sudden, quite inexplicable need to remain and witness Tarn's pain and humiliation.

The sergeant drew back his arm, and the ugly sound of leather hitting flesh broke the expectant silence, evoking a low sigh of pleasure from the watching crowd. But the blow was far softer than Rianna had expected. She knew the lash must have hurt Tarn, but there was no tearing of flesh, no drawing of blood, just a raised pink weal snaking over the golden skin of his right shoulder.

He didn't respond at all to the blow, his expression remaining aloof and disdainful. But that was not what the crowd wanted. Their disappointment showed in their faces. They were all desperate to gain satisfaction from witnessing Tarn's agony.

More blows followed, the lash hitting Tarn again and again, leaving a criss-cross pattern of weals across his back. Soon Tarn began to jerk in rhythm with the blows, his body automatically pulling away from the caressing sting of the whip. Beads of sweat broke out on his forehead; the cords in his neck stood out. Only the tightness of his cheek muscles betrayed his discomfort. As the beating continued without mercy, he clenched his fists, straining against his chains until the metal shackles cut into his wrists and ankles.

The sergeant began to aim lower so that the thin strips of leather painfully stroked Tarn's buttocks and upper thighs. His skin afire, he sucked in his breath. His belly grew concave, while tremors ran down his muscular thighs.

Rianna was enraptured, along with the watching soldiers, as they witnessed Tarn battling to overcome his pain. Glorious in his distress, Tarn took a deep shuddering breath. The soft noise sent a dart of fire straight to Rianna's lower belly. Her legs grew weak, her groin full and heavy. A strange heat gathered between her thighs, and moisture seeped hungrily from her sex, while her breasts seemed to swell in her tight bodice. She longed to pull Tarn's broken body into her arms and kiss away his agony.

The strands of the whip curled around Tarn's hips, the tips stroking his muscular stomach. Oddly enough his phallus was still hard, the shaft engorged. Rianna recalled what the sergeant had said about pain stirring the senses. She'd not believed it possible but, as she watched, Tarn's manhood appeared to harden even more. The exposed head grew darker, the skin stretched until it was shiny, while a tiny bead of moisture oozed from the tip.

Rianna shuddered, still overcome by a myriad of conflicting emotions, as the lash continued to deliver a caressing agony to Tarn's helpless flesh. There was a pronounced air of sensual excitement invading the clearing. It hung over the leafy glade like a dark palpable entity. The soldiers, open-mouthed and slack-eyed, were all intent on Tarn's writhing form. Some were red-faced, tense and breathing heavily. Others were openly massaging their cocks over their woollen breeches.,

An insistent pulsing heat permeated Rianna's groin. She was consumed by the need to feel that magnificent organ thrusting deep inside her. Filled with hungry desire she stared at Tarn. Almost unconsciously she clenched her fist and pushed it between her upper thighs, putting pressure on her wanton sex.

The lash embraced Tarn's body, stroking the shaft of his penis. It jerked, beating a rapid tattoo against his rigid stomach. Then the leather tips of the whip touched his balls. He groaned, and there was an accompanying gasp from the crowd. Again the lash snaked mercilessly over his sex, and he bucked against his constricting chains, trying to escape from the sweetly tearing agony.

Tarn's discomfort only served to increase the pressure in his penis, and it hardened into a rod of iron, standing out from his groin straight and proud. The glittering dewdrop at its summit grew larger, until it broke free and rolled slowly down the domed head. In unison, one sparkling tear slid damply down Tarn's taut cheek. He groaned harshly, drawing back his lips in a shameful mixture of pain and pleasure. He was well aware that his humiliation would soon be complete. He was steadily losing the battle with the contradicting demands of his own flesh.

'No,' he gasped, trying to deny the inevitable. He moved his head from side to side. His hair, darkened by perspiration, flapped lankly against his shoulders. The skin on his cock looked ready to burst. His sweat-soaked body tensed with sweet agony, his swollen veins visible under his golden skin. For a brief second he froze, looking like a statue of some warrior-like god carved out of solid gold.

Giving a harsh laugh, the sergeant dropped the whip and thrust his work-roughened finger deep into Tarn's anus. Tarn threw back his head and yelped, his muscles straining to breaking point. Then a creamy jet of seed spurted from his cock, followed by another and another.

Rianna gasped, pressing her bunched fist up towards her sex to relieve the throbbing pressure. An unfamiliar spasm of bliss consumed her completely. She shivered with pleasure as she experienced a climax for the very first time. The sensation astounded her, its aftermath leaving her spent, weak and exhausted.

She looked back at Tarn. He sagged between his chains, a thin trickle of semen running down one leg. His entire body trembled and his head was bowed in shame. It appeared his humiliation was complete. As the soldiers loosened his chains, he sank to his knees, immune to everything but his own despair. His arms hung limply at his sides, while his sweat-soaked locks tumbled untidily over his face.

The sergeant grinned and grabbed hold of Tarn's sodden hair, jerking his head back until his face was visible to all. It stood out luminously pale in the gradually darkening clearing. His lips were bloodless and two spots of livid colour stained his cheeks.

'What say you to resistance now, Tarn? Lord Sarin will

find you all too easy to subjugate,' the sergeant said gleefully.

Thrusting a booted foot in the prisoner's back, the sergeant forced him on to the ground. Tarn pressed his face into the thick grass, making no attempt to struggle, totally overcome by his despair.

Tarn did not see the crowd of soldiers part to allow Rorg to step forward. He moved painfully, obviously still in some discomfort from the blow to his groin. Reaching Tarn, he bent to pick up the whip, and stood over the prone form of the captive. He trailed the sweat-soaked leather strands across Tarn's fiery flesh and gave a low menacing laugh.

# Chapter Three

*R*ianna ran as fast as she could through the woods, and into the clearing where the rest of the caravan was camped. She had to find Chancellor Lesand – only he could put a stop to the prisoner's continued misery.

'Chancellor,' she cried out in agitation.

Lesand, who was standing in the middle of the clearing conversing with Captain Feroc, turned. 'My lady,' he said with concern as he moved swiftly to her side. 'What is amiss?'

'You must help,' she stuttered.

'Are you unwell? You are flushed. Perhaps you have a fever?' He put a cool hand to her hot damp forehead. 'I'll summon your maid –'

'No,' she interrupted, clinging on to his arm and digging her fingers into the sleeve of his black velvet robe. 'I am not ill, just distressed. I was walking in the woods, when I came upon Lord Sarin's soldiers abusing the prisoner.'

'Abusing?' Lesand frowned.

'They whipped him, and they . . .' she faltered, blushing deeply. 'I cannot say . . . it was so degrading.'

Rianna lowered her eyes, unable to forget the vision of Tarn writhing and straining against his chains. Neither could she forget the wrenching pleasure she'd experienced from witnessing the humiliation he was forced to endure.

'Go, Captain Feroc, put a stop to it now!' Lesand ordered.

Beckoning to two of his men to accompany him, Feroc ran swiftly through the trees towards the other encampment.

'Calm yourself,' Lesand said in a soothing voice as he guided Rianna towards her wagon. 'You must distress yourself no longer.'

'But you don't understand, we must help the poor prisoner,' she said anxiously. 'Not only was he hurt by the beating, he had other, more serious wounds.'

'Now, now, my lady.' Lesand placed a comforting hand on her shoulder. 'Feroc is my most experienced officer. He will deal with the matter.'

'Please let me offer my services. I'm skilled in the art of healing.' Like all chatelaines, Rianna cared for the medical needs of the servants and soldiers in the castle of Nort. She had also been taught much about herbs by Jenna's mother.

'There is a military surgeon in the caravan, Feroc can call on him. Now, I wish to hear no more on this matter.' Lesand's voice took on a harder tone. His dark eyes were cold and pitiless as he looked down at her. 'Your soft heart does you great justice, Lady Rianna, but the prisoner does not deserve your sympathy. My only concern at present is your own well-being.'

Rianna bit back her pleading reply, knowing it would be to no avail. 'A short rest, Chancellor, and I'm certain I will be fine.'

Lesand looked around the encampment. 'Where is your maid? She should be here, waiting to attend you.' Jenna was nowhere to be seen. Lesand sighed impatiently and beckoned to his personal body servant. 'Baral, you will attend to Lady Rianna.'

Baral approached and bowed to Rianna. With his soft features and large dark eyes, coupled with his slim, slightly built frame and long dark curly hair, Baral would make a very attractive woman. The gentle, pretty young man had a sweet, clear singing voice. In the evenings Baral often entertained the travellers with his lute-playing and songs. Rianna had noticed that Lesand treated him more like a friend than a servant.

'My lady, it is an honour,' Baral said.

Just as he was about to help Rianna up the steps of her wagon, Jenna arrived looking flushed and rather dishevelled as she strolled leisurely through the trees ringing the camp site, accompanied by one of Lesand's soldiers. She clung attentively to the young soldier's arm in an intimate manner. It was the first time Rianna had seen Jenna look happy since they left the castle of Nort.

'Jenna.' Lesand's icy tones rang loudly across the clearing. 'Come here, girl.'

Jenna stiffened and shot a glance in the Chancellor's direction. Lifting her crumpled, grass-stained skirts, she hurried towards her mistress.

Pink-faced and embarrassed, Jenna bobbed a brief curtsey. 'Lady Rianna, Chancellor Lesand.'

'Where have you been?' Lesand demanded to know. 'Your mistress has need of your services, while it appears that you are more interested in spending your time with one of my soldiers.'

'I was just taking a breath of fresh air,' Jenna lied. 'I've been but a few minutes.'

Lesand glared at the soldier. 'Be gone, man,' he growled. 'And you, Jenna, take this as a warning. Your task is to care for Lady Rianna, not to be off trifling in some lewd manner with my men.'

Jenna paled and looked at Rianna for reassurance. 'Forgive me, my lady.'

'Now take your mistress inside and attend to her needs.' Lesand smiled tight-lipped at Rianna. 'No more worries now, rest easy. We'll speak in the morning. Baral, come,' he ordered.

As Lesand strode away, followed by Baral, Jenna took hold of Rianna's arm, guiding her up the steps and into the privacy of their house on wheels. 'What is amiss?

You appear upset, and I've never seen the Chancellor so angry.'

'Neither have I.' Rianna was certain that Lesand's fury did not solely stem from Jenna's shortcomings. She felt it also had something to do with Tarn. 'I was upset by something I witnessed while walking in the woods.'

'You must rest,' Jenna said, leading her mistress to one of the narrow benches. 'You appear overheated. Let me cool you down.'

Rianna sat on the padded seat, while Jenna gently bathed her face with cool perfumed water. 'My head aches a little,' Rianna complained, feeling suddenly very weary. 'Take out the pins and let down my hair.'

Jenna deftly removed the pins and uncurled the long braid from Rianna's crown. Then she loosened the silken locks, fanning them around Rianna's shoulders and down her back. 'May I ask what you witnessed that upset you so?' Jenna enquired, unable to contain her curiosity any longer, as she brushed Rianna's shining red-gold hair with smooth restful strokes.

Rianna needed someone to confide in, and she could trust Jenna's discretion. 'You remember I told you about the prisoner in the cage at the rear of the caravan? I took a walk to the other campsite, merely to see if the Chancellor had arranged for the cage to be cleaned out as he had promised,' she confessed haltingly. 'The prisoner was in the lake washing. Curiosity prompted me to linger and see what the poor man looked like.'

'Was he handsome?' Jenna asked.

'Yes, amazingly so. Taller and far more well-favoured than any man of Harn,' Rianna said, colouring at the thought. 'They chained him between two trees, then whipped and abused him most terribly.'

'Why did you not leave?' Jenna asked, unlacing the back of Rianna's gown and sliding the bodice down to her waist.

More colour invaded Rianna's cheeks. 'I could not. I don't understand why . . .' she faltered. 'The prisoner's

49

distress and the degrading things they forced him to endure moved me in the strangest manner.'

Jenna gave a soft laugh. 'You felt aroused, excited. It's not unusual to feel so, my lady. I've experienced the same emotions when watching some handsome miscreant being punished with a whipping.'

'You have?' Rianna said in surprise. 'But the prisoner is no rough peasant, he is a nobleman. The soldiers' intentions were to humble him as well as to punish.'

Just speaking of Tarn made Rianna's breasts throb and her breathing quicken. Eager to be rid of her tight-fitting garments, she stood up and let her dress fall into a shining pool at her feet. Her shift felt impossibly restrictive, as it seemed to crush her breasts and rub enticingly against her rock-hard nipples. She hoped that Jenna didn't notice the way the tiny nubs stood out, lewdly distorting the fine silk of her undergarment.

'A nobleman,' Jenna repeated, lifting Rianna's gown and smoothing the shining folds before placing it in the storage chest. 'He is far more than that, my lady. Mircon, my soldier friend, told me that the prisoner is Tarn, the only son of the King of Kabra, and heir to the throne. How can so proud a prince reconcile himself to becoming a slave? Mircon says that is the fate Lord Sarin intends for him.'

'How can Lord Sarin allow a prince to be treated so cruelly?' Rianna asked. 'They did the most horrendous and degrading things to him.'

'While you stayed and watched,' Jenna reminded her.

As Jenna drew Rianna's shift up and over her head, the maid's cool fingers briefly brushed her over-sensitive flesh. Rianna shivered, finding the contact surprisingly pleasurable.

'I could not tear my gaze from him,' Rianna confessed, feeling conscious of her naked body. 'The whipping must have hurt, but the lash did not tear his flesh. There was no blood. It was purely to subjugate and humiliate . . .' She wanted to tell Jenna all that she witnessed and how aroused she felt, but she could not bring herself to voice the words.

'We all have a place of darkness within our souls.' Jenna slipped the finely embroidered, muslin nightgown over Rianna's head. The fine fabric fluttered downwards, gently caressing Rianna's febrile flesh. 'Watching pain being inflicted on a handsome warrior can be a potent spice to the senses.'

'I would never have believed such feelings possible, if I had not experienced them myself,' Rianna murmured.

'There are clearly many things you have yet to learn,' Jenna said with an understanding smile. 'Perhaps after all it is better that I accompanied you and not Veba. That dried-up old crone doesn't even know what it's like to bed a man.'

Rianna did not like the way Jenna spoke about Veba. She loved the old woman; however, she knew that in many ways Jenna was right. Veba was a spinster, with old-fashioned and restrictive views. Jenna was probably far more knowledgeable about matters of the flesh. 'Are you very experienced?' she asked shyly.

Jenna chuckled. 'I have known a number of men, if that is what you mean. You may ask me anything you want about the opposite sex, Lady Rianna. I'm certain to be able to provide you with a well-informed answer.'

'Anything?' Rianna asked, sitting down on her narrow bed.

'Anything,' Jenna confirmed, smiling affectionately at Rianna. 'I'll be happy to tell you about ways to pleasure a man. You'll no longer be a total innocent when you go to your husband's bed. But our discussions on this matter must cease now and continue on the morrow. Please, you must rest, I don't want to incur Chancellor Lesand's anger again.'

There were a multitude of questions Rianna wanted answered, but she knew Jenna was right, there was plenty of time for such discussions on the long journey to Aguilar, the capital city of Percheron. Rianna lay down on her bed, and smiled up at her maid as she covered her with a sheet. 'Thank you, Jenna.'

'Rest easy. I'll return later to see if you want anything to eat,' Jenna said, before she left the wagon.

With her head still full of images of the handsome warrior naked and in chains, Rianna eventually fell into a restless, dream-filled sleep.

Rianna's slumbers were disturbed by a sudden noise. 'Jenna, is that you?' she queried.

'Yes.' Jenna moved closer, striking the tinderbox to light a small oil lamp. 'I'm sorry to disturb you, my lady. But Chancellor Lesand wishes to speak with you urgently.'

Forcing herself into full wakefulness, Rianna sat up and brushed the tangled strands of hair from her face. 'It's the middle of the night, is it not?'

"Tis way past midnight. The Chancellor says he has urgent need of your healing skills.' Jenna handed Rianna a blue velvet cloak. 'No time to dress, wear this.'

'Who's ill?' Rianna asked, pushing her feet into a pair of velvet slippers as Jenna wrapped the cloak around her. 'Have you my bag?'

'It is outside with the Chancellor's servant,' Jenna replied. 'And I do not know who is ill. The Chancellor did not choose to confide in me.'

Rianna hurried down the steps of her wagon to where the Chancellor was standing with his servant. Baral was holding aloft a lantern, and at his feet was Rianna's bag of instruments and potions.

'I apologise for disturbing you,' Lesand said, appearing rather agitated. 'There was no other I could turn to. Your maid assures me that your healing skills are well-known in Harn.'

'I'll do what I can to help. Who is unwell?' Rianna asked.

'During a struggle with his guards, the prisoner received a blow to the head. He's been unconscious for hours,' Lesand explained hurriedly. 'The military surgeon who accompanies us can do nothing for him, so I crave your assistance. Baral will escort you, Lady Rianna, if you would care to examine the man.'

Concern for Tarn made Rianna decide she did not want to delay a moment longer. It was dark, no one would see she wore only a night-gown under her cloak. 'Of course, Chancellor. I'm ready,' she told Baral.

Baral picked up Rianna's bag. 'This way, my lady. Take care you do not trip on the rough ground.'

She followed him from the encampment and into the eerie darkness of the wood. Rianna had never been in a forest at night. She jumped nervously as she heard the distant scream of an unknown animal, and was relieved when she caught sight of the flickering flames of a campfire.

Three soldiers were sitting hunched around the fire, while the rest of the men appeared to be asleep, leaving Tarn unguarded. Unconscious, he lay on his stomach, close to the wagon that bore his cage. A rough piece of striped fabric was thrown over the lower half of Tarn's prone body, but there was nothing between him and the rough ground.

'Baral, I will need blankets for the prisoner,' Rianna said.

'Yes, my lady.' Placing the lantern and bag close to the prisoner's head, Baral moved over to speak to the soldiers by the fire. Meanwhile, Rianna examined Tarn's back. The flesh was red and angry, criss-crossed by raised scarlet weals. But there was no blood, no broken skin. The damage would heal swiftly and leave no disfiguring scars.

Opening her bag, Rianna took out a small clay pot containing a soothing ointment made of agrimony, rosemary and lavender oil. She spread it thinly over Tarn's damaged flesh, admiring the strength and hardness of the muscles under his skin. She had almost finished when Baral returned with the three soldiers, although she'd not yet lifted the strip of blanket to anoint Tarn's bare buttocks.

Under instructions from Rianna, the soldiers laid a blanket on the ground. She covered the top half with a clean cloth to prevent the rough fibres from sticking to the ointment on Tarn's back. Then she ordered the soldiers to lift him on to the blanket.

Tarn was a heavily built man, and a dead weight while unconscious. The three soldiers grunted in exertion as they lifted him and placed him atop the blanket. They decorously draped the piece of striped fabric across Tarn's hips to conceal his sex from her view. Then they insisted on putting manacles on his ankles and tethering his chains to the wheels of the wagon. However, because of Rianna's pleadings, they did not replace the manacles on the prisoner's wrists.

'You may leave,' Baral told the soldiers, who resumed their places by the campfire.

Rianna examined the wound on Tarn's head. The gash extended from his left temple deep into his scalp, surrounded by a matted mass of hair and congealed blood. She cleansed the gory mess with a cloth dampened in boiled water mixed with vinegar. The wound was bad, but the bone underneath appeared undamaged. Rianna's gentle probing fingers found no sign of a fracture, but even that did not ensure Tarn's survival.

'Is it bad?' Baral asked, unable to bring himself to look closely at the wound. 'The sight of blood sickens me.'

'It's hard to tell. I've seen men recover from worse, while others, with far less serious wounds, have died. Where the head is concerned, anything is possible.'

'Can you help him at all?' Baral stared sympathetically down at Tarn.

'A tisane of comfrey and valerian, mixed with mallow and borage will calm his blood and help relieve internal swelling,' she said thoughtfully. 'After that we will have to wait and see. Baral, will you go and seek out my maid, Jenna, and ask her to brew such a potion. In the meantime, I'll tend to these other wounds.' Rianna took a sharp silver scalpel from her bag. 'See here, on his shoulder.' She pressed an area of puffy, purplish-red flesh which bordered both sides of the long half-healed gash. 'There are bad humours here that have to be released, lest they drain into his blood and poison him.'

Baral turned pasty white. 'I'll find Jenna at once.' He smiled weakly. 'Will it trouble you to be left alone with the prisoner? I could call the guards.'

'No.' She looked down at her unconscious patient. 'What harm can he do me, Baral?'

'What harm indeed,' Baral agreed, moving quickly away before Rianna could use the scalpel.

Rianna worked with swift expertise, draining and cleaning the infected wound on Tarn's shoulder. Then she packed it with a healing unguent and covered it with a clean dressing.

Now she had but to examine the wound in Tarn's groin. She looked down at the unconscious warrior. He was quite the most beautiful man she had ever seen. His face was angelic in repose, the features bold but finely drawn. She wished she could see the colour of his eyes, now shaded by long dark lashes. She guessed they would be blue or grey because his hair was a pale shade of gold.

With the tips of her fingers she touched his mouth, easing it open a little. The lower lip was a little fuller than the upper, while his teeth were white and even. She trailed her hands down his corded neck to the firm planes of his chest. His heartbeat was regular, not thready, his breathing slow and even. These were good signs and she hoped with every fibre of her being that Tarn would recover.

Under the smooth unblemished flesh, lightly tanned by exposure to the sun, his body was a mesh of strong powerful muscles, honed to perfection by his life as a warrior. She continued her examination, her fingers brushing his nipples: two small dark nubbins surrounded by flat circles of copper. There was not even the faintest hint of a bulge at his belly; it was tight, iron-hard and infinitely appealing. Drawing her breath inwards, Rianna allowed her fingers to travel lower.

Gently she eased aside the striped fabric covering his groin. There was a dusting of pale blond hair on his lower belly, gradually thickening into the golden triangle of curls that covered his pubis. She couldn't resist staring at his male organs. Tarn's phallus was curled limply atop the bed of curls and behind it lay the sac of flesh which held his seed of life.

The skin of his manhood was a shade darker than that of the rest of his body, darkening even more at the domed tip. The organ was far from small, but she still found it difficult to understand how it could grow so impossibly large. Who would imagine that this curved, defenceless instrument could stiffen until it was much longer and thicker than the handle of the Great Broadsword of Harn? She recalled the phallus as she'd seen it earlier in the day – taut and shiny, a huge purplish bulb at its tip, poised and ready to pump spurts of creamy seed from his body.

Once again she felt the unquenchable fire burst into life, deep in the pit of her stomach, knifing through her feminine parts and filling them with lust. She could barely imagine what it would feel like to have Tarn's phallus thrusting deeper and deeper inside her, the smooth skin of his cock shaft polished to slick perfection by the copious dew of her own body.

Rianna recalled the feel of Lesand's fingers inside her, invading her virginal flesh. She'd never believed the experience could be so pleasurable. But what if those long thin fingers had been replaced by Tarn's huge rod of flesh? Would the pleasure increase or would it prove to be painful?

Sternly reminding herself that she had a task to perform, Rianna focused her thoughts on Tarn's well-being. She looked at the long sword gash extending from Tarn's groin to half-way down his thigh. It was still a little inflamed but the wound appeared clean. She judged it to be mending well. All it needed was regular applications of soothing unguent.

Rianna spread a thin layer of healing ointment along

the line of the wound. On finishing, she wiped her fingers, then rewarded her labours with another glimpse of Tarn's sex. The skin on the shaft of his penis looked wrinkled and rough. She touched it with the tip of her fingers, still finding it hard to comprehend how the organ could grow so swiftly. Surprisingly, the surface felt smooth and velvety, much like the skin of a ripe peach. She stroked the shaft, watching curiously as it slowly expanded. Before it straightened and hardened fully, she weighed the organ in her hand. How odd to spend one's life with this always hanging between one's legs. How much neater was a woman's body with everything tucked securely inside.

The head of Tarn's phallus was protected by a thick hood of skin. As she stroked and rubbed the shaft it grew larger, and the collar of skin slowly rolled back to reveal the tip of the expanding purple bulb that had so firmly imprinted itself on her fevered mind.

She was still marvelling at the amazing sight when she detected a slight trembling of Tarn's stomach. He gave a faint moan, and Rianna looked worriedly up at his face, but his eyes were closed and he still appeared to be unconscious. She glanced nervously over at the guards by the fire, fearful that they might be watching her intimately exploring Tarn's body, but they were all fast asleep.

Rianna was just about to return her attention to Tarn, when she felt a hand grab her wrist and jerk her forward. She fell across Tarn's chest, while arms, strong as steel bands, enfolded her.

'You've come to entrance me,' Tarn groaned. His sky-blue eyes raked her face, before he captured her lips with his.

As Tarn's tongue thrust between her lips, she gave a pleading moan. But as his searching tongue delved deeper, erotically exploring the moist crevices of her mouth, the fire in her belly blazed fully into life. She felt weak with wanting as she gave herself up to the sublime intimacy of his kiss. It was all she'd ever imagined and far, far more. Her heartbeat increased, turning into a helpless tattoo as she felt pure desire invade every nerve and fibre of her being.

Rianna forgot that Tarn was a captive, forgot that he was a stranger to her. She welcomed Tarn's touch as he ran his hands feverishly over her body. He stroked her lush curves through the fine muslin of her night-gown. His hand was so large it easily imprisoned one full breast, kneading and squeezing the sensitive mound of flesh.

She shivered with pleasure as Tarn's searching tongue continued to ruthlessly probe her mouth, his kisses and caresses wreaking havoc with her senses.

'Sweet faerie of the forest,' he murmured against her hot cheek. 'Bless you for coming to help wash away my shame.'

'No,' she gasped, but his ears were deaf to her pleadings as his searching fingers slid inside the loose neck of her night-gown. He stroked her nipple, pulling and squeezing the engorged nubbin until she cried out with the joy of it.

He kissed her again, with ruthless passion, enmeshed in a fantasy of his own making, prompted by the fevered confusion in his brain. One hand continued to fondle and stroke her breasts, while the other fumbled with the filmy folds of her night-gown, pushing the fabric away from her legs. Rianna's body felt boneless, her pudenda hot and moist. She wanted to open her legs and beg him to quell the slippery heat in her sex. She gasped as Tarn's hand moved up her thigh. His fingers slid higher to stroke the red-gold curls of her pubis and tenderly caress the engorged lips of her vulva.

Reason returned to Rianna in a sudden rush of heated concern. If she allowed Tarn to continue she would lose everything, and if anyone discovered her perfidy, Tarn would suffer even more, perhaps be put to death.

'No,' she wailed, trying to push his searching hand away from her sex. 'This must not be.'

Her struggles proved useless. Tarn was far stronger

than her, and still totally enmeshed in his feverish fantasy. Ignoring her protestations, he whispered soft words of love in her ear while the tips of his fingers slid between the swollen leaves of her labia to caress her sensitive, inner flesh. Fighting the urge to give up the battle and allow Tarn to continue on their mutual voyage of discovery, Rianna flailed her arms. Agitatedly she struck out at Tarn, unthinkingly catching his shoulder wound with the heel of her hand. Tarn groaned in agony, his hold on her lessening for a moment.

'Please stop,' she begged entreatingly. At last she managed to tear herself away from him and sit up. Pulling her cloak together with shaking fingers, Rianna struggled to contain the violent lustful urges that still consumed her inflamed flesh.

Tarn's arms fell limply to his sides as he stared at her in confusion. But a measure of rationality appeared to have returned to his mind. 'Who are you?' he asked hesitantly.

'I'm no faerie come to succour you,' she said, her breath still coming in nervous gasps. Rianna's skin was afire, and her wet sex throbbed. She fought the need to throw herself back into Tarn's arms and beg him to continue. The urgent desire he aroused in her refused to diminish and lust still simmered in her pudenda.

'Then I've not died and gone to heaven,' he groaned, closing his eyes as he put a shaky hand to the wound on his head.

Tarn's phallus was hard and fully erect, standing out at right angles from his prone body, a gleaming pearl of moisture crowning its bulbous tip. Rianna glanced over at it and blushed, realising how close she'd come to losing control and with it her precious virginity. Filled with embarrassment, she draped the striped fabric over Tarn's groin, but his erect organ held a portion of the fabric lewdly upwards, like the pole of a tent. Not knowing quite what to do next, she looked back at Tarn's face.

'You're certainly beautiful enough to be a forest wraith,' he murmured in confused bewilderment.

'I came to tend your wounds . . .' She hesitated, uncertain whether to use his name.

'Tend my wounds, sweet lady?' he questioned. Tarn's eyes were the deep blue of a clear summer sky. Briefly they clouded with pain as he tried to move his head. 'Ye gods, my head aches,' he muttered.

'Lie still. You've been unconscious for many hours.' She touched his forehead with trembling hands. His skin was now warm and slightly clammy. 'And you're a little feverish.'

'I've been insensible for that long?' Tarn gave a brittle laugh. 'I'm certain that swine Rorg must have suffered more. I hit his sex so hard he's unlikely ever to be able to father a bastard ag–' Tarn faltered, two spots of his colour appearing on his cheeks. 'Apologies, sweet lady, my words were crude and unnecessary.'

'Not unnecessary,' she said gently. 'Rorg deserved his fate.'

Tarn did not appear to realise that she knew who, and what, he was talking about. 'Lady, you must excuse my untoward behaviour . . .' he stuttered. 'To kiss and fondle you like that was unpardonable.'

'Your brain was fevered from the blow to your head.' She smiled tenderly. 'You did not know what you were doing. In your inflamed imagination you believed me to be some spirit of the forest come to claim you as her own.'

'I must have been dreaming most vividly,' Tarn said weakly. 'I could have sworn I felt gentle hands caressing me in the most intimate manner.'

Now it was Rianna's turn to blush. 'I was tending the wound close to your groin,' she said shyly. 'In my haste and concern it is possible I mistakenly touched your phal . . . touched you intimately,' she said in embarrassment, stumbling awkwardly over her words.

'I should be grateful that you showed such concern for my welfare.' Taking hold of her hand, he pressed it to his lips. 'I thank you for your kindness, sweet lady.' Tarn tried to lift his head but he grimaced in pain and perspiration broke out on his brow.

'No,' she pressed him back down. 'Your head wound is bad, and you must lie still for some time, until I deem it safe for you to move.'

'I will do as you say,' he said, attempting a shaky smile. 'What is your name, sweet lady?'

'Rianna.'

'And how came you to be on this journey? Judging by your unusual colouring, you are not from Percheron. I've never seen hair of such a glorious hue.'

'I'm travelling to Aguilar to be married,' she told him.

'Then you are the noble lady who is to wed Lord Sarin?' Tarn asked in harsh surprise. 'The daughter of the Protector of Harn.'

'Yes,' she confirmed a little uneasily. The cruelty inflicted on Tarn made her wonder even more about her future husband. She could only hope Lord Sarin knew nothing of Tarn's mistreatment.

'Sarin.' There was derision and abhorrence in the way Tarn spoke her bridegroom's name. 'How could your father sacrifice you to such a man?'

'It was necessary for the protection of my country,' she replied, 'lest he try to conquer Harn like he did Kabra. Fate has set my path, just as it has yours.'

'I made my fate, no one else had a hand in it. I brought about my own demise.' Tarn smiled wryly. 'Who would have thought the Prince of Kabra could fall so low?' He saw the apprehension and fear she felt reflected in her eyes. 'Do not be concerned, Lady Rianna. My situation is far different from yours.'

'We are both captives in our own way,' she admitted uneasily. 'Though my prison is far more comfortable than yours.'

His expression softened as he lifted a hand to touch her pale cheek. 'My hatred of what Sarin has done to Kabra colours my opinion of the man. He can be captivating and charming to those he admires. Sarin worships

61

beauty and you are lovely enough to turn the head of any man. I'm sure he will make you a fine husband.'

'You speak as if you know him well.'

'Very well,' Tarn confirmed. 'After he conquered Kabra, I resided at his court for a number of years. He treated me as a friend, a brother even; we were very close. I hear he was devastated when I chose to lead the insurrection in Kabra. Now he despises me as a traitor to our friendship as well as to Percheron.'

'Then I fear his plans for you will be harsh,' she said sadly. 'But do you not think that if he once cared for you he will temper his judgement with mercy?' She blushed awkwardly. 'I'm certain he would not approve of his soldiers abusing you as they did. The soldier, Rorg and his sergeant deserved any injuries you gave them.'

All the colour drained from Tarn's face and his features contorted in distress. 'You saw?'

'Yes,' she admitted, unable to meet his anguished gaze. 'When I discovered what terrible living conditions you were forced to endure, I persuaded Chancellor Lesand to allow you to cleanse yourself. I wanted to ensure he kept his promise so I came to this encampment and I unintentionally saw what they did to you.'

Tarn turned his head miserably away from her. 'I cannot believe you witnessed my humiliation,' he said, his voice cracking on the words.

'But it was not your fault.' She was filled with infinite pity for the suffering of this handsome prince. Tentatively she stroked his taut cheek. 'Do not blame yourself, Tarn, for what others inflicted upon you.'

'Say no more,' he groaned. 'If only I could find a way to erase the feel of those hands from my flesh.'

Leaning forward, she kissed his cheek with sympathetic understanding. 'Let me help you,' she whispered, her warm breath brushing his face. 'Please look at me, Tarn.'

Slowly he turned his head. Rianna was so agonisingly close to his trembling vulnerable mouth. She wanted to kiss those soft lips, inhale the breath from his body and help wipe away his pain. Resisting the temptation, she smiled tenderly at him.

'Rianna,' he murmured as he stared deep into her compassion-filled green eyes. 'Such a beautiful name, but nowhere near as beautiful as its owner. No mere mortal has ever been so lovely or so tender-hearted.'

She placed the palm of her hand on the hard planes of his chest, feeling the agitated beating of his heart. 'Tarn, you barely know me.'

'I know all that I need to know.' He covered her hand with his. 'Earlier, when I said I felt you touching me intimately, I was not dreaming, was I?' he asked entreatingly.

She couldn't lie to him. 'No, you were not dreaming,' she said shyly. 'Before you, I had never seen a naked man. I was admiring your body. You're beautiful also, Tarn.'

'No, I'm not, I'm tainted,' he said in disgust. 'Forever befouled.'

'Not forever.' She ran her fingers over his chest, feeling the hard muscles tremble beneath her caressing touch. 'I could wash away your degradation and make you whole again.'

'Please,' he begged as her hands trailed lower to tantalisingly stroke the iron hard planes of his stomach. 'Help me.'

She slid her hands under the fabric covering his groin, savouring the heat of his golden flesh, the springiness of the curls covering his pubis. Tarn's phallus was still partially engorged, but now lying prone against his stomach. She touched the velvety skin of his shaft, feeling it jerk excitedly. 'I'm inexperienced in these matters,' she whispered as she ran the pads of her fingers slowly down the side of his rod of hot male flesh.

With a trembling hand, Tarn pulled the striped fabric away, exposing all of his sex to her view. 'I ache for you, sweet Rianna,' he pleaded.

Cautiously she curled her fingers around his shaft, feeling the glorious power of his manhood throbbing gently beneath her fingertips. Then, unsure what she should do next, she recalled the sight of Tarn chained between the trees and the crude pumping motion the sergeant had employed when he'd forced Tarn's unwilling phallus into life. Using gentle, less vigorous strokes, she began to mimic the movement. At once, she felt Tarn's cock begin to harden, and she heard him give a soft encouraging moan.

The sound pierced her body like a sword, travelling deep to the pit of her stomach. Her womb throbbed. A sudden rush of moisture seeped from her sex, and coated her inner thighs. She was filled with the sudden need to be invaded and stretched by Tarn's rigid staff of flesh.

Trying to ignore her own desires, Rianna stroked his cock shaft, still employing smooth regular strokes. His organ grew rapidly until it was firm and hard. She slid her fingers higher, forcing the skin on his cock to roll back and expose the swollen purple head beneath. She milked the shaft with slow precision, until she saw a bead of moisture seep from the tiny mouth at its tip. Soon the collar of flesh tightly ringed the engorged head. It appeared to increase the pressure in the bulb; the skin of the plum stretched, becoming taut and shiny.

With her other hand, she caressed his trembling belly and the soft blond curls at his pubis. Then she stroked the smooth pliable skin of his balls, feeling them tighten and ripple under her gentle touch. Her innocent attempt to pleasure Tarn appeared to be working most admirably. He rolled his head from side to side as a soft, 'Yes,' drifted from his open lips.

Rianna wanted to kiss Tarn, to impale her throbbing sex on his iron-hard rod and feel him thrusting deep inside her feminine sheath. She pressed her legs tightly together and ignored the wetness seeping from her pudenda, instead taking pleasure from Tarn's steadily increasing excitement. Pumping and squeezing the stem of his penis ever harder, she disregarded the growing fire in the depths of her own sex.

The wrinkled skin of Tarn's seed sac hardened into two firm stones. A harsh groan came from Tarn's mouth as a shudder of pleasure traversed the muscles of his groin. His stomach tightened, his phallus jumped beneath her encircled fingers and his balls tensed. A great jet of creamy seed spurted from his cock head, followed by another and another.

Shivering with the strength of her emotion, Rianna looked up at Tarn's face. His eyes were closed and he was breathing heavily; he appeared to be at peace with himself.

'Sweet Rianna.' His lips curved into a contented smile. 'I adore you,' he murmured so softly it might have been but a whisper on the wind.

Glancing briefly in the direction of the guards to ensure they were still asleep, Rianna returned her attention to Tarn. Taking a cloth from her bag she cleaned the remains of Tarn's creamy emanations from his still trembling flesh. She took hold of the other blanket Baral had given her and gently placed it over him. Then she tenderly stroked his cheek.

'You must try and rest now,' she said, feeling a great affection for the handsome warrior. She had never realised how easy it was to give pleasure to a man. She stared at the handsome planes of his face, the tender vulnerability in his full lips. She was certain Tarn would recover from his injuries, but she feared for his eventual fate.

Suddenly, she was disturbed by the sound of movement behind her. Thinking it might be one of the guards, she turned her head. It was Baral walking towards her carrying a cup of the steaming potion.

'My lady,' Baral said anxiously. 'I'm sorry this has taken so long.'

'No matter.' She smiled tenderly down at Tarn, who had now opened his eyes and was staring up at her. 'The prisoner had but just regained consciousness. But the wound was as bad as I feared, and his brain is in total turmoil. He knows neither who or where he is. Also he has a fever. It appears I will have to tend to him for some days yet.'

As she spoke, Tarn gave a faint, barely perceptible nod and closed his eyes.

# Chapter Four

One of the herbs in the mixture Jenna had prepared would make Tarn sleep deeply. Rianna knew from experience that total rest and relaxation aided recovery, especially for wounds such as Tarn's. She ensured he was made more comfortable, with extra blankets and a soft pillow for his head, then she fed him the potion.

'It will be safe to leave him now,' she told Baral, once Tarn had drifted off into a peaceful slumber.

He nodded, then picked up her bag and the lantern. 'It's late, Lady Rianna. You'll not get much rest, it'll be morning soon.'

'No matter,' she replied as they walked out of the encampment and into the eerie stillness of the forest. Rianna knew it was unlikely that dangerous wild animals would venture close to the campsites, but she found the darkness menacing and frightening. 'I shall have to return first thing in the morning, before we depart, to ensure that the prisoner is transported in comfort. He cannot be returned to that terrible cage. He must be carried in a specially prepared wagon. Too much jarring will cause further damage to his head. If he's not treated gently I cannot be sure he will recover.'

'Lord Sarin would never forgive Chancellor Lesand, if Tarn of Kabra dies,' Baral admitted worriedly. 'His orders are for the rebel to be brought before him in chains, but unharmed.'

'Then you must tell the Chancellor, Baral. He must ensure that Tarn is treated with special care.'

'Indeed I will,' Baral replied as they came in sight of the other encampment. 'I'm sure he'll do everything you recommend.'

'Good.' Rianna smiled to herself. At least Tarn would travel in comfort from now on. If she acted with shrewd caution she could keep Tarn in her care until they reached Aguilar. The handsome prince fascinated her, and she wanted to get to know him better. Perhaps, under her persuasion, Sarin might relent a little and deal with Tarn less harshly. Who could blame a prince for trying to regain control of his own kingdom?

'Now you must rest,' Baral said as he escorted her to the steps of her wagon. He handed Rianna the leather bag containing her medicines.

'Thank you, Baral, and good night.'

'Sweet dreams, my lady,' he replied with a gentle smile.

As Baral walked away, she looked around expecting to find Jenna waiting for her, but she was nowhere to be seen. Rianna felt too weary to seek her out, but as she was about to climb the steps to her house on wheels, she heard a sound, like a low husky laugh, coming from the direction of the forest, followed by an audible moan.

The clouds covering the night sky had been blown away by a faint breeze, which heralded the steadily approaching sunrise. The bright moonlight made the forest appear less menacing. Rianna saw a golden glow coming from a patch of thick bushes just inside the trees ringing the campsite.

Putting down her bag, Rianna crept cautiously forward. She heard a breathy sighing coming from the undergrowth. She couldn't be certain but it sounded suspiciously like Jenna. Trying not to make a sound, she knelt and parted the interlaced branches.

Jenna and her soldier friend, Mircon, were indulging

in carnal pleasures. A lantern glowed beside them, bathing their bodies in a pool of golden light.

Rianna drew in her breath. Mircon was naked. The dusky skin of his chest was covered by a thick matt of black curls, which spread downwards over his belly to his groin. Jenna, also unclothed, crouched astride Mircon's thighs, kissing and stroking his engorged penis.

The organ was nowhere near as magnificent as Tarn's. It was shorter and slimmer, curving slightly at the end, while the bulb at its tip was a rich ruby red.

Jenna pulled Mircon's cock into her mouth and sucked on it lewdly. Rianna shivered excitedly. Her breasts suddenly started to throb and ache as she became conscious of every pore of her body. Heat spread downwards, filling her sex; powerfully erotic emotions suffused her thoughts. First it had been Tarn, now this. Her innocence was being eroded away. The sensual side of her nature had awakened from its youthful slumbers and overtaken every aspect of her existence.

'I want to come inside you,' Mircon groaned.

Jenna gave a soft laugh and eased her body higher. Straddling her lover's hips, she parted the lips of her labia with her fingers and slowly impaled herself on his cock, pushing down hard, until the brown curls at her pubis ground against the black curls circling the root of his penis.

Urgently, Mircon grabbed hold of Jenna's hips, digging his fingers into the full flesh. She lifted her body and thrust it downwards again, pumping herself up and down on the rigid stem. Rianna was overcome by their mutual lust. Opening her own thighs, she slid one cautious finger between the lips of her vulva. She was moist, the interior flesh warm and pleasantly slippery. With the tip of her finger she sought her clitoris and rubbed it gently, until it began to throb with a sweet heady fire of delight.

Unable to forget the wrenching pleasure she felt while watching Tarn climax as he strained against his chains, she rubbed the bud even harder, feeling a responsive tingling deep inside her womanly sheath.

She saw Mircon's shaft, gleaming wetly in the dim light, as it slid smoothly in and out of Jenna's vagina. Agitatedly, Rianna pressed her finger harder against her throbbing nubbin. The tiny clearing was filled with breathy moans and the sucking sound of flesh moving wetly on flesh as Jenna and Mircon approached their orgasms. Suddenly Jenna gave a high pitched squeal, her buttocks tensed and she ground her pelvis down against her lover's belly. Mircon grunted and heaved Jenna's body off him. She fell limply at his side as he climaxed, his face contorting with pleasure as creamy liquid spurted from the head of his cock.

Rianna shuddered, rubbing her fingers harder against her rosy pearl. It throbbed wildly, her flesh tensed and she was wracked by wave after wave of turbulent bliss. The pulsing pleasure slowly died away, leaving her weak, exhausted and trembling. She took a deep breath, and crawled away from the bushes. Then she rose to her feet and walked unsteadily back to her wagon.

Baral stifled a weary yawn as he escorted Rianna through the forest the following morning. The main encampment was a hive of activity. Most of the travellers had already breakfasted. Wagons were being packed and horses harnessed ready for their journey to recommence.

As Baral and Rianna approached the other encampment, it appeared far calmer. The soldiers worked with smooth military precision, packing up their bedrolls and donning their light body armour. A few of the men, however, still lingered around the fire talking and laughing together.

Rianna's arrival appeared to be of great interest to all the soldiers. They watched curiously as the young woman, destined to be their monarch's bride, walked into the clearing accompanied by Baral. Rianna blushed self-consciously under their scrutiny. Despite knowing it

70

was not the case, she regarded them as enemies not friends.

Rianna wore a travelling gown of turquoise sarsenet. The colour complimented her red-gold hair, which she wore loose around her shoulders. The shining waves spilled down her back and past her waist, confined only by a satin ribbon which matched her dress. She was tired; there were faint violet shadows beneath her eyes but she had rarely looked more lovely.

Ignoring the soldiers' admiring, lustful glances, and their lewd whispered asides, Rianna moved over to where Tarn lay. He appeared to still be asleep.

'Baral, could you check that a wagon is being prepared for the prisoner, just as I instructed.'

'Yes, my lady.' As Baral walked away, she knelt down beside Tarn, hoping he was awake. She wanted to be able to converse with him in private.

As she put a cool hand on Tarn's brow, his eyelids fluttered and then opened. His eyes were the most glorious blue, even more vivid than she remembered. Her memories of the handsome warrior faded into oblivion when she was confronted by the male perfection of Tarn in the flesh.

'Rianna, you've returned.' Tarn smiled warmly. 'For a time I feared you were just a wonderful dream.'

'Did you sleep well?' she asked, relieved that his fever appeared to have abated.

'Like a babe,' Tarn replied, wincing as she touched the wound on his head. 'It still aches a little.'

'Not surprising. The blow you took would have killed a lesser mortal.'

Baral had told Rianna what happened to Tarn after she'd departed. Captain Feroc had arrived to find Tarn violently attacking Rorg, while the other soldiers vainly tried to drag him away from their comrade. The blow which felled Tarn had come from the heavy hilt of Captain Feroc's broadsword.

'I never saw it coming,' Tarn confessed with a shaky smile.

'You are lucky to be alive.' She placed a small covered basket by his side. 'I've brought you breakfast. Honey cakes, freshly baked and still warm.'

The delicious odour of the cakes made Rianna feel hungry, but she could eat later. Tarn's needs were more important. Baral had told her that Tarn had been fed only weak gruel and sour ale since they left Harn.

'They smell delicious.' He wrinkled his nose in the most endearing manner. 'I just hope my stomach doesn't rebel against such luxury after the swill I've been forced to eat.'

'Eat slowly, and you'll be fine,' she replied. 'And be assured that from now on you will be well fed. Chancellor Lesand insists on that.'

'Fattening me up for the kill?' Tarn said with a wry grin.

'You should not jest about such matters.' She did not bother to hide her concern for him. 'If there was something I could do . . .'

'You've done enough already, sweet Rianna,' Tarn said in a voice heavy with meaning. 'More than enough for any man.'

She blushed. 'No more than I deemed necessary.'

'If it were possible I would ask for far more,' he replied. 'I long to once again kiss your ruby lips and to experience the tender touch of your hands on my body. I know it is not likely, but I can always live with the hope.'

'Anything is possible if you want it enough,' she whispered huskily, inwardly quailing at her boldness.

'I could not place you in danger. If Lesand were to discover how kind you have been to me, he would never forgive your behaviour.'

'The Chancellor will not find out.' She took hold of his hand. 'From henceforth you must be cautious, Tarn. We need to convince everyone that your head wound is far worse than it is. Seem confused, not knowing who or where you are. Ensure the soldiers see that you are in pain.'

72

Rianna found Tarn's full lips impossibly tempting as she recalled his passionate kisses. She was filled with an unquenchable need to throw herself into his arms. Her mind was in turmoil. She desired Tarn, yet she was promised to his enemy, Lord Sarin; and Sarin held the power of life and death over Tarn.

Rianna's thoughts had been aroused and inflamed. First by witnessing Tarn's punishment, then by watching Jenna and Mircon together. Her pudenda throbbed as she craved sensual fulfilment, but she was forced to deny the wanting.

'Is something amiss?' Tarn said worriedly. 'You appear troubled.' He tried to sit up but fell back with a groan of agony.

'It seems you have no need to pretend to be in pain,' she said tenderly.

'There is a pounding in my head. It feels like a dagger twisting deep within my skull,' he gasped weakly.

'Only time will heal the damage,' she told him. 'Remember, the weaker you appear the longer I can justify caring for you, Tarn.'

'Then I'll appear weak for my entire life.' His eyes darkened with the intensity of his emotion. 'I could wish nothing more wonderful than to have you always by my side.'

'Move yourself, barbarian!' a harsh voice interrupted. The sergeant, who had punished Tarn, marched over to them. 'Get up,' he snapped.

Angrily, Rianna jumped to her feet and glared furiously at the sergeant. 'What do you think you are doing?' she said icily.

He coloured in embarrassment. 'Forgive me for speaking so boldly, Lady Rianna. The prisoner needs to be moved to the wagon.'

'Chancellor Lesand has assigned the prisoner to my care,' she said in a determined voice. 'He cannot walk, he will have to be carried. The slightest jolt could cause irreparable damage.'

Turning, the sergeant shouted some instructions to his

men, then he looked back at Rianna. 'The wagon is prepared as instructed, my lady. It is sufficiently padded. No further harm will befall the captive, you can be assured of that.'

'Your men did the damage in the first place,' she snapped, watching the sergeant shift his feet awkwardly as she glared at him. 'If my instructions are not carried out to the letter and any harm befalls him, I shall speak to Lord Sarin myself. Do you understand what I'm saying, sergeant?'

'I do,' he stuttered, nodding vigorously. 'I'll ensure he's treated with every care.'

'Be sure he is,' she said sternly. The sergeant attempted a cautious smile. His teeth were stained and broken; he was quite the most repulsive man Rianna had ever come across. She hated him more than she believed she could hate any man. 'And give the captive this to wear. It is not fitting for him to be unclothed in my presence.'

She thrust the rolled-up garment she'd so recently acquired from Chancellor Lesand at the sergeant. The loose-legged trousers were made of the finest silk. No other man in the caravan could provide a suitable garment. Lesand was the closest to Tarn's height but still a head shorter than him.

'Of course, my lady,' the sergeant said obsequiously. Frowning, he looked down at the blue silk garment. Prisoners were not usually given such fine attire. 'We'll be departing soon. If you'll excuse me, my lady, the prisoner must be put in the wagon.'

He beckoned to four men, who now held between them a hastily constructed stretcher. They approached and encircled Tarn while one removed the manacles from his ankles. As they lifted him on the stretcher, Tarn grimaced in pain. The sergeant, meanwhile, pursed his lips in disgust, clearly resenting having to be so gentle with the captive.

The men carried Tarn over to a large baggage wagon and loaded him inside.

'Lady Rianna,' Baral touched her arm. 'We should leave. The caravan will be departing soon.'

'I wish to ensure that my patient is comfortable first,' she replied. 'You return to the other camp. I'll be with you shortly.'

'As you wish.' Baral bowed and departed.

Rianna waited until the soldiers had left the baggage wagon and Tarn was alone. Then she picked up the basket of honey cakes and walked over to the wagon. It was quite high off the ground and without steps it did not prove easy for her to climb inside.

Tarn, now discreetly clad in the silk trousers that barely reached his calves, smiled at her. He was lying on a pile of sacks stuffed with straw, which would help protect him from the jolting of the wagon. His face was pale, and perspiration covered his brow; visible proof that being moved had proved painful to him.

'Who thought this necessary?' Rianna asked in irritation as she saw the manacles on Tarn's wrists and ankles, attached by heavy chains to a ring bolted in the side of the wagon.

'The soldiers seem to think I might try and escape. They are not wrong,' Tarn said weakly. 'Although the way I feel at this moment, I doubt I would get more than a few paces.'

'You've tried escaping before, I hear?' She sank to her knees beside him and put down the basket of cakes.

'Twice so far. It is also rumoured that some of my comrades from Kabra may try to launch some kind of rescue attempt. I had hoped those rumours might be true, but the closer we get to Aguilar the less that seems likely.'

'If only you could escape,' she said with a sigh.

'Who knows, maybe the chance will still arise.' Tarn did not sound as though he thought it likely. 'Why even talk of such matters when I'm too weak to try?'

'Then we have to make you stronger.'

He lifted his manacled hand to stroke her pale cheek. 'You are so beautiful, Rianna.'

Meshing his hands in her hair, Tarn pulled her towards him and captured her lips with his. For a long, wonderful moment she melted in his arms, and gave herself up to the kiss. Entwining her tongue with his, she responded with warmth and passion, losing herself in ecstasy.

Tarn stroked her breasts through the fine sarsenet of her gown, and the simmering heat of desire in her sex burst into a blazing inferno. Rianna was brought back to brutal reality by the heavy weight of Tarn's chains as they fell across her waist. She forced herself to pull away from him, knowing one of the guards could appear at any moment.

'I must leave, but I'll return this evening,' she said breathlessly.

'I'll count the hours until you return,' he said in a voice husky with unrestrained passion.

By the time the caravan stopped for the night, Rianna was in a state of nervous excitement, all too eager to see Tarn again. During the long hours of travel she and Jenna had talked. Jenna told Rianna about the young men she'd known, her distress at being forced to leave Harn, and her growing affection for Mircon. Rianna spoke about her fears for the future and the life she envisaged in Percheron, but she could not find the courage to say anything about Tarn. The emotions raging within her head were far too complex to put into words.

Out of her limited travelling wardrobe, Rianna chose a deep pink silk gown, heavily embroidered with silver, which had been a gift from Lord Sarin. It fastened at the front with a multitude of tiny silver buttons and was far more loose fitting than her garments made in Harn.

The Chancellor had ordered that henceforth Tarn's guards should stay close to the main camp. She had to walk less than two hundred paces across an open, flower-filled meadow, so she chose not to bother with an escort.

Rianna found Tarn still chained inside the wagon,

resting on his pile of straw-filled sacks. The day had been warm but now the sky had clouded over and it looked likely to rain at any moment. The heavy metal hoops fitted across the wagon had been draped with canvas in order to protect the contents, affording Rianna and Tarn a measure of privacy.

'Rianna,' Tarn smiled and dragged himself into a sitting position.

'I have come to check on your wounds,' she said, trying to ignore the upsetting clanking of his chains as he moved.

'I've been desperate for you to return,' he confessed.

Rianna could not bring herself to admit that she felt the same. 'I trust you were given something palatable to eat?'

'A delicious stew. Quite the best I've ever tasted.' He pointed at the empty wooden bowl by his side. 'The first time I've eaten meat for weeks.'

'Good food will give you strength and help you recover.' Rianna's hand shook as she knelt down beside him and opened her bag. 'I'll examine and then redress your wounds. First let me look at your head.'

Tarn stayed silent, his blue eyes fixed on her face, as she thoughtfully probed his head wound, then examined his chest and shoulder. Tarn didn't wince or complain as she pulled off the stale bloodstained dressings.

'The pain in my head has decreased,' he volunteered as she spread soothing unguent over the now clean sword gash on his chest. The skin appeared healthier and far less inflamed, much to her relief.

'It's possible the pain may became worse again at times,' she said, pausing to smile tenderly at him. 'What of your back? Does that trouble you?'

'The skin feels tight and it smarts a little,' he replied with a twisted ironic smile. 'But it does not concern me. The whipping was intended to scar my mind not my body.'

'At least until we reach Aguilar I can ensure you will not have to endure such mistreatment again. After that . . .' she faltered, busying herself with taking more clean cloths from her bag.

'Let us not speak of the future, Rianna. I wish to live only for the present.' The look on Tarn's face made her tremble. She shivered with pleasure as he took hold of her hand and covered her palm with gentle kisses that set her skin on fire. 'I should remind you,' he whispered softly, 'that there is another wound you have yet to attend to.'

Rianna tried to quell the agitated beating of her heart. 'Indeed there is,' she huskily acknowledged.

He let go of her hand and relaxed back on the sacks, his blue eyes still fixed on her flushed face. Struggling to appear calm, Rianna unfastened the cord which held up Tarn's silk trousers. Cautiously she eased the fabric downwards, trying to keep his phallus and balls modestly covered. But the fine silk clung enticingly to his semi-erect shaft and the musky male scent of him made her knees feel weak with wanting. Faint with desire, Rianna tried to keep her attention on Tarn's wound. If the blow had been but a fraction to the right, his manhood would have been at risk. She shuddered at the thought as she spread unguent over the long gash. The strong smelling ointment would help him heal faster and it also served to mask the heady, compelling odour of Tarn's sex.

'Why so shy?' Tarn murmured. 'You were not so coy last night.'

'Tarn, I . . .' She tried to smile. 'Perhaps it would be better if you applied the ointment yourself.' She placed the pot by his side.

Tarn laughed softly and lifted his hand to touch her face. Tenderly, he ran his thumb over her trembling mouth. 'I know, my sweet one, I feel the same,' he said with understanding. 'Desire is a powerful emotion,' he finished, the need he felt for her plainly reflected on his face.

''Tis getting dark in here,' she said unsteadily. 'I should light the lamp.'

'Leave it a while.' He pulled his trousers together and retied the cord. 'I prefer the darkness, it hides us from prying eyes.'

The chains restraining Tarn clanked noisily as he leant forward to pull her into his arms. 'Should we be doing this?' she whispered in concern.

'No,' he groaned. 'Yet I cannot help myself. You're too tempting to resist.'

Tarn kissed her with anguished longing. Rianna's heart raced as she clung on to him, overwhelmed by passion. Her arms slid around him. She splayed her hands across his back, feeling the strength and hardness of his muscles. Beneath her fingertips she could just detect the raised weals which still marred the surface of his smooth golden skin.

'Order me to stop and I'll obey,' he whispered against her hair, as he struggled to unfasten the tiny buttons at the front of her gown. 'I just want to give you some of the pleasure you gave me.'

Tarn's musky male warmth enchanted her senses and she could feel the rapid beating of his heart. She shivered with impatience as Tarn's large hands struggled with the tiny buttons. Twisting them roughly from their confining loops, he opened her gown to well past her waist. He slid one hand in the opening to stroke her burgeoning flesh, then his fingers closed possessively around one naked breast. He caressed the creamy globes, first one then the other, kneading and squeezing them until she whimpered with pleasure.

As he kissed her again, she tasted the sweetness of his breath. His tongue invaded her mouth, stroking and probing the moist interior, making her desire grow to a fiery heat that knew no bounds. Rianna strained against Tarn as his searching fingers pulled and tweaked her nipple, forcing it to swell into a rigid cone. The throbbing bliss caused a responsive pulling in her belly. Unconsciously she moaned and opened her legs.

Pulling the pink silk further apart, Tarn pressed his face to the opening to kiss and lick her breasts. He nuzzled her nipple, closing his lips around the tiny teat. Pulling the nubbin deeper into his mouth, he sucked on it hard. Rianna whimpered and pressed herself even closer to Tarn as the pleasure rippled downwards, like the spreading flames of a fire. Heat filled her belly, increasing the pulsing warmth between her thighs.

She heard the clink of the chains as Tarn moved to slide his hand slowly up her leg. He paused to stroke the sensitive skin of her inner thigh. Rianna trembled with longing, wanting Tarn to continue and quell the slippery heat in her sex.

He meshed his fingers in her pubic hair and gently stroked the engorged lips of her vulva. Using the pad of his thumb, he traced the line of the crack of her sex. But still to her frustration he did not venture inside.

'I need your approval,' he said softly, as if expecting her to deny him entrance to her secret flesh.

'Please,' she moaned, in eager longing.

As he parted the lips of her labia and slid his fingers inside, the sudden rush of pleasure Rianna experienced was astounding. She had never know such bliss. Tarn moved his fingers smoothly along the rosy divide to her kernel of delight. First he circled the throbbing root, then rubbed and squeezed it gently. The power of her response made her realise the best was yet to come. She trembled, overcome with emotion, as Tarn caressed her bud of pleasure until it expanded and grew into the ultimate focus of her existence. Nothing else mattered but the feel of his fingers on her most intimate flesh as he drew her closer and closer to her climax.

Just when Rianna thought she could take no more of the pleasure, Tarn slowly slid one finger into her womanly sheath. He stroked the silken walls, careful always not to probe too deeply.

Rianna moaned, wanting to be stretched and filled by Tarn's flesh. Well aware what she desired, he thrust another finger inside her. But when she lifted her hips, trying to force him to venture deeper, he held back. 'No,' he said huskily. 'I'll not be the one to destroy the proof of your virginity.'

With care and precision he thrust his bunched fingers in and out of her vagina, all the while continuing to stroke her pleasure pearl with the pad of his thumb. Rianna was beyond ecstasy. She clutched agitatedly at Tarn's back, heedless of any discomfort it caused him, as he stimulated her to the ultimate peak of arousal. She reached the summit, her body tensing while her inner flesh pulsed. Consumed by the wrenching bliss she gave a muffled moan.

The spasms peaked and slowly died away, leaving her replete and exhausted. She laid her head against Tarn's chest as tears slid silently down her cheeks.

'I sought only to give you pleasure,' Tarn said worriedly. 'Now I've made you unhappy.'

'No, you have not.' She smiled tremulously. 'I never knew it could be so wonderful.'

Tarn pulled her skirt down over her legs and began to refasten the row of tiny buttons down the front of her gown. 'If only life were different,' he said sadly. 'You could have been travelling to Kabra to become my bride. I would have been the happiest man alive if that were so.'

'Life is cruel, is it not?' she replied shakily, still overcome by the strength of her climax.

'Our fate is set. It appears there is nothing we can do to change it.' He smiled tenderly at her. 'You should leave now, the guards may become curious if you linger too long.'

A few drops of rain spattered on the canvas above them. 'I have no wish to be drenched,' she said, attempting to lighten the mood. Rianna felt almost too weak to walk. She did not want to leave, her only desire was to remain with Tarn. 'I'll leave my bag here for when I return in the morning.'

Still feeling unsteady on her feet, she clambered to the back of the wagon and climbed down the wooden steps the soldiers had provided for her comfort. Before she departed, she allowed herself one long lingering look at Tarn. He was staring at her, his expression a mixture of longing and undisguised despair.

After Rianna's departure, Tarn sighed heavily and lay back on the straw-filled sacks. His penis was engorged, throbbing for a release that was denied him. He longed to plunge it deep inside sweet Rianna's feminine sheath and feel the velvety flesh close around him, then watch her face wracked by pleasure as his thrusting cock brought her once again to the peak of fulfilment.

Never before had he desired a woman so much. Rianna was beautiful, the loveliest creature he'd ever laid eyes on, but there was a tenderness and compassion within her that moved him even more completely. He recalled the delicious scent of her, the smooth softness of her ivory skin, the round lushness of her breasts and the sweet fiery heat of her sex.

Tarn's erect penis jumped at the thought and there was an unbearable pressure in his scrotum. However, he had no wish to bring himself to a brief, unsatisfactory climax with his own hands. He wanted to feel Rianna's gentle intoxicating fingers caressing his aroused flesh.

He did not know how long Lesand would allow Rianna to tend him, or how many more opportunities there would be for them to be together. Each meeting would bring him exquisite pleasure, but also unbearable pain. Rianna, the woman he wanted and desired above all others, was destined to wed his greatest enemy, Sarin. Up to the moment Tarn had first set eyes on Rianna, he'd almost come to accept his fate, well aware that he might be put to death, or worse still, be forced to become Sarin's slave. Sarin was a clever but selfish man, obsessed with sensuality and carnal pleasure. Tarn knew that Sarin secretly desired him, and now he would be taken before Sarin in chains, totally at his mercy; forced to genuflect before him and accept whatever punishment Sarin's devious mind could contrive.

Tarn did not fear pain or death, but he feared Sarin.

The noble lord knew him too well. Sarin was well aware of Tarn's weaknesses and he would enjoy humbling and degrading him. However, Tarn was more concerned for Rianna. The brave, beautiful lady deserved a husband who would love and cherish her, treat her with honour and respect. She knew little of the licentious life that awaited her at Sarin's court. Sarin would lure her into his web of carnal sensuality, entrap her and devour her completely. Sarin surrounded himself with acolytes, both male and female; some were slaves, others were there because of circumstance, or of their own choosing. But they all found pleasure in the decadent sensuality of their existence.

Pressing his hands to his throbbing cock, Tarn tried to ignore his unfulfilled desires. He closed his eyes, but visions of Rianna invaded his mind. How could the Protector of Harn allow his daughter to wed Lord Sarin? Sadly, it was not unusual for a royal maiden to be used as a pawn to ensure peace between two opposing lands.

Pain knifed through Tarn's heart; if only his bid to free Kabra had not failed. His father, weakened by old age and remorse, had become Sarin's puppet king, no longer able to make decisions for himself. Fearful of Sarin, the king had refused to let his personal guard or any of his soldiers fight in the rebellion. Tarn's army had not been strong enough to defeat the superior forces of Percheron, and many good men of Kabra had died in the ensuing battle. If they had won, Tarn could have asked for Rianna's hand in marriage.

Filled with despair, Tarn rolled on to his side. The delicious scent of Rianna still clung to his flesh. He lifted his hand close to his face and inhaled deeply.

Never-ending rain drummed noisily down on the wooden roof of Rianna's wagon. Large pools of water covered the grass at the sides of the road, and the wagons sloshed uncomfortably through the steadily thickening mud. If it rained much longer, Rianna feared the roads would become impassable and they would be unable to continue their journey. By nightfall the downpour had lessened a little, but not enough to allow Rianna to make her way to the other camp to visit Tarn.

The rain died away just after midnight, and in the morning the ground had dried out enough for the caravan to proceed. Lesand issued orders for the caravan to set out earlier than usual, so Rianna found the opportunity to visit Tarn only briefly. However, she contented herself with the thought that she could spend more time with him that evening.

Because of the sodden ground, the horses and wagons moved slowly, and it was almost dark by the time they stopped for the night. 'I'm going to see Tarn,' Rianna announced after swiftly eating her meal. Swinging a cloak around her shoulders, she picked up a lantern.

'It's very dark for you to be walking about alone,' Jenna pointed out. 'Someone should accompany you. Mircon is waiting for me, at least allow us to walk with you to the other encampment.'

'If that is your wish.' Rianna was secretly relieved to have an escort.

She accompanied Jenna outside. Mircon bowed politely, a little overcome by Rianna's presence. He said nothing, staying totally silent as he walked with Rianna and Jenna to the other encampment.

'Be sure you get someone to walk you back,' Jenna fussed. 'It's rumoured that a group of strange warriors has been sighted in the vicinity. The local peasants think they are bandits.'

'I'll be careful,' Rianna replied with a smile. She watched Jenna and Mircon walk away then strode into the soldiers' encampment. The first person she saw was the sergeant who had so cruelly beaten Tarn.

'My lady.' He approached her and bowed ingratiatingly. 'I have a favour to ask.'

'A favour?' she queried, wanting to get away from this unpleasant oaf.

'I'm told you are a skilled healer. The prisoner appears

to be greatly improving under your care. Could I therefore trouble you to examine one of my men?'

'If you wish,' she agreed, hiding her impatience.

'Come here,' the sergeant shouted to a soldier lurking
in the shadows of a nearby baggage wagon. In the dim
light Rianna could not see the man's face, but as he
stepped forward she recognised him at once. It was Rorg.
She wanted to turn away in disgust but she managed to
conceal her loathing. 'What is wrong with the man?'

'During a struggle with the prisoner, Rorg was badly
hurt. Even now, he can barely manage to walk, my lady.
The damage is centred in a most sensitive part of his
anatomy,' the sergeant explained, awkwardly.

'I think I have a potion that might aide him, and an
ointment of arnica to help heal the bruising,' she replied,
thinking swiftly. 'I'll have my maid prepare them in the
morning.'

'I would be most grateful,' Rorg stuttered.

'The potion tastes most unpalatable,' she warned him.
'But it will work swiftly, ensuring that you completely
forget your present discomfort.'

'My thanks, Lady Rianna,' the two men echoed.

'My pleasure. Now I must go and dress the prisoner's
wounds. Please see that I am not disturbed.'

She walked swiftly away from then, and climbed into
Tarn's wagon. With the canvas still draped over the
wagon, the interior was dark and gloomy.

'I feared you were not coming,' Tarn said, as she
hooked her lantern on to one of the bars supporting the
canvas.

She smiled. 'I would not forget you, Tarn.'

'You appear light-hearted,' he said, smiling adoringly
at her.

'No wonder.' She gave a bitter laugh. 'The sergeant
who whipped you just stopped me and begged me to
tend Rorg's injury. It appears he still suffers great pain.'

'He deserves every moment of his agony,' Tarn replied
venomously. He then frowned. 'Why does this amuse
you so? I thought you too hated Rorg.'

'Mightily.' She knelt at Tarn's side and kissed his cheek. 'The potion I intend to give him will be the strongest purgative in existence. Rorg will be forced to take refuge behind every tree and bush on the road to Aguilar. He'll be in such distress, he'll forget all about the wound you gave him,' she said, with immense satisfaction.

'Rianna, I never believed you to be so cruel,' he teased.

'Oh, I am cruel.' She ran her hands slowly over his chest, pausing to pull and squeeze at his copper-coloured nipples. Then she leant forward and nibbled at them with her teeth.

'Most cruel,' he agreed with a moan of longing.

'Last night my maid spent the evening instructing me in matters of the flesh,' she purred. 'I'm most eager to put what I've learnt into practice.' She slid her hands under the top of his silk trousers and stroked his firm stomach.

'What pray has she been teaching you?' he asked huskily.

She trailed her fingers over his sex, feeling his belly tremble and his penis jerk excitedly. 'How to pleasure a man . . . in the most intimate of manners.' Rianna conquered her shyness, urged on by her desire for Tarn. 'With my mouth,' she added as her fingers closed around the stem of his manhood and began to stroke it softly.

'Perhaps this is not wise,' Tarn said with a groan of pleasure. 'You're promised to another.'

'Then let me enjoy being with you while I can,' she insisted. 'This is what I want, Tarn.'

'How can the gods have punished me, yet allowed me to taste such bliss in your arms,' he groaned.

Rianna unfastened the tie of his trousers and pulled the fabric down his body, pooling it on his thighs. She cupped the loose flesh of his testicles, caressing them gently, then she stroked the sensitive ridge of skin behind them. Tarn shuddered, reduced to helplessness by the arousing touch of her fingers.

Boldly grasping his cock stem, Rianna milked the shaft

with long smooth strokes, watching it harden until the foreskin rolled back to reveal the luscious plum hidden beneath. Increasing the pressure of her fingers, she intensified the pace of her movements until his rod hardened even more, turning into a rigid inflexible stem. The collar of skin ringing the head tightened, forcing the bulb to grow even more in size. It became taut and shiny, and a tiny bead of moisture seeped from the mouth at the tip, trembling like a tear on the summit. She scooped it up with her finger and placed it on the tip of her tongue.

The juice of Tarn's body tasted salty, with a faintly musky tang. Wanting to savour more, she milked the shaft harder. Tarn gave a groan as more liquid seeped from the tiny mouth. This time she captured the dew-drop with her tongue. She lapped at his sex head, licking it with long tantalising strokes.

Tarn shuddered. 'Rianna,' he murmured.

She tipped her head forward and silken strands of her hair tumbled across Tarn's stomach and thighs, stroking his aroused flesh. Sliding her lips over the glans of his penis, she pulled the entire head into her mouth. She ran her tongue around the ridge of flesh collaring the rim, savouring the taste of the salty emanations which seeped from his body.

Tarn made an entreating sound from deep in his throat, wanting her to take more of his penis inside her mouth. She slipped her lips lower, acutely aware of the throbbing heat in her own sex. The pulsing hardness of Tarn's manhood pressed against the soft interior of her mouth, as she accommodated as much of the shaft as she could, feeling the tip hit the back of her throat. Knowing she was not yet skilful enough to swallow the rest of his sex without gagging, she began to squeeze and stroke the base of the long, thick rod with her fingertips. She cupped the swollen sac of his balls, feeling them contract into two firm stones.

Tarn arched his back, thrusting his hips upwards as she moved her tongue sensuously up and down his manly shaft. Rianna slid her lips smoothly upwards, until she held only his cock head in her mouth. Then she slid her lips downwards again, gradually increasing the speed of her movement until she was milking the stem with her mouth.

Defenceless in his bliss, Tarn moaned. She felt his penis jerk as the pressure built inside him. The strength and power of his orgasm surprised her; as he climaxed, the seed spurted deep inside her throat. She swallowed, fascinated by the taste and texture of the creamy substance. Squeezing her legs tightly together, she ignored her own desire, gaining pleasure from Tarn's joyous release.

As the intense climax died away, she felt his organ soften and his body grow limp and relaxed. Releasing her hold on him, she raised her head.

'My sweet.' Tarn pulled her into his arms, kissing her long and deeply. 'I love you, Rianna,' he murmured as he cradled her lovingly in his arms.

# Chapter Five

*R*ianna wanted to remain with Tarn all night, but she knew she could not afford to tarry too long. She pulled herself from his embrace and with swift precision tended and redressed his wounds. Then she bade him a reluctant farewell, promising to return early the following morning.

She took little notice of the soldier who escorted her back to the other encampment. She was engrossed by her thoughts of Tarn, and all too aware of the taste of his sex still lingering in her mouth.

Rianna was just about to enter her wagon when she heard Lesand call to her. Turning, she waited for him to approach. 'How fares the prisoner?' Lesand asked as he joined her.

'He is slowly improving,' she replied with caution. 'But his head wound still troubles me. It is not unknown for warriors with such wounds to appear to recover, then suddenly relapse.'

'Quite so,' Lesand said gravely, staring at Rianna very intently. 'Baral seems to think you hold great sympathy for the prisoner.'

'He is a gentle and noble warrior,' she replied. 'Tarn is the prince of Kabra and deserves to be treated with honour and respect. Do you not agree, Chancellor?'

'My personal opinions are of no consequence,' he replied brusquely. 'Lord Sarin had issued certain orders concerning the prisoner's treatment. I do not question my sovereign and neither should you.'

'You appear to be avoiding a direct answer, Chancellor. This leads me to believe that you too feel some sympathy for Tarn's sad predicament.'

Lesand appeared pensive. 'You have a stubborn streak in your nature that you'd be wise to suppress.'

'I inherited it from my mother, Kitara. She was a warrior princess,' Rianna said with pride. 'Tell me, Chancellor, do you think Lord Sarin would be prepared to grant me a boon on the celebration of our marriage?'

'A plea of clemency for Tarn of Kabra, no doubt?' There was an unreadable expression on Lesand's face.

'Why not?' she asked. 'Surely Lord Sarin can understand that it was necessary for Tarn to try and regain what was once destined to be his.'

'You are venturing on very dangerous ground,' Lesand warned. 'Such matters are best left alone, and certainly not discussed in public.'

'Then I will stay silent for the moment.' Some time in the near future, Rianna intended to find the right opportunity to speak to Lesand in private about Tarn.

'There is a matter which concerns me,' Lesand added. 'The propriety of your constant visits to Tarn. I hear you have been spending much time alone with him.'

'Only as much is as necessary,' she argued. 'He still needs my healing skills.'

'I will allow you to continue tending him, but in future you should be accompanied by your maid or Baral. You cannot be alone again with Tarn.'

'But he can do me no harm. He's chained hand and foot.'

'Tarn would never hurt a woman, I know that,' Lesand replied. 'My concerns centres on your position as Lord Sarin's bride. An unwed maid should not spend time alone with a young man who has at least partially regained his strength. It's not seemly, Lady Rianna.'

* * *

'Jenna, I have a favour to ask of you,' Rianna said as they approached the prisoner's encampment the following evening. 'After I've dressed Tarn's wounds, I wish to spend some time alone with him.'

'Contrary to the Chancellor's orders?' Jenna smiled understandingly. 'I saw the way the prisoner looked at you when you tended him this morning. The prince of Kabra is totally smitten, Lady Rianna.'

'Smitten?' Rianna glanced at her maid who seemed vastly amused.

'As smitten as you are,' Jenna gently teased. 'I have eyes in my head, it was obvious to me. Just take care you do not reveal your secret to any other. It would not bode well for either of you if Lord Sarin discovered the truth. Prince Tarn is handsome and charming. What woman wouldn't fall in love with him? 'Tis a pity your prince lost the battle to regain control of Kabra, then you could have married him instead.'

The two women were surprised by the unexpected commotion as they walked into the encampment. The sergeant was shouting orders and men were hurrying hither and thither, saddling horses, donning body armour and readying themselves for battle.

'What is happening?' Jenna asked one of the soldiers as he brushed past her.

'A group of warriors has been sighted five leagues from here,' the soldier hurriedly explained. 'It's thought the men might be from Kabra, intent on freeing our prisoner. We are to hunt them down and stop them reaching the caravan.'

Hope filled Rianna's heart. She prayed that Tarn could be rescued, but whatever happened it was bound to lead to bloodshed.

As they continued on towards the wagon where Tarn was chained, Rorg approached them. 'I've been left in charge, my lady,' he said gruffly. 'If you wish to tend to the prisoner you will have to work swiftly. We've orders to move all our wagons close to the rest of the caravan.'

He suddenly paled, clutching at his stomach. 'Ye gods,' he grunted, and then sped towards the cover of the trees.

Rianna laughed. 'Your potion appears to be working most admirably, Jenna. Now we must hurry.'

Lifting up her skirts, she climbed into the wagon.

'What is amiss?' Tarn asked as he saw her. 'Why all the commotion?'

'A group of warriors have been seen about five leagues from here. It's feared they are a rescue party from Kabra.' She smiled and moved to his side. 'Let us hope it is your friends.'

'They'll be greatly outnumbered,' Tarn said with concern. 'It's doubtful they'd manage to reach me.' He glanced over at Jenna who stood just inside the entrance to the wagon, then back at Rianna as she sank down beside him. 'Did you have to bring your maid again?' he asked in a low voice.

'The Chancellor has ordered that from henceforth we are not to be left alone. He fears for my honour, Tarn.'

'A little late for such niceties,' Tarn whispered under his breath as he smiled lovingly at her.

'I'm most discreet,' came Jenna's cheerful voice from the rear of the wagon. 'I forget most of everything I see.'

'Can you trust her?' Tarn asked Rianna.

'Of course,' Rianna confirmed as she swiftly examined Tarn's wounds, applying more ointment before redressing the cut on his shoulder.

There was the clink of weapons and the wagon suddenly shook as a troop of horsemen cantered by.

'Most of the soldiers are leaving,' Jenna announced. 'The rest are probably too busy guarding the camp and looking out for attackers to trouble themselves with what you are doing, my lady.' She laughed. 'And Rorg is nowhere to be seen. He's probably crouching behind some bush with his trousers round his ankles.'

Tarn took hold of Rianna's hand and smothered it with kisses. 'I long to be alone with you,' he groaned. 'Will we manage even a few moments of privacy, my love?'

Jenna stretched lazily. ''Tis odd, I suddenly feel most unwell,' she said, never having sounded healthier. 'I beg leave to step outside for a breath of fresh air.'

'Of course, Jenna. Stay outside as long as you like.' Rianna flashed her maid a grateful smile.

Jenna took no time in leaving the wagon. As she disappeared, Tarn pulled Rianna into his arms. 'Very discreet,' he murmured, capturing her lips with his and kissing her with unrestrained passion until she was breathless with desire for him. 'I adore you, Rianna,' he murmured, pressing gentle kisses on the unruly red-gold curls that spilled untidily over her shoulders and down her back.

The sound of gruff male voices close to the wagon disturbed the intimacy of the moment. Nervously, Rianna pulled away from Tarn.

'My lady,' Jenna pushed her head through the canvas opening, pointedly not looking in their direction.

'What is it, Jenna?' Rianna asked.

'The soldiers are hitching the team to the wagon. It's their intention to join the main body of the caravan.'

'Best you come inside. Why walk back to the other camp when we can ride?' Rianna resented the fact that she'd shared only brief moments with Tarn, but the fault was not Jenna's.

As Jenna joined them, there was a shout from the driver and the wagon jerked forward, trundling noisily over the rough ground. It only took them a moment to join the rest of the caravan, entering the circle of wagons and coming to a halt close to the Chancellor's tent.

'I should leave,' Rianna said with regret. She did not know when they would have the opportunity to be alone again. Here, in full sight of all the other travellers, there was little chance of privacy. She leant towards Tarn. 'I love you,' she whispered in his ear.

Overcome by her honest declaration of feelings, he looked at her in surprise. 'Rianna,' he murmured.

Before Tarn had time to say anything more, Rianna clambered swiftly from the wagon. Jenna was already outside, speaking to Baral. The encampment appeared to be in total chaos as the travellers and the soldiers packed up their belongings and hitched teams of horses to the wagons.

'Baral tells me that we will be departing soon,' Jenna announced.

Rianna looked questioningly at Baral, who nodded. 'Indeed we are. You've heard that a band of warriors has been sighted close by?'

'Yes,' she confirmed.

'In the circumstances, Chancellor Lesand has decided it would be safer to seek shelter within the estate of a local nobleman, Seigneur Wernock. He is a close friend of Lord Sarin and his country estate is only a short distance away. Messages have been sent to the Seigneur, and he is eagerly awaiting your arrival, Lady Rianna.'

'The Chancellor cares greatly for your welfare, my lady,' Jenna said with a caustic smile.

'It appears so,' Rianna agreed, certain that the Chancellor was more concerned about Tarn escaping. Even if his comrades were in the area, it was unlikely they could rescue him from a nobleman's stronghold.

In no time at all the caravan was on the move, with Rianna's conveyance escorted on both sides by Lesand's soldiers. The darkness and the rough roads slowed down the large cortège and it was almost midnight when they arrived at the Seigneur's estate. The house and outbuildings were set in huge grounds surrounded by a high stone wall. The area within the walls was so large it could accommodate their entire caravan without appearing crowded.

Most of the travellers made camp, while Rianna, Chancellor Lesand and his senior officers entered the manor house. They were greeted by the Seigneur, a portly, dark-haired gentleman with a hooked nose who was inordinately pleased to see them. He immediately handed Rianna and Jenna into the care of a gaggle of serving maids. Chattering excitedly, they fussed around

Rianna as they led her to a large, elaborately furnished chamber.

Rianna shivered with tiredness as they brushed her long hair and divested her of her clothes. They dressed her in a delicately embroidered silk night-gown, and helped her climb into the large bed. It was warm, soft and incredibly comfortable, and Rianna relaxed back on the pillows watching Jenna undress.

'Sleep with me tonight, Jenna,' she said with a yawn.

'There's a pallet made up for me at the end of your bed,' Jenna pointed out.

'I'm lonely, I don't want to sleep alone.'

Rianna was feeling sad, knowing now that there was little chance of Tarn being rescued, as there appeared to be a large number of soldiers guarding the Seigneur's estate.

Jenna smiled with understanding. 'If my lady wishes it,' she acknowledged, joining Rianna. She waited until the maids had departed before looking over at her mistress. 'I know how troubled you are. I managed to exchange a few brief words with Mircon. The Prince is to be confined in the cellars of the house.'

Rianna sighed unhappily. 'I wonder if I will ever be able to speak to him again. Let alone . . .' she faltered, her voice trembling with distress.

Jenna edged closer to Rianna and slipped a comforting arm around her shoulders. 'Don't be downcast, the future may not be as grim as you think. In the morning I'll seek out Mircon. He's sure to be able to get a message to Prince Tarn.'

By the end of the first day in Seigneur Wernock's house, Rianna was heartily sick of her host's company. He insisted on spending every moment by her side, and unfortunately he was an incredibly irksome companion.

After a long evening meal, consisting of many rich, highly spiced courses, Rianna retired. It appeared she would have to endure her host's continued attentions on the morrow, as the Chancellor had decided to spend at least another day here before recommencing their journey.

Jenna was awaiting Rianna in her bedchamber. 'Any news?' Rianna asked her, having shooed all the other maids from the room.

'The group of warriors has yet to be captured. There's been no sign of them so far,' Jenna replied.

Rianna wondered why Jenna seemed so uncomfortable. 'What is amiss?'

'The Seigneur is a rich and powerful man. He even brings his personal surgeon when travelling to his country estate. I hear the man is very well respected and considered to be a great healer,' Jenna replied awkwardly. 'The Seigneur had him examine Tarn. He has concluded that Tarn is recovering well, and Mircon does not think you will be allowed to tend him further. It has been decided that Tarn is now fit enough to be returned to his cage for the final few days of travel to Aguilar.'

The colour drained from Rianna's face. Never before had she felt such despair. 'This cannot be.'

'Come, sit down.' Jenna took her arm and made her sit on the bed. 'You must be strong. Be of good heart, it is not quite as bad as it appears to be. I've spoken to Mircon and it is all arranged. But be warned, what I propose will be dangerous for you.'

'What is arranged?' Rianna asked in confusion.

'You are to see Tarn tonight. Let us hope it is not for the last time,' Jenna replied. 'You wish it, do you not?'

'Oh yes. But how?' Rianna struggled to hold back her tears of pain.

'Mircon has ensured that he will be one of the two guards on duty outside Tarn's cell tonight. I will be taking Mircon down a flask of a red wine, and he will offer some to his comrade. I have spiked the wine with a strong potion which will make the other soldier sleep like a babe for hours.'

'Jenna, how can I ever thank you?' Rianna said with relief as she embraced her maid.

'By allowing me to continue seeing Mircon.' Jenna

jumped to her feet. 'Now I must take the wine down to the cellars. Wait here, my lady, until I return.'

Rianna waited impatiently, desperate to see Tarn as she paced restlessly around the chamber. It seemed like a lifetime had passed before Jenna returned. When she did, Rianna stepped eagerly forward. She had already changed into her loose pink gown, and she wore a dark cloak around her shoulders.

'Ready?' asked Jenna.

'Yes.' Rianna felt nervous as she took hold of Jenna's hand, fearing she might be discovered before she was able to reach Tarn.

The manor house was silent, and the long winding corridors were dimly lit. The two women hurried to the rear of the building and down the stone steps that led to the cellars. The underground corridor was well illuminated. Mircon stood to attention beside a thick wooden door. The other guard was slumped on the floor snoring noisily.

'I will reward you for this, Mircon,' Rianna said with gratitude as Mircon drew back the heavy bolts on the door of Tarn's cell.

'Jenna is all the reward I need, Lady Rianna,' Mircon replied. 'I knew Prince Tarn in Aguilar before he returned to Kabra and led the rebellion. He's a good man, and deserves to be treated with honour.'

Smiling her gratitude, Rianna slipped into Tarn's cell. She was relieved to find that it was no dank dungeon, it was dry and warm but a little stuffy. The only illumination came from a small oil lamp suspended from the ceiling. Tarn was sitting on a pallet laid against the far wall.

He looked up at her, hardly able to believe what he was seeing. 'I'm not dreaming?'

'No, my love.' She flung herself into his arms. Tarn embraced Rianna, holding her so close he almost squeezed the breath from her body.

It was then that Rianna realised there were no cruel

manacles around Tarn's wrists and ankles. She kissed Tarn and he responded with passion as he thrust his tongue deep into her mouth. Sighing with pleasure, Rianna meshed her fingers in his long silky blond hair, but they brushed against something hard and metallic encircling his neck.

'What is this? A heavy chain ran from Tarn's collar to the wall.

'It's nothing,' he said lightly. 'The chain's long enough to allow me movement. At least my arms are free to embrace you without restrictions. Seigneur Wernock has made it plain he has no wish for me to escape while in his custody.'

'I think it's barbaric,' she said with disgust, then added, 'the soldiers have found no sign of your rescuers as yet.'

She stared at his handsome face, drinking in the beauty of his sky blue eyes, and wondered how she could exist without him.

'I've come to doubt my rescuers exist,' he said with a frown. 'They're probably a figment of some nervous peasant's imagination. If my former comrades did plan to mount a rescue, it would have been attempted before we entered Percheron.' He hesitated, then added anxiously. 'You endanger yourself by coming here, my sweet.'

'This may be our last chance to be together,' she told him sadly. 'Mircon, Jenna's soldier friend, has discovered that you are to be returned to that terrible cage. In all probability I will not be allowed to attend you again.'

Pulling herself from his embrace, she rose to her knees and threw aside her cloak. With trembling fingers she began to unfasten the buttons at the front of her dress.

'Is this wise?' Tarn glanced worriedly towards the door.

'Mircon is on guard duty outside. He will ensure we are not disturbed.' She ripped the buttons apart and let the gown slide from her shoulders. Rianna wore nothing beneath it. She knelt before Tarn naked and unadorned.

Then lifting her hands she undid the ribbon holding her hair. The red-gold strands fell around her shoulders and down her back.

'You're so beautiful.' Tarn's eyes darkened with desire.

'I want you to pleasure me, Tarn,' she said, all the love she felt for him reflected on her face. 'I want you to make me yours completely.'

She leant forward to unfasten the cord holding his trousers together, her long hair brushing his stomach and thighs.

'No.' Tarn put his hand atop hers, preventing her from drawing the silk downwards. 'I long to make love to you, but I cannot commit the ultimate act. It's impossible, you must go to your husband a virgin.'

'My virginity is the only thing which is mine to give,' she insisted with determination. 'I want you to have it, not Sarin.'

Tarn's mouth was set in a stubborn line, but Rianna knew he was deeply moved by her nudity. His hand trembled as he tried to push her away from him. 'Please do not torture me, Rianna. However much I want you I cannot let you do this.'

'And I will not let you stop me,' she replied with equal determination. She kissed the corner of his mouth, moving her lips lower to caress the tense cording of his neck and the firm planes of his chest. As her teeth nibbled at his left nipple, Tarn groaned and relaxed his hold on her hand. She jerked the silk away from his sex to free his engorged rod.

'No, Rianna,' Tarn pleaded, helpless in his desire for her.

'Tarn, I adore you.' She slid her arms around him and pressed herself close, rubbing her bare breasts against his chest. It was the first time they'd been naked together, flesh to flesh. Rianna cherished the warm smoothness of his skin as she felt the rapid beat of his heart. Her nipples hardened, while her knees felt weak with wanting.

'I cannot resist,' he groaned, unable to stop his hands feverishly caressing her delectable curves.

Tarn's mouth covered hers, kissing her with anguished longing, worshipping at the fountain of her lips. As his tongue invaded her mouth the breath of their bodies mingled as one.

'You may be a warrior, but you're still not strong enough to fight me, Tarn. If fortune would permit, I would take you as my husband, not Sarin. So why should I give him the most precious gift I can bestow?'

She caressed Tarn's trembling flesh, feeling more empowered now than she had in her entire life. This was what she wanted, this was what she would have. She would be Tarn's completely, always and forever.

Tarn's manhood twitched restlessly as she ran her fingers though the silky curls of his pubis. Smiling, she touched the engorged shaft, stroking it tenderly, feeling it harden even more. A tremor ran across Tarn's stomach and thighs. With a soft groan, he resumed his possession of her lips, kissing her passionately and thrusting his tongue deep inside her mouth. Rianna's pudenda throbbed, longing to be invaded in a similar manner by his thick rod of manly flesh. Twining his arms around her, Tarn clasped Rianna close, as though he never wanted to let her go.

'My dearest love,' she whispered. The need Rianna felt for this man was stronger than anything else in her life. She no longer cared for the future, only for this precious moment in time.

She pulled away from him, and straddled his thighs. Bending her head to lap at the engorged head of his penis, she ran her tongue teasingly around the rim, then she drank the pearl of moisture that trembled on the tip.

'I love you with all my heart, Rianna,' Tarn gasped. 'If you do not desist I'll not find the strength to repel you again,' he added, in a voice shaking with emotion.

'Do not fight your desires, Tarn.' She raised her eyes to his. 'I want you. I need you to pleasure me. I long to feel your glorious staff of life thrusting deep inside my body.'

'I always knew you were a forest wraith come to tempt me beyond any man's endurance,' he groaned softly. 'I can no longer fight the erotic spell you've woven around me.'

Tarn pressed gentle kisses on her cheek, her mouth, the curve of her jaw. Sliding his lips down her neck, he mouthed her breast, lapping on her nipple and concentrating on the tiny peak until it swelled into a rigid cone. He collared the nubbin, sucking hard, drawing it deeper into his mouth. As he nibbled at it with his teeth, the painful pleasure made her gasp with delight.

With the flat of his hand he stroked her belly, then ran his fingers through her pubic curls. Her pudenda was hot and ready for him. Moisture seeped from her feminine sheath, coating the secret valley of her sex. Parting the red-gold fleece, he slid his fingers between the full labial lips to caress the moist divide. Her vulva throbbed, alive with longing. She sighed aloud as his searching fingers found her pleasure bud, pressing and stroking the aching nubbin until its tiny hood rolled back to expose the extra sensitive flesh beneath.

He touched the entrance to her feminine sheath, circling the opening before sliding his fingers inside. As he stroked the velvety interior, he kissed the underside of her breasts and lapped at the perspiration gathered there. Rianna pressed her face to his long blond hair, pulling the familiar scent of him deep into her lungs, wanting it to remain forever a part of her – a constant reminder of the man she loved. This moment was special, never to be repeated. She was gifting Tarn with her innocence. He was her life, her very existence. Rianna vowed that in her heart he would always be her soul mate, her true husband.

Tarn stroked and teased her pearl of ultimate bliss while his fingers probed her honeyed folds, seeking the centre of her creation. The tips of his fingers brushed the barrier that denied him further entrance and she felt him pull back.

'No,' she complained. 'Continue.'

'Rianna, Rianna.' He repeated her name like a litany. 'You are all I've ever wanted and far, far more. I cannot destroy your future with this one selfish act.'

'You'll destroy me if we do not continue,' she said huskily, her desire aroused to fever pitch. Her only need was to be impaled on his thick male shaft, and to feel him thrust deep inside her. Then she would be joined to him completely.

She eased her hips forward until the tip of his glans pressed against the crack of her sex. She was so moist it slid easily between her swollen leaves. Tarn shook his head, wanting to desist but not having the strength to pull away from her. She felt his penis jerk beneath her fingertips as it slid along the valley and brushed the taut pearl of her existence. The nubbin throbbed sweetly and she gave a soft pleading moan.

'It's too late, Tarn.' She positioned herself so that the head of his cock rested against the entrance to her vagina, then she bore down enough to let it stretch the entrance. As she lowered her hips his cock slid inside, stretching the soft, velvety flesh. The sensation was wonderful and she wanted the pressure, the stretching to increase. Very cautiously, she eased her hips lower, feeling her sheath welcome the intimate intrusion as it expanded to accommodate more of the bulky shaft.

'No!' Tarn clutched at her hips as if trying to pull her off him. 'We can stop this, now.'

'You cannot stop me, Tarn.'

Placing her hands on his shoulders, Rianna thrust her hips downwards. His penis slid deeper, breaking through the membrane that had barred its way. The pain was sharp but momentary. It faded away to be replaced be a feeling of intense pleasure as Tarn's flesh filled her completely.

Impaled on Tarn's shaft of life, she leant forward and took possession of his mouth. She felt his lips soften and his resistance dissolve as he kissed her with unrestrained passion. Tightening his hold on her hips, he lifted her and then pulled her down again, increasing the depth of the penetration until the head of his cock hit the neck of her womb. The feeling of stretched fullness was totally exquisite.

Tarn began to move his hips, employing a smooth seductive rhythm. Rianna instinctively began to move her hips in an accompanying beat. Every thrust half-emptied and then filled her, caressing the sensitive walls of her feminine sheath. She dug her fingers into Tarn's muscular shoulders as his movements became stronger, the accompanying thrusts harder.

Perspiration broke out on Tarn's brow, and his beautiful face was transfixed by the intensity of his passion. Every thrust brought them closer and closer to release. Their mutual pleasure expanded until it grew into a rosy, all-enveloping haze, their souls merging and becoming one.

'I love you,' Tarn gasped.

As she felt his penis jerk inside her, Tarn's body tensed, trying vainly to pull away from her. Rianna clung on to him, grinding her pelvis against his. Then her climax came in a sudden rush of pleasure. As her flesh tube contracted, milking his cock, Tarn lost control completely. His penis pulsed as he spilt his seed deep inside her body.

The sweetly tearing bliss of Rianna's orgasm seemed to go on forever. When at last it began to die away, she made a vain attempt to cling on to it, but it slipped through her fingers like grains of sand to be blown away on the winds of time.

'Rianna, my love,' Tarn whispered brokenly. 'How can I live without you?'

'We must find a way to be together.' She clung on to him unable to comprehend how life could go on if they were parted.

Tarn's eyes were bright with unshed tears as he lifted her body from his and cradled her in his arms. Very gently he touched the blood that now stained her inner thighs. 'I did not hurt you, did I?'

'No,' she replied lovingly, conscious only of a slight soreness deep inside her feminine sheath. She did not regret for a moment what she had just done.

'It is not safe for you to remain here,' Tarn said worriedly.

'A moment more,' she begged, relishing the loving closeness.

'A lifetime more is what I would ask.' Tarn stroked her hair and pressed gentle kisses on her flushed face. 'That is what I will pray for.'

Rianna felt Tarn stiffen as they heard a faint noise in the corridor outside. The door swung open and they both glanced up anxiously, unable to make out the identity of the dark figure silhouetted against the brightness of the corridor.

Presuming it was Mircon come to warn her that their time together must finish, Rianna grabbed hold of her dress and held it in front of her to cover her nakedness.

'Ye gods!' a man growled in a voice choked with fury. It was Lesand.

Terror enveloped Rianna, weighing her down, but Tarn reacted with the instincts of a warrior. Springing to his feet, he stepped protectively in front of Rianna.

'Don't hurt her,' he said, making no attempt to cover his own nudity as he stared challengingly at Chancellor Lesand.

Lesand appeared transfixed by the enormity of his discovery. 'This is insane,' Lesand's voice shook with disbelief. He turned to glare at Mircon who hovered in the doorway. 'Leave,' he snapped.

The soldier stepped back, pulling the door shut while Tarn helped Rianna to her feet and wrapped her cloak around her trembling shoulders. 'The blame is mine,' Tarn said, turning back to Lesand.

The Chancellor's skin had turned ashen, making the fiery anger in his eyes even more pronounced. 'I cannot believe this is happening,' he said almost to himself.

'Tarn, how can you expect me to accept that the blame is yours alone. You are chained and confined here. Are you a sorcerer? Did you summon Rianna here by magic, make her strip naked and . . .' He shook his head, appearing choked with emotion. 'Why?' he asked, turning to look with anguished fury at Rianna.

'It's simple enough, Chancellor,' she replied. 'I love Tarn. Blame me, not him.'

'You would have me believe that you forced a warrior at least twice your size to couple with you?'

'Indeed I did,' she confirmed, with a smile that spoke more eloquently than words ever could. 'Tarn loves me deeply. When I came here and begged him to take me, he was so overcome he could not resist my charms.'

'Why do the gods test me like this?' Lesand raised his eyes to the ceiling. 'What have I done to deserve such wretched vexations?' He looked with exasperation at Rianna. 'You were an innocent maiden, afforded the honour of becoming Lord Sarin's bride. You have thrown it all away; sacrificed your entire future for a brief moment of rapture with this traitor to Percheron. What am I to do now?'

'Forget what you have seen, forget this ever happened,' Tarn suggested.

'And by doing so, betray my sovereign,' Lesand said in disbelief.

'Consider it aiding Rianna, not betraying Sarin,' Tarn corrected. 'And by doing so you will be saving yourself. Do you honestly believe Lord Sarin will forgive you, Lesand, for allowing this to happen?'

A mixture of complex emotions flashed across Lesand's taut features. 'With my position comes responsibilities, Tarn. I have to accept that, but your punishment will be far worse.'

'I am already to be punished for my supposed crimes. Sarin cannot execute me twice,' Tarn calmly pointed out.

'Maybe not,' Lesand agreed. 'However, he can force you to endure unimaginable pain.'

'And do you want that to happen?' Rianna said,

stepping forward and placing a pleading hand on Lesand's arm. 'I know you were once Tarn's friend. Does that not count for anything now?'

'Do not ask this of me,' Lesand grated, his mouth set in a thin line.

'Betray us if you must,' Tarn interjected. 'But if you do your career will be finished, Chancellor. Even if Sarin doesn't punish you physically, it's likely you'll be sent into permanent exile.'

'Lady Rianna, go to your room,' Lesand said. 'I have much to consider before I make my decision on this matter. I'll speak to you again in the morning.'

'No.' She looked worriedly over at Tarn, then back at the Chancellor. 'I won't leave,' she said determinedly.

'Lesand will not harm me tonight,' Tarn assured her. 'Whatever he decides, my retribution lies in Sarin's hands alone. Please leave, Rianna.'

Lesand pushed open the heavy oak door. 'Soldier, you are to escort Lady Rianna to her room, then return here,' he told Mircon.

Rianna cast one last anguished glance at Tarn. Then, hugging her cloak around her, she slipped silently away into the night.

Once Rianna had departed, Lesand looked back at Tarn. The tendons in the Chancellor's neck stood out like strands of twisted rope. A red flush stained his cheeks and it was clear he was still very angry. Nevertheless, Tarn was not afraid of Lesand and never would be. There was a nobility of purpose inside this man that even Sarin could not extinguish.

'You blame yourself, don't you?' Tarn said with understanding. 'You think it's your fault because it was you who brought us together.'

'Rianna was an innocent maid and beautiful enough to tempt any man, while you are a handsome nobleman in distress. I should have realised your position would have evoked more than sympathy from one as vulnerable and kind-hearted as Rianna.'

'You were not to know, Lesand,' Tarn replied. 'It was my weakness that caused this tragedy. I should have resisted her charms, but I allowed emotion to overrule logic and took her virginity. I would willingly give my life for her, but if Sarin discovers the truth it will not only be me that suffers.'

'I have no wish for Sarin to vent his wrath on Rianna,' Lesand said. 'Neither, if I am honest, do I wish to have Sarin's anger directed towards me.'

'Then conceal the truth. Forget what happened.'

'I am not the only witness,' Lesand pointed out.

'The guard, Mircon, will not betray Rianna. Her maid, Jenna, is Mircon's sweetheart. It was Mircon who helped Rianna to meet me here in secret. If Mircon exposes the truth, he also betrays himself.'

'And how do I explain to Sarin that his bride is no longer a virgin?' Lesand argued.

'Women have ways of concealing such truths. Do you not have someone you can trust within the confines of Sarin's seraglio?'

'You ask a lot of me, Tarn,' Lesand said thoughtfully.

'You were once my friend.' Tarn looked deep into Lesand's eyes. 'Of all those at Sarin's court, you were the man I respected most of all. You may not agree with my attempts to free Kabra. However, I know that deep in your heart you understand why I had to betray Sarin and try to regain control of my own kingdom. I'll fall to my knees and beg you to help Rianna if I have to, Lesand.'

Since that fateful night in Seigneur Wernock's cellar, Rianna had not seen Tarn or spoken to Chancellor Lesand. The caravan had departed early the following morning and for the last three days Rianna and Jenna had been confined to their wagon, only allowed out for a short time in the evening to stretch their legs. They had been told to speak to no one, but Jenna had managed to discover that Mircon was now assigned to Lesand's personal staff, while Tarn was once again locked in the barbaric cage.

The weather became much warmer as they travelled further south. The interior of the wagon was unbearably hot and stuffy but they were allowed no respite. So they were relieved when, on the third day, early in the afternoon, the caravan came to a stop in a grove of olive trees. The gnarled branches at least protected them partially from the heat of the sun. Glancing out of the window, Rianna saw Chancellor Lesand gallop up and dismount from his horse.

He stepped into her wagon unannounced. 'We'll be in Aguilar within the hour,' he said brusquely. 'I suggest you change into something more suitable to greet your future husband.' He looked pointedly at her crumpled gown. 'A moment alone with your lady,' he added, turning to address Jenna.

Jenna hurried from the wagon, while the Chancellor stared penetratingly at Rianna. Her heart had sunk when he mentioned her future husband. Part of her had hoped she would be packed off home in disgrace and not obliged to marry Sarin. Now she was unsure what the future held for her. 'Chancellor,' Rianna said hesitantly. 'About the night –'

'Best you forget that ever happened,' he interrupted. 'Against my better judgement, I've done as Tarn requested and chosen to ignore your traitorous actions. Lord Sarin will never learn the truth from me.'

'So I'm still to marry him?'

Lesand nodded. 'Certain arrangements will have to be made in order to conceal the loss of your virginity. Lord Sarin will expect proof of that when he beds you, but there are ways he can be deceived. Once in the palace my representative will make herself known to you by showing you a ring bearing my personal crest. Be advised, trust no one but her.'

'And Tarn?' She was more worried for him than she was for herself.

'Tarn is no longer your concern,' Lesand said curtly. 'Forget you ever knew him.' His expression softened. 'Never fear, Rianna, I do not believe Lord Sarin has any intention of executing Tarn.'

'I've much to thank you for, Chancellor.'

'Fate may not have been overly kind to you, Lady Rianna. I wish you good fortune and hope that one day you will find happiness in your new life.'

'Happiness is no longer within my grasp.' She turned away from him, tears filling her eyes.

# Chapter Six

*T*hey reached the summit of the hill. Below them, banded by the sparkling blue sea on one side, was the city Aguilar. It was the largest seaport in Percheron, a sprawling mass of white buildings surrounded by orange and lemon groves. Dust rose from the horses' hooves, choking Rianna and Jenna's throats and stinging their eyes as the caravan made its slow descent into the fertile valley.

The hard-packed roads were uncomfortable enough to travel on, but the city streets were even worse as the wooden wheels of the wagons trundled over the uneven cobblestones. White-painted shops and houses bordered the streets, and brightly coloured fabric hung from wrought iron balconies. Now and then through open doorways, Rianna caught a glimpse of shady, blue-tiled courtyards. It was beautiful and exotic, yet there was something a little sinister and secretive about this city.

The heat was suffocating. Smells of spices and jasmine mingled with the odour of cooked meats and honeyed pastries. There were people everywhere; a sea of dark-eyed and dusky-skinned onlookers watched curiously as the caravan passed by. Some of the looks were inquiring, others openly hostile, making Rianna draw back from the window, wondering anxiously how Tarn was faring trapped in his cage and fully exposed to the taunts of the crowds.

Soon the streets became wider. The stone walls of the houses backing on to the road were swathed with scarlet bougainvillaea. They passed through the entrance of the palace protected by ornate gold-painted gates. Here most of the caravan stopped, and only Rianna's wagon and her military escorts moved forwards into a large square with an ornate fountain in its centre. The palace was a huge white marble-fronted building, its windows covered by elaborate wrought iron screens.

A large number of elaborately-dressed people were gathered in the courtyard. Rianna was conscious of the agitated beating of her heart as she nervously descended the steps of her wagon. Chancellor Lesand took her arm and escorted her towards those waiting to greet her. The heat was intense, the sun searing through her gown. Moisture pooled under her breasts and between her thighs, and strands of her hair stuck uncomfortably to the back of her neck.

At the front of the crowd was a tall man, protected from the sun by a mushroom-shaped, heavily fringed umbrella.

'Lord Sarin, may I present Lady Rianna of Harn.' Lesand bowed, and Rianna sank into a deep curtsey, keeping her eyes firmly fixed on the ground.

'Welcome, my lady.' A strong, cool hand grasped hers, urging her to rise to her feet, then a questing finger tipped up her chin. 'Your portrait did not do you justice, Rianna.'

The way he spoke her name made her shiver. Sarin's voice was deep and compelling, like liquid velvet. Shyly she raised her eyes to his; the irises were so dark they appeared black in the bright sunlight. His face was as she'd remembered it from the painting, but stronger, and dare she say, more handsome. Rianna's heart missed a beat as Sarin's lips curved into a spellbinding smile.

'My lord,' she murmured.

Sarin wore a deep blue robe heavily embroidered in

silver, slashed to the waist to reveal trousers in a paler blue silk and long, leather boots. He looked every inch a sovereign, while she felt rather underdressed in her green brocade gown.

'Let us go inside, it is even warmer than usual today. I am sure that at first you will find the heat uncomfortable.' He led her through an arched doorway into a wide marble-floored corridor, and on into an opulently furnished, high-ceilinged room. It was far cooler in here. A gentle breeze brushed her pink, over-heated face, making her conscious of the perspiration beading her brow and the sweat which was beginning to stain the underarms of her gown.

'I find the weather overpowering,' she admitted. 'Harn is far cooler.'

From under the cover of her long eyelashes, Rianna examined Sarin again. His skin was a pale olive, and his features though well-defined were a little hard, but he did not strike her as a cruel man. She began to feel more composed. His manner was gentle and protective as he led her to a long, low seat upholstered in ivory velvet.

'Then you must rest before you face the rest of the court.'

Rianna was relieved. She smiled shyly and lowered her eyes. Although Sarin was to be her husband, this all had a dream-like quality; Tarn was her only true reality.

She was conscious of Sarin's eyes scouring her body from head to toe as she sat on the couch, accepting a goblet filled with cool fruit juice from one of the servants. 'Is it usually so hot?' she asked, unable to think of anything else to say. She knew virtually nothing about Sarin, his interests, or what he expected of her as a wife. Except one thing, he would most likely wish to bed her. After Tarn she had no desire to couple with another man.

'Not always so hot.' Sarin remained standing in front of her. 'It is our custom in Percheron to rest in the heat of the day.'

The fruit juice was so cold it set her teeth on edge as

she drank it, but it was delicious and most refreshing. 'Thank you.' Rianna returned the goblet to the servant.

'There is no need to give thanks to a slave,' Sarin said curtly.

'I was not aware he was slave. We have none in Harn, my father does not hold with slavery.'

'It is clear you have much to learn. I will teach you,' Sarin said, his tone deepening as he stared at her with his piercing dark eyes.

'Yes,' she said blushing shyly.

'Come.' Sarin took hold of her hand and helped her to her feet. 'I'll have you shown to your rooms.'

Before her courage deserted her, she had one thing to do. 'Lord Sarin, I have a boon to ask,' she said, her breath catching in her throat.

'Boon?' he queried.

'A prisoner travelled with my party – a nobleman.' She tried to control her feelings as she spoke Tarn's name. 'Prince Tarn of Kabra.' Rianna sank to her knees. 'I would ask you to show mercy towards this prisoner.'

'You seem overly concerned for his fate,' Sarin said coldly.

'Yes.' Rianna continued to stare at Sarin's soft leather boots, not daring to look at him. 'Tarn is a distant kinsman on my mother Kitara's side of the family,' she lied. 'I thought it only right to take it upon myself to plead for clemency on his behalf. I know you consider him a traitor, but he is a good and gentle man, only doing what he thought was right.'

Had she gone too far? she asked herself, as Sarin stayed silent. Then she felt his hand drawing her to her feet. Forcing herself to be courageous, she looked him boldly in the eyes and was relieved to see he did not appear angry.

'Tarn is your kinsman?' Sarin frowned thoughtfully. 'I was not aware of that. However, I know little of your mother's origins, Rianna. Perhaps you could tell me more about her sometime?' He lifted her hand to his lips.

'How can I refuse such a request from my beautiful bride? If you wish clemency for Tarn you shall have it.'

'Then he'll not be executed?'

'No,' Sarin said gently. 'Neither will he be sent to the mines as was suggested by some of my advisors. To be truthful, Rianna, I still hold some fondness for Tarn myself. He was once my friend. Despite his disloyalty and treachery, I had already decided to be lenient in my dealings with him.'

Rianna smiled tremulously at Sarin. 'I'm grateful to you, very grateful.'

'That is how it should always be, my dear,' he said, kissing her hand again.

The dungeons of the palace were carved out of living rock. Because of their depth they retained a constant temperature both day and night, never too cold, never too hot. Tarn had visited them before, but not as a prisoner.

Chained hand and foot, he was led down the stone steps into a world of despair and pain. A gaoler stepped forward. He was short and bulkily built with lank greasy hair. Layers of fat covered his chest, giving him small pendulous breasts, and a thick roll of flesh hung obscenely over the waistband of his sagging leather trousers.

'So, the noble prince is here to visit us at last,' the gaoler leered, rubbing his hands with glee. He accompanied Tarn into a cell. Tarn had expected darkness, but the small room was brightly lit by lanterns hung high on the walls, way out of reach. The cell was windowless and smelt stale, as if it had not been used for some time.

'Special accommodation for a special prisoner,' the gaoler said with sarcastic cheerfulness. 'I trust you approve, my lord?'

Tarn stayed silent as the soldiers accompanying him attached the manacles around his ankles to metal rings set in the stone flags. His wrist manacles were fixed to heavy chains hanging from the ceiling. Using a pulley at the side of the cell, the gaoler tightened the chains until Tarn's arms were stretched taut above him. He knew that in an hour or so his muscles would cramp and ache with the strain.

The soldiers and gaoler departed, leaving Tarn alone with his dark thoughts. It was difficult to calculate the passage of time, but it didn't seem long before the door of his cell opened.

'Tarn.' Sarin's smile was cruel and calculating. 'It seems so long since we last parted.'

'Not long enough,' Tarn said boldly.

Sarin was not alone. He was accompanied by a pale-haired beauty. Tarn didn't recognise her, but that wasn't surprising as Tarn had been away from court for two years, and Sarin changed his female companions often. Tarn had never seen such pale blue eyes. Her hair was so blonde it almost appeared silver in the bright light. She gave a narrow-lipped smile, and Tarn saw that her side teeth had been filed into sharp points.

'This is my wife, Niska,' Sarin announced, amused by Tarn's expression of surprise. 'When you knew me, Tarn, I had vowed never to marry. Now you find me with one wife and about to take another.'

'So this is the famous rebel, Tarn, former Prince of Kabra,' Niska said in a husky, strongly-accented voice. She wore a tight-fitting, low-cut bodice in emerald satin, a skirt of matching emerald silk heavily embroidered with gold, and a necklace of huge emeralds around her neck. The colour contrasted vividly with her silver-gilt hair and pale skin. 'May I touch the slave, my lord?'

Sarin nodded, his dark eyes never leaving Tarn. 'Remove those silk trousers, they are not a fitting garment for a prisoner.'

Niska glided closer to Tarn. He was already a little light-headed, as he had not eaten or drunk today. Her strong perfume made his head spin as she ran her hands over his chest.

'His muscles are firm and well-honed,' she said, tracing the red line of the scar on his shoulder downwards.

Smiling, she leant even closer to Tarn. Her warm breath brushed his cheek as she caressed his nipples, then dug her fingers into the tiny teats. 'Do you desire me, slave?' she whispered in a voice too low for Sarin to hear.

Tarn clenched his lips together and stoically ignored her.

'His manner needs to change if he is to make a good slave,' she commented, as she ran her hands through Tarn's tangled blond hair and pulled down his lips to examine his teeth. 'But I wager he would command an uncommonly high price in the slave market. Many a rich lady would pay a thousand pistole or more to own such a superb specimen.'

She put a hand to his groin, gauging the size of his manhood through the thin trousers.

'A nobleman or wealthy merchant would bid even higher for such a handsome plaything.' Sarin watched Tarn tense as he spoke.

'He should be bathed and oiled,' Niska sniffed in disgust. 'He smells of dirt and sour sweat.'

'If you had joined me in my cage you would have smelled much the same,' Tarn purred seductively.

'Watch your tongue,' she sneered, as she removed a pearl-handled dagger from the sheath on her girdle.

The sharp blade caught the light as she placed the tip close to Tarn's stomach. Taking hold of his trousers, she began to cut the fabric from his body, throwing the tattered remnants on the flagstones at his feet.

Once Tarn was naked, Niska stepped back and slowly examined his body. The lack of exercise had not softened his muscles. They were even more well-defined than usual because his poor diet during most of the journey had caused him to lose weight.

'Also his hair and skin need attention,' she said, running the tip of her tongue provocatively along her lower lip. 'He is mightily well-endowed,' she added as she stared at his sex, lust darkening her odd-coloured eyes.

Stepping forward again, she touched his sex, weighing

the seed sac in her hand. Tarn shuddered, his blood running cold as she curved her fingers around his cock shaft and began to milk it with slow precision. Despite Tarn's best efforts to stem his body's natural response, lust stirred like a serpent deep within his belly.

Niska smiled with satisfaction as his penis stretched and hardened. She pressed herself closer to Tarn and licked his nipples. Sucking lewdly on the tiny nubs, she began to pump his cock faster, her long fingernails digging cruelly into the engorged flesh.

'Contain yourself, Niska,' Sarin hissed as he stepped forward, his eyes lit up with anger. He wrenched Niska away from Tarn with such fury that she slammed against the cell wall.

Pouting and rubbing her bruised arm, she moved over to the door of the cell. 'Do you wish to be alone with him, my lord?'

'Go and tell the gaoler to have the gold slave collar and chains prepared.' As Niska departed, Sarin smiled mockingly at Tarn. 'A prince should be properly attired.'

Tarn stared coolly at Sarin, ably hiding his true feelings. He knew the Lord of Percheron well, and had always thought it unlikely that Sarin would execute him. Tarn was expecting a far more ignoble fate.

'Why so jealous of what Niska was doing to me?' Tarn taunted. 'I've always known how you feel about me, Sarin, and I find your pathetic desire totally abhorrent,' he continued vehemently.

Frustration briefly flared in Sarin's eyes. 'Now you no longer have a choice, Tarn. You are my prisoner, and I intend to make you my personal body slave.' Stepping close to his prisoner, Sarin trailed his fingers down over Tarn's chest and rigid stomach. 'I shall use you as I wish.'

'Never,' Tarn hissed.

'When I order it you will spread yourself for me.' Sarin slid an arm around Tarn and squeezed his buttocks. Invading the narrow crack, he probed the tight muscle ring of Tarn's nether mouth. 'I will take you in any manner of my choosing.'

'I'd rather die.' A scarlet flush of humiliation stained Tarn's face.

'Then I've judged your punishment well,' Sarin replied with intense satisfaction. Gently, he cupped Tarn's balls, then his fingers drifted teasingly across his penis. 'I should, of course, consider having you circumcised. But perhaps I'll find the difference from my other male slaves even more tempting.'

Tarn gritted his teeth, forced to endure the unwanted caresses, and trying to appear indifferent to Sarin's sensual touch. 'I cannot prevent you enslaving me, Sarin. But I'll never willingly submit to any of your vile demands on my flesh. I'll fight you with every measure of my strength and will. Eventually you are bound to tire of the conflict and come to accept that I am a lost cause.'

'You seem very determined, Tarn. But remember that even the strongest will can be broken.' He stroked Tarn's cock stem with his long slim fingers. 'I'll have your nether mouth oiled and trained to accommodate me. My gaolers are well used to preparing slaves for my use.'

Tarn closed his eyes, filled with a sense of foreboding. Sarin appeared so confident, so certain.

'They use ivory phalluses of ever increasing sizes,' Sarin continued, sliding his hand between Tarn's thighs to probe his nether mouth with the tip of an index finger. 'At first, of course, the ivory rods are uncomfortable. But as your inner flesh is stretched and accustoms itself, you'll come to welcome the cool feel of the phallus as it's slowly inserted into your helpless body.'

Tarn's mouth twisted in contempt, his eyes as cold as ice. 'You disgust me, Sarin.'

'Now that you are a slave, Tarn, you are not permitted to use my name. In future you will address me as master.' Sarin watched Tarn wince as his index finger probed deeper into the virginal opening. 'Imagine how it will feel, Tarn, to be continually forced to wear the phallus of servitude inside your anus; a constant reminder of what is now required of you. Eventually you will learn that submission itself brings the sweetest of pleasures.'

The memory of the whipping was still fresh in Tarn's mind; the humiliation of his release being witnessed by all those soldiers. He was certain Sarin had ordered it, and he could not have hated the Lord of Percheron more than he did at this moment.

'One day you will thank me for this, Tarn,' Sarin said with calm assurance. He kissed Tarn's taut cheek, then fastened his lips on his prisoner's mouth. However, he gave a growl of pain and jumped back, blood welling from his lip.

'So I'll submit, will I?' Tarn challenged, watching Sarin dab angrily at his bleeding mouth.

'Yes,' Sarin snapped furiously. 'Your defiance will disappear in a matter of moments. I'll have you taken to a cell close to this one. There you'll find a prisoner you know only too well.'

For the first time Tarn felt deep concern. 'Who?' he asked harshly.

'Your own kinsman. Your cousin, Cador.'

'Cador?' Tarn grated in surprise. 'That cannot be. I left him in a place of safety far beyond the borders of Kabra.'

'It appears that Cador devised a foolish plan to try and rescue you, Tarn. It failed, of course, and Cador and his comrades were captured.'

'No.' Tarn shook his head. 'I will not believe you, Sarin. You're trying to trick me.'

'Then you shall see Cador for yourself.' Sarin smiled. 'I never promise what I cannot produce. I assure you, Cador is my prisoner.'

'You have Cador,' Tarn said brokenly. The young man was like a brother to him. With Cador's capture, Tarn's last hopes for Kabra were lost. Cador had been his staunchest ally and one of his battle commanders.

'Every time you refuse me, Tarn, every little sign of disobedience will cause Cador to suffer. He will be punished in your place. Cador is young and far less strong-willed and determined than you. Can you live with the knowledge that if you resist me, Cador will be forced to endure unimaginable pain?'

Rianna ate a light meal and rested for almost three hours. She was unused to sleeping during the day, but she awoke feeling refreshed. Her new home was a delight, even to one who had no desire to be there at all. The apartment consisted of five opulently furnished rooms. The main reception room had an impressive gilded ceiling, and her sleeping chamber contained the largest bed she had ever seen, draped with curtains of the sheerest muslin.

Soon after she awoke, a young woman arrived. Introducing herself as Yasmin, she informed Rianna she had come to escort her to the bath house. It appeared it was not the custom for maids to accompany their mistresses to the bath house, so Rianna left Jenna to oversee the unpacking.

Yasmin gave no clue as to her position in Sarin's household as she led Rianna through a beautifully tended garden. She was tiny and slightly built, scarcely reaching Rianna's shoulders. Her skin was the colour of dark honey and her hair as black as night. It was piled high on her head and decorated with loops of lustrous pearls.

'You must have found the long journey wearisome,' Yasmin said, smiling shyly at Rianna. Her large almond-shaped eyes reminded Rianna of a startled fawn she'd once come across in the forest.

'I confess I found it most enlightening,' Rianna replied, wondering why she couldn't have a bathing chamber in her own quarters.

'Most find time spent in the hammam most relaxing,' Yasmin said as they entered a massive chamber, with long slender columns supporting its high roof. The entire chamber was covered in tiny blue, green and gold tiles set out in elaborate patterns, and the pool at its centre was the size of a small lake.

There were a number of young women present, all strikingly beautiful. The soft sound of their voices echoed through the warm, vapour-filled chamber. They fell almost silent as Yasmin and Rianna walked across the room.

'Do all the ladies of the court bathe here?' Rianna asked.

'No.' Yasmin gave a soft laugh. 'Only a privileged few.'

'In Harn we bathe alone,' Rianna said, a little embarrassed by so many women in a state of undress. Some were in the water, while others lazed, indolent and naked, on low couches.

'Not in so much comfort, I wager,' Yasmin replied, glancing anxiously towards a naked blonde on one of the couches.

The blonde rose to her feet and walked towards Rianna, never taking her eyes off the new arrivals. She moved with a feline grace that bore an uneasy resemblance to a wild animal stalking its prey.

'Who is she?' Rianna asked. The woman's hair was so fair it appeared to be silver until the light caught it, showing the faintest glint of pale gold.

'That's Niska. Beware of her, Rianna, she can be dangerous,' Yasmin whispered.

Quite how dangerous a lady of the court could be, Rianna didn't know. Nevertheless, she did feel a little uncomfortable as Niska approached.

Niska's breasts were small and up-tilted, the nipples almost as pale as her ivory skin. Something flashed, catching the light, and Rianna saw that Niska's left nipple was pierced, and hung with a teardrop-shaped diamond that shimmered as she moved. Her pubis was totally denuded; it was rounded and quite smooth, with the pouting pink slit of her sex plainly visible.

'So you are Rianna, the Lady of Harn,' Niska sneered.

Her eyes were unnaturally pale with glacial-blue irises

surrounded by a darker rim. They had a predatory quality, and Rianna shivered, taking an instant and total dislike to Niska.

'You should show the noble lady respect,' Yasmin reminded Niska. 'Lady Rianna's position is far superior to yours.'

'I am also Lord Sarin's wife,' Niska snapped, pursing her thin lips.

'You are only a secondary wife.' Yasmin heard Rianna's gasp of surprise and turned anxiously towards her charge. 'You did not know?'

'I was not aware that my future husband was already married,' Rianna replied. She recalled that Jenna had learnt from Mircon that it was acceptable in Percheron for a man to take more than one wife. Had her father known she would not be Sarin's only wife? Somehow she thought not.

'Do not be concerned, Lady Rianna, Niska's position is of little importance compared to yours. Lord Sarin wants you at his side, and only you can bear an heir to the throne,' Yasmin assured her.

'My blood is as good as hers,' Niska retorted jealously, as she tossed her head in anger, making the diamond on her nipple tremble enticingly. 'Just because she's the daughter of the Protector of Harn.'

'And you are the result of a hasty coupling between a northern raider and a lowly slave,' Yasmin mocked. 'Not quite the bloodline for an heir to the throne of Percheron. Lord Sarin honoured you by bedding you.'

'He did so because it is I who can pleasure him better than anyone.' Niska looked Rianna up and down with derision. 'He'll soon tire of this mawkish maiden.'

'Come.' Yasmin took Rianna's hand and led her though an open doorway away from Niska. 'We'll bathe here in private.'

The room was filed with warm steam and contained a much smaller pool. Four young, bare-breasted female slaves, wearing only short linen skirts to cover their nudity, stepped forward to attend them.

'I confess I did not find Niska altogether likeable,' Rianna said haltingly, unsure if she could wholly trust Yasmin.

'Stay away from her, until you've established yourself both in Lord Sarin's bed and his affections. When that time comes you can have Niska banished to one of the other palaces, far away from the court,' Yasmin replied, as she removed her slippers and shrugged off her satin robe.

She squatted on one of the low wooden stools, her thighs splayed lewdly apart, quite unconcerned that her pudenda was open and visible to Rianna. Like Niska, she had no body hair. Her mound was naked, and her labia gaped, revealing the moist red interior. Rianna turned her eyes away from her companion as the slaves divested her of the satin robe, and led her to another stool opposite Yasmin. Rianna sat down, making sure her thighs were pressed modestly together.

'I forgot.' Yasmin leant towards Rianna and held out her hand. She twisted the gold ring she wore, so that Lesand's crest, which had been concealed in her palm, was visible to Rianna. 'I am truly your friend,' she whispered, quietly enough to ensure the slaves attending them would not hear what she said.

'Perhaps we should talk later,' Rianna suggested with a nod of acknowledgement.

'Later,' Yasmin agreed.

The slaves poured basins of warm water over the two young women and began to cleanse them with perfumed soap. Rianna heard her companion give a soft sigh as one of the slaves reached between her legs and massaged the sweet-smelling cream into her sex. The slave's fingers slipped between the fleshy folds, gently caressing the entire length of Yasmin's vulva. Rianna coloured as she heard her new friend give a soft, breathy moan.

Another slave began to massage the creamy soap over Rianna's breasts. 'I'll wash myself,' she said, pushing the slave away. She grabbed hold of a sponge and spread the lather over her body, all too conscious that the slave's hand was still between Yasmin's thighs, expertly manipulating her to a climax.

Rianna coloured, ignoring the sudden warmth forming in her belly, as she heard Yasmin moan again. She glanced awkwardly in Yasmin's direction. Yasmin lifted her hips while holding the slave's hand hard against her pubis as her orgasm came. Determinedly, Rianna concentrated on washing herself, pushing away the constant helping hands of the slaves.

Yasmin, now pink-faced and happy, smiled at Rianna. 'Your upbringing has clearly denied you much pleasure. Lord Sarin will find your innocence appealing.'

'Life here is very different,' Rianna replied, unsure how much Chancellor Lesand had told Yasmin.

Once Rianna and Yasmin were thoroughly cleansed and their hair washed, they spent some time lazing in the pool of perfumed water. Yasmin stayed silent, leaving Rianna alone with her thoughts, most of which were of Tarn. As yet she knew nothing of his fate.

Slaves appeared with linen towels. They were dried and led into an adjoining room. 'Lie down.' Yasmin pointed to one of the divans. 'Now we rest. The slaves will bring refreshment.'

Rianna lay back on a divan covered by a linen towel, and supported by pillows, which slaves rushed to place behind her head. She sipped a cool sherbet while one of the slaves ran a wide-toothed comb through her long, damp hair. Despite having slept less than two hours ago, Rianna began to feel weary. She closed her eyes and relaxed, but was forced into wakefulness when the linen towel was lifted from her body.

'Leave me be,' Rianna complained as one slave tried to ease her legs apart and another attempted to stuff a pillow beneath her buttocks.

'Do not chastise them.' Yasmin sat up. 'They have orders to remove your body hair.' She pointed at her own denuded mound. 'It is our custom. Did you not notice the other women in the baths?'

124

'Yes, but it is not my custom.' Rianna eyed the steaming bowl, being brought into the room, with suspicion.

'Lord Sarin wishes you to abide by our customs,' Yasmin insisted, sounding a little anxious. 'It would not be wise to resist.'

There was no point in antagonising Sarin, Rianna thought. She squeezed her eyes shut and tried to relax, too embarrassed to watch what the slaves intended to do to her. She jumped agitatedly as her thighs were spread wider and her arms lifted above her head.

'It's sugar paste,' Yasmin explained as the hot paste was spread slowly over the red-gold curls nestling in Rianna's armpits.

She had expected it to be more painful than it was. The heat was uncomfortable for a few seconds, but died swiftly. Gentle fingers glided over her pubic fleece applying the thick, sticky paste, careful to keep it from invading the crack of her sex.

'It's not so bad,' Rianna said through gritted teeth, doing her best not to jump uncontrollably when the nubile fingers strayed too close to her most sensitive parts. She was unused to female hands touching her so intimately. The paste itself was warm, but her pudenda was steadily growing hotter, and she felt a film of moisture start to seep along her rosy divide.

'The next part will hurt a little, but the discomfort will pass swiftly,' Yasmin warned.

A soft muslin cloth was pressed to the sticky paste just before it hardened. The cloth was held there for a moment, then ripped off with a deft flick of the slave's wrist. Rianna squealed in pain, but found she was left with only a dull tingling sensation in its wake.

It did prove to be a little more uncomfortable on the most sensitive portions of her sex. She held her breath as one of the slaves held her labial lips together, putting extra pressure on her already throbbing nubbin, while another removed the paste. However, the brief, ripping pain served to increase, not decrease, the lustful fire in her sex.

'See, it is nearly finished. The next time it is done it will be far less uncomfortable,' Yasmin assured her, as she climbed off her divan and stared at Rianna's denuded sex. 'Your skin is so pale, like thick cream with a swirl of delicate red fruit at its centre.' She ran her fingertips over the smooth flesh and Rianna shivered, feeling suddenly vulnerable without her red-gold fleece.

'I'm relieved they have finished.' She went to press her legs together, but Yasmin held them apart. 'Just a few stray curls to be removed that the sugaring missed.'

Yasmin stepped aside, and a slave holding a small pair of tweezers stared intently at Rianna's pubis. Rianna had never felt more exposed and humiliated, yet she was also aroused. She bit her lip, hating the embarrassment as the slave carefully removed the few stray hairs until the entire area was smooth and totally unprotected.

'The skin will be sore for a short while,' Yasmin said, examining Rianna's flesh which had become quite pink in places. 'This cream will quell any discomfort.'

A small knot of excitement formed in Rianna's belly as Yasmin spread the thick cream over her denuded flesh. She trembled as Yasmin's fingers moved caressingly over her sex, desperately wanting them to slip inside the pouting lips and quell the mounting tension in her pudenda.

'Does that feel better?' Yasmin asked as she straightened. There was a half-smile on her lips, as if she secretly knew that Rianna was aroused. 'Now we must return to your rooms and prepare you to go to Lord Sarin.'

Tarn had been bathed and his skin freshly oiled with a sweet-smelling balm that added a soft sheen to his tanned flesh. His hair, washed and perfumed, hung in rich golden strands past his shoulders. He'd rarely looked more handsome, but his eyes were dull, his expression glum. Filled with despair, he sat on a bench in an ante-room leading to Lord Sarin's quarters.

After he had spoken to Sarin, Tarn had been taken to a secret hatch in a corridor where he could look into an adjoining cell. He had discovered that Sarin spoke the truth; Cador was a prisoner. Chained and confined, Cador looked weary, but appeared physically unharmed and in reasonably good health.

Tarn's strong will had crumbled. A broken man, he was led back to his cell to face Lord Sarin's mocking pleasure. Still, it had not been easy for Tarn to fall to his knees in front of Sarin, but he had done so for Cador's sake. He could not allow his young kinsman to suffer for his crimes.

A slave collar fashioned out of pure gold had been bolted around Tarn's neck. Around his waist was a thick gold chain, joined at each side by shorter chains which could be clipped to the elaborately fashioned gold bracelets he wore around his wrists. Once confined, he had been obliged to promise to serve and obey Sarin, acknowledging him as his master. Each word of submission seemed a betrayal of everything he stood for.

Tarn glanced up anxiously as Sarin strode into the room wearing a blue velvet robe. His dark hair was loose around his shoulders.

'Tarn.' Sarin approached his new slave and fingered the collar around Tarn's neck. 'Your nakedness enhances the subtle beauty of your chains,' he gloated. Looking deep into Tarn's eyes, he frowned. 'Why so listless? Is this the way a slave greets his master?'

Swallowing the last remnants of his pride, Tarn sank to his knees, inwardly quailing as he realised that Sarin appeared to be naked under his robe. Tarn had expected it to be some time before he had to face his final and ultimate act of humiliation.

'My lord.' Tarn's voice was low-pitched and husky, wracked by pain.

Sarin stroked Tarn's golden hair, almost with affection. 'You've visited my private quarters often, Tarn, but never as a pleasure slave. I confess I prefer it this way, but I fear you do not.' He hesitated and gave a brutal laugh. 'What, no defiant reply! You're learning fast, Tarn. Come into the other room.'

Rising smoothly to his feet, Tarn followed Sarin. Some time in the future it was likely he would have to face the members of Sarin's court in this pitiful state. The thought frightened him, but what terrified Tarn even more now was Sarin. He was filled with apprehension, not that Sarin might punish or hurt him, but that he might eventually come to like what Sarin intended to do to him. Sarin was a clever man, well able to devise many devious ways to cow Tarn's spirit, and forced him to find joy in absolute submission.

Since arriving in Aguilar, Tarn had not allowed himself to think of Rianna. To dwell on what might have been only heaped coals on the fire of his humiliating agony.

'I've decided to extend you a great honour,' Sarin smiled at his new pleasure slave.

'Honour, my lord?' Tarn said with a wry twist of his lips.

The room they had just entered contained a number of odd-looking contraptions. Tarn was uneasily reminded of a torture chamber. That thought was compounded as he saw the table covered with different restraints fashioned out of metal and leather.

'I intend to fit you with this myself.' Sarin picked up an ivory phallus. It was slimmer and shorter than Tarn had expected, but that gave him little relief. However, he managed to hide his concern.

Two muscular Nubian slaves, their dark skins oiled and gleaming, stood in the centre of the room, watching Tarn intently. Clearly Sarin was taking no chances, perhaps not yet able to accept how much Tarn was prepared to sacrifice for the well-being of his kinsman. Sarin did not know that on his death-bed Cador's father had extracted a promise from Tarn that he would always protect and care for Cador. Tarn did not take such promises lightly.

'Kneel and bend over that pole.' Sarin pointed to a

thick gilded pole, just above knee height, supported at each end by an ornate stand.

Mutely, Tarn did as he was ordered.

'Part your knees wide and lean forward so that your belly is supported by the pole,' Sarin continued.

Stretching forwards, Tarn leant his belly against the gilded pole and waited. The soft, exposed flesh of his scrotum dangled unprotected between his open legs, while his buttocks were open and vulnerable.

One of the Nubians moved forward and Tarn gritted his teeth. The slave anointed the valley between Tarn's buttocks with oil, forcing open the tight ring of muscle to allow it to dribble inside his nether mouth. With his large hands, the slave held Tarn's buttock cheeks apart and looked expectantly at Sarin.

'Ready?' Sarin asked softly, as he placed the cool tip of the phallus at the entrance to Tarn's anus. He pushed gently, easing the oil-coated muscles apart to allow the ivory shaft to enter. Tarn could not repress a groan as the phallus slid deeper, stretching the virginal walls. He tried consciously to relax, knowing that if he resisted, the discomfort would be far worse.

His thighs trembled as Sarin inserted the entire phallus, burying it deep in Tarn's anus. The cool ivory rod seemed to fill him completely. Fighting the desire to bear down and try to force it out, Tarn involuntarily clenched his muscles around the shaft. A wave of something akin to pleasure rippled through his belly, catching him totally by surprise.

The pleasure vanished, to be replaced by an all-encompassing despair as a wide leather belt was buckled around his waist. A thin padded strap, attached to the centre back, was fed between his buttock cheeks to keep the phallus in place. 'Move back a little,' Sarin ordered.

As Tarn straightened, the strap was slipped between his legs. Then his balls and cock were fed through an oval ring that sat flat against his pelvis, while the strap attached to the ring was fastened to the front of the belt.

Restrained in the harness, Tarn's sex was thrust into even greater prominence, the tight leather and metal putting a subtle pressure on the whole of the sensitive area.

Unable to find the strength to look down and see the visible proof of his servitude, Tarn rose to his feet, his gaze fixed straight ahead. The briefest movement caused the restraint to pull against his flesh and emphasise the feeling of fullness inside his anus. What troubled Tarn most was that a part of him found a subtle pleasure in the intrusive distension of his inner flesh and the tight feel of the harness restricting his sex. The leather rubbing against the sensitive ridge of skin between his balls and nether mouth was causing his phallus to visibly harden.

'Very good, Tarn. It feels most agreeable, does it not?' Sarin gloated, clearly pleased with Tarn's unbidden arousal. He stroked the now semi-erect shaft, curiously examining the thick ridge of flesh which still covered the head. 'Odd that your people do not remove this soon after birth as we do in Percheron. The lack of it makes stimulation even more pleasurable.'

Tarn concentrated on trying to ignore Sarin's presence, and the gentle stroking motion, as his supposed master caressed his cock shaft.

'Would you wish it removed, knowing it could enhance sensual pleasure?' Sarin asked.

'My wishes are of no importance,' Tarn replied, looking coldly at Sarin.

'What of your foolish pride now, Tarn?' Sarin asked as a faint tremor passed over Tarn's firm stomach.

By now the padded strap was pressing tightly into the groove of Tarn's buttocks, adding to the mounting pressure in his groin. His body might be reacting automatically to Sarin's unwanted attentions, but his mind would not. His humiliation almost complete, Tarn shook his head, unable to answer Sarin. Then the last vestiges of his pride made him lift his head. 'I do this for Cador.

If he were not your prisoner, Lord Sarin, I would deny you constantly and willingly embrace death.'

'What a waste that would be, Tarn,' Sarin said softly, as he beckoned to the Nubian slaves. 'Confine this one in the room I've had prepared.'

# Chapter Seven

*T*he clothes that Rianna had brought with her from Harn were all deemed unsuitable for her new position and packed away in cedarwood chests. In future, Rianna would wear the opulent garments provided by Lord Sarin. They were all beautiful, fashioned from silks and satins in every colour of the rainbow. However, Rianna was troubled by the scanty nature of the garments. It appeared that all the ladies of the court walked around half-clothed, in a state that would have been considered indecent in Harn.

Jenna, like the other maidservants, now wore a tight black bodice that left her arms, upper breasts and midriff bare, and a silky skirt edged at the hem with elaborate embroidery.

Rianna's garments were similar; a tight-fitting silver bodice which left her breasts barely covered, a silver girdle set with precious stones, and a full skirt made out of layers of silver gauze. Rianna's midriff was also bare, and to her embarrassment, Yasmin insisted on her wearing a diamond the size of her thumbnail in her belly button. As she moved it caught the light, shimmering enticingly.

'Come, it is time,' said Yasmin as she wrapped a deep pink satin cloak around Rianna's shoulders. 'Lord Sarin's quarters are close by.'

As they walked along the wide corridor, Rianna's sandalled feet made no sound on the smooth marble floor. Ahead were the beaten copper doors leading to Lord Sarin's apartment, guarded by two soldiers holding sabres.

A musky cloud of perfume surrounded Rianna which had been applied to her body before she had dressed. The maids had painted her eyelids and ringed her eyes with kohl, but her hair had been left loose as befitting a maiden.

The stony-faced soldiers did not move a muscle as Yasmin pushed open the doors. Rianna stepped nervously inside, automatically turning to look at Yasmin for a smile of support, but realising with a jolt of unease that her new-found friend had disappeared.

Lord Sarin was awaiting her, looking splendidly regal in violet silk trousers and a richly embroidered deep purple tunic. His long dark hair was tied at the nape of his neck and he wore diamond studs in his ears.

'My lord.' She sank into a low curtsey, her knees shaking slightly.

'Rianna, your beauty astounds me.' Sarin helped her to her feet, divested her of her cloak, and led her towards a velvet-covered divan.

Rianna had been feeling strangely languid ever since she arrived here. She felt overcome by the sensuality of this exotic palace and the man who ruled it. The silver fabric of her bodice rubbed teasingly against her nipples, while her gauze skirts brushed tantalisingly against her denuded sex. She sat down next to Sarin, suppressing a nervous shiver as he lifted her hand to his cool lips.

Gently Sarin turned her hand over and examined her palm. 'I see a life full of warmth and joy,' he said softly. 'All that you are lies in the lines of your hand. Fate led you to me, Rianna.'

He kissed her exposed palm, his lips lingering on the sensitive skin of her inner wrist. Rianna trembled. Sarin smelt of lemons and verbena, sharp yet sweet. She felt a gentle breeze from the open window brush her cheek and catch stray strands of her hair. In the distance she could hear the eerie call of the peacocks that roamed the palace gardens.

Entranced by the feel of Sarin's hands caressing her body, Rianna trembled on the edge of some erotic dream, a step away from reality. Her senses swam; time had no meaning. Sarin whispered something sensual in her ear, but she couldn't quite make out the words.

Meshing his fingers in her hair, Sarin stroked the nape of her neck, trailing his hands downwards to stroke her shoulders and the curve of her bosom. 'How pale your skin is, how green your eyes,' he murmured. 'I'll have a necklace of emeralds fashioned to drape over these sweet breasts.'

Rianna floated on a cloud of bliss, sighing with pleasure as her bodice was eased apart so that Sarin could caress her breasts. He pulled and teased her nipples, watching the tiny teats surge into life.

'So pretty. Nubbins like berries, sweet and entrancing,' he purred as he bent his head and took one between his lips, mouthing it expertly until she gave a pleading moan. 'Your clothing should be designed to reveal these sweet teats.'

Rianna coloured, regaining some control over her over-heightened senses. 'I could not,' she said breathlessly. 'It would not be proper.'

'Only in the privacy of my quarters, sweet Rianna,' he assured her. 'Now let me look at your denuded pudenda.'

'We are not yet wed,' she replied as he began to pull aside her skirt.

'Tomorrow, in the late afternoon the ceremony will take place. I'll soon be your husband. Do not deny me what you've already shown my Chancellor. Lesand assures me your sex is quite entrancing.'

His words almost took her breath away. She disliked the thought of Lesand and Sarin speaking in such intimate terms about her body. Yet it was not in her power to deny Sarin anything, except for her heart of course. That belonged to Tarn and no one else.

'As you wish, my lord.' Her cheeks flushed as he moved the silver skirt to around her waist and stared down at her denuded sex. When she tried to pull her legs together, he eased them apart. 'Yasmin likens your pudenda to cream with a swirl of sweet red fruit at its centre,' Sarin said, his voice thick with desire.

Did everyone in this palace discuss her in such intimate detail, she wondered anxiously, as she coloured even more.

At first Sarin didn't touch her, he just stared at her sex while continuing to tease and tweak her nipples. Running his hand over the soft planes of her belly, he stroked the curve of her pubis. Rianna's sex lips still felt full and heavy, and moisture started to flood her divide. The desire she had experienced in the hammam reignited. Unconsciously she spread her thighs wider, lifting her hips up towards Sarin.

'I think you will please me well in bed,' Sarin remarked as his fingers slid inside the sensitive valley to gauge how moist she was already. 'One touch and your body prepares itself for my intrusion. I'll be counting the hours until we are wed.'

To her surprise, he pulled down her skirt and rose to his feet. Rianna meanwhile took an unsteady breath, realising how easily she had denied her feelings for Tarn, just by responding to Sarin's caresses. The sensual desires Tarn had aroused within her would not be easily quelled.

'Have I displeased you?' she asked Sarin as he stepped away from her.

'Indeed not,' he smiled at her. 'You please me greatly, Rianna. Your innocence excites me.' He lifted his fingers, still covered with the dew of her body, to his lips. 'Your honeyed flesh tastes so sweet.' Watching Rianna's cheeks turn a hot pink, he added, 'You look tired, my dear. It is time you retired.'

* * *

Jenna glanced nervously behind her as she heard the sound of footsteps. The wide corridor was silent and empty, pools of shadow lining its edges. She shivered. There were so many corridors and rooms in this huge palace it was easy to lose one's bearings. Next time, she vowed, she would ask Mircon to escort her at least part of the way.

Their long evening of lovemaking had left her feeling tired and languid. Rather than endure a long walk along endless, empty corridors, she decided to take a short cut across the gardens. Turning left, she stepped through an archway, crossed the narrow path and began to walk across the springy grass. She could see the outline of palm trees, silhouetted against the star-spattered sky, swaying gently in the breeze.

Jenna was in such a hurry she almost walked into the dark figure of a man. She gave a squeak of surprise. 'Sir, you startled me,' Jenna said nervously.

The bright moonlight enabled her to make out his features, and she saw he was young and good-looking.

'These gardens are out of bounds to slaves after dusk,' he told her curtly.

'I am no slave,' she protested. 'I'm maidservant to the Lady of Harn.'

'You are Lady Rianna's maid?' he asked with interest.

'I am honoured to serve Lady Rianna,' she said proudly. 'My name is Jenna.'

'You travelled with her from Harn?' He moved closer, smiling in a friendly manner.

'Yes, sir.' She nodded, thinking him most handsome and well-spoken.

'I hear your mistress is as kind and tender-hearted as she is beautiful?'

'I can attest to that, sir. At home, in Harn, she often spent her days tending the sick and helping those less fortunate.'

'Did she not tend the wounds of the traitor, Tarn of Kabra?' he questioned.

'She did,' Jenna confirmed. 'But only at Chancellor

Lesand's behest. He feared for the prisoner's life and there was nothing more the military surgeon could do for him.'

'So it was *she* who saved the traitorous swine,' he hissed.

'Lady Rianna believes all life sacred,' Jenna replied hotly. 'Now I should leave, sir. My lady will be wondering where I am.'

'Wait.' He grabbed hold of her arm.

'Please unhand me, sir,' she said agitatedly. 'I have to go.'

'You will leave when I say you can,' he growled, his pleasant demeanour vanishing.

Jenna struggled to get away from him, but the nobleman dug his fingers into her arm. As he wrenched her cloak from her shoulders, the fragile lacing of her bodice parted and her breasts broke free.

His eyes fastened on the full globes. Pulling Jenna closer, he roughly stroked her bosom, squeezing the soft flesh between his fingers. 'Please leave me be,' Jenna begged, frightened but excited by the crude caresses.

'I'm a close friend of Lord Sarin, and of noble blood, while you are but a lowly maidservant,' he said thickly as he pulled her to the ground. 'You should be honoured that I even show an interest in you, wench. If you know what's good for you, Jenna, you'll welcome my attentions.'

Jenna froze. This man was not unattractive, quite the contrary, and she knew her place in the order of things. For Mircon's sake she had no wish to anger someone close to Lord Sarin.

'That's better,' he smiled as she ceased her struggles. 'It's a while since I took a wench like this. A hasty coupling will be most pleasurable. I find the cloying attentions of the women here less than stimulating.'

Jenna wondered if he would reward her, as she needed a goodly sum if she and Mircon were to wed. She adored her soldier lover, but sometimes she daydreamed about a stolen sexual interlude with a handsome stranger.

Mircon would never know, she thought as she lay back on the soft grass.

The stranger lifted her skirts. 'How I've longed for this,' he grunted as he saw the thick brown curls of her pubis. 'I've become weary of soft, scented, hairless women, growing lazy and indolent in their luxury. A lusty wench is just what I need.'

Jerking open his breeches, he pulled out his penis. It was already erect, and of a splendid size. Jenna's eyes widened and her belly grew hot with lust. His cock was longer and much thicker than her soldier lover's. She could feel the remnants of Mircon's semen still sticking to her thighs, increasing the musky odour of her sex.

The nobleman ran his hands through her fleece. Without preamble he grabbed hold of her hips and thrust into her, heedless of causing her any discomfort, but Jenna was wet and ready. She sighed with bliss as his magnificent organ slid deep inside her feminine sheath.

Leaning forward, he buried his face in her full breasts, pulling one teat deep into his mouth. All the while he thrust into her, grinding his pelvis roughly against hers. The onslaught was swift and harsh. In no time at all Jenna was moaning loudly, having reached the point of no return. As he grazed her nipple with his teeth and thrust even harder, the pulsing pleasure swept Jenna over the summit and into the dark abyss.

With a grunt of satisfaction, the stranger reached his climax, spilling his seed while digging his teeth into her breast. Pain and pleasure combined into a myriad of wonderful sensations, leaving Jenna exhausted and replete.

The stranger rose to his feet, readjusted his clothing and looked down at her. 'Here.' He tossed two gold coins on to her belly. 'I look forward to our next meeting,' he said with a salacious grin. Then he turned and was soon swallowed up in the dark shadows of the garden.

Yasmin waited in silence as the hunched old woman examined the elaborate henna patterns on the backs of

Rianna's hands, similar decorations covering her feet. Smiling toothlessly, the old crone inclined her head at Yasmin and Rianna before walking slowly from the room.

'She likes to oversee her slave's handiwork. Her eyes are too bad, her hands too shaky to do it herself. It is said she has served the Lords of Percheron for nigh on sixty years,' Yasmin explained. She turned to the other servants. 'Leave now.'

Rianna wore her wedding gown: a bodice and skirt of scarlet silk covered by a long sleeved robe of cloth-of-gold. Her hair was loose as befitting a bride, but her long red-gold locks were entwined with strands of emeralds worth a king's ransom. They were part of her wedding gifts from Sarin.

'Do you have the bladder in place?' Yasmin asked once they were alone.

Rianna nodded anxiously. 'Are you certain it will work?'

'Of course it will,' Yasmin assured her. 'It would have been far more difficult if Lord Sarin had not accepted Chancellor Lesand's advice, and decided to deflower you himself. Lord Sarin has bedded a number of virgins, and it is likely he would have realised you were trying to deceive him.'

Chancellor Lesand, in Rianna's best interest, had persuaded Sarin to revive the ancient ceremony of the ritual of deflowerment. It had been a common custom among the nobility for centuries in Percheron, but Sarin's grandfather had declined to carry on the custom. During the ceremony, the bride's virginity was taken by a silver phallus, and the witnesses to the ritual were the bridegroom and his concubines.

Rianna now knew that the women in the bath house were members of Sarin's seraglio. Some he kept purely for his own pleasure, but the less important concubines he was happy to share with his friends.

Yasmin had resided in the seraglio since the tender age of fourteen. She came from a land far across the sea,

139

where women were considered mere chattels. Her father, a merchant, had owed Sarin a great amount of money and had offered his youngest daughter in place of the debt. Sarin had refused, bringing shame to Yasmin and her family, until Chancellor Lesand had intervened and persuaded the Lord of Percheron to change his mind.

'You're sure the bladder will burst at the right moment,' Rianna pressed, knowing that if she did not produce visible proof of her virginity Sarin might investigate and discover the truth. She feared more for Tarn than herself, still not having any idea of his fate.

'It will burst, the blood will flow and all will believe you to be a virgin.' Yasmin kissed her cheek. 'You owe a great debt to the Chancellor, Rianna, just as I do.' She handed her friend a small vial of clear liquid. 'Now drink this. It's a mild mixture of valerian and other herbs which will help you relax. The marriage ceremony is long and wearisome. I don't want you worrying all the time about what will happen at the deflowerment.'

Rianna remembered little of the marriage ceremony. She sat on a dais, her head and face covered by a silk veil, her breathing choked by the overpowering smell of incense, enveloped in a happy haze of euphoria.

Gifts were heaped in front of her. At one point Lord Sarin moved to sit beside her, and lifted her veil to kiss her cheek. She knew he spoke but she had no idea what he said, as she was still overcome by the relaxing potion Yasmin had given her.

Eventually, as her conscious mind began to find its way though the haze, she felt Sarin remove her veil and help her to her feet. Rianna almost stumbled as her legs were stiff from sitting cross-legged for so long. She heard the sound of music, and saw slaves move forward to serve food and drink to the many guests.

'Soon you will be mine completely,' Sarin whispered in her ear as he led her into an adjoining room.

The air in the other room was bereft of the choking incense and far cooler. Rianna was unsure why there

140

were so many women gathered here. Something was about to happen, but the valerian potion Yasmin had given her still muddled her thoughts.

Sarin led her to a dais on which stood a table covered with a white cloth. Yasmin was waiting for them. She smiled encouragingly at Rianna and took hold of her hand.

'Let the ceremony begin,' Sarin said, moving off the dais.

'This will all be finished soon,' Yasmin said.

At last, Rianna began to recall why she was here. Paling visibly, she glanced nervously at the expectant female audience, then back at Yasmin.

'I had hoped the potion would dull your senses for a while longer,' Yasmin said with concern. 'Be brave, Rianna, and remember why this has to be done. Now you must ready yourself for the brief ceremony. Lie down on the table.'

Rianna climbed on to the hard table and lay back, trying to hide her apprehension. She hoped their deception would work, and Sarin would be convinced she was still a virgin. Yet even now, as this troubling time, she did not regret giving her innocence to Tarn.

'When the moment comes, bend your knees, as it will make the entrance easier,' Yasmin said as she looped silken ropes around Rianna's ankles. 'I've left the ropes long enough to afford you movement.'

As Yasmin moved away to take part in the blessing of the phallus, which preceded the taking of Rianna's virginity, a familiar female figure leant over Rianna. 'Niska!' she gasped in surprise.

Niska gave an evil smile. 'As Sarin's wife, I have claimed the right to wield the ritual phallus myself. Have you seen the object? It is magnificent,' she gloated. 'With a splendid girth and length. I almost envy you Rianna, yet I think still prefer hard male flesh for myself.'

Rianna became even more apprehensive, dreading what Niska might try to do to her. She would find a cruel pleasure in causing pain. There was a rustle of silk

141

as Niska stepped from the dais to take part in the blessing. It was supposed to ensure that the deflowered maiden became fertile and would soon present her husband with a lusty male heir. Soft music filled the room, the steady rhythmic beat masking Niska's footfalls as she returned to the dais.

As Niska pulled Rianna's skirt up around her waist, she felt the cool air brush her legs, belly and naked sex. Rianna was exposed in an intimate manner to all the residents of the seraglio.

Pushing Rianna's thighs apart, Niska forced her to bend her legs and lift her pelvis. The ropes were tightened so that Rianna was held fast and helpless. With her legs spread so wide, Rianna was certain that her flesh lips must be gaping open, revealing the entrance to her womanly sheath. The bladder rested close to the neck of her womb and she feared that someone might see it.

Niska trickled cool oil over Rianna's pudenda, and it coated her engorged labial lips and ran down between her thighs. With the tips of her fingers, Niska spread it thickly over the narrow divide, pouring more in the valley to slickly coat Rianna's inner flesh.

'Would that I had you all to myself,' Niska whispered, roughly caressing the tip of Rianna's pleasure bud, and watching her wince with painful bliss. She squeezed the sensitive pearl between her fingers, surging it into life. It throbbed excitedly, welcoming Niska's touch. Rianna tried to ignore the feel of Niska's fingers stroking her pudenda, but her body responded. Niska brushed back the protective hood of Rianna's clitoris and ran the tip of her long nail over the sensitive flesh beneath. Rianna whimpered; it hurt, but the stinging agony was also pleasurable.

Placing her fingers either side of Rianna's engorged labial lips, Niska pressed hard, putting more pressure on the taut bud, making it throb sweetly for release.

'Now for the phallus,' Niska said gloatingly.

She lifted the heavy silver object and Rianna saw it for the first time. The centuries-old, silver phallus, with its ornate fashioned silver handle, glimmered softly, looking impossibly large. Rianna felt faint with apprehension. She wondered how would it ever fit inside her, and watched nervously as Niska carefully coated the phallus with oil.

Rianna's knees trembled as Niska placed the tip of the object against the entrance to her vagina.

'Ready yourself for its caressing strength. You're a virgin, your flesh has never been stretched so it's bound to hurt,' Niska said malevolently. 'I feel no pity for your predicament. Another time I will plunge this deep into your nether mouth. You'd suffer even more then.'

Rianna shivered, knowing no one could come to her aid, not even Sarin. Once commenced, the ceremony could not be interrupted until her virginity had been proven. The phallus felt hard and icy cold. She steeled herself, determined not to reveal any discomfort as the phallus was thrust into her body.

At first Niska was surprisingly gentle, as she pushed the phallus into Rianna slowly. As Rianna's soft sheath began to stretch, Niska employed a steady twisting movement, burying it deeper. Partway she halted, and looked down at Rianna. 'Now for the virginal barrier,' she mocked, smiling with cruel pleasure.

Quite unexpectedly, she thrust the phallus deep into Rianna's vagina. Rianna gave a sharp squeak of surprise which appeared to the onlookers to be a maiden's cry of anguish. Unconcerned by Rianna's supposed discomfort, Niska buried the sheath up to its elaborately carved handle. With a flick of her wrist she rotated the phallus. Rianna groaned as the bladder inside her burst and a sudden rush of wetness trickled downwards.

Rianna would have preferred Tarn's hot male flesh to be stretching her so, but the sensation was still superbly pleasurable. As Niska began to move the phallus in a thrusting twisting movement, Rianna bit her lip, trying to imagine that it was Tarn's cock buried deep inside her, tantalisingly stretching and caressing her silken walls. She felt the heat in her groin grow, and wondered

143

whether this symbolic lovemaking was intended to make her climax. Her desire was mounting, while Niska clearly thought the phallus was causing great discomfort and was determined to continue the torture as long as she could.

'Enough.' Sarin stepped forward and put a restraining hand on Niska's arm. 'You forget she is a virgin, you'll hurt her.'

'Was a virgin,' Niska amended with a mocking smile. 'And I forgot nothing. I wanted her to suffer.'

'I'll have you punished for your behaviour,' Sarin growled.

'I was counting on it,' Niska replied with a smile. She flung a brief, derisive glance at Rianna and moved out of her sight.

Rianna saw Lord Sarin look worriedly down at her exposed sex. She knew the outer lips must be bulging obscenely around the rim of the invading silver phallus. Taking hold of the handle, he withdrew the dildo slowly and with great care. Its removal left a void in Rianna, an aching emptiness in her sheath that needed to be filled.

The proof of Rianna's virginity was exposed; blood streaked her inner thighs. Sarin smiled, wiped the phallus, then held up the bloodstained cloth for all to see. There was a soft sigh of appreciation from the audience, followed by the sound of many chattering voices.

Unfastening the ropes that held her, Sarin swept Rianna into his arms. Carrying her from the room, he gave her over to the care of one of his waiting Nubian slaves. The man held Rianna protectively against his huge chest as he carried her to Sarin's chambers. She was laid on a bed, where slaves surrounded her to strip off her wedding garments and bathe her soiled flesh. As they left the room, Yasmin appeared to help Rianna remove any remnants of their deception before Lord Sarin arrive to claim her for himself.

'I told you all would be well,' Yasmin said with a smile of encouragement before she departed.

Naked and alone, Rianna lay in Lord Sarin's bed.

There was an aching emptiness between her thighs that only Tarn could extinguish. But he was cruelly confined somewhere deep in the bowels of this great palace.

'Rianna, my dear.' Sarin's arrival disturbed her troubled thoughts. 'Did Niska hurt you?' he asked worriedly. With his dark hair loose around his shoulders, his features appeared softer, less threatening.

'No,' she admitted. 'I was more humiliated than harmed.'

'She had no reason to be so brutal,' he replied with concern. 'I could not refuse her request to take part in the ceremony. By reason of her position, the right was hers. Now, I can help you forget your discomfort and show you what pleasures life here can offer you.' Sarin slipped off his velvet robe. 'Together we will find the pathway to true ecstasy.'

The lights were dim enough to allow Rianna only a brief glimpse of his naked form as he joined her in bed. There were no visible signs of an indolent monarch; Sarin's body was firm and hard, like that of a warrior.

As Sarin pulled her into his arms and took possession of her mouth, Rianna closed her eyes, wishing she could be with her one true love. The thought that Sarin was now her husband made her quail inwardly, yet she found she was not unmoved by his sensual kisses. Her heartbeat quickened as he stroked and caressed her. Sarin was a connoisseur of women, an acknowledged expert in the art of carnal pleasure, and knew exactly how best to arouse the senses of an inexperienced maiden.

Rianna trembled beneath him as he employed every seductive technique he knew to further inflame her desires. He stroked and squeezed her bosom, massaged her nipples and caressed the sensitive undersides of her breasts. Gently, he trailed his hands downwards, allowing his fingers to just brush her naked mound of Venus. Pulling the sheet from her body, he caressed her with his lips, kissing and licking every inch of her soft, smooth skin. He nuzzled her nipples and sucked on them gently.

Sliding downwards he lapped at her belly and drew moist circles on her pubis with the tip of his tongue.

Rianna tensed, feeling suddenly apprehensive as he spread her thighs. 'I seek to give only pleasure,' he purred huskily. 'Let me taste your honeyed folds.'

She lay back on the pillows, trying to relax as she felt his warm breath brush her pudenda. Parting her labial lips, Sarin delicately licked her most intimate flesh, his saliva contributing to the growing moisture as she became steadily more aroused. His tongue teased and stroked the rosy flesh, adding to her already inflamed passion. Rianna gave a soft moan, not having expected him to be so unselfish in his lovemaking. He had any number of women to serve his every sensual need, but Sarin was intent on giving pleasure to his new bride. As his tongue swirled delicately around her aching pleasure pearl, she was consumed by bliss. He sucked at the bud, forcing it to stiffen, filling her sex with a fiery warmth.

She felt him probe the entrance to her womanly sheath and shivered apprehensively. It felt stretched and sore from Niska's brutal invasion, but the teasing caresses served to relax her abused flesh and the soft, stabbing warmth of his tongue as it ventured deeper, made Rianna gasp with delight. Unconsciously, she lifted her hips up towards Sarin, now welcoming each searching thrust. Her desire increased to fever pitch. She was filled with the longing to mesh her hands in his hair and force his face closer to her vulva, but she feared Sarin would think her far too demanding.

Sarin sucked on her throbbing pearl, while his tongue delved deeper. Soon Rianna's pleasure started to peak, the exquisite sensations growing stronger. She felt the walls of her vagina pulse and her orgasm came swiftly in a sudden rush of white-hot, fiery bliss. As the pulsing died away, it left a sweet, heavy warmth deep in the pit of her belly.

'In time you'll become more experienced,' Sarin said thickly as he lifted his head. 'And you'll learn to hold back on your release. By doing so you become able to reach the ultimate peak of pure pleasure. I find your innocence surprisingly pleasing, Rianna. I look forward to teaching you to appreciate every different facet of carnal delight.'

Rianna blushed, not from innocent embarrassment, but because she felt she had betrayed Tarn by finding such unbound pleasure in Sarin's skilful lovemaking. She had thought she would not enjoy his intimate attentions, but unfortunately she had.

'I feared you would find my innocence tiresome, my lord,' she said coyly as she hid her inner shame.

Sarin's manhood was erect, standing stiffly out from his groin. It looked different from Tarn's; there was no thick ridge of skin collaring the bulbous head, and the taut skin was far darker than that of her golden-skinned warrior. Yet she was filled with the desire to feel it thrusting inside her. The sensuality Sarin exuded was overwhelming in its intensity and far too strong for her to resist.

Leaning towards her, Sarin deftly slid his penis into her soft, open sheath, at last filling the aching void left by the silver phallus. He began to move his hips, thrusting in and out of her, pushing and twisting slightly so that he caressed every portion of the velvety walls, putting even more pressure on her already sensitised sex.

A master of technique, Sarin led her swiftly towards the summit, ensuring that with every pull and thrust the shaft of his member rubbed tantalisingly against her aching pleasure nubbin. Still enfolded in the aftermath of her previous climax she reached the peak of fulfilment all too swiftly. Holding her close, Sarin joined her and they tumbled together into the fiery chasm of bliss.

There was still a warmth blazing in her belly when Sarin withdrew and lay down by her side. Sated and exhausted, she fell asleep in his arms.

Jenna left her quarters on her way to meet Mircon. Yasmin had informed her that Lady Rianna would be remaining with Lord Sarin until morning, and it meant she could spend the entire night with Mircon in his new quarters. Now that he was officially part of Chancellor Lesand's personal guard, he had his own room within the palace, and it would be far easier for them to spend time together.

She walked briskly through the quiet corridors. A few courtiers were around, but most were still at the wedding feast. Jenna turned a corner, and to her surprise saw the handsome nobleman who'd pleasured her so roughly in the garden.

'Why in such a hurry, Jenna?' he asked, looking even more handsome now that she could see him clearly in the bright light of the passageway. Tall, and richly dressed, he had glossy chestnut hair and brown eyes.

'I have an urgent matter to attend to,' she replied. Their recent brief encounter had been constantly in her thoughts. She went to pass the nobleman but he grabbed hold of her arm.

'I've missed you.' He smiled mercilessly as he dragged her through an open doorway and into an opulently-furnished bedchamber. 'Now you surprise me with an unexpected visit.'

'Sir, you presume wrongly,' she stuttered. 'I did not intend –'

'Jenna,' he interrupted. 'Don't tease me by pretending to resist, when you know very well you want this just as much as I do,' he said in a soft but commanding tone. Pulling her close he roughly fondled her breasts. 'Your noble mistress is busy pleasuring Lord Sarin. So you are free to find your entertainment elsewhere.'

He kissed her, pushing his tongue deep into her mouth, continuing to caress her in a brutal fashion. Grabbing hold of Jenna's hand he thrust it on to his huge erection. Lust speared Jenna's belly and she began to feel exhilarated.

'Perhaps you are not the entertainment I seek.' She pulled away from him, knowing she should resist and run to Mircon, but she wanted to stay. 'Why the sudden interest in a lowly maidservant such as me, sir? You are a wealthy nobleman. You can call upon any number of the court ladies to pleasure you.'

'I told you before, Jenna. I prefer lusty wenches,' he growled, preventing her from pulling away. He held her fast with one hand while he removed his velvet doublet. His fine linen shirt was open to the waist. In contrast to Mircon his skin was pale and virtually hairless. 'However, perhaps I did choose you precisely because you are Lady Rianna's maid. Tell me, are you as free with your affections as your mistress?'

'I don't know what you mean,' she replied nervously.

'Come now, Jenna.' He smiled mockingly. 'I hear Lady Rianna became mightily fond of the prisoner, Tarn. She spent many hours tending his wounds, and much of that time she was alone with him. Strange behaviour for one destined to wed Lord Sarin, Tarn's greatest enemy.'

He let go of Jenna but she didn't run, she wanted to stay. Hungrily, she watched him slip off his shirt and breeches, overcome by a sudden lust. The nobleman smiled provocatively, magnificent in his nakedness, his cock standing lewdly out from his body. There was a thick, gold bracelet around his right wrist, set with rubies and diamonds, a further indication of his status and wealth. Jenna noticed a small heart-shaped birthmark just above his left nipple. An incongruous mark for such a hard man.

'The prisoner was unconscious most of the time that Lady Rianna was alone with him,' she replied, wondering how this nobleman had acquired such intimate knowledge of their journey to Percheron. 'My lady would treat any wounded man in a similar fashion, whether he be freeman or prisoner.'

'Your loyalty is commendable,' he chuckled. 'You must care deeply for your lady.' Grabbing hold of Jenna, he threw her on to the bed and wrenched her skirt up around her waist. 'How I love this thick brown fleece,' he muttered hungrily as he opened her sex lips with his thumbs. Without any sign of finesse, he stabbed at her intimate flesh with his tongue and sucked hard on her pleasure bud.

Jenna moaned as he thrust his tongue deep inside her vagina and a fiery warmth flooded her belly. She relaxed, letting the lust flow over her as she tossed all other thoughts aside. She could try to discover more about this man later, but first she had to find her release.

He licked and sucked her pudenda with a rough passion that took her breath away. Her pleasure built swiftly and she had almost obtained her fulfilment when he pulled away from her. Springing forward, he sat astride her heaving bosom, almost crushing her with his weight. She took a shallow, laboured breath as he pushed his erect phallus close to her face.

'Suck it,' he ordered.

A sharp thrill ran through her. 'No!' she gasped.

Ignoring her reluctance, he pushed his cock into her mouth, pressing the smooth hardness of his shaft between her teeth. She began to mouth the member, lovingly circling the bulbous head with her tongue. She heard him give a harsh groan as he pressed himself closer, trying to force more of the organ into her mouth.

Jenna wanted her release, and longed to feel that massive cock thrusting deep inside her. Wrenching her head to the right, she pulled his phallus from her mouth and glared challengingly at her oppressor.

'Greedy whore,' he growled. 'I suppose you want it inside you.'

Lifting his weight from her, he slid his body downwards and penetrated her with a forceful lunge. His iron-hard shaft parted her soft flesh as he thrust into her with long, powerful strokes. Jenna moaned and twined her legs around his waist, meeting each thrust with passion, her desire aroused to fever pitch. Jenna's orgasm came in a sudden, unexpected rush of pleasure. Her vagina pulsed excitedly as the intense climax washed over her.

The nobleman pulled away from her and spilt his hot

seed on her stomach. 'I'll not father a babe for you to foist on to your soldier lover,' he said brusquely.

Sinking down beside her, he lay on his back looking up at the ceiling. Jenna grabbed hold of a crumpled shirt. 'Who are you?' she asked, wiping his semen from her stomach.

'What concern is that of yours?' he replied coolly.

'I only wish to know your name.'

'Why?' he countered.

'Why not? Is it wrong to know who I couple with?'

'Just accept I desire you, Jenna,' he growled.

'Yet you constantly question me about my mistress. Why such an interest in her, sir?'

'Interest?' He raised one eyebrow. 'Sheer curiosity – that is all, Jenna. Lord Sarin happened to mention that the Lady Rianna went down on her knees to him and pleaded for Tarn's life. I thought it strange that she seemed so concerned for the fate of a traitor.'

'She did do because Tarn of Kabra is a distant kinsman of her mother, Lady Kitara.' Jenna voiced the excuse Rianna had used. It could not be disproved because little was known of Kitara's heritage. No doubt Tarn would not deny it even if Lord Sarin questioned him on the matter.

'So Lord Sarin tells me,' the nobleman said thoughtfully. Sitting up, he took three gold coins from a pile on a table beside the bed. 'For you, Jenna,' he said, tossing them on to the bed beside her. 'Now begone before your idle chatter begins to anger me.'

'Yes, sir.' Jenna gathered up the coins, pulled down her skirts and walked swiftly to the door.

'I look forward to our next encounter, Jenna,' he said with a soft, menacing laugh. 'You have another orifice I've yet to penetrate.'

His words rang in her ears as she left the room. She began to run down the corridor, eager to get away from him. The ruthless way he took her and his searching questions troubled her. She was certain his desires were driven by something darker than lust. Somehow she had to find out who he was.

She was breathless with haste by the time she found Mircon waiting in the garden where they had arranged to meet. 'I was worried,' he said, pulling her into his arms. 'What's wrong, my sweet?'

'Nothing,' she lied, holding him close, feeling safe in his embrace. 'What possible harm could come to me within the confines of the palace?'

'Jenna, don't lie to me.' He lifted her chin and stared deep into her troubled eyes.

'It's a nobleman. I don't know his name but he has taken a sudden interest in me. Twice he has questioned me about Lady Rianna and her relationship with Tarn. He knows too much, Mircon. His suspicions might well prove dangerous for my lady.'

'Let us get inside my room before we discuss this further,' Mircon whispered. 'We would not wish to be overheard.' He said nothing more until they were safely in his room with the door bolted and barred. 'I've heard rumours,' he told her. 'Someone has been questioning the soldiers who travelled with us from Harn. It's said that Rorg suddenly seems to be in possession of a large amount of silver which he has been spending in the local taverns.'

'You think it is the nobleman?' Jenna asked.

Mircon shrugged his shoulders. 'Perhaps him, or someone working for him.'

'What will be gained from harming Lady Rianna?' Jenna said worriedly.

'I don't know,' replied Mircon. 'But for her sake we have to do our best to discover more.'

# Chapter Eight

$R$ianna sighed softly in her sleep. Sarin raised himself on one elbow and looked down at her, a faint smile on his lips. She lay on her back, not moving, her red-gold hair splayed across the pillow, looking beautiful and quite innocent.

Sarin was captivated by Rianna's innocence. It was a unique quality within a seraglio filled with women whose sole purpose in life was to give him pleasure in any and every conceivable fashion. They were taught to disregard their own needs and take their joy from his release. Only Niska was different. She defied the rules and demanded satisfaction when he bedded her. She was also a willing participant in all his varied licentious excesses. Nothing was too strange or bizarre for Niska. Sometimes Sarin regretted marrying her. Nevertheless, there was something unique in Niska that he recognised, a reflection of himself. She was his darkness, while Rianna would be his light.

Lesand had warned him that Rianna was stubborn and self-willed, a trait she had inherited from her warrior mother. Because of that, and the reluctance Rianna had displayed over being forced into a political marriage, Sarin had ensured that her food and drink contained a potion that dulled any natural reluctance and heightened her senses, so that their first encounters would arouse her natural feminine passions. Last night she had given herself to him unreservedly, but Sarin had no intention of feeding her any more of the potion. After the effects wore off, Rianna might begin to display some reluctance. Sarin thought that a measure of resistance would add an extra facet of pleasure to their future relationship. Soon, of course, she would come to want him as much as he now wanted her. After that it would be easy to capture her heart.

Gently, trying not to wake her, Sarin rolled Rianna on to her side. He slid closer to her, until her back was pressed to his chest, her buttocks to his belly. She moaned and moved her legs restlessly, throwing one forward and opening her sex to his embrace. Sarin slid his fingers into her velvety sheath and her soft flesh welcomed the intrusion. As it wrapped around his fingers, her moisture began to flow, gently coating her honeyed folds.

It was a long time since he'd been so aroused without previous stimulus. His need for Rianna was like an aching heat in his lower stomach. Sarin slid his engorged cock past her nether mouth and into her vagina. He felt as if he could take her a thousand times, and yet not be sated. He knew from experience that such depth of feeling rarely lasted long. He tired of most women in time, regardless of their fragile beauty, their personalities or their varied talents. Love was forever denied to him. Sarin thought it a sign of weakness and would never allow himself to succumb to such a profoundly crippling emotion.

He lay there deep inside Rianna, feeling her womanly sheath embrace his cock. Gently he began to move, careful not to push too hard in case she awoke. She was even more innocently vulnerable when she was asleep. Sarin continued to thrust into her, savouring his pleasure, letting it slowly grow. He felt her vagina start to contract in strong waves, and his cock jerked in response as the seed spurted from his body.

Sarin held Rianna close as the climax overwhelmed him, buffeting his body with waves of sweetly tearing agony. 'My treasure,' he murmured, burying his face in her jasmine-scented hair.

He waited until his organ had softened before withdrawing. Bereft of his closeness, she rolled on to her back and looked up at him, a faint flush staining her ivory cheeks. 'I thought I was dreaming,' she whispered.

'You were not.' He smiled tenderly at her. 'You learn swiftly and you please me greatly. I look forward to welcoming you in my bed tonight.' Leaning forward, he kissed her soft, inviting mouth, fighting the urge to take her again.

'You honour me,' she blushed, appearing confused, and his heart warmed to her even more.

'I have important matters of state to attend to. Until this evening.' Sarin climbed from the bed and slipped on his velvet robe. Usually one of his Nubian slaves was in attendance at all times. For Rianna's sake, he had forgone their presence last night.

'Yes, my lord.' She pulled up the sheet to cover her nakedness.

Amused by her modesty, Sarin left the room. Two of his Nubians were waiting outside the bedchamber. Ordering them to follow him, Sarin strode briskly onwards. As he approached the special chambers which were set aside for his most secret pleasures, his thoughts turned to Tarn. Because of her innocence, he had treated Rianna with care. Sarin knew it would be some time before she was ready to learn that pleasure could be gained in many diverse and devious ways. However, he had no intention of treating Tarn so delicately. His induction would be swift, and judging by Tarn's wilful determination, necessarily harsh.

The two Nubian slaves accompanying Sarin were tall and muscular, their skin dark like polished ebony. After their purchase Sarin ordered their tongues cut out. So that his privacy could always be assured, he had only mute slaves to guard his pleasure vault.

Tarn was already in the inner chamber. He stood by a bench, waiting patiently, looking beautiful and wonderfully vulnerable. A length of chain ran from his gold collar to a ring in the wall. His arms were still chained to his sides, and he was naked apart from the leather harness. Despite Tarn's apparently docile demeanour, Sarin could not bring himself to wholly trust his new pleasure slave. In the past he'd been a strong, skilful warrior, and if he were pushed too far there was always the chance he would rebel.

'You may sit if you wish, Tarn,' Sarin said, his desire aroused just by seeing Tarn in his provocative leather harness. The constant pressure on his sex ensured Tarn was always partially aroused. 'Perhaps you find sitting uncomfortable with the phallus in place,' Sarin continued tauntingly.

A number of emotions flashed across Tarn's features, among them rebellion and anger. He clenched his hands, demonstrating to Sarin how difficult it was for him to rigidly control his feelings. 'I prefer to stand,' Tarn replied coldly.

'You should kneel when you greet me,' Sarin reminded him. 'But I'll ignore the oversight as it's obvious the collar chain does not permit you to do so.' He smiled wryly. 'In time you'll come to accept your position, Tarn. Even learn to welcome the pleasure that comes with absolute submission.'

He stepped over to Tarn and ran his finger over the slave's full bottom lip, then he meshed his fingers in the long, perfumed hair. In total contrast to Rianna, Tarn's body was firm and unyielding, but sweet just the same.

The first time Sarin had laid eyes on Tarn, the young warrior had been sixteen years old, just growing into manhood. He had been beautiful then, and Sarin had desired him. They'd become friends, close almost as brothers for a time. Sarin had always wanted a much deeper relationship, but he'd always been forced to hold back on his unrequited lust. Tarn seemed unable to accept that one man could desire another. Now of course it was different.

Tarn's features were calm and impassive but his mind was in turmoil as he stared at Sarin. 'You may control my body, Sarin. But you'll never control my mind.'

'We shall see.' Sarin smiled, appearing confident in his powers of persuasion. 'As you know, Tarn, over the years I've had a number of male pleasure slaves. Some I purchased, others were warriors captured in battle. Most were as strong-willed and determined as you are, but in time they all succumbed and willingly embraced their slavery. All were content to accept me as their master.'

'For Cador's sake I follow your orders, but I'll never willingly submit,' Tarn grated, unsure whether he would be strong enough to resist Sarin's merciless, seductive onslaughts on his senses.

Tarn had known this pleasure vault existed but he'd never been inside it before, or known exactly what happened here. Now he was about to find out. He looked at the low, wide bed, the wall chains, and the two saddle-like devices. They were all subtle instruments of exquisite, tortuous pleasure, like the strange contraptions in the other room, where he'd been fitted with his restrictive harness.

He became certain he was about to undergo his first test of strength as Sarin smiled cruelly and said, 'Of course I don't expect you to accept submission swiftly. It will take time to break your indomitable spirit. I confess the challenge excites me.'

As Sarin spoke, a young female slave entered the room. She was naked, her long, light brown hair falling almost to her pubis. 'You sent for me, master?' she said in a fearful voice as she prostrated herself at Sarin's feet.

'Get up, girl,' he said in a gentle tone. 'I'm not intending to punish you.'

Relief lightened her face as she rose gracefully to her feet. She wasn't beautiful, but she was comely, with sweet, innocent-looking features and large, hazel eyes.

Her pale skin was lightly dusted with freckles, while her breasts were high and full, the nipples firm and red as berries.

As Tarn stared at the young woman, a sudden surge of lust speared his belly. He tensed without thinking, but that only served to remind him of the ivory rod still buried in his anus. He had been allowed the blessed relief of sleeping without either harness or phallus, but the replacement rod one of the Nubians had thrust into him this morning had been visibly thicker and longer. What troubled Tarn even more, was that his abused flesh had practically welcomed the new intrusion.

When he moved, the hardness and the stretching inside him became almost pleasurable. His inner flesh contracted around the smooth ivory, filling his sex with a fiery lust. That, coupled with the tight leather straps around his groin, and the constant chafing of the sensitive skin of his perineum, overwhelmed his mind with erotic thoughts. Often he craved release, but that was denied him. Tarn's wrists were kept chained to his waist, the links only long enough to allow very limited movement. There was no way he could use his hands to pleasure himself.

'Remove the slave's harness,' Sarin told the young woman. She nodded and stepped nervously towards Tarn. 'Don't worry, he won't harm you,' Sarin assured her.

She smiled tremulously at Tarn as she unbuckled the wide belt and carefully removed the harness. Tarn could not hold back a soft sigh of relief as the pressure on his sex was released. The slave girl dropped the harness, darkened in places by his sweat, on to the bench. She then stepped behind Tarn. Exerting a gentle pressure on his nether mouth, she slightly rotated the phallus to make it slide smoothly from his body. Bereft of its intrusion, the virginal opening ached, feeling oddly empty. Tarn tensed his buttocks, trying to ignore the unwanted sensation.

'What now, my lord?' She looked at Sarin.

'You are to pleasure him, but first he must be securely confined. Step back,' Sarin replied.

Tarn hid his surprise. This was not what he'd expected. He had presumed that Sarin wanted him only for himself. One of the Nubian slaves unclipped Tarn's chain from the wall and led him into the centre of the chamber. Tarn's wrists were unclasped from his waist, his arms drawn high above his head and fixed to a chain hanging from the ceiling.

A padded chair was moved into position to allow Sarin to watch in comfort. 'You see, Tarn,' Sarin said with a smile, as he sank on to the chair, 'I'm not so cruel after all. The wench is comely, is she not?'

He clapped his hands and the young woman moved over to Tarn. She smiled, appearing pleased with her orders. 'My name is Brigit,' she whispered so softly that Tarn could barely hear her. 'I'm honoured, Prince Tarn.'

She kissed his cheek, then rubbed her body provocatively against his. Pressing her naked breasts and their cherry-like nubbins against his bare chest, she stroked and caressed him, pulling teasingly at the fine, blond hair in his exposed armpits.

Tarn had no intention of responding. He resented being expected to provide Sarin with salacious entertainment. Staring stoically ahead, his blue eyes icily fixed on Sarin's expectant face, he appeared unmoved by Brigit's seductive attentions. He was determined to display no desire or feeling, telling himself he wanted no one but Rianna.

Brigit's caresses became more intimate as she lapped and teased his nipples. Tarn did his best to disregard the growing heat in his groin, determinedly turning his mind to other thoughts.

Sarin frowned, angered by the contempt in Tarn's challenging stare. 'Take care, Tarn,' he warned. 'Have you so quickly forgotten Cador's plight? If you don't respond, I promise you Cador will be punished.'

Anger flared in Tarn's eyes for a brief moment, before

159

he capitulated. 'As you wish, my lord,' he grated reluctantly.

'Blindfold him. He'll respond better deprived of one of his senses,' Sarin said curtly.

A thick, silk blindfold was placed over Tarn's eyes. For a moment nothing happened, then he felt hands caressing his body again. This time he noticed the perfume, sweet and musky, strong enough to titillate his senses. No longer pressing her body against his, the slave girl concentrated on touching him with just her hands and lips.

Strands of her hair brushed his chest as she sucked on his nipples, pulling at the tiny nubbins with her mouth and nibbling them with her teeth. He felt her lips trail downwards, and her tongue lapped at the taut skin of his stomach. Tarn shivered; despite himself, he was aroused. Desire slithered into his groin like a lustful snake.

As she stroked his pubic hair, he gave up the struggle and succumbed to his arousal. Her breath brushed his semi-erect penis and it twitched excitedly, longing for the teasing caresses of her fingers and lips.

Tarn tried to forget that Sarin was watching his every move, finding pleasure in his unwilling response. Instead, he imagined that it was Rianna's lips and hands that were stroking his engorged flesh.

The slave sank lower, running her hands up the inside of his thighs, easing his legs further apart so that she could cup the soft sac of his scrotum. Her fingers felt surprisingly strong as they kneaded and squeezed his buttocks, and stroked the tortured flesh of his nether mouth. He tensed, willing her fingers to slide inside, but they drifted away to caress his penis.

Circling the shaft, she pumped the organ, urging it gently into full life. It hardened, the bulb at the end swelling as the foreskin slid slowly back to reveal the taut, purple glans beneath. She captured the bead of moisture seeping from its summit, and probed the tiny slitted mouth.

Tarn gasped and pressed his hips forward, sighing with relief as he felt her lips close around his cock head. She ringed the thick collar of flesh with her tongue, and coated the glans with her saliva. As she drew it deeper into her mouth, Tarn clenched his hands, digging his nails into the palms. She slid her lips further down the shaft, licking and sucking in a smooth, erotic rhythm. By now, Tarn was beyond anything other than his imminent release. Jerking his pelvis forward, he tried to force even more of his penis into the willing orifice.

She stroked the sensitive flesh of his perineum and squeezed his seed sac; it tightened, his balls hardening into two firm stones. Then her fingers probed his nether mouth. Tarn groaned loudly.

'Please,' he unconsciously murmured as her fingers slid inside.

They delved deeper, pausing to press on an achingly sensitive spot. The pleasure was so intense that Tarn could hold back no longer. His climax came, profound and frighteningly intense, as he spilled his seed deep inside Brigit's throat.

Tarn sagged on his chains, his arms supporting his weight as his thighs trembled from the strength of his orgasm. The slave girl straightened and fastened her lips on his. Apart from his brief moments with Rianna, Tarn had never felt such desire. The taste of his seed still lingered in Brigit's mouth as their tongues entwined.

Later, Tarn couldn't be certain of the exact point he came to realise how cruelly he had been deceived. Perhaps it was the kiss, or the moment later, when a firm, naked body pressed itself intimately against his. 'No!' he cried with anguish and pain as he jerked his head away.

'Why not, Tarn?' Sarin whispered. 'You were not so reluctant a moment ago.' He pressed his body even closer so that his penis was trapped between their hard, male bodies. 'Despite your denials I now know that deep in your heart you do desire me.'

'It's a lie, you deceived me,' Tarn groaned, feeling Sarin's penis pulse against his hot flesh.

The blindfold was eased from Tarn's eyes. He blinked in the sudden light as he stared at Sarin, not wanting to accept that which he knew was true. How could he not have realised that it wasn't Brigit touching him? When she'd first pressed herself against him, Tarn had smelt no perfume, and her hands were smaller and weaker than Sarin's. The two men had spent enough time together in the past, so why hadn't he recognised Sarin's sweet musky scent? Pain constricted Tarn's heart, his fear profound and all-encompassing. He had to accept that even if he had been duped he'd still been aroused by Sarin's touch.

'*Your* mind deceived you, Tarn, because you wanted to be deceived,' Sarin told him with a self-satisfied smile. 'I suggest you think hard on that.'

'I cannot,' Tarn said, filled with self-loathing.

Sarin beckoned to Brigit, who crouched in the corner of the room staring at them. 'Come here,' he ordered.

She approached Sarin and bent forward over the chair arm, parting her buttock cheeks with her hands, holding them so wide that both Tarn and Sarin could see her rosy nether mouth. It looked moist and shiny, as though it had already been well oiled.

Tarn's knees felt weak as he watched Sarin move over to Brigit. Soon it was likely he would be in her place, submissively offering his body to his master. His mind cried no, while his traitorous flesh almost ached with longing as he watched Sarin gently ease his manhood in Brigit's nether mouth. She gasped, as if in discomfort, when Sarin first entered her. But as he grasped hold of her hips and pounded into her, she lifted her buttocks to meet each welcoming thrust.

Tarn was aroused by the sight of Sarin's red, shiny stem thrusting erotically in and out of Brigit. Would he one day appear so willing, he asked himself, feeling weak and trembling at the thought. He would betray himself and all he believed in if he willingly submitted to Sarin. Yet a moment ago he gained immense pleasure from the caresses of a man he professed to hate. Alone and enslaved, his life was crumbling around him as dark and light began to merge into one.

He heard Brigit moan softly and Sarin grunt with pleasure as their thrashing movements became more frantic. She was bent low over the chair, her bottom high in the air. Tarn saw her hand slide under the chair arm and slip between her thighs. She fingered her sex, rubbing her nubbin while Sarin's cock still slid smoothly in and out of her nether mouth. Tarn was transfixed, unable to tear his gaze away as Brigit and Sarin climaxed at the same time.

As Sarin gave a satisfied sigh and withdrew from Brigit, Tarn lowered his eyes, not wanting Sarin to know how aroused he'd been while watching the hasty coupling.

Dismissing Brigit with a casual wave of his hand, Sarin moved to address Tarn with a voice full of soft menace. 'Now that you've demonstrated your true feelings, and the desires you've so far kept hidden, I can reassess our relationship and decide what will happen next.'

Lamps, set in the interlaced branches of lemon trees, bathed Sarin's private gardens in a soft light. The evening was warm, but still pleasantly cool after the oppressive heat of the day. Nearby, a caged nightingale sang sweetly.

Time flowed like a never-ending stream in the palace, one day of indolent pleasure merging into another. The constant luxury, the exotic food and the sensuality of Sarin's lovemaking, had captivated Rianna. She still thought of Tarn often, her remembrance tinged with guilt. So far she had done nothing to help him, and by willingly indulging in the erotic excesses Sarin offered her, she had betrayed her one true love. But there was no way she could escape the luxury, no way to avoid the constant pleasuring of her senses.

She had been married to Sarin for almost three weeks, and in that time she had changed. Modesty no longer concerned her, and she felt comfortable in the scanty provocative garments she was obliged to wear. Also, she had learnt that gratification could be gained in many different ways. In the last few days she had been happy to welcome Yasmin in her bed along with Sarin.

Tonight, she lay naked on a soft blanket in the lamp-lit garden, Sarin's head resting on her stomach, while she watched Yasmin pleasure him with her mouth. The vision of Yasmin's full, red lips sliding up and down Sarin's engorged shaft, and the soft sucking sounds, were deeply erotic and infinitely arousing.

Rianna bent forward and ran the tip of her tongue over Sarin's mouth, kissing him with passion. He returned the kiss, before turning his head to lick her full breast. His lips closed around her nipple. She gave a faint moan as he sucked the teat, pulling at the sensitive nubbin. Rianna's body was becoming conditioned to accept a constant diet of carnal pleasure. She thought about it all the time, constantly craving Sarin's touch and eagerly joining him in his chamber at night. Often she dreamt of their lovemaking, but always in the background was Tarn, staring reproachfully at his lost love.

She closed her eyes, enmeshed in her erotic daydreams. Her belly contracted as Sarin sucked harder, digging his teeth teasingly into her nipples. But as she heard the unexpected sound of movement, her eyes flew open.

'Master.' Niska knelt on the grass in front of Sarin, her head bowed.

He frowned at the intrusion, but didn't chastise her. 'Don't stop, Yasmin,' he said harshly, as Yasmin ceased her ministrations.

Yasmin returned to her task, expertly pulling his entire shaft into her mouth. Sarin closed his eyes and gave himself up to the pleasure. As his climax came he pushed Yasmin's face hard against his pelvis and groaned loudly.

There was a short silence, punctuated by the sound of Sarin's heavy breathing. He let go of Yasmin and smiled at her with unusual warmth. 'Leave now, Yasmin. But not you, Rianna,' he added, before looking coldly at Niska. 'What do you want of me?'

'I come to beg your forgiveness, my lord.'

Niska wore a provocative breast harness made of finely wrought silver that supported her bosom but left her silver-painted nipples exposed. A belt made of looped silver chains encircled her waist, the lower chain just reaching her naked pubis. She was dressed as a supplicant, her wrists bound at the front with ropes of white silk.

'You have yet to be punished.' Sarin took hold of the diamond attached to Niska's nipple and tugged on it, stretching the flesh so hard she winced in pain.

Niska bit her lip, enduring the discomfort. 'I've been waiting for you to decide my punishment,' she said softly.

Sarin let go of the diamond. 'I've stayed away from your chambers for nigh on three weeks. Do you consider that punishment enough, Niska?'

Niska cast a sly glance at Rianna, then looked back at Sarin. 'Only you can decide that, my master.'

'As Rianna was wronged, perhaps I should let her decide.' He smiled at Rianna. 'How say you, my dear?'

'I leave it in your hands, Sarin,' she replied, fighting the need to cover her nakedness in front of Niska.

'Then I'll let you administer the chastisement.' He beckoned to one of the ever-present, stony-faced Nubian slaves. 'Fetch the red leather harness,' he commanded.

The Nubian ran swiftly off, returning only moments later with one of the strangest articles Rianna had ever seen. Two carved objects, made to resemble male organs in every detail, were joined at their bases by a replica of a scrotum. The two phalluses were bent upwards at a curved angle, and one had a leather harness at its base as though it was to be worn.

Rianna coloured in surprise, imagining the contraption

fitted to her groin. One phallus would nestle deep inside her, while the other would stand stiffly out, a lewd representation of an erect penis. She watched nervously as the Nubian placed the magnificent double dildo at Sarin's side.

'Put it on, Rianna. You can punish Niska and pleasure yourself at the same time,' Sarin said with a smile.

'No,' she shook her head. 'I cannot do this, Sarin, not with Niska.' Rianna wasn't altogether repulsed by the object. Perhaps in the midst of desire she would be prepared to slip on the harness and play erotic games with Yasmin. But not here in the garden, in front of Sarin and his Nubians, and certainly not with Niska.

'Your shyness becomes you,' Sarin said indulgently. 'Cast aside that now, my sweet. It would please me to watch as you do this. And would be a fitting retribution for Niska's brutality at your deflowerment. I honour you, Rianna, by allowing you to exact such a punishment on Niska.'

Rianna rose to her knees, and pulled her silk robe in front of her to cover her nakedness. 'I'm sorry I cannot do this. Please do not ask me.'

'I do not ask. I order,' Sarin replied curtly.

'Still I cannot comply,' Rianna countered, her lips set in a defiant line. 'I'm your wife, Sarin, not some pleasure slave.'

'You are anything I say you are,' he growled, suddenly angry. Ripping the robe from her hands, he tossed it aside. 'Put the harness on, Rianna, and penetrate Niska. Despite your initial reluctance, you'll find it a uniquely pleasurable experience. I think such a punishment most fitting.'

'Look at her, Sarin, she wants me to do it. It will be no punishment,' Rianna flared, having watched Niska's response when she'd seen the harness. All the resentment Rianna's indolent life had suppressed came to the fore. 'I will not, and that's an end to it!'

'End to it,' he growled, cruelly pinching and twisting her left nipple.

166

'That hurts.' Rianna pushed him away.

She paled as Sarin's face contorted in fury. 'You dare lay a hand on me, woman,' he said through clenched teeth. 'Hold her down,' he ordered the Nubians.

The two huge slaves grabbed Rianna, one holding her arms, one her feet, as she was pinned face down on the rug. At first she was more angry than terrified, until she felt the first stinging pain across her buttocks. She gave a loud gasp of anguished surprise, hardly able to believe this was happening.

Rianna caught sight of the thin leather riding crop in Sarin's hand before he hit her again. The pain was worse, sharp and fierce. It sent a fiery heat through her buttocks and down into her groin. She pressed her face to the blanket, holding back her angry sobs, filled with a sudden, quite vicious hatred of Sarin. How dare he treat her like this; she was his wife.

Her buttocks grew hot, the skin stinging painfully as Sarin continued to abuse her already inflamed flesh. He held her buttocks apart for one blow and flicked the tip of the crop against her exposed nether mouth. Unbelievably, despite the humiliating agony, she felt a sudden, spiked warmth fill her belly. It was as if the beating were arousing her senses, and the heat increased to a dull, pleasurable ache that sang enticingly through her veins.

She remembered witnessing Tarn's arousal when he had been similarly abused. The punishment, the pain she was enduring, and her steadily mounting desire, caused her to feel at one with her lost love. Like Tarn, she fought the unwanted sensations, knowing that if she gave in to the spiked pleasure she would be surrendering her soul to Sarin.

Rianna caught her breath as she was forced to endure one last sharp, agonising blow. Tossing the riding crop aside, Sarin ordered the Nubians away and crouched between Rianna's open thighs. He entered her with one powerful lunge that filled her completely, his cock head venturing so deep it pressed against the neck of her womb. Despite herself, Rianna's passions were excited.

She wanted Sarin, she welcomed his pounding thrusts, but there was no one she hated more at this moment in time.

As he pressed his body against hers, she lifted her sore, reddened buttocks, relishing the slippery wetness as the shaft of Sarin's cock caressed the walls of her vagina. Fiery heat speared her belly, consuming her in a whirlpool of lust as Sarin drove into her again and again. She felt him push the heavy fall of her hair aside to kiss her neck while he continued to brutally pound his body against hers.

She shuddered as her climax came, washing over her in a tumultuous wave of bliss that merged with the glowing pain in her buttocks, turning into a kaleidoscope of painful pleasure. As her vagina pulsed around Sarin's cock shaft, he trembled, and mouthed the nape of her neck, whispering her name as his own orgasm consumed him.

Silently he rolled off her, and pulled her to her feet. Rianna could not bring herself to look at him. If she did she knew she would see no sign of sorrow or regret. He had enjoyed punishing and then pleasuring her.

Rianna swallowed hard and brushed the unwanted tears from her cheeks. She glanced down at the double phallus still lying on the ground in front of Niska, vowing that she would never use it, no matter how many times Sarin punished her. Kitara's warrior blood ran in her veins, and Rianna had never felt that as strongly as she did now.

Niska appeared to have enjoyed Rianna's humiliation. 'Stupid bitch,' she mouthed while Sarin wasn't looking.

Rianna ignored Niska and turned to glare proudly at Sarin, determined not to appear cowed. 'I beg leave to depart,' she said coldly.

Sarin smiled. 'Lesand told me that you were strong and self-willed. I never quite believed him until now,' he said, appearing pleased that she'd dared to refuse him. 'I admire that strength, Rianna. Once you've come to accept that I will always be in command, you'll become a fitting wife and consort.'

It was then that Rianna realised he was using her for his pleasure, just as he did every other concubine in his seraglio. Sarin considered her a challenge, but he would never truly care for her as a husband should his wife. She meant no more to him than any other pleasure slave in the palace; she existed only to serve him and do his bidding.

Tarn strode briskly across Sarin's private garden. It was good to be in the open air. He felt the sun on his back, and the soft breeze brush his long hair. For once he felt at peace, at least for a brief, fanciful moment.

Tarn was only required to wear his harness for a few hours at a time now, in the privacy of his room, or Sarin's pleasure vault. The rest of his day was spent in more normal pursuits. Sarin had deemed it necessary for Tarn to take regular exercise to keep his body in shape, his muscles taut and toned. Afterwards, he spent hours in the bath house being scrubbed, massaged and oiled, kept in the peak of physical condition so that he could be beautiful for Sarin.

Now that Sarin had decided Tarn could be trusted a little, his hands had been freed from his chains, although the slave collar remained, as did the wrist and ankle bracelets so that he could be restrained at any time. In Sarin's private quarters, Tarn had not been allowed clothing. Once he had been given permission to move about certain areas of the palace, Tarn had been given a thin muslin breechclout, and short, leather skirt to wear. The garments were similar to those worn by the other male slaves, and designed to accentuate his muscular physique. Some of the other slaves had their intimate body parts pierced, but so far Tarn had escaped that form of humiliation.

Tarn had yet to see Rianna. He had no wish for her to discover his degradation, and yet he longed to lay eyes upon her again. Of late, he had attended a number of

169

Sarin's private entertainments. Having spent a number of years at court, he was well-used to the licentious excesses, but as a guest who could choose his pleasures wisely and not as a slave who was expected to do whatever was asked of him. Thankfully, so far Sarin declined to share him with any of his courtiers. Those whom Tarn had once considered friends often chose not to notice him. Others glared at him accusingly, but even worse were the few who threw sad pitying glances in his direction when he passed.

Tarn did his best to ignore all those around him. His former life was over; his existence now revolved around Sarin and his visits to his master's pleasure vault.

Sarin appeared to be in no great hurry to vanquish Tarn. He worked on him slowly, breaking him like a horse to a saddle, not forcing him to accept the ultimate humiliation until the time was right. Sarin seemed convinced that eventually Tarn would submit all too willingly, but Tarn could not allow himself to think that was even remotely possible.

However, he looked upon his times in Sarin's vault with mixed emotions. Female slaves were often brought to pleasure him in front of Sarin. Sometimes Tarn was allowed his release, but often he was not. If he didn't perform to Sarin's satisfaction, he was punished. Sarin enjoyed inflicting pain, but he was subtle with his chastisements, and Tarn found himself experiencing the familiar spiked pleasure he'd first discovered during the beating he'd been given on the journey to Percheron.

Tarn knew that Sarin was slowly winning the battle with his senses. Layers of reluctance were slowly being peeled away, but Tarn's true needs and feelings were hidden deep inside him. It was a place that so far Sarin had failed to touch, but once he had come frighteningly close.

A few days ago, Sarin had ordered Tarn to fall to his knees and pleasure his master with his hands and mouth. Tarn had refused. Surprisingly, Sarin had not threatened to hurt Cador; instead he punished Tarn with a tender caressing reverence that left him aroused and wanting. Sarin then stroked and teased Tarn's helpless flesh, until Tarn could not find the strength to resist his lustful desires, reaching the point where he'd closed his eyes and welcomed the feel of Sarin's mouth and hands on his body. When his climax came, in a sudden rush of illicit pleasure, Tarn was filled with confused self-loathing.

Sarin now knew how much Tarn feared the dark desires that tainted his soul. With that knowledge came an awesome power. When Tarn faced the ultimate challenge, he had to accept the terrifying possibility that he would lose and be forced to surrender to Sarin.

As Tarn entered Sarin's private chambers, he smelt the familiar perfume that always made him think of Rianna. A number of the concubines used the same jasmine-based scent. He sniffed and smiled, reminded painfully of his lost love. What he did not expect was to find her standing in Sarin's bedchamber.

For a moment, joy overwhelmed all other emotions. She was even more beautiful than he remembered, and his heart almost exploded with love.

'Tarn?' The colour drained from her perfect face. He feared she might faint but he dared not touch her, it would be just too much to bear. 'I never . . .' she faltered as she saw the gold collar around his neck, and his slave's clothing.

'No!' he grated in anguish, stepping back as she moved to touch him. 'Lady Rianna, you're looking pale, perhaps you should sit for a moment,' he said, trying to hide the painful depth of his feelings.

'What are you doing here, Tarn?' She stared at him with hurt confusion.

'My punishment was slavery,' Tarn replied, fighting the need to pull her into his arms. 'I serve Lord Sarin.'

'Why? How? I don't understand,' she stuttered.

'Rianna.' Sarin strode into the room, just having returned from hunting. He halted and looked from one to the other, staring mercilessly at Tarn before turning to smile pleasantly at Rianna. 'My dear, you are early.'

'You didn't tell me,' she accused Sarin, casting a lovingly compassionate glance at Tarn.

'I presume you refer to my new slave,' Sarin said icily, turning his penetrating gaze on Tarn. Tarn's blood ran cold, fearing that Sarin might suspect their involvement, as he silently willed Rianna to hide her true feelings. 'Well, Tarn?'

'Master,' Tarn mumbled, sinking reluctantly to his knees.

Now that Tarn's mortification was complete, Sarin turned back to Rianna. 'My dear, you begged me to spare Tarn, so I did.' He smiled and took hold of her hand. 'I always had a deep fondness for him, so I've made him my personal pleasure slave.'

'Pleasure slave?' Rianna repeated in disbelief. It was obvious from her expression that she knew exactly what Sarin meant. With a superb strength of purpose she pulled herself swiftly together. 'Of course, I thank you, husband. It is far better than being executed or sent to the mines.'

'Indeed so, Rianna.' Sarin looked down at Tarn still on his knees, now staring mutely at the ground. 'Wait here, Tarn, until I return. Now, my dear, let us go into the other room; there are some matters we need to discuss,' he said, leading Rianna from his bedchamber.

Filled with frustration, Rianna sought the privacy of her chambers. Ever since she had discovered Tarn's terrible plight she had been seeking an opportunity to speak to him. She could not understand how Sarin had so easily broken her handsome warrior's spirit. The Tarn she knew would never have willingly accepted the life of a pleasure slave. The sight of Tarn sinking to his knees and acknowledging Sarin as his master haunted her dreams at night.

It had not been easy to find the opportunity to speak to Tarn without the chance of being overheard. So far she had managed to do so only twice. Overcome by emotion, she begged Tarn to tell her why he had so easily capitulated to Sarin. Tarn declined to tell her, treating Rianna with polite reverence, behaving just as a slave should towards his master's wife. Yet Rianna saw the tortured anguish in his blue eyes and she knew he was hiding the truth.

After her beating, then her discovery of Tarn's fate, Rianna's opinion of Sarin had drastically changed. He had no kindness in his heart; he was cruel, selfish and merciless. She had allowed herself to be deceived by his lies and seduced by his licentious excesses. Never again would she trust her husband, never again would she go willingly to his bed.

The morning after her beating, Rianna received a message from Sarin. It had been decided that she would be allowed a little more freedom. Adequately escorted, she could visit the city, or ride her mare, Freya, in the surrounding countryside. She welcomed the extension of her boundaries, but she knew they were a bribe. An attempt by Sarin to atone for her humiliation in front of Niska.

Sarin had not sent for her since and she was relieved, yet her body ached with longing and she was haunted by visions of Tarn and Sarin together. She knew what Sarin expected of his male pleasure slaves. She could hardly bear to imagine Tarn being forced to pleasure Sarin. Visions filled her head of her beautiful, blond warrior and her swarthy, sensual husband naked together, enmeshed in a dark world of sensual delight.

'What's wrong?' Jenna asked as Rianna entered her chamber. 'You appear distressed.'

'Tarn still will not speak to me,' Rianna replied, sighing in frustration.

'Take care. It's not wise for you to be seen together,' Jenna warned, leading her mistress into her bedchamber. 'Mircon has found out what you need to know.'

'Tell me,' Rianna said agitatedly.

'There's much I have to tell you.' Jenna appeared tense

and uneasy as she glanced around the bedchamber. 'I've dismissed the slaves. Told them you wish to rest for a while, undisturbed.'

'Why so secretive, Jenna?' Rianna asked.

Jenna was her one true friend here. Yasmin knew about Rianna's lost virginity, but she thought it had happened before she left the Castle of Nort. She had no knowledge of Rianna's involvement with Tarn.

'It's complicated.' Jenna sat on the bed beside Rianna and wrung her hands. 'Very complicated. Mircon and I are to be married.'

Rianna smiled with delight. 'But that is good news. You should be happy. Do not be troubled about money, Sarin is generous with me. I'll give you two hundred gold pistoles as a wedding gift. You'll be able to purchase a fine house and have your own maidservant as well.'

'Your generosity is much appreciated.' Jenna looked with affection at her mistress. 'I know you will not be so happy when I tell you that Mircon and I wish to settle in Harn.'

Rianna paled. 'Harn! But I thought that Mircon was content with his new position serving Chancellor Lesand.'

'Harn will be safer.' Jenna's voice shook with feeling. 'If only I could take you with us, my lady. I am concerned for your safety. I know there are some who plot against you, just as they plotted against Prince Tarn in the past.'

'I do not understand,' Rianna said in confusion.

'Soon after we arrived here a nobleman of the court sought me out. On a number of occasions he has questioned me, then forced me to pleasure him. Now his attentions are becoming more frequent and more demanding. He frightens me. I dare not tell Mircon about the sexual favours I'm forced to provide but I've told him about the constant questions. I'm certain the nobleman suspects an involvement between you and Prince Tarn.'

'I cannot believe this.' Rianna tried to hide her rising concern. 'Why is he doing this? Why would he ever suspect such a thing?'

'I am not certain,' Jenna replied. 'But he appears to hate Prince Tarn. Mircon made some enquiries and discovered that someone had been questioning the guards who accompanied us from Harn. Both the sergeant in command of the prisoner's guards, and Rorg appear to have become quite wealthy of late. They've been spending large quantities of silver in the local brothels and taverns.'

'They cannot reveal what they do not know,' Rianna said with shaky confidence. 'Apart from you and Mircon, only Lesand knows the whole truth. I'm certain he'll not betray me. Whatever anyone else says, Jenna, nothing can be proven.'

'But the seeds of suspicion can take root. You must take care not to nourish them in any way,' Jenna replied anxiously. 'The palace is a hotbed of intrigue. Mircon tells me that when Tarn was leading the rebellion against Sarin, rumours abounded that someone who knew his plans was revealing them to Lord Sarin. By knowing Tarn's strategy in advance, Sarin was able to gain the upper hand and crush the rebellion. Perhaps this same traitor now pursues you, my lady.'

'Do not distress yourself, Jenna. I will speak to the chancellor. He has the power to ensure I am safe. You marry Mircon and be happy.'

'There is something else,' Jenna said unhappily. 'It's said that Lord Sarin told Tarn that he holds a kinsman of his prisoner. He threatened to harm the man if Tarn did not agree to become his slave. Nevertheless, Mircon cannot as yet locate the whereabouts of this prisoner, as none of the gaolers will talk.'

'I married a monster!' Rianna said with anguish, relieved in a strange way to know that Tarn had not surrendered willingly.

# Chapter Nine

With Rianna's blessing, Jenna and Mircon decided to depart for Harn almost immediately. Rianna tried, with little success, to discovery the identity of the nobleman who'd persecuted her maidservant. Eventually she was sure she would find out who he was, as Jenna had provided her with a very accurate description of the man. At present Chancellor Lesand was away from court, negotiating a treaty with a neighbouring land. When he returned, Rianna intended to seek out his help. Even if the nobleman tried to move against her in some way, she knew the Chancellor would do everything in his power to protect her.

The evening after Jenna and Mircon set out for Harn, Rianna was required to attend a reception to honour a number of foreign noblemen whose lands had forged strong trading connections with Percheron. The great hall of the palace was specially decorated for the occasion with garlands of sweet-smelling flowers and brightly coloured silk banners. Rich carpets covered the marble floor, and the divans scattered around the central area, which was left free for the entertainment, were already overflowing with guests.

Everyone was bejewelled and richly dressed in brocades, silks, satins and velvets. Rianna stood out among all the women because of the simplicity of her garments: a bodice and skirt of white silk, edged with silver.

Sarin, dressed in cloth-of-gold, escorted her regally across the great hall to their seats on a raised dais at one end of the chamber. Rianna sat beside him on the velvet-covered divan, while Niska, as befitting her position, was obliged to perch on a low stool at Rianna's side. All of Sarin's other concubines were present, the majority to provide comfort and sexual favours to the guests, most of whom were male. His favourites sat apart in a special section of the chamber.

Rianna cast a sideways glance at Sarin. She had never noticed before the hard set of his mouth, the coldness in his dark eyes. She found it difficult to look at him now without revealing her hatred and resentment, yet despite everything she still desired him. Rianna could only presume he had somehow cast a spell over her senses.

It was then that she saw Tarn making his way through the crowds of guests towards Sarin. Tarn looked magnificent, every inch a Prince of Kabra. He was bare-chested, and his golden skin glistened in the soft light, bringing extra emphasis to his muscular physique. His hair was freshly washed and gleaming, lying like a glowing halo around his head and down over his shoulders. Tarn wore full, white silk trousers tucked into cream suede boots, and a wide, gold-linked belt around his waist. Only the narrow metal collar around his neck and the ornate wrist manacles betrayed his position as a slave.

One of the guests, a nobleman from a distant land, turned to smile warmly at Tarn, perhaps not aware of how far he had fallen since they last met. Tarn ignored the greeting and continued onwards until he reached the dais. Stopping, he stared up at Sarin for a long heart-stopping moment, then fell to his knees and uttered one auspicious word, 'Master.'

'Come, slave. You may stand at my side and serve me,' Sarin said with a self-satisfied smile.

As Tarn moved closer, Rianna was filled with a sudden rush of desire. Even in his distress he was achingly beautiful. 'Handsome, is he not?' Niska leant forward and whispered in Rianna's ear. 'I intend to have him for myself once Lord Sarin tires of him.'

Rianna ignored Niska's words; her only interest was Tarn. She saw the determined set of her beloved's mouth, the raw pain in his blue eyes. She could see his agony even if others could not. For the briefest of seconds their eyes made contact. A spark of joy lit up his face before he managed to hide his feelings and compose himself again. Trembling with the intensity of her emotions, Rianna tried to ignore the sudden fire in her pudenda as her body cried out for him.

Tarn stood behind Sarin, so close she could almost reach out and touch his smooth, golden flesh. Rianna closed her eyes, remembering the feel of his hands caressing her, the bliss of his naked body pressed against hers, and the wondrous fulfilment when he'd made love to her. Whatever Sarin did to them both, he could never take their memories away.

Time seemed to pass quickly as the slaves moved among the guests, serving food and drink. Rianna tried to make it appear she was watching the slave girls dancing, the jugglers and the acrobats, but in reality all her thoughts were directed towards Tarn. Sarin made him sit on the floor by his side. Now and then, Rianna saw Sarin reach out and touch his pleasure slave almost with affection. There was an atmosphere, a tension between the two men, that made her shiver with apprehension. They were opposing ends of the same spectrum, one dark, one light.

Rianna felt a sharp stab of jealousy every time Sarin patted Tarn's shoulder or played absent-mindedly with his blond hair. It was clear that Sarin desired Tarn, but she could not even begin to imagine how Tarn felt about his supposed master. To Rianna's disappointment, when Sarin left the dais to talk to his many guests, he insisted Tarn accompany him. She'd hoped she would have the opportunity to discreetly try and speak to Tarn again.

'So I'm not the only one who lusts after Lord Sarin's

new pleasure slave,' Niska commented thoughtfully, as Rianna closely watched the two men make their way across the great hall.

'You're imagining things, Niska,' Rianna snapped. 'Not all my thoughts revolve around lust, like yours.'

'You lie badly,' Niska mocked. 'He's quite the handsomest man I've ever seen, and he's mightily well-endowed. I can vouch that for myself,' she said with a husky laugh. 'But I wager you know that already, dear, sweet, innocent Rianna.'

'You're mad,' Rianna said uneasily.

'I hear you spent an inordinate amount of time on the journey from Harn tending Tarn's wounds. I see pain and something else in your eyes when you look at him.'

'Why not,' Rianna replied boldly. 'He's a distant kinsman, and of royal blood. He does not deserve such an ignoble fate.'

'Perhaps he does not, but Tarn is his own worst enemy. He should not believe all Sarin tells him. One day Tarn will discover the true extent of the treachery surrounding him. By then of course it will be too late. Sarin will have worked his sensual magic and subdued Tarn completely.'

'You speak in riddles,' Rianna said curtly. 'And you're wrong if you think Tarn will ever willingly accept his slavery.'

'Mark my words, he will, because Sarin has the ability to see our darkest desires and use them against us. Deep in his heart, Tarn wants Sarin, I'm certain of that.'

'You're wrong, so very wrong,' Rianna insisted.

'Careful, Rianna, you reveal too much of your inner feelings.' Niska narrowed her eyes and stared at her rival. 'You care deeply for Tarn, do you not? Such emotions are dangerous for a wife of Lord Sarin.'

'I care nothing for Tarn,' Rianna lied, hot colour staining her pale cheeks. 'If Lord Sarin returns, tell him I've retired as I feel unwell.'

Rising to her feet, Rianna stepped from the dais and made her way to the side of the great hall. Niska's words made her fearful and agitated. She was surrounded by those who wished her nothing but harm. The only people she felt she could remotely trust were Yasmin and Lesand.

She stepped into a chamber leading off the great hall. Lit only by a few lamps, the edges of the room were in darkness. Later the room would be put to good use, by those seeking privacy for their casual sexual encounters. Thankfully, at present it was empty. Rianna leant her head against a cool, marble pillar and closed her eyes, trying to quell the agitated beating of her heart.

'Lady Rianna.' The deep male voice was unknown to her. 'Are you unwell?' the tall, good-looking man asked as he stepped from the shadows.

'I'm just a little over-heated,' she said breathlessly, thinking there was something familiar about his features, although she could not recall meeting him before. 'I am afraid I do not know you, sir.'

'As yet, you do not.' Any sign of his previous concern vanished as his tone hardened. 'But I know you all too well. Have you retired because you cannot bear to watch Tarn meekly serving Lord Sarin? How can one so great have fallen so far?' he continued, mockingly.

'I must leave.' She went to move away, but he grabbed hold of her. Rianna caught sight of the thick gold bracelet set with precious stones on his right wrist. 'You forget your manners,' she said haughtily, knowing without a doubt this was Jenna's persecutor.

'Why did you allow Jenna to leave?' he growled. 'I intended to have her for myself. She would have made a good pleasure slave. She has spirit and she enjoys sex with a lusty abandonment. Perhaps you feared that she knew too much and some day might betray you?'

'Jenna left to return to her family. It had been arranged long before we first left Harn,' Rianna replied, knowing she had to discover this man's identity. Perhaps that would give her some clue as to his motives and his hatred of Tarn.

'You're trying to deceive me, Rianna.' Smiling mercilessly, he ran his fingers through her hair and stroked the exposed curves of her breasts.

'When Lord Sarin learns of your behaviour, you'll find yourself in the dungeons,' she threatened, beginning to feel fearful.

'Dungeons?' He gave a harsh laugh. 'Don't be sure of that, beautiful one. You'll tell Sarin nothing of this encounter.' Snapping the laces of her bodice, he jerked the fabric apart to expose her breasts. 'Such sweet teats,' he said hungrily, as he squeezed her rosy nipples.

Despite her anguish and fear, Rianna felt a sudden rush of lust spear her belly. Sarin had conditioned her body to crave carnal pleasure. Denied his attention for some time, her traitorous flesh ached for fulfilment. 'Leave me be,' she flared. 'How dare you treat me like this, I'm Lord Sarin's wife.'

'In flesh perhaps, but not in spirit. You gave your heart to Tarn when you tended his wounds. I would venture to guess that you gave even more than just your affection.' He squeezed her nipples hard, making her wince with pain. 'Soon I intend to find out the entire truth.'

'You're mad,' she said, terrified by the lust in his dark eyes.

'I'm frighteningly sane.' He pulled up her skirts and touched her sex. 'It's a shame you're denuded,' he commented as he caressed her naked mound of Venus. 'I'd hoped you might have retained your fleece like Jenna. Sadly, Sarin prefers his maidens hairless. However, I'll enjoy you just the same.' He parted her labial lips, his fingers feeling the sudden rush of moisture as he stroked the entrance to her vagina. 'Sarin has taught you well. Your flesh readies itself for me.'

Rianna wrenched herself away from him, and tried to run, but he grabbed hold of her, digging his fingers cruelly into her arms. 'You're wrong about everything,' she gasped. 'I love my husband. He'll not forgive you for this.'

'Tell Sarin anything and you'll regret it,' he threatened.

'I can bring witnesses who will testify that you spent many hours alone with Tarn. Once his suspicions have been aroused, Sarin will do anything to find the truth. He is merciless and cold-blooded, and will not balk at torture to aid his investigation. How long do you think it will take him to discover the true extent of your involvement with Tarn?'

'I keep telling you that you are mistaken,' she insisted, as he began to pull her towards a divan in the shadowy depths of the room.

'So there you are.' For once Rianna was pleased to hear Niska's voice. Her captor swung round, still holding on to her tightly. 'Don't you think this a little foolish?' Niska sounded angry. 'Are you really prepared to risk everything for a quick coupling with *her*?'

'I just wanted to punish the whore,' Rianna's tormentor replied.

'Because Tarn cares for her. And all that was his must be yours? Is that not right, Cador?'

'Yes,' he hissed. 'Everything.'

'So you risk alienating Sarin.' Niska looked derisively at Rianna. 'Believe me, Cador, she's not worth it. Lord Sarin is still enamoured of her. It won't last, it never does. You can find your pleasure elsewhere until Sarin tires of Rianna.'

'Just like he tired of you,' the nobleman sneered.

'None of this is important.' Niska stepped over to Rianna. 'I should introduce you to my good friend, Cador, nobleman of Kabra. This is Tarn's kinsman, and he is an even greater enemy to Tarn than Lord Sarin. Cador wants Tarn dead, while Sarin only wishes to slake his lust upon him. Sarin's desires for Tarn are a weakness he'll eventually regret.'

'Are you the man Lord Sarin threatened to harm if Tarn did not submit?' Rianna asked in horror.

'Incongruous, is it not?' Niska said gleefully. 'Tarn sacrificed himself in order save Cador, believing him Sarin's prisoner. Cador might have been in the dungeon for a brief moment to help Sarin fool Tarn, but he was not a prisoner; on the contrary, he is Tarn's betrayer. If it wasn't for Cador, the rebellion might well have succeeded and Kabra would be free.'

'Why?' Rianna looked at Cador in disbelief. 'If you are his kinsman, why betray him?'

'Because Tarn's father, the puppet king, is dying. Now that Tarn is enslaved, Sarin intends to make Cador heir to the throne. Soon he'll rule as king, with me by his side.'

Rianna looked from one to the other, hardly able to believe how cruelly Tarn had been betrayed.

'Before you retire, I have something to show you,' Niska said, having insisted on accompanying Rianna back to her chambers. Rianna had no wish for Niska's company, but it had at least protected her from Cador's unwanted attentions. Now she knew the truth, and as soon as the opportunity arose, Rianna planned to tell Tarn about Cador's treachery. Sarin would no longer be able to blackmail Tarn with threats against his kinsman.

'I've no wish to see it,' Rianna replied coldly.

'But this involves Tarn. You wish to see him, do you not?' Niska added with a smile. 'There's no point in denying your feelings any longer. Both Cador and I know you care deeply for him. Why else would you have fallen to your knees and begged Lord Sarin to show him mercy? Cador knows your mother is no distant kinswoman of Tarn's. Fortunately for you, Rianna, Cador has decided not to tell Sarin that you lied in an effort to gain clemency for the former Prince of Kabra.'

'I did so because I pity him,' Rianna countered.

'Your pathetic attempts to conceal the truth do not convince me,' Niska sneered. 'It is this way,' she added, taking hold of Rianna's arm.

They moved through a number of unoccupied, dusty rooms, into a narrow passageway, and through a metal-banded door which Niska opened with a brass key. The chamber they entered was tiny, only a few paces square, and there were wide, wooden steps leading up to a narrow slit set high in the far wall.

'You must keep silent,' Niska warned. 'It will be the worse for us if we are discovered.'

She led Rianna up the steps. Breasts pressed against the smooth wall, they peered through the slit. Rianna found herself looking down on to a spacious chamber which contained nothing but a wide bed. Tarn was lying face down on the black satin coverlet, naked and chained hand and foot, his arms and legs spread wide apart.

Niska drew in her breath sharply, her eyes fixed on Tarn's naked body. 'I want him,' she whispered very softly, as she turned to smile challengingly at Rianna. 'And one day soon, with Cador's help, Tarn will be *my* slave.'

Rianna ignored Niska's pointless threat, all her attention directed towards her beloved. Desire flooded her veins. She longed to feel Tarn's thick stem thrusting inside her again. Despite Sarin's seductive charms, she had never felt such bliss in his embrace. Her sex grew hot and moist with yearning.

She stiffened nervously as she saw Sarin, wearing only a loose velvet robe, enter the room. In his hand he carried a short, leather-covered switch. 'Tarn, you displeased me this evening,' Sarin said with soft menace.

'So now you've come to beat me into submission, and take pleasure from my pain,' Tarn mocked, his words muffled by the coverlet.

'You know you like the punishments,' Sarin said teasingly, as he stood by the bed looking down at his naked slave. 'You have to learn that it is most unwise to even consider disobeying my orders.'

'You asked too much of me. I could not debase myself completely in front of a former friend and ally.' Tarn was angry and resentful as he turned his head to stare at Sarin.

'Still so much pride, Tarn?' Sarin chastised, as he ran the tip of the switch slowly down Tarn's back and over his taut buttocks. 'I also noticed the look you gave Lady

Rianna this evening. It appears you have a fondness for my wife.'

'I'm grateful to her, that is all. The noble lady was once kind enough to tend my wounds. She's beautiful and tender-hearted, far too good for you, Sarin,' Tarn grated, taking a hissing breath as Sarin placed a stinging blow across his left buttock.

'Will you never learn?' With great care Sarin laid a number of blows across Tarn's back and buttocks. 'You will continue to be chastised until you accept that your only function in life is to serve, obey and respect your master.'

'It seems I am unable to grasp that lesson,' Tarn jibed.

'It's a pity, because I'll have to continue marring your beautiful flesh,' Sarin said softly as he traced the red line of the last lash mark with his fingertip. 'You're quite the handsomest slave I've ever owned. I hate to damage you so badly that you lose your worth.'

'If I were not well-favoured, would you still lust after me?' Tarn questioned contemptuously. 'I think not. Would that I were as ugly as sin.'

'But you are not ugly.' Sarin brushed Tarn's long, blond hair to one side and gently kissed the nape of his neck. 'Let me give you a choice, the lash or my lips?'

Tarn tensed. 'The lash causes me less pain,' he groaned.

'Remember the last time I beat you, slave,' Sarin said as he stroked Tarn's back, running his fingers teasingly down the curve of his spine. 'Eventually, your abused flesh welcomed my caressing touch and you found pleasure in the feel of my hands and lips.'

'No,' Tarn said in a voice wracked with anguish. 'I just could not find the strength to resist any longer. My unwilling release was no pleasure, Sarin.'

'Deceive yourself if you must,' Sarin said, as he removed his velvet robe. 'But you'll soon be forced to accept the depth of your need for me.'

Sarin's penis was already erect, standing stiffly out from his body. The head and shaft glistened as though the organ had recently been oiled. Rianna shivered, knowing what Sarin intended to do in order to further subjugate Tarn.

She stared at the two men who had possessed her. One she loved, one she hated, yet in a perverse way she desired Sarin almost as much as Tarn. How this could be she didn't know. She failed to understand the complex nature of her own emotions. She wanted to tear her eyes away from Tarn and Sarin, run from this place and pretend that none of this was happening, but conversely she had to stay and watch.

As Sarin climbed on to the bed, Tarn began to pull at his chains, struggling uselessly to get away. 'No,' he grated.

'Why resist the inevitable?' Sarin appeared excited by Tarn's struggles. He brushed the underside of Tarn's arm, where the muscles stood stiffly out as he strained to escape.

'I'll never submit,' Tarn said, cursing under his breath.

'Your resistance only serves to increase my arousal,' Sarin replied, lust lighting his dark eyes as he watched Tarn try to pull away from him.

'If you take me now, by force, you lose, Sarin,' Tarn gasped breathlessly. 'You vowed that when the time came I would be all too willing to surrender.'

'Perhaps I'm just tired of waiting,' Sarin retorted. 'If you continue to fight, Tarn, it will only cause you pain.'

Sarin knelt between Tarn's thighs. His muscular arms strained with the pressure as he held down Tarn's hips. Employing his full body weight, he pinned down his captive and parted the globes of Tarn's buttocks.

'Damn you,' he spat, as Sarin rubbed the pads of his thumbs over Tarn's exposed nether mouth.

'Have you so swiftly forgotten your imprisoned kinsman?' Sarin asked with cruel menace.

Tarn ceased his struggles and collapsed limply on the bed. 'No,' he said in a strained voice. 'I've not forgotten, but I fear I cannot do this, even for him.'

'You fear the consequences, because deep inside you

desire me. That one thought terrifies you, Tarn. Accept your need for me, accept your slavery and you will find freedom in the very act of submission,' Sarin said in a low hypnotic voice.

Tarn shivered, but made no more efforts to resist as Sarin pressed the head of his cock against Tarn's exposed nether mouth. Gently, Sarin parted the puckered ring with his hard, oiled shaft. As Sarin's organ slid inside the virginal opening, Tarn gave a deep groan of anguish.

'You're so tight, so delicious,' Sarin purred as he thrust into his helpless captive. Tarn made a faint sound and pressed his pelvis down against the satin coverlet, but there was no escape from the invasion of his most intimate flesh and the ruthless onslaught on his senses.

Rianna held a hand to her mouth, biting her knuckles as Sarin plundered Tarn's defenceless body. He grasped hold of Tarn's hips and thrust harder, employing a smooth seductive rhythm that caused the glowing fire in Rianna's sex to burst into life. Tarn lay limply on the bed, his face buried in the satin coverlet, now and then giving a soft moan, whether from pain or pleasure Rianna didn't know. She hated herself for continuing to watch, knowing she was unable to help him. She still found the sight of the two men powerfully arousing and a warm damp heat invaded her pudenda.

Then something changed, Rianna didn't quite know what. Sarin's movements became slower, more seductive, and she saw Tarn lift his buttocks to meet the next thrusts. 'You see, Tarn.' Sarin leant forward, pressing gentle kisses on the muscular planes of Tarn's back as he meshed his fingers in his slave's long blond hair. 'I knew you would be willing in the end.'

'I'm not willing,' Tarn grunted harshly. 'I've no desire for this.'

'You still continue to deceive yourself.' Sarin, smiling confidently, reached up to free his captive's wrists from their chains. Withdrawing from Tarn, he bent to remove the chains from his ankles. 'Now you may fight me unhindered. Will this be a battle of strength or self-will?'

He employed the head of his cock to the rim of Tarn's nether mouth with exquisite tenderness before he slid his shaft into the tight male sheath. Despite the fact that he was no longer chained and helpless, Tarn made no attempt to resist. He lay silent, his face still pressed to the satin coverlet as Sarin thrust into him again. This time Sarin's movements were tenderly erotic. It appeared he was doing all he could to arouse Tarn as he varied the pace and depths of his thrusts, sometimes pausing to lovingly rim the pulsing mouth before sliding deep inside again.

Sarin buried his cock deep inside Tarn, until his pelvis was pressed close to his slave's buttocks. Gently he rolled over on to his side, pulling Tarn with him. Cradling the slack body against his, Sarin mouthed the nape of Tarn's neck while stroking his copper-coloured nipples, pulling teasingly at the teats until they hardened into firm cones.

'Please,' Tarn moaned, agonised confusion apparent in that one brief word.

'Tell me you want me,' Sarin pressed, his hands sliding lower to stroke Tarn's trembling stomach.

Tarn pressed back against the hard, male flesh that pierced him so completely as Sarin's hand brushed tantalisingly against his penis. It was already engorged and achingly hard. Curving his hand around the solid shaft, Sarin began to milk it with slow precision. As he increased the pace, he began to move his hips, thrusting into Tarn in an accompanying rhythm.

'Tell me,' he urged in Tarn's ear. 'Or would you prefer me to desist right now?'

Rianna felt a sharp spear of jealousy pierce her heart as she heard Tarn reluctantly whisper, 'No, don't. I want you. By the gods I do and the wanting mortifies me,' he continued in a guilt-filled voice.

Sarin laughed triumphantly and began to thrust harder and faster, while continuing to stroke and caress Tarn's engorged penis, moving his hand briskly up and down the stem, and collaring the bulb as it throbbed against his palm. Tarn's suppressed passion was unleashed. He pressed his sweat slicked flesh against Sarin, his body welcoming the plundering of his senses.

With a loud grunt of pleasure, Sarin's orgasm came. He spilt his seed inside Tarn as he too gained his release. The creamy liquid spurted from the head of Tarn's cock, coating his belly and Sarin's hand.

'Don't you find that arousing?' Niska whispered in Rianna's ear. 'I look forward to joining Tarn and Lord Sarin in bed. I've no doubt that my lord will soon afford me that privilege. Never you, Rianna, only Sarin's seed can be allowed to take root in your belly.'

'I loathe and despise you,' Rianna flared in a low voice, her eyes never leaving the two figures still melded together on the bed, her agony, her unrequited desire and her love for Tarn combined into a fierce emotion that almost rent her asunder.

'Would you like me to ask Lord Sarin to allow you to watch Tarn pleasuring me?' Niska smiled, her eyes cold and cruel.

'Damn you, Niska.' Rianna turned to glare at her tormentor. Her pain magnified as she looked back into the room to see Sarin tenderly caressing Tarn. He was unresponsive as he struggled to regain control of his shattered emotions. Rianna was certain that she could see tears on Tarn's cheeks.

'Now you have your victory,' Tarn said tremulously. 'Will you not gloat over one you vanquished, and tell me how wrong I've been?'

'Do you wish me to?' Sarin eased himself away from Tarn and moved over the prone body of his humbled opponent so that they lay facing each other. Lifting his hands he cupped Tarn's face and stared deep into his pain-filled blue eyes. 'I've always desired you, Tarn. Your betrayal hurt me more than you'll ever know,' he continued, a faint catch in his voice.

Bending forwards, he claimed Tarn's mouth with a fierce possessive passion. Tarn responded, returning the kiss with an unfettered need that left Rianna breathless with jealousy. It felt as if she had been betrayed, yet she knew that she had betrayed Tarn in a far more terrible way. Tarn had endured unimaginable misery to reach this point, while she had succumbed so willingly to Sarin's demanding onslaughts on her flesh.

Sarin was evil. He'd woven a dark erotic spell around them both, and she feared that neither she nor Tarn would ever escape its consequences.

All was well in the castle of Nort. Gerek, the Protector of Harn, laughed aloud as Elise, his new mistress, pushed him down on to the bed. Tossing back her midnight-black ringlets Elise leapt astride his naked body and sheathed herself on his sex.

Gerek stifled a loud moan of pleasure as she ground her pelvis against his. Elise made love with a wild abandon that reminded him of Kitara. Physically they were very different. In contrast to Kitara's tall, auburn beauty, Elise was tiny with narrow boyish hips and small sharp-pointed breasts. However, she had the same proud fire in her eyes, the same energy and sheer exuberance for life.

The first time Gerek had laid eyes on Elise she'd been dressed as a boy, living among a group of travelling mummers as they moved from town to town performing their plays. Elise never stayed in one place long, but Gerek had persuaded her to remain at the castle.

'You have that far-away look in your eyes again, my lord,' Elise said. She treated Gerek with far less respect than his other bed-mates, but he enjoyed her company all the same, and found her irreverent manner refreshing.

'How could I ignore such a lusty wench?' Gerek grinned as she began to bounce vigorously up and down on his throbbing cock.

'If I please you, Protector, will you reward me?' She began to milk his engorged shaft with her internal muscles. Elise had the most unique control over her vagina; she was capable of bringing Gerek to orgasm without outwardly moving a muscle.

'How about the silver necklace that pleased you so much?' Gerek suggested. It was but a small trinket in his estimation.

'The necklace will do very well.' She smiled provocatively, then bit her lip with concentration as she began to caress his stem with just the walls of her feminine sheath.

'That feels so good,' Gerek grated. 'Hot and very tight,' he gasped as her sheath clasped his cock in a strong embrace. The walls started to ripple, alternately squeezing and releasing his engorged shaft.

'I also want my pleasure,' she purred. 'Don't climax too swiftly, my sweet lord.'

She lifted her hips and ground them down against his pelvis, repeating the movement again and again, still gripping him firmly with her vagina. Flinging back her head, Elise rode Gerek with wild abandon, always continuing the subtle, inner pressure until Gerek thought he might explode with bliss.

Reaching towards her, he slid his fingers inside her slit and tugged and pulled at her pleasure nubbin. 'Yes,' she gasped, her hips moving harder and faster. Her vagina pulsed as her climax came, and at the same moment, Gerek achieved his own release.

His cock pulsed, while Elise's internal muscles contracted around the stem so strongly that it felt as if she were emptying him completely. 'I've no more seed to give,' he groaned. 'You'll wear me out, Elise,' he added as the pulsing bliss died, leaving him drained and exhausted.

She rolled off him and lay down by his side, rubbing her naked body tantalisingly against his. 'I was hoping you might consider using your tongue on my slit. You know you like to taste your own leavings on my pudenda.'

'Greedy whore,' Gerek teased, moving to bury his face in her warm, moist sex. He tensed as there was a loud knock on the door. 'What?' he growled, irritated by the unexpected intrusion.

'Two travellers await you, my lord, in the great hall,'

the soldier shouted through the barred door. 'One of them is the maidservant, Jenna.'

Gerek stiffened, concern etched on his face. 'Jenna?'

'Is something amiss?' Elise asked as she sat up.

'Tell the travellers I will be with them shortly,' Gerek replied. 'Serve them food and drink.'

'Yes, Protector.'

As the man's footsteps moved away from the door, Gerek sprang from the bed.

'Is this Jenna important?' Elise asked.

'It depends why she is here,' Gerek said anxiously, as he threw on his clothes. 'She is my daughter's maidservant.'


Tarn knelt submissively in front of his master, hating himself as the familiar, unwanted desire for Sarin came flooding back. He longed to set it aside, forget it existed, but in these sensual erotic surroundings it would not disappear.

Tarn felt as if he had fallen into a bottomless pit, and somewhere in the dark depths was a place he never wanted to reach. A place where pleasure, pain and submission combined into an all-encompassing torrent that would consume him completely. He would become Sarin's slave always and forever, and the knowledge that he was steadily growing closer to that destination filled him with fear.

He had shared Sarin's bed for the last five nights, and he dared not allow himself to think of the many dark pleasures they had shared. The brief moment of tenderness Sarin had shown Tarn that first night had never been repeated, and he had almost come to doubt it had ever existed anywhere but inside his tortured mind.

'Why so sad?' Sarin smiled and beckoned to Tarn. He went to rise to his feet. 'No, on your hands and knees,' Sarin ordered.

Tarn had learnt his lesson well. He emptied his mind of thoughts as he crawled over to Sarin and crouched at his feet. He felt Sarin stroke his hair. Then a gentle hand tipped up his chin and stared into his sky-blue eyes. They were dull and expressionless, devoid of feeling.

'What is your desire, master?' Tarn asked. There was little that would shock him now. Sarin's training was thorough. Why even try to resist? Tarn asked himself, when he had already committed the ultimate act of submission many times over.

'I miss your defiance, Tarn,' Sarin mused, then he smiled. 'But I've known you a long time. I'm certain there is still a small spark of resistance somewhere deep inside. If fanned it could well flare into life.'

'I see no point in resistance,' Tarn murmured. 'I've already betrayed everything I ever believed in.'

'Have you?' Sarin eyed him thoughtfully. 'We shall see tonight, when we attend a small gathering for some of my closest friends.'

Tarn said nothing. He had discovered that despair had a numbing effect on the mind. It helped to erase self-will, pride and feeling. Tarn still experienced carnal desire in a cold, rather detached way. The brief surge of satisfaction he gained from his release was nothing compared to the flame of love he'd once known. That had burnt like a bright beacon in the darkness of life. Now he had nothing, no future, no past, just the cruel eternity of the present, where Sarin ruled sublime.

'You've attended some of my more intimate gatherings in the past,' Sarin continued. 'Most of my slaves are well used to performing and pandering to the pleasures of my friends, but you are not.' He beckoned to the ever-present Nubians. 'Have this slave taken to the bath house to be prepared for this evening's entertainment. Naked and in chains he'll play a central part in tonight's erotic tableaux.'

'Haven't you done enough to me?' Tarn asked harshly, as fear pierced his apathetic numbness. 'You must hate me greatly to force me so low,' he added as he was hauled to his feet by the Nubian slaves.

Sarin gave a soft laugh. 'I knew you weren't yet totally subdued. The fire still burns within you, Tarn. Tonight

193

I'll extinguish it forever. Many you know will be there. My wife, Chancellor Lesand, old friends from the past, and of course your kinsman, Cador!'

By the time evening came Tarn felt tense and apprehensive. He had thought himself beyond emotion but unfortunately that was not the case. Now he feared his last spark of resistance would be erased. He had spent many hours in the bath house being steamed, scrubbed, and massaged with oil and exotic perfume. His skin glowed with health and his hair, which was steadily growing longer, fell in silken waves down his back. Tarn's only ornament was a gold circlet around his brow, perhaps chosen to remind him of his former position in life.

Naked and chained, he was taken to the part of the palace where the banquet was being held. Most of the guest were already present. As he waited in the small ante-room he could hear them talking and laughing.

'Tarn,' Sarin said with a smile, as he strode into the chamber. 'I think I should always keep you naked and in chains. The sight titillates my senses.'

He beckoned to the two Nubians who followed him. They were the tallest and most muscular of Sarin's mute slaves. The Nubians were impressive even in their nudity, their black skin glistening like polished ebony.

'A perfect contrast,' Sarin commented, as the Nubians took hold of the chains attached to Tarn's wrists. 'Darkness and light.' He turned to the slave who'd accompanied Tarn from the bath house. 'Has he been properly prepared, his nether mouth oiled?'

'Yes, master,' the man replied.

Sarin pressed a small jar into the man's hand. 'Anoint him with this to ensure he stays fully aroused.' Without glancing back at Tarn, Sarin strode through the curtained doorway into the banqueting chamber.

'Why, Tarn,' a husky female voice purred, as a cool hand caressed his bare buttocks. 'Don't you look beautifully vulnerable tonight.' Tarn smelt her familiar musky scent as Niska moved round to face him. 'I'm looking forward to watching you take part in tonight's entertainment.' She ran possessive hands over his chest. 'And if Lord Sarin permits, I intend to use you myself later. He enjoys watching me don a phallus harness and penetrate his pleasure slaves. It will prove a stimulating end to the evening.'

Tarn gritted his teeth and said nothing in reply, trying to appear unmoved as Niska stroked his sex. She wore a pale pink bodice cut so low it revealed the tips of her rouged nipples, while her gauzy skirt was so fine he could see her veiled pudenda through the folds. Despite himself, Tarn felt his desire rise and a heavy warmth invaded his groin.

'I'll apply the ointment.' Niska took the jar from the slave. She dipped her fingers in the thick, spicy-smelling cream and began to spread it over the shaft and head of Tarn's penis. Already aroused, Tarn trembled as the fire in his loins increased. Unrelentingly, she coated the base of his shaft, his balls and even the thin skin of his perineum with the cream. A tingling warmth began to spread across his entire sex, growing into a fiery heat that made his erection increase until his cock stood stiffly out from his groin.

'It will keep you erect and ready for hours,' Niska said, her cold eyes gleaming as she stared at his engorged organ. 'I can hardly wait to feel that magnificent shaft inside me,' she whispered, before she glided gracefully from the room.

Tarn was led forward through the curtained doorway into the banqueting chamber. The room was crowded but the corners of the chamber were in darkness, and for a moment he could watch unobserved. He saw Sarin lounging on a divan with Rianna at his side, looking as beautiful as ever in emerald green silk. Chancellor Lesand sat close by, surrounded by men Tarn had known in the past.

Naked slave girls moved around the room, serving drinks or pausing to allow the guests to kiss and fondle their bodies. The entire chamber was filled with a darkly sensual atmosphere of carnal delight. Tarn could see it on the slack, indolent faces of the guests and the concubines who lounged by their sides. Only one person in the room appeared immune to the atmosphere; Rianna had a tense, troubled expression on her beautiful face which told Tarn that she knew of his fate.

A dancing girl had just finished discarding her many veils. She was replaced by a troupe of acrobats, slim and lithe naked men and women who contorted their bodies in lewd, unnatural poses which exposed their most intimate parts and aroused the guests.

The dancer, her nakedness now covered with a loose robe, moved over to Tarn. 'My name is Yasmin,' she said breathlessly. 'I have a message for you from Lady Rianna. She has been trying to reach you for days. You must do nothing for Cador's sake. He is no friend, he is your enemy.'

'Cador, my enemy?' Tarn frowned in confusion. 'You must be mistaken.'

'Believe me I am not, but it is not safe to talk here,' she said agitatedly, then rushed through the curtained doorway.

# Chapter Ten

*T*aking a tight hold on Tarn's chains, the Nubians
urged him forwards. Holding his head high he
walked to the centre of the room, all too conscious of his
very visible arousal. He heard the whispered remarks
and the lewd comments, but he had no choice but to
ignore them all. The lights were bright in the centre,
blinding him a little and making it impossible to see the
individual faces of the audience. His chains were clipped
to rings set in the marble floor, and he was forced to
stand there naked and exposed while Sarin proudly
announced that this was his new slave – the traitor, Tarn,
former Prince of Kabra.

'May I examine him more closely?' Tarn heard one
guest ask.

'By all means,' agreed Sarin as he rose to his feet and
escorted the guest forward.

Tarn recognised the tall man with pock-marked skin;
he was a lesser prince from desert land across the sea.
Tarn had always disliked him because it was said he
was unnecessarily cruel to his slaves.

'Ensure he behaves,' Sarin said to one of the naked
Nubians.

The Nubian stepped behind Tarn and took hold of the
short chain leading from his gold slave collar. He stood

so close that Tarn could perceive the heat emanating from his oiled flesh, smell his cinnamon-scented breath and feel the man's huge cock pressing against the small of his back.

'I remember you, Tarn. Once the proud prince and rebel, now this.' The guest ran an appreciative hand over Tarn's muscular chest. 'You're even more magnificent naked.' Hungrily he touched Tarn's erect penis. 'How much do you want for this slave, Sarin? He's trained, I suppose?'

'He's trained.' Sarin slid an arm around Tarn and stroked his taut buttocks. 'Most agreeably so. But he's not for sale at any price.'

'Then would you consider loaning him to me tonight?' the man pressed.

'Tarn pleases me at present. While he continues to do so I'll keep him for myself,' Sarin said firmly. 'Come, let us return to our seats.'

As Sarin and his guest resumed their places, Tarn felt the Nubian step closer. Hard male flesh pressed against his back. The Nubian's erection felt impossibly huge. Tarn hoped Sarin didn't intend to allow this man to take him, as he felt the slave's hands stroke his chest and stomach. Tarn stood there, fearing the worst as other naked slaves, both male and female, joined them. Many gentle hands began to stroke and caress Tarn's legs, arms and chest. A woman crawled forward on her hands and knees to kiss his feet. He felt naked breasts being pressed against his body, while the Nubian ran the head of his cock slowly down the crease of Tarn's buttocks. Lovingly, it rimmed the tight opening, but never ventured inside.

Tarn closed his eyes as more hands and lips began to tantalisingly stroke his naked flesh. It felt as if every portion of his skin was being teased by fingers, lips or moist tongues. His arousal increased. He gave a soft moan as a searching finger slid inside his nether mouth. Lips fastened around his penis, sucking on the head of his cock, while other lips brushed the ever-stiffening shaft. Hands and fingers cupped his balls, and stroked the paper-fine skin of his perineum. Then a wet tongue followed the same erotic path.

He no longer knew who was touching him, whether the slave was male or female, as his pleasure increased. He just relaxed and allowed the myriad of sensations to overwhelm his senses, as the bliss enfolded him in its gentle waves. Teeth nipped at his nipples, fingers ventured deeper into his anus, and a willing mouth swallowed more and more of his achingly aroused cock.

The constant, all-encompassing assault on his helpless body sent him wild with lust. There was no escape from the onslaught whichever way he turned. As he gave a soft moan of pleasure, a hot mouth covered his. A tongue speared his mouth, and the long kiss seemed to suck the essence from his being while the hands and lips continued the invasion of his defenceless flesh. A warm tongue licked his balls, another lapped at the base of his penis, while the ever-present lips rimmed the head of his cock and then swallowed most of the thick shaft, making it grow so tight he felt it might explode.

The combination of different sensations was exquisite. The fire in Tarn's loins increased, the skin of his sex hot and stretched taut. He thrust his hips forward, pressing more of his manhood into the willing mouth, while the searching fingers ventured even deeper into his anus. A swelling crescendo of sensations drew him upwards. He reached out for the summit and the sweet pleasure consumed him. Losing control, Tarn spasmed helplessly in a violent, all-encompassing climax.

His limbs still trembling from the strength of his orgasm, Tarn reluctantly opened his eyes. Other slaves lay at his feet, gaining their pleasure now by coupling in every conceivable manner and combination, while he heard the soft wet sounds of sex coming from dim corners of the chamber.

'Release him.' Sarin's voice was tense with restrained passion. 'Then come here to me, Tarn.'

One of the Nubians was thrusting mercilessly into a

groaning slave girl. Obediently he withdrew and rose to his feet, his engorged cock gleamed wetly as he walked over to Tarn. Bending he released Tarn's chains, grabbed his arm and pulled him forward. Sarin waved the slave away as Tarn fell to his knees in front of Sarin. His legs felt so weak he'd thought they would buckle under him, but he still hated abasing himself in front of all these people. He bowed his head and sweat-stained strands of his hair fell across his taut cheeks, helping to hide his shame.

'Tarn,' said Sarin in a low voice as he leant forward. 'You should feel how hard I am. I almost envied you for a moment. I'm certain my guests enjoyed the spectacle as much as I did.' His face was slack with desire as he added, 'Now 'tis your turn to pleasure me. Do I choose your lips or that tight, rosy nether mouth?'

Tarn raised his anguished eyes to Sarin, conscious of Rianna's pitying gaze. There were two spots of hot colour on her cheeks and it appeared even she had been aroused by the erotic tableau.

'You wish me to pleasure you here and now, my lord?' Tarn asked hesitantly.

'Would you prefer something else?' Sarin asked mockingly. 'Perhaps you'd like to offer your buttocks to Niska. She longs to pleasure you with her toy phallus. I confess I find watching her quite stimulating.'

Tarn paled, then murmured in a resentful voice. 'Whatever it is you wish, my lord.'

'How you must hate and despise me at this moment,' Sarin said mercilessly. 'I knew there was a small spark of defiance that still needed to be extinguished. I shall miss it when it is gone forever.'

There was the rustle of silk as Niska moved forward to whisper in Sarin's ear. As she finished, his eyes lit up. 'It would be the final test of obedience,' Sarin agreed. 'But I'm not certain he is ready.'

'The truth is common knowledge around the court. Do you wish him to learn it from overhearing some loose-mouthed talk?' she replied. 'And it would heap coals on this final humiliation, would it not?'

'Perhaps you are right,' Sarin said thoughtfully. 'Now is as good a time as any.' He looked back at Tarn. 'It's decided then. You'll not pleasure me, you'll pleasure my special guest in any way he chooses.'

Sarin pointed to a man seated deep in the shadows. Tarn stared into the darkness, just able to make out a tall figure as the guest stood up. When he saw the man's face Tarn was overcome by surprise. 'Guest?' he repeated, as he stared in disbelief at Cador. 'But I thought . . .'

'I was never a prisoner, Tarn,' Cador sneered. 'All the sacrifices you made to keep me safe were for nought.'

Nothing made sense to Tarn any more as he stared at his kinsman, the man he'd cared for like a brother. He saw the hate and derision on Cador's face, and a pain pierced his heart. 'But Cador, you were apprehended when you tried to rescue me.'

'I never tried to rescue you, Tarn. On the contrary, I revealed your whereabouts to your pursuers and that was why you were captured.'

'Cador was never your friend, Tarn,' Rianna interjected, unable to stay silent a moment longer. 'He betrayed you,' she added, conscious of Sarin's surprise at her temerity. 'If it had not been for Cador's treachery, your rebellion might have been a success. Cador revealed all your plans to Lord Sarin.'

Cador gave a harsh laugh. 'Madam, you've denied me the pleasure of telling Tarn that myself. I'm proud of what I did.'

'Why?' Tarn asked incredulously.

'Because your weak-willed father will die soon. Now you are deposed, Tarn, I, as your closest kinsman, become heir to the throne.'

A knot of anguish started in the pit of Tarn's stomach, travelling upwards to spew out of his mouth in a roar of pure fury. Springing to his feet, Tarn lunged at Cador.

The impetus sent the two men staggering back before they crashed to the ground.

'Guards!' yelled Sarin.

Cador tried to resist, but Tarn pinned him down, pummelling him with his fist, consumed by a white-hot anger that knew no bounds. Cador was almost senseless by the time Tarn wrapped the chain, still attached to his wrist, around his kinsman's neck.

'I'll kill you, Cador,' Tarn grated, his handsome face contorted in rage.

'Kill me and you kill yourself,' Cador choked, pulling uselessly at the chain which cut into his throat.

'I'm dead already,' Tarn yelled. 'Your treachery killed me. Now I want to bring about your death!'

Cador gave a rattling gurgle, his arms flailing wildly. The Nubians and a number of guards grabbed hold of Tarn and tried to haul him off. He fought them as best he could, while still attempting to throttle the life from his treacherous kinsman. Eventually, they managed to prise him off his victim, holding him down while they unravelled the chain from Cador's neck, which left a bloody trail where the links had cut into his flesh.

Tarn was dragged in front of Sarin, a booted foot placed across his neck as he lay prostrate on the marble floor, while Cador lay some distance away trying desperately to pull deep, rasping breaths into his starved lungs.

'It appears the spark of resistance is far from extinguished, Tarn,' Sarin said coldly as he stared down at his slave.

Rianna made no attempt to resist as Sarin grabbed hold of her, pulling her along behind him as he walked briskly to his private quarters. When they were alone, he turned to glare at her. 'Well, madam, what is your involvement in this?'

'No more than Cador wants there to be,' she replied coldly. 'He persecuted my maid until I was forced to send her back to Harn for her own safety. He spreads cruel lies about me, and a few days ago he tried to assault me.'

She watched Sarin's expression turn to one of disbelief. 'And what does Cador gain by all this?'

'I wish I knew, husband.' She smiled tremulously at him. 'I should have told you sooner, but you have so many other concerns and responsibilities.' She frowned thoughtfully. 'I know he wants Tarn dead, because then he will truly be heir apparent to the Kabran throne. But he also appears intent on causing unrest within your court and dissent between you and I.'

Sarin's interest appeared aroused. 'What would he gain from that, I wonder?'

'Cador is clever and ruthless. His true aims may not be clear to us at present. Think back to before Prince Tarn left here to visit his ailing father. Did you have any reason to mistrust him? Had he showed any inclination to rebel against your rule?'

'No.' Sarin shook his head. 'We were close, as close almost as brothers.'

'Is it not strange that within a few months of arriving in Kabra and meeting his kinsman Cador again, Tarn began to raise an army to fight you, my lord? What suddenly made him decide to rebel? Perhaps it was Cador himself who persuaded Tarn to do so. Is it not possible that Cador planned everything, including the failed rebellion, to ensure that Tarn was enslaved and he gain the throne?'

Sarin shook his head. 'I have never considered it before.'

Rianna hoped her seeds of mistrust might grow into something stronger. For all she knew, her wild theory might even be partially right. 'Perhaps it might be wise to become more cautious in your dealings with Cador in future. At least until you discover the truth of the matter.'

'So there is a quick mind inside that beautiful head of yours,' Sarin said admiringly, as he led her into his bedchamber.

Rianna was beginning to feel a little more hopeful until she caught sight of Tarn chained hand and foot to the wall. 'I did not know you had him brought here,' she stuttered, hardly able to look at Tarn in case she revealed her true feelings to Sarin. If her attempt to raise suspicion about Cador was to succeed, Sarin must trust her loyalty implicitly.

'I'd thought to punish Tarn for his outrageous behaviour myself before I sent him to the dungeons,' Sarin said, with a shrug of his shoulders.

'But if Cador was involved in inciting Tarn to rebel in the first place,' she said worriedly, 'will Tarn's punishment now be necessary? He harmed Cador, not you, my lord.'

'Tarn is my slave. He must still be punished for his flagrant disobedience if nothing else. I'd thought him broken, but that does not appear to be the case.'

'If by chance you discover the rebellion was Cador's idea?' she pressed. 'What will happen then?'

'Cador will never be allowed to rule Kabra.' Sarin took the pearl-headed pins from her hair, and ran his hands through her red-gold locks, letting them fall in loose waves around her shoulders. 'But I'll not free Tarn. He led the rebellion, massacred many of my soldiers and betrayed my trust in him. No matter what, Tarn will remain my slave.'

Rianna could not hide her contempt, and Sarin frowned. 'I'm too soft-hearted, my lord,' she said regretfully. 'It pains me to see a proud warrior so humiliated.'

'I understand, my dear.' He caressed her cheek. 'I would have you no other way,' he added before fastening his lips on hers. Sarin kissed her passionately, and she was breathless by the time he pulled away from her. Then to her consternation, he began to unfasten the laces of her bodice.

'My lord, the slave,' she said hesitantly.

'I thought your shyness gone.' Sarin lifted her into his arms and carried her to the bed. 'The presence of my

Nubians does not trouble you, so why should Tarn?' he asked, as he lay her down on the brocade coverlet.

Rianna could just see Tarn pinned against the wall, chained and helpless. His handsome face paled and contorted with despair as he watched Sarin caress her breasts, then lap at and tease her nipples. Lifting her skirts, Sarin stroked her sex, sliding his fingers between her labial lips to squeeze her pleasure nubbin. As he invaded her feminine sheath, the familiar rush of wetness betrayed her, flooding her pudenda. Rianna's body wanted Sarin even if she did not.

Filled with hot shame, she could not repress a soft moan as Sarin's searching fingers ventured deeper. She strained against the invading hand, knowing that her every sensual move filled Tarn with more distress. She wanted to close her eyes as Sarin ripped open his breeches, but he'd chastised her for doing so in the past. Her breath caught in her throat and fearful desire filled her groin as she saw his stiff, dark manhood rear out of the opening.

Sarin thrust into her without preamble, his hard rod piercing her moist flesh. 'It's a long time since I took a woman in such haste,' he growled. 'This evening's occurrences incited my lust.'

Rianna clenched her fists at her sides, intending to remain unmoved by this rough assault on her senses. Sarin thrust harder, pounding into her with a wild abandon. Sadly, she'd been starved of attention, and her body was now conditioned for constant carnal pleasure. Filled with anguish, she felt her desires become aroused to fever pitch. She welcomed the weight of Sarin crushing her, and the lustful heat of his spear as it penetrated her helpless flesh.

As he ground his pelvis against hers, she was caught up by the dark torrent and dragged under, to be buffeted by the infernal waves of sexual pleasure that dragged her deep into the abyss.

Sarin withdrew from her, his manhood still stiffly erect and wet from the dew of her body. Rianna lay there, shaken by the strength of her climax, staring wide-eyed at her husband, unable to even glance in Tarn's direction. If she did, her shame would become even more difficult to bear. She waited fearfully for Sarin to order her to bring him to his own climax with her hands and mouth. He did not, but just pulled down her skirt and drew her gently to her feet.

'You should leave now, my dear. I have to arrange for Tarn to be taken to the dungeons.'

The cell was small and dingier than the one Tarn had been confined in before, but it was clean and there was fresh straw on the floor. None of this meant anything to Tarn, as he was pushed into the small room by Sarin's guards. Unwittingly, Sarin had just caused him the greatest agony he had ever known.

What pained Tarn most was that Rianna had been visibly aroused but then hadn't he also fallen under Sarin's seductive carnal spell? Rianna's moans of pleasure, and her breathy sigh when she reached her climax, had pierced Tarn's heart like the sharpest sword. His distress had been almost unbearable. Fortunately, Sarin was unaware of his agony, and for that Tarn was grateful.

The guards took hold of a chain attached to the cell wall and fastened it to the back of Tarn's collar. Leaving his hands still tied securely behind his back with thin strips of leather, they left the cell. Only Sarin remained, staring sternly at Tarn.

'You know why you've been punished, slave?'

'Because despite everything you've not yet managed to subdue me.' Tarn's eyes were full of hate. 'It now appears you didn't even trust in your own ability to vanquish me,' Tarn jeered. 'So you deceived me with your lies about Cador. It seems I won after all, Sarin!'

'You did not.' With a growl of anger, Sarin grabbed hold of Tarn and threw him across the low wooden shelf that served as a bed. He landed so hard that the breath was forced from his lungs and the rough wood boards cut into his bare stomach.

Tarn had no chance to recover before he felt a hot shaft pierce the tight opening of his oiled nether mouth. As Sarin thrust deep into his anus, the discomfort was intense for a moment. But his inner flesh was now well-used to this erotic abuse, and a dark part of himself even welcomed the cruel invasion.

He was still aroused by the initial events of the evening, and the spicy cream Niska had spread on his sex. Despite his pain, Tarn had even been moved by the sight of Sarin taking Rianna. Now this crude invasion served to incite his lust even more. Biting his lips to stifle his groans of pleasure, he endured the intrusion as his body once again became Sarin's completely.

Sarin's angry thrusts became harder, more determined, as he dug his hands into Tarn's buttocks. Tarn strained back against the cock that pierced him, as his dark lustful pleasure grew in intensity. Images of Sarin and Rianna together filled his brain. The white-hot jealousy and rage consumed him, just as he was consumed by Sarin's penetrating thrust as his body jerked heavily against Tarn's.

Tears streamed down Tarn's anguished face as his own erection grew harder. His cock pulsed as the onslaught continued, but there were no gentle hands to bring him to a climax today; Sarin was intent only on revenge.

Sarin gave one last forceful thrust, his heavy weight pressing Tarn's bound hands into the small of his back, while splinters of wood dug into his flesh. With a loud grunt, Sarin spilt his seed deep inside Tarn. Then, breathing heavily, he withdrew, pausing only to grimly clean his shaft with Tarn's long hair. It was a final and complete end to his act of subjugation before he strode wordlessly from the cell.

Tarn's sex ached for release, but that torment was the least of his concerns. He lay there, his body filled with pain and unrequited lust, while humiliating agony filled his thoughts. With a groan, he pulled his body from the rough shelf and fell on to the straw-covered floor, his face still wet with tears.

Tarn tensed as he heard footsteps approach his cell, relaxing only once they had passed. He was constantly prepared to protect himself against another attempted assault by his gaoler, and the painful punishment that usually followed the event.

After Sarin left that fateful night, the fat, greedy gaoler he now knew as Gan entered his cell. Gan appeared almost sympathetic as he untied Tarn's hands and gave him a blanket to cover himself. Then Gan opened his breeches, pulled out his short, stubby cock and ordered Tarn to take it in his mouth. His refusal brought him a brutal beating with a thick leather strap.

The sexual demands of his gaoler had continued. Tarn soon learnt that Gan had specific orders. He could do anything but penetrate the prisoner – that pleasure was Sarin's alone. Tarn was forced to endure Gan's crude fumbling as the gaoler slobbered lewdly over his firm flesh. If he did not, he was denied food and water. Yet when Gan had taken out his stubby cock again and ordered him to suck it, Tarn still refused. Tarn grinned and bared his teeth, threatening to sever the paltry organ with one clean bite. So Gan found his pleasure by beating Tarn instead. To further subdue him, Tarn's wrists were kept constantly chained together.

Once again Tarn heard footsteps approach, and this time his cell door swung open. It wasn't the gaoler, however, it was Niska, dressed in vibrant scarlet, a heavy rope of diamonds around her neck. 'Tarn,' she smiled, as the door clanged shut behind her.

'Do you not fear for your life, lady?' Tarn growled. 'The gaolers think I'm dangerous.'

'No, I do not fear you,' she laughed. 'You're far more suited to being a warrior than Sarin's pampered pleasure slave.'

208

Tarn saw her eyes hungrily rove over his naked body. 'To what do I owe the pleasure of this visit?' he asked.

Niska moved closer, and ran her hands over Tarn's chest, brushing away the pieces of straw that clung to his skin. 'Sarin spends all his time pleasuring Rianna,' Niska said, witnessing the brief flash of jealousy in Tarn's blue eyes. 'There's no need to hide your emotion. I know how much you care for her, and she you.'

'I care nought for the lady,' Tarn replied. 'Why should I?'

'Why bother to lie to me, Tarn, when I know the truth.' She picked a piece of straw from his tangled hair. 'I still find you desirable, even in these wretched surroundings. Would that you were still a warrior. You have nobility that Cador and Sarin lack. With you beside me, I could be happy.'

'But I could never be happy with you, Niska,' Tarn replied. 'How could any man desire a wanton bitch such as you?' Even as he spoke, Tarn felt lust spear his loins. After the crude, smelling gaolers he longed for the soft-scented sweetness of female flesh. Niska was standing so close in her brief, provocative garments. His desire increased as he smelt her musky perfume, and he remembered the diamond droplet that pierced her nipple.

'You flatter me,' she smiled coldly. 'Now you are about to discover just how wanton I can be.' She pulled open her skirt to reveal her naked sex. 'Get down on your knees and pleasure me.'

'No,' Tarn grated, as a hot excitement grew in him.

'Don't even consider refusing me.' Niska ran her hands over his taut stomach. She cupped his sac, feeling the heavy weight of his balls. Then she ran her fingers along his manhood, watching it stiffen. 'Slaves do as they are ordered.'

'Not this slave,' Tarn replied with a harsh laugh.

'You wish Rianna to be safe?' she asked. Roughly, Niska rubbed his shaft between her fingers, coaxing the organ to harden even more, pinching the tip of the head, before pushing back the hood of skin to reveal the sensitive glans beneath. 'If you pleasure me, I'll keep what I know to myself. Sarin will never learn that you and she were lovers.'

'You deceive yourself, Niska. I admit I admire the lady, but she is Lord Sarin's wife.'

'I am no fool, Tarn. It is you that cannot deceive me.' Niska sat down on the wooden bed, pulled apart her skirts and opened her thighs so that Tarn could see the pink gaping leaves of her sex. 'Rianna loves you, Tarn, I see it every time she looks at you. During all the times you were alone together, would you have me believe you never touched her?' She pointed to the floor between her thighs. 'Kneel.'

Fighting his unbidden arousal, Tarn stepped over to the bed and knelt in front of Niska. 'You have no proof,' he challenged.

'Proof? All I need do is arouse Sarin's suspicions. He'll do all he can then to discover the truth. Neither Lesand, or his little spy Yasmin, will be able to help Rianna then.'

Tarn knew how right Niska was. Even a mere suggestion might harm Rianna, and she was more important to him than anything else. He leant towards Niska's sex, inhaling her heady scent. Niska pulled her outer lips apart with her fingers and gave a soft sigh as Tarn buried his face in her pudenda. His warm tongue slid slowly up each side of her moist divide, circling her clitoris with gentle, teasing strokes. He stimulated the sensitive bud with the tip of his tongue, flicking the tiny hood back as it stiffened.

'Yes,' Niska moaned as he closed his lips around her pleasure pearl and sucked on it hard. He ground his mouth into her soaking folds, savouring the sweet, musky taste of her. When his tongue invaded her vagina she arched her back and meshed her hands in his hair. Tarn pressed his tongue deeper, teasing the silken walls. Niska's body tensed as her pleasure washed over her in strong unrelenting waves, her vagina pulsing around his questing tongue.

As Tarn lifted his head, Niska gave a lazy, satisfied smile. Glancing hungrily down at his engorged sex, she eased her buttocks closer to him. Tarn's lust was aroused and he entered her with one smooth stroke, feeling her curl her legs possessively around his hips. He placed his chained hands on her narrow waist to help support his weight. As her muscles tightened around his cock, he gave a soft groan. He had been denied his release for so long, and his pleasure peaked swiftly as he savoured the silken heat of her sex.

'You fill me so completely,' Niska gasped as he rode her hard, thrusting into her relentlessly, until his climax came in a sudden rush of sinful bliss.

Niska pulled him closer and took possession of his mouth, kissing him with unrestrained fervour as her second orgasm overwhelmed her. Tarn felt her vagina pulse hungrily around his cock, draining him of the last vestiges of his passion.

Niska gave another satisfied sigh and tenderly stroked Tarn's cheek as he withdrew from her. 'If only I could persuade Sarin to give you to me. I can see now why he keeps you for himself. You were magnificent, Tarn.' She rose to her feet, pulling her skirt together to cover her sex. 'I'll come again, perhaps tomorrow,' she added with a malicious smile. 'I'll expect you to display even more ardour than you did today.'

Rianna left Sarin's bed, and returned to her quarters. Since Tarn's attack on Cador, Sarin had insisted she lay with him every night. He was no longer heedful of her feelings, expecting her to partake in all manner of erotic delights. Rianna shared her husband with his pleasure slaves, both female and male. However, Sarin never allowed the men to touch her too intimately. If they ever had a child he intended to ensure it was from his seed and none other.

Rianna was helplessly enmeshed in Sarin's sensual web of carnal delight, which indulged her senses and drained her of all emotion. She missed Jenna, and had become very reliant on Yasmin of late, yet she could never speak of her feelings for Tarn, for that might prove to be too dangerous. Yasmin was in Lesand's employ but she still had some sense of loyalty towards Sarin.

'My lady, you have a visitor,' a maidservant announced, as Rianna entered her chambers.

Rianna sighed; she was in no mood for company. She felt warm, sticky and incredibly weary after her night of indulgent excesses. She knew it would not be Chancellor Lesand, even though she'd been trying to obtain an audience with him for a number of days. Male visitors were not allowed in this part of the palace. It was out of bounds, even to Sarin's male slaves.

She tensed in surprise as she walked into the main reception room and discovered her visitor was Niska.

'This is quite unexpected,' Rianna exclaimed.

Niska rose to her feet and smiled politely. 'Lady Rianna, forgive the intrusion. I wish to speak to you on a very personal matter,' she said, glancing pointedly at the maidservant.

'You may leave us.' Rianna dismissed the girl with a wave of her hand, and seated herself on the divan opposite Niska's chair. 'What do you want?' Rianna asked coldly.

'I've come to offer you my help.'

Rianna stared at her suspiciously. 'Why would I want *your* help?'

'You wish to leave this place, do you not?' Without waiting for an answer Niska added, 'I've no reason to hide that my one aim is to be rid of you. With you gone, Lord Sarin and I can become close again.'

'I thought your intention was to leave Lord Sarin and go to Kabra with Cador. You told me so yourself.'

'That was my initial plan,' Niska replied. 'Because of you, Sarin is now suspicious of Cador. It's likely he won't offer him the throne of Kabra, as he now seems to think that Cador might try to raise another army, and lead a second rebellion. With the royal coffers of Kabra open to him, and the king's guards on his side, Cador might well succeed where Tarn failed.' Niska smiled conspiratorially. 'In the circumstances it seems sensible to keep all my options open.'

Remaining suspicious of her unwanted visitor's motives, Rianna stared penetratingly at Niska. 'What exactly are you suggesting?'

'I will help you escape. You will disappear, and Lord Sarin will eventually become weary of looking for you. Then he will be mine completely. However, you cannot return to Harn. I can arrange a ship's passage to another country, preferably one that has no ties to Percheron.'

'Why should I leave?' Rianna challenged. 'I'm Lord Sarin's wife.'

'His unwilling wife,' Niska corrected. 'Your lover languishes in the dungeons. If he were ever to be released it will only be to become Lord Sarin's pleasure slave again, or be sold on the block. With my help you and Tarn can be together at last.'

'You mean for Tarn to leave as well?' Rianna asked incredulously. 'You'd help us both to get away?'

'I know you'd never be willing to leave without him,' Niska replied. 'Tarn is in good health at present. I visited him in the dungeons and found him even more defiant than ever. Sarin hasn't truly tamed Tarn, and I doubt he ever will.'

'But your accomplice, Cador, wants Tarn dead,' Rianna continued.

'Just because Cador wants Tarn dead doesn't mean I do. I am my own woman,' Niska said proudly. 'I've risen high for the daughter of a slave, and I intend to rise even higher. I'll never allow any man to totally control me, neither Cador nor Sarin.'

'I cannot believe I am hearing this,' Rianna said.

'You first instinct is to refuse my help, is it not?' Niska continued. 'In your position I would feel just the same. Consider this: do you have any other options? If you want to spend the rest of your life with Tarn, you have to put aside your suspicions and trust me.'

Rianna shook her head. 'I'm not certain . . .'

213

'Then be certain,' Niska said frustratedly. 'I am doing this to achieve my own selfish ends. In order to get what I want, I must help you and Tarn. But if you do not want my help . . .' She rose to her feet. 'Then I bid you good day, Lady Rianna, and promise I will not speak of this again.'

She began to move towards the door. 'No,' Rianna said. 'Wait. Let us discuss this matter further.'

Niska smiled. 'So you are interested in what I have to offer.' She stepped back to Rianna and lowered her voice. 'I have more power than you know. There are a number of guards and slaves in the palace in my employ, and I have contacts in the city, merchants who will find me the captain of a vessel who'll give safe passage to you and Tarn.'

Baral hurried up the steps that led to the bowels of the palace. He hated the dungeons, they made his flesh creep. Of late he'd been forced to visit them a number of times. Chancellor Lesand insisted on regular reports about Tarn. He'd interceded on the prisoner's behalf to ensure that he was properly fed, but he had been unable to improve the conditions Tarn was kept in; that was Lords Sarin's prerogative alone.

Much of Baral's time was spent moving about the palace, gleaning news from those secretly in the Chancellor's pay. Lesand liked to be aware of everything that went on at Court, however small and insignificant it might appear. It was well past noon, and the reception rooms of the palace were empty; most of the courtiers were resting in the heat of the day. Baral wished he too was resting, as he mopped the perspiration from his brow with the edge of his sleeve.

Just ahead, he spotted Cador, striding purposefully along the empty corridor. Baral's instructions were to find out all he could about Cador, so it seemed circumspect to delay his return to Chancellor Lesand and follow the nobleman.

Cador turned right, into an open-sided corridor which

overlooked a small courtyard. A woman was sitting on a bench waiting for him. Baral recognised Niska's pale, silvery hair. Baral crept forward to hide behind a large marble statue, just able to overhear their conversation.

'Is it settled?' Cador asked agitatedly.

'Yes,' Niska confirmed. 'She was naturally suspicious at first, but I eventually persuaded her to trust me.'

Cador gave a harsh laugh. 'All is arranged for tomorrow night?' Niska nodded as he added, 'We'll be rid of that interfering whore forever. I loathe her even more now for causing Sarin to doubt my loyalty.'

'It may take some time before he begins to trust you again,' Niska pointed out.

'It will be easier when both Tarn and Rianna are dead.'

'You're convinced that Sarin will decide to execute them both if Rianna is caught helping Tarn to escape?'

'He'll have no other choice,' Cador assured her confidently. 'It would make him appear weak if he did not. Sarin likes to appear a strong, ruthless monarch.' Frowning at her troubled expression, he continued, 'I thought you wanted this as much as I?'

'Rianna, yes,' she confirmed. 'I'll not shed a tear for her. But Tarn is different.'

'So you still lust after him?' Cador's face contorted with fury. 'He has to die, otherwise it is possible Lord Sarin might question him, torture him into revealing how great a hand I had in persuading Tarn to lead the rebellion. If Sarin discovers the truth, he'll never trust me again.'

'I would rather Tarn did not die,' Niska said determinedly. 'If that appears so, I want you to plead for his life. A show of mercy on your part might help assuage Sarin's suspicions of you. Then you can persuade Sarin to sell Tarn instead. If Sarin is offered a large enough sum, greed will make him agree.'

'All that, just so you can make Tarn *your* pleasure slave,' Cador growled. 'Is he worth the trouble?'

'Yes.' Her pale eyes lightened with excitement. 'Imagine it, Cador, Tarn would be your slave also.'

'The thought does have some merit.' He touched the bruises that ringed his neck. 'Death does seem too easy an option for him.'

'Then promise me we can keep him as our slave at least for a short while. Owning Tarn will give you the power of life and death over him, Cador.' She kissed his cheek and pressed the palm of her hand against his groin.

'How can I refuse you anything?' He groaned as she pulled open his breeches and lowered her head.


'Chancellor?' Rianna exclaimed in surprise, as she found him waiting in her bedchamber after she returned from the bath house. 'I did not expect to find you here.'

Lesand smiled tightly. 'I doubt Sarin would chastise me for flouting his rules. No part of the palaces is out of bounds to the Chancellor of the kingdom. I ensured that no one saw me enter.' He pushed the door of her bedchamber shut. 'This conversation must be between us alone, that is why I decided not to call you to my chambers. I had no wish to arouse any suspicion.'

'What is it?' Rianna asked, fearing the worst.

'I've heard of your plan,' Lesand said grimly. 'And I cannot allow it.'

'You've witnessed Tarn's fate, Chancellor, the way Sarin has enslaved and humiliated him,' she said, her eyes filling with unshed tears. 'Can you deny Tarn the chance to break free from his misery?'

'If Niska's scheme goes ahead tomorrow night, you will be far from free,' he replied, looking at her with deep concern. 'The guards will be told in advance of your plan to free Tarn and escape with him. You will both be apprehended when you try to leave the palace. There is only one punishment for such a crime; do you know what it is, Rianna?'

She swallowed hard and shook her head. 'No,' she said quietly.

'Public beheading,' Lesand replied. 'Both you and Tarn.'

'So Niska wants us dead?'

'Cador,' he corrected. 'He is the prime instigator of this plan. Cador knows it was you who planted seeds of suspicion in Lord Sarin's head. If you are apprehended while helping Tarn escape, he rids himself of two troublesome problems at the same time.'

'What can I do, Chancellor?' she said, clutching at his sleeve, knowing that all her hopes for the future were now extinguished. 'I fear for my life and Tarn's. If Tarn doesn't escape he will either die in the dungeons or be forced to resume his position as Lord Sarin's pleasure slave. You helped us once, can you not do so again?'

Lesand frowned. 'I hoped never to be faced with a decision such as this, Rianna. I feared it might come to this when I helped you in the first place. What I have learnt of late leads me to presume that Cador was one of the Kabran nobles who persuaded Tarn to lead the rebellion. Why should Tarn be punished while Cador is not? Tarn is a far nobler and more trustworthy man than Cador.' Lesand's expression softened as he took hold of her hand. 'Your suspicions about Cador were valid, Rianna. If Cador comes to the throne of Kabra, he will eventually persuade others to join him in invading Percheron and deposing Lord Sarin, but with Tarn free, the noblemen and lesser princes from surrounding kingdoms will not support such a plan. If I help free Tarn, I effectively help Percheron.'

'So you'll come to our aid?' she asked eagerly.

'The garment you're wearing isn't suitable for travelling,' he remarked.

'We leave now?' she queried incredulously.

'Just as soon as you are suitably clad,' he agreed. 'Lord Sarin is detained on matters of state, so he'll not send for you this evening. I did not inform you earlier, just in case my plans were forced to change.' Lesand watched Rianna rummage in a cedarwood chest and pull out the breeches and doublet she had worn for riding at home in Harn. 'Far more suitable. Make haste,' he added.

Swiftly, she changed, donning her riding boots and a

plain, black wool cloak. Dusk had already fallen. The night was warm, but it could turn cold later and they would be travelling far, so the cloak was a necessity.

'This way.' Lesand led her into the anteroom leading off her bedchamber and pulled back a heavy wall hanging to reveal a small door. She followed him through the door into a dusty passageway. 'This is one of many similar corridors all over the palace,' Lesand explained, as he picked up the lantern he had left ready.

They walked along a twisting passageway. There were other narrow corridors branching off at angles. It would be an easy place in which to get totally lost.

Eventually Lesand opened a door and guided her into a large chamber, with dark, rather gloomy furnishings. 'My quarters,' he explained, handing her into Baral's care. 'Now wait here and be very quiet.' He strode briskly through a curtained doorway.

'Through there is the Chancellor's office,' Baral whispered. 'You can watch, but ensure you're not seen,' he added.

Rianna tiptoed to the curtain and peered through a narrow opening at the side of the fabric. Lesand was seated in a large imposing chair. 'Enter,' he said, as there was a sharp rap at the door of the chamber.

Two guards escorted Tarn into the room. Tarn's skin was damp and his hair wet. Before leaving the dungeon, the gaoler had thrown a couple of buckets of icy-cold water over him to wash away the dirt and grime of his squalid cell.

'Chancellor,' Tarn acknowledged, with a brief bow of his head.

'Leave,' Lesand told the soldiers. 'I have instructions from Lord Sarin that this prisoner is to be questioned.'

'But Chancellor,' the guard interrupted.

'Be gone,' Lesand snapped. 'The prisoner is chained, I'll come to no harm.'

Tarn remained silent until the guards had left, then he said coldly, 'Are you certain I won't harm you, Lesand?'

He lifted his manacled hands. 'I've managed to do my guards harm chained as I am.'

'I am certain,' Lesand said, rising to his feet. 'It's safe to come in now, Baral.'

Rianna didn't wait for Lesand to call her. She rushed into the room and flung her arms around Tarn. 'My love!'

Tarn looked at her in bewilderment. 'Rianna?'

'The Chancellor is to help us escape,' she said, hugging Tarn, then kissing him passionately.

'Rianna,' Lesand said agitatedly. 'Baral has horses, weapons and provisions waiting. Step back. Baral has to remove Tarn's chains before he can dress. We must hurry!'

# Chapter Eleven

When daylight came, Tarn and Rianna were well away from the city of Aguilar, heading in a northeasterly direction. Tarn had decided to head for Kabra, as he wanted to see his ailing father one last time. Also, there were friends in Kabra who would help them travel to lands in the east where Lord Sarin's influence did not reach.

The cool breeze brushed Rianna's face and ruffled her tangled hair. At last she felt free and happy. She knew Sarin's men would soon give chase, but the guards would be under the impression that Tarn was alone, still chained and on foot. First they would look for him in the palace, and then the confines of the city. Her disappearance would probably not be discovered until this morning, so they should have a good few hours head start.

Her only sadness was that she'd been forced to leave her pretty mare, Freya. She was too gentle a mount for the rough journey they faced.

'Do you think we could stop to eat and water the horses?' she asked Tarn. They had been travelling swiftly in order to put a distance between them and any pursuers.

'Are you weary, my love?' he asked anxiously.

'No more than you,' she smiled. 'Neither of us have ridden much of late.'

'A short rest will ease the stiffness from our limbs.' He followed her gaze to his groin. 'You need not worry,' he added with a wicked grin. 'Only one thing will ease the stiffness from that!'

Taking hold of the reins of her mount, Tarn guided the horses beneath the shelter of a thick clump of trees. Dismounting, he tethered the horses, then held out his arms to her. Rianna gave a soft, happy laugh as she fell into his embrace.

'I never dreamt such a moment as this would ever exist,' Tarn said, kissing her with unrestrained passion.

She was shaking with need by the time he let go of her. Almost stumbling in her haste, Rianna threw off her leather doublet. 'I want you now, Tarn,' she said breathlessly.

His hands trembled as they slid under her linen shirt to caress her naked breasts. Rianna moaned, pushing herself closer to him, her fingers fumbling with the fastening of his breeches.

'Let me.' Tarn undressed hastily, while Rianna removed her clothes. He placed a soft blanket on the rough, uneven ground and pulled her gently down beside him. They embraced, Tarn's hard body pressed against hers, his engorged manhood digging temptingly into the soft curve of her stomach.

'I love you,' she whispered.

'You are my life, Rianna,' he said, his voice full of emotion.

'And you are mine,' she replied, almost crying with joy. Tarn kissed her, sliding his tongue into her mouth, savouring the sweetness of her lips. But their need was urgent, their desire for each other overwhelming. 'Take me now,' she pleaded, rolling on to her back.

Tarn positioned himself between her thighs. 'My dearest love,' he said softly. 'This sweet union will cleanse us both.'

He entered her, his hot shaft parting her soft, moist flesh. Once she was filled completely, he lay there for a moment cradled inside her body, kissing her face, her neck, her breasts. Then Tarn began to move, thrusting smoothly into her, his engorged manhood lovingly caressing her silken sheath and rubbing teasingly against her taut pleasure pearl. The passion Rianna felt for Tarn was beyond anything she'd ever known, her love stronger than life itself.

The warm, musky scent of Tarn's flesh surrounded her; soft strands of his hair brushed her breasts. The sheer power and strength of his body thrusting into her was even more wonderful than she remembered, or thought it could ever be again. She felt Tarn's hard shaft filling her completely, rubbing and stroking every part of her vagina, giving her a pleasure that knew no boundaries.

She wound her arms around his neck, holding him close as the glorious sensations he aroused within her started to peak. She reached the summit, and her inner flesh pulsed. Tarn lost control completely as her sheath tightly enfolded his penis, drawing his life essence deep into her body. Joined in their mutual climax, they floated upwards on a happy cloud of bliss.

When the strong pulsing ebbed away, Tarn held her close. They kissed, cuddled, shared intimate words and their deepest thoughts. All the while, Tarn's shaft remained inside her, until their need for each other sprang into life again. This time their lovemaking was slow and leisurely, with no need for the frantic haste of their first coupling. Her climax was longer and more drawn out, just as pleasurable and just as overwhelming. Once again she felt her soul soar into the deep blue yonder to join with Tarn's.

'We should leave,' Tarn said, holding her close. 'We can tarry here no longer. Lord Sarin's men may be close behind us.'

She smiled lovingly at him. 'If the gods are willing, we can look forward to a lifetime of moments as beautiful as this.'

* * *

'Have you found the fugitive yet?' Sarin asked irritably, as the captain of the palace guards entered the room. When Sarin didn't receive a reply he angrily thumped his fist on the table in front of him. 'How can one naked, chained prisoner disappear so completely?' he said in disbelief. 'It is not possible.'

'We've searched the palace and its grounds more than once, my lord,' the captain replied. 'Now my men are combing the city streets.'

'Search the palace again,' Sarin blazed. 'A thousand times over if needs be. If the prisoner is not found, you and your men will suffer my wrath. What now,' he snapped as Captain Feroc paused hesitantly just inside the door of the large chamber.

'I have something for you to see, my lord.' Feroc strode forwards and bowed low. 'These were found hidden in some bushes close to the armoury.' He placed the manacles on the table.

'Ye gods!' Sarin growled, his face contorted by angry frustration. 'Tarn is no longer chained. Doubtless he managed to steal weapons and clothing?' He looked questioningly at Feroc. 'How fares Chancellor Lesand?'

'The Chancellor still complains of pains in his head. The blow the prisoner gave him left only a small wound, but it appears to have robbed him of any memory of the incident. We should give thanks that Tarn did not harm him further.'

'Indeed we should,' Sarin replied. 'However, I can think of nothing but recapturing the fugitive.' He thumped the table again, making the chains of the discarded manacles rattle. 'Have the stables been checked? Tarn might well have stolen a mount.'

'Twice, sire,' replied his captain of the guard. 'No horses are missing.'

'What about the horses Chancellor Lesand had shipped in two days ago, as replacement mounts for his men. Are they all accounted for?' asked Feroc.

'Well?' Sarin stared at the man whose cheeks had turned bright red.

'I was not aware of their arrival, sire,' he mumbled.

'I'll speak to the Chancellor's Master of the Horse at once,' Feroc said. 'And report back to you straight away, Lord Sarin.'

'Thank you, Captain Feroc.' Sarin glared at his captain of the guard. 'If Tarn has a horse he will be miles away by now.' He glanced over at Cador, who lounged in a chair, tapping his booted foot with his riding crop. 'It seems we have underestimated Tarn.'

Cador straightened. 'I never underestimated him, my lord,' he replied. 'May I suggest that if you send out men to search for him, you instruct them to travel northeast. Tarn will be heading for Kabra.'

'Surely he'll not return there?' Sarin questioned, as Feroc silently departed.

'I know Tarn well. I'm certain he'll want to see his father,' Cador continued.

Sarin glared at the palace guard who had just stepped into the room. 'Be gone,' he growled. 'I wish to be alone.'

'But, my lord, there's a visitor to see you,' the guard stuttered.

'Visitor?' Sarin enquired.

Someone brushed past the guard and strode boldly into the room. 'Lord Sarin,' Gerek acknowledged with a brief brow. 'I am Rianna's father.'

'Protector, this is an unexpected honour,' Sarin said coldly.

'Forgive the intrusion,' Gerek smiled, ignoring the chilly greeting. 'I had business in southern Harn, so I came to enquire of my daughter's health. She has not written me for some time.'

'Welcome to my house,' Sarin said, hiding his irritation. 'I'll have rooms prepared and advise Lady Rianna you are here.'

'I took it upon myself to ask one of the servants to seek her out.' Gerek looked thoughtfully at Sarin. 'You appear somewhat preoccupied. Is something amiss?'

'A prisoner has escaped,' Sarin explained hurriedly.

'My men are such incompetent fools they seem unable to find him.'

'The prisoner is of some importance?' Gerek questioned curiously.

'If you think the former Prince of Kabra important,' Cador interjected, looking towards the door as he heard a sudden commotion outside.

'What is wrong now?' Sarin grumbled.

Cador stepped over to the door, exchanged a few words with someone, then grabbed hold of a maidservant and hauled her before Sarin. She fell to her knees, tears streaming down her cheeks.

'It was not my fault, master, forgive me.'

'What is she babbling about?' Sarin looked at Cador.

'It appears that Lady Rianna has also disappeared,' Cador grinned slyly. 'Somewhat of a coincidence, my lord.'

'Has the fugitive abducted my daughter?' Gerek asked anxiously. 'Perhaps he intends to use her as a hostage to ensure we do not pursue him.'

'I fear that might be possible,' Sarin replied worriedly, while Cador held his tongue.


'Are you certain it is safe to have a fire?' Rianna asked, as she pulled her thick cloak tighter around her chilled body.

'We're not close to any towns or villages that I know of.' Tarn threw more wood on the flames and sat down beside her, pulling her close. 'I don't want you to freeze, my love.'

Rianna smiled at Tarn. There were dark shadows under her eyes as they had managed little sleep over the last three days, only pausing to rest when the horses became too tired to continue. At the next town Tarn had decided to buy two more mounts so that they could carry spare horses with them.

'With you beside me, Tarn, I'll always be safe.' She glanced at the thick trees that ringed their small camp site. 'Do you know exactly where we are?'

'The constellations help me to plot our path.' He pointed up at the dark, star-spattered sky. 'See that bright star in the north? Kabra is that way.'

Rianna looked up at the sky. The star looked brighter than all the others and she thought that an auspicious omen. She never even heard a sound, just felt a body press against her back as the sharp knife touched her throat. Tarn stiffened, and out of the corner of her eye Rianna glimpsed the cruel blade held to her lover's neck.

'Stand up slowly,' ordered a female voice. 'You're outnumbered. We won't hesitate to kill you if you make any attempt to resist.'

'Do as they say, Rianna,' Tarn said in a reassuring voice. 'They won't harm us if we obey.' The dagger was removed from Tarn's neck and he rose very slowly to his feet. Tarn turned to face his opponents, five armoured, heavily-armed, female warriors. 'We mean no harm. We are travelling to Kabra, and strayed into your land by accident. Release us and we will be on our way as soon as it is light.'

'Only our Queen can accord you that privilege,' the tallest woman replied, pointing a sword straight at Tarn's stomach. 'All strangers have to be taken before her. Hands behind your back.'

'As you wish,' Tarn said, placing his arms behind his back. One of the women stepped around him and lashed his wrists together with strips of leather that cut cruelly into his flesh. They were kinder to Rianna. Taking the dagger from her throat, they tied her hands in front of her. One of the women gave a piercing whistle and a sixth warrior appeared leading a number of horses. Rianna and Tarn were allowed to mount their own steeds. The group set off, wending their way through the thick forest until they reached a narrow path which led upwards into the mountains, eventually turning into a narrow road.

Their captors urged the horses into a fast gallop. Rianna was able to hang on to the pommel of her saddle. Tarn, hands tied behind his back, gritted his teeth, grasping the saddle with his knees. The muscles of his thighs ached by the time the castle came in sight; a large imposing stone edifice, which almost seemed part of the rocky summit on which it stood.

Female warriors guarded the entrance. They pulled open the heavy oak gates to allow the warriors and their captives inside. Torches, set on high wooden poles, lit the bailey. Tarn could see only a few guards on duty inside; the walkways running along the high battlement walls were empty. Tarn felt heartened, as the lack of guards would make it easier to attempt an escape.

The group of riders stopped in front of a large, stone building which was the main body of the castle. Other, smaller buildings could be seen within the keep.

'Dismount,' ordered one of the warriors who had captured them.

Tarn slid from his horse, tensing his muscles to stop his weary legs from buckling under him, and moved closer to Rianna. She looked anxiously at him.

'I do not think this is as bad as it first seemed,' he whispered, smiling at her reassuringly. 'As soon as they realise who you are, we shall be safe.'

'What do you –'

'Silence,' snapped one of the warriors. 'This way,' she ordered, taking a firm hold on Tarn's arm and leading him up the wide stone steps. Rianna followed them.

They entered the great hall, which was brightly lit and sumptuously appointed. It had a striking floor made of slabs of marble in rich shades of cream and brown. Silk banners and brightly coloured tapestries covered the thick stone walls. There were ornately carved chairs and tables, and huge silver candle holders. The smell of sweet incense scented the air, a contrast to the smelly, smoky atmosphere prevalent in most castles Tarn had visited.

The warriors tossed aside their cloaks, revealing their beaten metal breastplates and short leather skirts. Tarn's initial conclusions were right. They had unwittingly strayed over the border into the land of Freygard, the ancestral home of Rianna's mother, Kitara.

A woman severed Rianna's bonds but left Tarn's hands tied, leading them forward to stand in front of a raised dais on which stood an ornately carved gold throne.

Tarn drew in his breath as the Queen entered. She was probably twenty years older than Rianna, but still extraordinarily beautiful, with a superb figure and long, dark auburn hair. She too was dressed as a warrior, with a breastplate of beaten gold covering her upper torso, and white silk breeches which clung tightly to her shapely legs.

'Queen Danara,' a warrior whispered in Tarn's ear as the queen seated herself on the imposing throne.

'So these are the strangers?' The Queen glanced dismissively at Tarn, then looked thoughtfully at Rianna. 'What is your name, child?'

'Rianna,' she replied. 'Lady Rianna of Harn.'

'Your father is the Protector?' Queen Danara queried, leaning forward intently.

'Rianna's mother, Kitara, was one of your people,' Tarn interjected.

'I did not address you,' Queen Danara said regally, as she glared angrily at Tarn.

'I appreciate that it is not usually permitted for a man to address your majesty directly, without first receiving permission. But I beg leave to speak,' Tarn said boldly.

'Who is he?' Queen Danara asked Rianna.

'Prince Tarn of Kabra.' Rianna looked lovingly at Tarn. 'We are fleeing from my husband, Lord Sarin of Percheron.'

'You fear Lord Sarin, child?' The Queen smiled warmly at Rianna. 'Do not be concerned. He has no control over this land. Our laws do not recognise the union of marriage.' Relenting, she turned to Tarn. 'So you are the rebel prince who dared to oppose Sarin of Percheron?'

He nodded. 'I am, your majesty. Could I ask you to

228

give Lady Rianna sanctuary for the sake of her birthright, if nothing else? We are being pursued by Lord Sarin's soldiers and I fear they are not far behind us.'

'We welcome all our lost sheep back to the fold, Prince Tarn.' She honoured Tarn by inclining her head as a measure of respect. 'As Lady Rianna's companion, we also offer you sanctuary. However, while you reside here you must abide by our customs.'

'Thank you, your majesty,' he acknowledged.

'Rianna, I bid you welcome.' The Queen stepped down from the dais and embraced Rianna. 'Your mother and I were raised together as children. You are my kinswoman. If it please you, Rianna, you may address me as Danara. You've travelled far, you must be weary. You need good food and rest.'

'Indeed we do.' Rianna looked over at Tarn. 'Surely, Queen Danara, you do not leave those you welcome restrained?'

'You have a fiery spirit like your mother.' The Queen nodded to Tarn's guard. Taking out her dagger, the warrior sliced through Tarn's bonds. 'Come, my dear. I'll guide you to your chamber,' she said to Rianna. 'In this castle, the different sexes live apart. Tarn will stay in the men's quarters.'

'He'll be treated well?' Rianna insisted. 'I've heard you can be harsh with your male slaves. Tarn is no slave, he's my dearest companion.'

The Queen gave a soft laugh. 'Many of the stories about Freygard are just that – wild tales told by troubadours who know nothing of our land. Prince Tarn will be shown to a comfortable chamber and have all his needs attended to.'

'I'll see you on the morrow,' Rianna said anxiously, as she smiled at Tarn.

He smiled encouragingly back at her. Tarn had no wish for them to be parted, but it appeared they had little choice. Despite the Queen's words of welcome, he had the uneasy feeling they were still as much prisoners now as they had been before. With one last fleeting glance at Rianna, he followed his warrior escort from the great hall. They walked down the steps and across the chilly keep to a low, stone building nestling against the castle walls.

Rianna sat in the warm, scented water, which eased the stiffness from her travel-weary limbs. This bathing tub in front of a blazing fire in her bedchamber was a far cry from the luxury of Sarin's bath house, but infinitely preferable all the same. She wished Tarn could be here with her. For the last three days they'd spent every moment together, and she wanted the rest of her life to be the same. She had vowed that they would never again be parted. Unfortunately, the customs of Freygard did not permit them to share a bedchamber.

They had been offered sanctuary by her kinfolk, yet still Rianna did not feel at ease. She couldn't bring herself to wholly trust Queen Danara.

'Rianna, are you feeling better now you've eaten and bathed?' Danara asked, as she entered the room. 'Here, I've brought you clean towels.' She placed the white linen cloths on a stool by the side of the tub.

'Much better.' Rianna smiled at Danara, who looked a little more approachable now that she had changed into a loose robe. 'Thank you for the towels.'

There appeared to be no female servants in the castle. Rianna had seen just two male slaves who brought the water for her bath. They hadn't even dared look at her, keeping their eyes lowered. After the plethora of slaves and servants eager to attend to her every need in the palace of Aguilar, the sight of the queen bringing her fresh towels was a little strange.

'You should get out of the bath before your flesh wrinkles like a prune,' Danara teased with a soft laugh. 'We've no slaves here to massage scented oil into your skin. Life in Freygard has none of the luxuries of Lord Sarin's court.'

Danara shook a linen towel free of its folds and held it out to Rianna. She stood up, water streaming from her body, her skin pink from the warmth. As Rianna stepped from the tub, Danara wrapped the towel around her, but not before her gaze briefly darted down to Rianna's denuded sex.

'So you know what life is like in Sarin's court?' Rianna asked in surprise.

'We do not encourage strangers to visit our lands. Yet some of our warriors do choose to travel, merely in order to learn more about other countries,' Danara replied. 'We like to keep well acquainted with what happens in kingdoms close to our boundaries. For safety's sake if nothing else. We have never been invaded, but that does not mean it will never happen.' She led Rianna over to the four-poster bed. 'Sit and I'll comb your hair.'

'It's knotted and tangled. I've had little time to tend it on our journey,' Rianna replied. When they had paused to rest, if they weren't eating or sleeping, she and Tarn had been making love.

'I'll try not to hurt.' Danara unpinned the red-gold locks. Gently, she began to run a wide-toothed ivory comb through the tangled strands.

'Has Tarn been made comfortable?' Rianna asked, wincing as the comb caught on a knot.

'I did not lie,' Danara gently chided. 'He's been given one of our best chambers and a nourishing meal. By now he's most likely asleep.'

'Life had been hard for him of late,' Rianna confessed.

'We heard he was captured by Lord Sarin's troops after his rebellion failed. I was surprised to discover he was still alive. We have heard much of Lord Sarin's cruelty and excesses. It is said that he keeps both male and female slaves to pander to his strange desires. Marriage to such a man could not have been easy. If you ever feel the need to talk, I will be happy to listen.'

'Some time, perhaps.' Rianna felt a need to unburden her soul. If Danara learnt more about what Sarin had done to her and Tarn, she might be more sympathetic to their plight. She intended to ask Danara to grant them

231

safe passage through Freygard, when the time was right. 'Not tonight. The pain is too fresh in my mind.'

'I understand,' Danara said gently, as she fastened Rianna's hair at the nape of her neck with a thin ribbon.

'I'm weary. I should rest now,' Rianna said sleepily.

'First, I have a gift for you.' Danara took a small wooden box from the bedside table and handed it to Rianna. 'All our warriors are given these when they reach maturity.'

Curiously, Rianna lifted the lid of the box. Initially she thought the pair of exquisitely wrought silver clamps with dangling chains, tipped by tear-shaped sapphires, were meant to be worn on her ears. She looked up at Danara, who smiled and pushed aside the front of her robe to reveal one perfect breast. Her nipple was teased into a firm peak. Attached to the tiny cone was a similar silver clamp, the chains tipped by sparkling pink stones.

'I never imagined . . .' Rianna murmured, wondering what it would feel like to have her nipples constantly compressed by the snug clamps.

'These are only worn in private, when we are with those closest to us,' Danara explained. 'Here,' she said as she picked up one of the clamps. 'Let me fit it for you. Kitara had some almost exactly like these on her six-teenth birthday.'

She pushed the towel away from Rianna's breasts and teased one pert, rosy nipple between her finger and thumb until it hardened. Danara carefully attached the clamp, then turned to do the same to Rianna's other nipple.

'It feels strange.' The pinching caress of the clamps imprisoning her nipples caused a warmth to dart through Rianna's breasts. Her cheeks flushed and her breathing quickened as she looked down at her decorated teats.

'They look so pretty,' Danara said in a low, husky voice. 'You're beautiful, Rianna. So like my beloved Kitara.'

'What do you want of me?' Rianna asked breathlessly

as Danara gently pulled down her towel. Danara's eyes roved the soft curve of Rianna's belly and the denuded mound of her sex.

'What every other warrior would want if they saw you like this,' Danara purred hungrily. 'To give you pleasure. To show you what sweet bliss life here has to offer you.'

'I know what it's like to lie with a woman,' Rianna confessed as Danara's hands glided tenderly over each curve and hollow of her body, setting her nerve endings on fire. Rianna did not have the strength to resist this gentle seduction. Curiosity about her heritage drove her onwards. Perhaps the need for this was in her blood?

'Maybe so, but you've never been pleasured by one of your sisterhood.' Danara touched Rianna's naked sex. 'Without its fleece your pudenda looks so innocent, the pretty pouting lips so very tempting.'

'Sometimes one of the concubines would join Sarin and I in bed. My husband liked to watch us pleasuring each other. When he became sufficiently aroused, he would pull us apart and insist we pleasure him instead.'

'How cruel,' said Danara in disgust. 'I cannot imagine how terrible it must have been to be forced to pleasure a man, and to submit to all his vile demands on your flesh.' She shivered. 'How you must have suffered. Now lie back, relax. Let me show you what bliss we can share.'

'But, Danara,' Rianna protested.

'Hush, my sweet,' Danara said, as she tugged at the cluster of chains attached to one of Rianna's nipples. The pulling sensation caused a responsive tug deep in the pit of Rianna's belly.

'So tight,' Rianna gasped.

Danara pushed her back on to the pillows. 'My only desire is to please you,' she murmured. Her fingers stroked the sensitive skin of Rianna's inner thigh, then drifted higher to brush the swollen lips of her vulva. 'See how eagerly your body welcomes me.'

She squeezed one of Rianna's breasts, close to the nipple, increasing the pressure on the imprisoned teat.

The aching bliss magnified the moist heat between Rianna's thighs. Then Danara slipped her fingers between Rianna's labial lips and tenderly stroked the damp cleft. 'Is that not better?' she whispered.

'Yes,' Rianna groaned, as Danara leant forward to pull an imprisoned nipple into her mouth.

She sucked hard, drawing the soft flesh deeper, increasing the pulling and pinching sensations until Rianna whimpered. The sweetly tearing agony was sending her wild with lust. Her sex felt molten, like liquid fire. She lifted her hips as Danara stroked and teased the root of her pleasure bud. Grasping it between her fingers, Danara eased the tiny hood backwards and forwards, putting constant friction on the sensitive pearl beneath. By now Rianna was desperately craving her release.

'Danara,' she murmured, restlessly moving her hips.

'My sweet.' Danara slid her bunched fingers into Rianna's vagina to caress the silken walls. As she increased the pace and depth of her thrusts, she sucked on Rianna's breast and rubbed her pleasure bud with the pad of her thumb.

Rianna's arousal began to peak as pain and pleasure merged into one. She closed her eyes, as an image of Tarn, naked and aroused, invaded her fevered mind. Now it was his lips and hands passionately caressing her flesh.

'Tarn,' she gasped, as the powerful climax washed over her.

Tarn awoke with a start as someone touched his arm. 'What?' he growled, jumping to his feet, pulling the sheet with him to cover his nakedness.

'I've brought you food.' The middle-aged man backed fearfully away from Tarn. 'Milk and honey cakes.'

'Milk?' Tarn queried with a grimace, as he glanced at the platter left beside his bed. 'That's for babes and small children.'

'Not here,' the man replied. 'We only have ale and wine on special occasions.'

'Where are my clothes?' Tarn asked. He'd slept well and felt surprisingly refreshed.

The man pointed to a blue tunic on a nearby chair. 'The mistress had them taken away to be washed. Eat, then I'll be back to take you to the stables.'

'I won't leave without my own clothes,' Tarn insisted. 'I can't travel in a garment like that.' The tunic appeared to be similar to the one the middle-aged man wore. His garment was sleeveless and barely reached his mid-thigh, revealing a pair of scrawny, hairy legs.

'Travel?' the man scoffed. 'You're not going anywhere. You're to work in the stables. The mistress says only light duties at present.' He looked Tarn up and down, noting the handsome features, the perfect physique. 'Though I doubt you'll have to work there for long. The mistress has yet to see you. When she does she'll probably insist you spend most of your days and nights in this chamber.'

'I prefer not to spend all my time in the guest quarters.' Tarn glanced around the room. It was comfortable enough, but he'd rather work for his keep than laze around here.

The man gave a harsh laugh. 'Guest quarters,' he repeated mockingly. 'This is a coupling chamber, stranger. You're no guest, you're a slave just like all the other men in Freygard.'

'You're mistaken,' Tarn insisted. 'Queen Danara herself granted us sanctuary. We'll soon be on our way again.' Even as Tarn spoke he had the uneasy feeling the man might be right. Tarn hadn't trusted the Queen from the moment he'd laid eyes on her.

'Think what you like,' the man replied. 'You'll learn the truth soon enough. You're not the first stranger to stray over the border by mistake and find himself enslaved. I'll be back in a moment,' he added, stepping over to the door. 'I was told to bring the largest tunic we had. But the mistress didn't know the size of your feet.'

235

He stepped outside and shut the heavy wood door. As Tarn heard the bolt slide into place, he strode over to the window and pulled open the shutters, only to be faced with a thick metal grille. Anxiously, he wondered if Rianna was in a similar position. He could only hope that because of her heritage she at least would be safe.

Tarn grinned wryly. So they thought to make him a stud, constantly coupling to help breed children. He supposed some men might enjoy such a fate, but he wanted only two things, his freedom and Rianna. He intended to have both. Tarn had endured enough enforced sexual pleasure to last him a lifetime.

Deciding there was no point in starving, he hungrily consumed the honey cakes, and drank the milk, finding it more palatable than he'd expected. He was prowling the room restlessly, when the door opened again.

'Aren't you dressed yet?' the woman snapped, throwing a pair of sandals at his feet. Her lean, rather gaunt figure was accentuated by her tight-fitting leather trousers and snug leather jerkin.

'You're the mistress, I presume?' Tarn looked her up and down in the same derisive way that she'd just examined him. 'The woman in charge of the male slaves?'

'I am,' she confirmed, her mouth set in a grim line. 'You've yet to learn respect, slave.'

'Others have tried to subjugate me, but not succeeded,' Tarn responded confidently. 'I doubt you'll have any more success.'

'Bold words for a mere man,' she sneered scathingly, as she tapped the thin cane she carried on the palm of her gloved hand. 'Now dress,' she paused and smiled coldly. 'Or do I have to bring some slaves in here to do it for you?'

'I'll do as you ask, for the moment.' Tarn smiled, which only served to irritate her more.

'Hurry,' she snapped, stepping forward to slap the cane against his bare arm.

Tarn picked up the tunic with a derisory grimace. He

pulled it on over his head, making sure he was adequately covered before he removed the sheet from his waist. The tunic wasn't Tarn's idea of proper clothing. He had worn less as Sarin's slave most of the time, but this felt different. Now his sex hung loose under the ill-fitting tunic, making him feel acutely vulnerable. Because of his height, the tunic was very short. If he bent too far in any direction his manhood would be exposed. Swiftly, he pushed his feet into the sandals, then stared challengingly at the mistress.

'Follow me,' she said curtly.

She strode from the room, with Tarn following close behind. Through an open doorway at the end of the short passage, he saw the slaves' quarters, a long barrack room with pallets ranged along each side. They didn't go that way, but left the building by the entrance he'd used last night, and walked across the bailey. As far as Tarn could see, there were still only a few warriors guarding the walls. But he did notice a number of men in blue tunics similar to his. Most of them looked cowed and pathetic, barely men at all.

The stables were large and airy, filled with many splendid horses. His and Rianna's mounts were housed in two stalls side by side. One man was moving bales of hay in a corner, but there was no one else around.

'You know how to care for horses?' the mistress asked.

'Of course, I'm a warrior,' Tarn replied.

'You're a warrior no longer, just a slave,' she said irritably. 'The sooner you accept that the better. You may tend the horses. Ensure they are fed and groomed. I'll inspect your work later. If it's acceptable, you'll eat tonight.' She paused and stared at him sternly. 'Remember, don't leave the stables without permission.'

She turned and strode away, Tarn staring at her retreating figure in surprise. He'd expected to have someone watching his every move. The warriors apparently felt no need to guard their slaves too closely. Centuries of oppression must have completely subjugated the men of Freygard.

Tarn knew that he needed to know more about the layout of the castle, and discover where Rianna was before he formed any plan of escape. For the present, he must appear compliant. He was just tending to the needs of a large black stallion, who appeared far more highly strung than the other animals, when he realised that he was being watched by a number of female warriors who had just entered the stables.

'So you're the new slave,' a tall, pretty brunette said, as she moved towards Tarn. He ignored her as he stepped away from the stallion's stall. 'You reply when I address you,' she ordered. She strode forward and slapped his shoulder with the leather crop she carried.

'I've only recently arrived here,' he said condescendingly.

'This one is bolder than the other slaves,' a woman with copper-coloured hair said, appearing amused. 'And far more handsome.' She looked Tarn up and down. 'Very well favoured. Take off your tunic, slave.'

Tarn stared at her coldly. 'No, I prefer to remain clothed,' he said stubbornly. There were six women, all heavily armed. Too many for him to handle with ease. 'Now please excuse me,' he added. 'I have work to do.'

As he went to move, the brunette stepped in front of him, barring his way. 'When you're told to do something by a woman, you do it without question.'

'Not where I come from,' he said challengingly.

'I am due to visit the coupling chambers,' the copper-haired vixen said, with a soft laugh. 'I'm going to tell the slave mistress I want him. This slave is bold and arrogant, his seed will produce fine daughters.'

'Why wait, Zene?' asked the brunette, glancing back at her companions. 'Let's try him out now and see how bold he truly is.' She pulled her dagger from her belt and went to cut the shoulder laces of Tarn's tunic.

'I think not.' He grabbed hold of her wrist and twisted the dagger from her grasp.

'Damn you!' She reddened in fearful embarrassment.

'Damn yourself,' he replied with a defiant grin. 'I'll not strip for your pleasure.'

Tarn turned, pulling her with him, to confront the others, holding the dagger loosely in his hand. Unfortunately, the copper-haired Zene was swift on her feet and she managed to dart behind him. He froze as he felt the point of her sword dig threateningly into the small of his back.

'Drop the dagger. I don't want to kill you, slave,' she said with soft menace. 'I can think of far better punishments.'

As Tarn reluctantly dropped the dagger, the point of the sword moved lower, lifting his tunic to slide menacingly between his legs until it touched the exposed sac of his scrotum. He took an unsteady breath and let go of the brunette. She picked up her dagger and moved angrily away from him.

'On your knees if you don't want to lose your manhood,' Zene ordered.

Tarn nodded. As the sword point moved away from his sex, he sank to his knees. Zene moved closer and grabbed hold of his hair, pulling his head first to one side then the other, so that she could slice through the shoulder laces of his tunic. The blue linen slid downwards to pool around his knees.

'You've chosen well,' one of the women commented, as they feasted their eyes on his broad, muscular chest, flat belly and generous sex. 'I've never seen such a specimen. His seed will be of the finest quality.'

They pushed him forwards on to the trampled straw, while the tunic was pulled from his legs. A hot excitement formed in the pit of Tarn's stomach, a mixture of fearful lust, tinged with sweet helplessness – much like the emotion Sarin always managed to arouse in him.

'That's for your disobedience.'

A sharp, stinging pain seared Tarn's buttocks. The second blow caught the side of his hip as he rolled swiftly over. Before he could spring to his feet and defend himself, hands caught hold of his wrists and ankles. They were surprisingly strong for women and, despite his best efforts, he was pinned spread-eagled on the prickly straw.

Zene stared down at him with lustful dark eyes as she unbuckled her leather skirt. She wore only a thin scrap of dark fabric between her legs to cover her intimate parts. Jerking it away, she stood over him. Tarn stared at her dark, coppery fleece and the thin red line of her sex. A dull heat flooded his groin and his cock began to harden. Tarn could smell the sweet herbal scent of his oppressors, feel their warm breath on his flesh as they leant over him. He wanted to fight, to resist them, but there was a lustful ache building in his loins, an eagerness that could not be denied. Despite everything, part of him now craved the excitement of enforced sexual submission. Sarin had trained him far too well.

'His manhood is huge,' gasped the brunette. She leant forward to examine his sex more closely, pinning his arm down with the weight of her knee. Her hair tantalisingly brushed his chest and the sensitive skin of his armpits.

Zene smiled and crouched down between Tarn's outstretched thighs. 'It will grow even larger,' she said huskily. She ran her fingers slowly along the shaft, watching it twitch and stiffen even more. 'The touch of hands and lips arouses them just as it does us,' she laughed. 'Do you suppose they pleasure each other, like we do?'

'Do you?' the brunette asked Tarn as she stroked his muscular chest, pausing briefly to rub and squeeze his nipples.

Tarn didn't deign to answer, yet the memories of Sarin's erotic attentions caused two spots of high colour to stain his cheeks.

'It appears they do.' Zene curved her fingers around the stem of Tarn's penis and pumped it crudely. Then she pinched the loose skin of the head of his cock until she saw the bead of clear liquid seep from the tiny slitted mouth. 'The seed,' she said, working the loose skin backwards until the engorged plum was fully exposed.

Tarn groaned and tried to pull away from them. The women determinedly held him down as he bucked and writhed beneath them. 'Let me be,' he begged.

'So he begs at last,' the brunette mocked. 'Stop fighting us, or you'll feel the cruel sting of the lash,' she added menacingly. Tarn gave up the struggle and lay limply on the straw-covered ground.

'Don't you want to couple with Zene, slave?' another teased, tugging at the soft hair in his armpits.

'Zene wants your seed,' the woman holding his left leg said as she stared hungrily at Tarn's rampant cock. 'But she's scared because your manhood is so large.'

'I'm not scared,' Zene scoffed. Kneeling, she straddled Tarn's hips. 'I'll have him right now.'

Cautiously, she lowered herself until the tip of his glans was pressing against the entrance to her feminine sheath, then she paused. Tarn, grunting with the effort, jerked his hips upwards with all his strength, desperate to savour the soft heat of her pudenda. His cock invaded the soft, moist opening, sliding near halfway into her vagina.

Startled by his temerity, Zene stared wide-eyed at Tarn. Then, biting her lip with concentration, she delicately sheathed herself on the entire length of his iron-hard rod. The tightness of her vagina embracing his engorged flesh was infinitely pleasurable, yet it still managed to stretch enough to fully accommodate his entire shaft. He felt the head of his cock press against her womb as he pierced her completely.

'Now ride him like a stallion,' the brunette urged.

Digging her fingers into Tarn's hips, Zene began to pump herself up and down on his shaft. Her internal muscles tightened even more as she lifted her body and thrust down again. The different sensations were maddening. Tarn could smell the scent of his oppressors' desire, feel their strong hands holding him down. Zene's suede boots rubbed against his outer thighs, while her vaginal muscles vigorously embraced his cock.

She ground her vulva down against his pelvis, her face taut with concentration, her breath coming in laboured gasps. Tarn's lustful desires were beyond redemption. He revelled in the sensation of helplessness as Zene worked herself up and down on his straining member.

Zene's pleasure peaked swiftly. As the climax washed over her, Tarn felt her internal muscles pulse rhythmically. What little control he had deserted him. He gave a hoarse gasp as his orgasm overwhelmed him and his seed jetted deep inside her.

The strength of her own response appeared to take Zene by surprise and she fell limply forward across Tarn's chest. Lifting his head, Tarn took possession of her lips, thrusting his tongue deep into her mouth. She returned the kiss with a greedy passion that astounded him. Suddenly realising that she had totally lost control of her senses, Zene pulled away from Tarn and sat up, her cheeks flushed with embarrassment.

'Zene?' the brunette said in confusion, appearing quite overcome herself. 'What happened?'

'I don't know.' Zene's legs trembled as she moved away from Tarn and knelt on the straw-covered floor. 'I never knew one could feel like that when coupling with a man,' she muttered, picking up her leather skirt.

'What is going on here?' a harsh voice asked. The women moved nervously away from Tarn as the slave mistress angrily approached. She looked down at Tarn, her face contorted in disgust. 'Get up, slave, and cover yourself.'

Tarn rose shakily to his knees, grabbed his discarded tunic and held it protectively in front of his sex. He struggled to his feet, hearing the slave mistress harshly berate the women. It soon became clear that unauthorised coupling between warrior and slave was not allowed. He brushed the straw from his skin and hair, then draped the tunic around his waist, certain that he was next in line for the slave mistress's wrath.

'You!' She turned as the warriors slunk guiltily away. 'I knew that bringing an outsider here would cause trouble. If you wish to survive, you'd better learn to become far more submissive, slave.' She grabbed hold of Tarn's arm. 'Come with me. I have orders to keep you under lock and key until further notice.'

# Chapter Twelve

$S$arin turned to look at his companions as they reined in their horses beside his. 'Do you think we've lost their trail?' he asked Cador and Gerek.

'Surely they cannot be far ahead,' Gerek replied, glancing back at the weary troop of soldiers accompanying them. 'Rianna may be well used to riding but she's still a woman.'

'She doesn't appear to be slowing Tarn down,' Cador pointed out frustratedly.

They had discovered that Tarn and Rianna stopped yesterday morning, in a small village twenty leagues from there, to purchase extra feed for their horses. Their trail had been all too clear at first, but as they reached rougher, thickly-forested ground, their tracks became far less easy to follow.

'Why did they come this way?' Sarin looked at the dense forests and high mountain peaks in the distance. 'We must be close to the border of Freygard.'

'Perhaps they came this way because Rianna intends to seek help from her kinsfolk,' Cador suggested, drawing his cloak tighter around him. The weather was turning steadily colder.

'How can she do so, when she is Tarn's prisoner?' Gerek said irritably. On a number of occasions Cador had insinuated that Rianna was no hostage, and was in some way aiding Tarn's escape.

'I understand you've no wish to believe ill of your daughter,' Cador replied. 'But it's obvious that Tarn could never have travelled so far, and so swiftly, burdened with a reluctant female prisoner. Everyone we've spoken to said that Rianna looked well and quite happy in his company. How so, Protector?'

Gerek grunted crossly and turned away from Cador. 'Until it's proved otherwise, Sarin, I intend to go on believing in my daughter. Rianna would never take her marriage vow so lightly.'

'She never gave me any cause to believe she would help Tarn,' Sarin faltered, frowning thoughtfully.

'Doesn't pleading for Tarn's life count?' Cador said harshly. 'You know she lied to you about her mother being Tarn's kinswoman, Sarin. And she displayed great sympathy for his plight.'

'I've had more than enough, Cador.' Gerek drew his sword. 'I'm prepared to defend my daughter's honour.'

'Wait!' Sarin held up his hand. 'This has gone on long enough. When we catch up with them, we'll discover the truth. Until then you keep your opinions to yourself, Cador.'

'My lord,' the captain of the troop interjected. 'One of the soldiers we sent ahead is returning.'

The soldier galloped up to them and pulled his mount to a halt. 'Any sign of the fugitive?' asked Sarin

'They camped close by last night, my lord,' the soldier replied breathlessly. 'But there are signs of more than two horses. At least seven or eight.' He glanced back from whence he had come. 'My companions thought they spotted a lone rider and set off in pursuit.'

Sarin's mount stamped its feet restlessly. He moved it forward a few paces, in order to calm it a little, just as the other two soldiers came in sight, accompanied by another rider. 'Let us hope they have some positive news,' he muttered.

Gerek tensed as the soldiers came closer. 'I rather

think we've miscalculated our position, Sarin,' he said anxiously, as he stared at the woman the soldiers had apprehended. 'I wager we are already in Freygard.'

'You obviously have some knowledge of this race, because of your late wife,' Sarin said, seeming unconcerned by the news. 'We'll ask for their aid in tracking the fugitive,' he added, disregarding all cautionary tales about not venturing into Freygard uninvited. 'They are your daughter's kinswomen, they are bound to want to help us capture her kidnapper.'

'Danara, I'm not staying here another moment,' Rianna said as the Queen entered her chamber. 'I insist on seeing Tarn.'

'All in good time,' Danara said, with an understanding smile. 'Calm yourself, my sweet. There are good reasons why I've issued orders confining you to your room, just as I've ordered that Tarn be confined in the men's quarters.'

'What good reason can there be?' Rianna pressed irritably. 'I ask for your help, then find myself a prisoner. I expected to see you hours ago.' She went a little pink, then whispered, 'Especially after what happened last night.'

'I've been busy.' Danara put an arm around her and kissed her cheek. 'I received some troubling information. I've been sending messages to the surrounding villages, calling my warriors here to the castle. I intend to be prepared for all eventualities.' She led Rianna to the bed and sat her down. Twining an arm around her she gently stroked her breasts.

'What eventualities?' Rianna asked, trying to remain unmoved by Danara's intimate attentions. Last night she'd succumbed out of curiosity as well as lust, but now all she felt was an uneasy sense of guilt.

'We're expecting company. A large troop of soldiers led by Lord Sarin have been spotted in the area. They're fast approaching the castle. It appears your deserted husband wants you back, Rianna.'

'No, he wants Tarn more than I,' Rianna replied anxiously. 'You must not surrender Tarn to them. Please, Danara, I'll do anything if you'll help.'

'Anything?' Danara said huskily.

'Anything,' Rianna confirmed. 'But you must know that my heart belongs to none but Tarn.'

Danara pursed her lips. 'You called out his name in the midst of your pleasure last night. In a way I felt betrayed. Nevertheless, in time I am sure your feelings will change.'

Rianna felt uneasy as she heard Danara's words. 'So you'll help us?' she pressed.

'Our sisterhood safeguards its own. I cannot refuse you protection. And while you remain here with me, I'll also give shelter to Tarn. He will not be handed over to face Sarin's bleak justice. Tarn is part of our community now, just as you are,' she said reassuringly. 'So do not look so concerned.'

'But Sarin might attack the castle.'

'Not if he thinks you gone,' Danara smiled confidently. 'I'll open my gates to him. Offer him and his men food and a warm bed for the night. I intend to tell him that you passed by the castle early this morning.'

'You think he'll be deceived?'

'Lord Sarin has no reason to mistrust me.' She took Rianna's face between her hands. 'Now that I've found you, Rianna, I intend to keep you safe.'

The fervent desire in Danara's eyes was immensely troubling, but at present Rianna was more fearful of Sarin. Once she was sure Lord Sarin and his soldiers were far from here, she and Tarn could plan their escape from this castle.

'Very impressive,' Sarin whispered to Gerek as they entered the great hall of the castle. 'I didn't expect such luxury, and such an obvious display of wealth.'

Gerek was unimpressed by the show of wealth. His only concern was the large number of warriors ranged along the side of the large chamber. Most of them were young and attractive, but also very fit-looking and well-armed. Gerek knew just how brave the women of Freygard could be in battle. He felt uneasy with this obvious show of hospitality. Strangers were usually not welcome in Freygard, even those of royal blood.

'Women dressed as warriors and armed to the teeth make me uncomfortable,' Cador muttered. 'So do those male slaves,' he added, staring at the men laying the table at one end of the hall. 'I cannot believe that every man in Freygard is a slave.'

'Believe it,' Gerek said in a low voice. 'That's why this charade troubles me so much. They have little or no respect for men,' he added.

Unconsciously, he found himself looking at all the female faces, seeking some likeness to Kitara. He knew she had sisters and cousins, but he had no idea of their positions or names. The loss of her was made even more poignant in these surroundings.

'Lord Sarin,' said a female voice. 'I bid you and your companions welcome.' They turned to see a tall, elegant woman approach them, dressed in regal purple, a gold circlet on her brow.

'Queen Danara,' Sarin bowed politely. 'I thank you for agreeing to see us.'

'The pleasure is mine, Lord Sarin.' She smiled but her eyes were cold, like emerald chips.

'May I introduce my companions,' Sarin said swiftly. 'Cador, a nobleman of Kabra.' Then he turned with a flourish. 'And of course, Gerek, Protector of Harn.'

Danara appeared taken aback for a moment, before she recovered herself. 'I've heard much of you, Protector.'

'And I you, Queen Danara.' Gerek was certain Danara was a close relative of Kitara. There was a strong family resemblance, even down to the colour of the eyes and hair. He bowed, then placed his hand on his heart, an ancient Freygardian custom he'd learnt from Kitara.

She appeared to appreciate the gesture. 'You pay honour to our heritage, Protector.' Once again she smiled, still with little genuine feeling. 'I can begin to see why our sister Kitara decided to remain by your side.'

'I was blessed with her affection, but she never forgot Freygard. Unfortunately at that time no strangers were welcome in your land. It saddened her that we could not visit the land of her birth,' Gerek said in all seriousness. 'To be truthful, I am surprised that you welcome us now, I believed that the borders of Freygard were still closed to outsiders.'

'Lord Sarin is a powerful monarch. Now that you and he are allies, you would prove to be formidable opponents,' she replied. 'It seemed prudent to discover why you ventured into our lands without prior warning, before we displayed any show of force.'

'You must excuse the oversight, Queen Danara,' Sarin interjected. 'I should have sent a messenger to seek your permission before entering Freygard. We became over-zealous in our pursuit of a fugitive and crossed the border without thinking,' he explained.

'Fugitive?' she enquired innocently.

'The man who led the rebellion in Kabra.' Sarin's face was wracked by concern. 'The swine kidnapped my wife, Lady Rianna, your kinswoman.'

'Kitara's daughter?' Danara appeared surprised. 'If only we had known about this, we could have aided you earlier. I presume this man still holds your lady captive?'

'Sadly, he does,' Sarin sighed. 'I'm greatly concerned for her well-being.'

Gerek was painfully aware that Sarin's display of feeling was purely for Danara's benefit. Sarin hated the thought that Tarn had taken Rianna, but he had shown little genuine concern for his wife's welfare. He seemed to consider her a possession and little else. After what Jenna had told him about Sarin, Gerek was deeply troubled. Once Rianna was safely recovered he intended to insist on taking her back to Harn for a time.

'Permit me.' Danara beckoned to one of her warriors, a brawny, rather masculine-looking woman. She stepped over to the Queen and they exchanged a few private words. As the woman departed, accompanied by a number of warriors, Danara turned back to Sarin and Gerek. 'I'm told that two riders were seen passing close to the castle yesterday morning. I've sent some of my best warriors to track them down. My people know the countryside, they are bound to be more successful than your soldiers.'

'I hope they are. I'm obliged to you, Queen Danara,' Sarin said gratefully. 'How can we thank you?'

'By dining with me this evening.' She pointed to the table now laden with steaming, delicious-smelling dishes. 'We can share a pleasant meal, while your chambers are prepared. Tonight you will sleep on a soft bed instead of the hard ground.'

Gerek was woken by a sudden stinging pain in his left thigh, to find his bedchamber illuminated by the soft light of many candles. At the same moment his mind was assailed by a multitude of sensations. The pain in his thigh had diminished, but his skin was chilled by the lack of bedclothes. He lay naked on his bed, his hands tied behind his back and a restrictive tightness around his neck.

'So you're awake.' The woman's voice was husky, low-pitched and sounded a little strained.

Gerek experienced a sudden rush of fear. Queen Danara had betrayed their trust and he was a prisoner. He didn't bother to reason why; his only concern was the second stinging pain as something hit his stomach. It felt like a hundred tiny pins pricking his flesh.

Lifting his head, as far as the stiff leather collar would allow, he looked to his left. The chain attached to the collar was fixed to the bedpost. Then his eyes alighted on the woman. She wore the most provocative outfit he'd ever seen, and he felt an immediate lustful desire for his captor.

A tight, black leather corset encased her shapely torso. The top was gently cupped to support her full, naked breasts. The creamy globes were tipped by prominent rusty brown nipples and silver clamps imprisoned her delectable teats. The clamps were decorated by fine silver chains, tipped with diamonds, which swayed tantalisingly as she moved. His gaze slid downwards to where the corset curved at the base of her belly in order to best display her thick, auburn fleece. A skirt of silver chains looped away at the front, bringing even more emphasis to her exposed sex.

Gerek wanted to see her face, but only her lush red lips were visible. The rest was covered by an elaborate silver mask. Her eyes glittered through the almond-shaped slits as she swung the small whip she carried against the side of her shapely thigh. The leather strands of the whip were tipped by small silver beads, and he remembered the cruel pain they'd inflicted on his flesh.

'Who are you? What do you want of me?' Gerek said harshly. He was aroused by the sheer sight of her. Blood surged into his loins and his penis twitched excitedly.

'I am your Mistress, slave,' she said coldly. 'I'm here to punish you for your misdeeds.'

'What misdeeds?' Gerek croaked, attempting to move in order to ease the pressure of his body weight on his bound hands.

'Your crimes against women.' She stepped forward and pushed him back down as he strained to sit up. 'Only here in Freygard have men found their rightful place in the order of things.'

She trailed the strands of the whip over his sex, then flicked them teasingly against his balls. Gerek winced with discomfort, but the caressing agony was also arousing. He felt nervous sweat pool in his armpits and between his thighs. Never had he felt more helpless, or more vulnerable.

'You cannot restrain me like this. I am the Protector of Harn,' he protested.

'In this room you are nothing more than my slave,' she said in a soft menacing voice. 'If you please me, I'll reward you. If you don't, you'll be punished.' She flicked the ends of the whip across the tender skin of his lower stomach. The stinging agony made his flesh tremble. 'Does pain arouse you, Gerek?'

'No,' he growled as the lash stung his thighs, only just missing his sex.

'Are you sure?'

She ran the metal-tipped strands slowly across his penis. Then, with a flick of her wrist, she stroked the soft skin of his scrotum with the fiery filaments. Gerek drew in his breath as the pricking pain caught the side of his member, and curved in a sharp caress over the skin protecting the head of his cock. The discomfort was becoming more and more pleasurable. When the lash caught his thighs again, he pressed them tightly together, but that only served to bring his sex into greater prominence.

'You seem aroused,' she said softly, as she ran the tip of her finger over his reddened, tender flesh. 'You want more, don't you Gerek?'

'No,' he groaned, powerless to resist whatever she cared to do to him.

She climbed on to the bed and sat astride his thighs. He felt the soft curls of her pubis rub enticingly against his bare legs. By the gods, he wanted her so much. She ran her tongue over her full lower lip, then lifted her hand to tug teasingly at the left nipple clamps. Gerek longed to pull one of those imprisoned teats into his mouth and suck on it hard.

'How does it feel to know you're a prisoner?' she mocked. 'You fear me, don't you, slave?'

'I fear no one,' he grated, feeling her fingers gently stroke the soft skin of his scrotum.

She touched his penis, gauging its stiffness. 'Not very impressive,' she said with derision. 'You're barely hard.' Gripping the stem, she pumped it crudely. 'I want proof of your virility, slave.'

Gerek could not repress a groan as she roughly pulled back the collar of skin to expose the taut purple bulb hidden beneath. She dragged the metal ends of the whip slowly over the exposed head, gently tapping the sensitive tip. 'Please,' Gerek begged, fearing she might hit it harder.

'Address me as mistress.' Her eyes glittered cruelly behind the silver mask.

'You're not my mistress,' he replied with obstinate determination, readying himself to endure unimaginable pain.

'You're too proud and stubborn for a slave,' she said coldly.

His tormentor moved to sit astride his hips, pressing the slit of her sex against his stomach. Gerek drew in his breath as the tip of his engorged penis pressed against her firm buttocks, while the heavy weight of her chained skirt fell across his sex. Grabbing hold of his shoulders, she pulled him upright so swiftly that the chain holding him stretched taut and the leather collar cut into his neck. At his strangled gasp, she released the pressure enough to let him draw breath.

'The collar is uncomfortable, isn't it?' she mocked, pushing her body closer to his. At that moment Gerek bent his head, heedless of the leather biting into his throat, and grabbed hold of the hanging chains of the nipple clamp with his teeth. He pulled the clamp away from her nipple with a rough jerk, and spat the object from his mouth. Her moan of discomfort was stifled by a gasp of surprise, as Gerek locked his lips around the abused teat. Sucking hard he pulled it deep into his mouth.

'Greedy and disobedient,' she murmured, as he sucked and licked her breast. She slid her arms around him and pressed herself closer as he pulled more of her soft flesh into his mouth.

She was flushed and breathing heavily by the time she pulled away from him. Gerek smiled, watching with perverse satisfaction as she eased her body backward. When she crouched over his sex, he could see the soft sheen of moisture now coating her labial lips.

'Is my cock hard enough for you now?' he asked

boldly as she curved her hand around the base of his penis, gauging his readiness.

'No, not quite!' Picking up the nipple clamp, she fastened it around one of his brown teats. Gerek winced as it bit into the sensitive nubbin, but he found the pressure arousing. 'Now it should be,' she added, pushing him back against the pillows.

She lowered herself until she was fully transfixed by his rigid flesh. Gerek suppressed a groan of pleasure as she ground her vulva against his pelvis. The hot tightness of her vagina was exquisite. Her inner muscles firmly gripped his shaft as she began to move herself up and down on his cock, intent only on her own release.

With cruel deliberation, she rode Gerek hard and fast. With each vigorous thrust, Gerek's bound hands dug uncomfortably into the small of his back, but that only served to increase his arousal. As her pleasure mounted, she arched her body and threw her head back, exposing her pale throat.

The myriad of conflicting sensations were drawing Gerek towards lustful fulfilment. He heard her give a faint gasp as her vagina pulsed and her inner muscles contracted around his shaft. Gerek's helpless desire began to peak, drawing him deep into the dark whirlpool of passion as the rippling bliss consumed him.

She fell forward, half supporting herself with her arms, and she took a deep, gasping breath. Her limbs were still trembling in the aftermath of her violent climax as she looked down at Gerek.

He smiled. 'Did I please you, mistress?' he asked in voice laced with sarcasm.

'Your behaviour does not wholly please me. You're way too bold, way too defiant.' To his surprise, she pressed her lips to his for a brief, almost affectionate, kiss. 'Far too bold,' she said tenderly. Swiftly she recovered her composure. Pulling the clamp from his nipple, she tossed it aside. 'Now you can cleanse me,' she said curtly, moving forward so that her damp pudenda was just above his face. 'Lick it clean.'

Gerek could smell the musky scent of her sex, mixed with the lusty odour of his own semen. 'No, I will not,' he said angrily. He could see the moist secretions coating her vulva, and he was so very tempted to do as she ordered. But her demands made him feel abused and degraded.

She lowered her body until her open sex was only a hair's-breadth from Gerek's face. Lustful desire consumed him. He felt humiliated, yet aroused. He began to appreciate how it must feel to be a slave. The overwhelming sensation of submissive need was far too powerful to ignore.

He began to lap at her moist sex, savouring the mingling essence of their desires. It acted on his senses, like strong wine. He became drunk with passion as his head spun. Despite his determination not be subjugated, he revelled in the sensations of vulnerability and helplessness she aroused in him. Tenderly twining his tongue around her hot little pleasure bud, he teased it until he felt it stiffen and harden into a perfect pink pearl. She lowered her body just a fraction, so that he could imprison the bud with his lips and draw it deeper into his mouth. Her sex was hot, the pearl throbbing. Grabbing hold of his shoulders, she pressed her soaking vulva to his face. He felt her flesh pulse against his mouth and she shivered as her release came in a sudden rush of unexpected pleasure.

She pulled away from him and crouched on the bed, staring at him through the impenetrable barrier of her silver mask. Very cautiously, she touched his cheek, running her fingers over the hard planes of his face. Gerek was filled with a sudden, quite unexpected sensation. A feeling of knowing, intimacy, oneness that he'd not experienced for a very long time. He took a deep, troubled breath as it grew in strength.

'You did not follow orders, slave,' her voice shook as she spoke.

'Did I not?' he challenged. 'You wanted me to pleasure

you, that was obvious. Yet you would have me believe you hate all men.'

'I do,' she said with vicious fury. 'They are ruled by their basest instincts. They care for no one but themselves. They take what they want and then throw you aside. Only here, in Freygard, are they properly controlled.'

'I fear you were hurt badly by someone,' Gerek said gently, trying to disregard the strange feelings that would not go away. This woman reminded him so strongly of Kitara, it was frightening.

'Their affections do not withstand the test of time. Love and sex are the same to them. Unlike women, they are incapable of deep feeling,' she sneered.

'Not all men are like that,' he protested. 'You see only two kinds. Your slaves, and brutal strangers who prowl the borders of your land. You're wrong, mistress, so very wrong.'

Gerek couldn't understand why he felt the need to convince her she was mistaken. He doubted it would make any difference to her attitude towards him. He knew he was at present her captive, but he did not fear slavery. His people would offer a generous ransom for his safe return and Queen Danara was bound to accept the offer. She was well aware her army could never resist the combined might of Percheron and Harn.

'You lie, Gerek, just as you always have.' The timbre of her voice had changed. Gerek knew what he was hearing, yet he still did not wholly believe it. The pain squeezed his heart and he shook with the strength of his emotion.

'Who are you?' he asked haltingly. 'Kitara's sister? Cousin? You sound so like her, feel so like her.' She stared at him, saying nothing. 'Tell me, I must know,' he pleaded. 'I've suffered so much anguish, so much pain,' he faltered, closing his eyes and swallowing hard. 'I sometimes wish . . . even though I know it impossible.'

'What do you wish, Gerek?' He opened his eyes as he

felt her unfasten the collar from his neck. 'Tell me,' she added as he struggled to sit up.

'I wish Kitara wasn't dead. That I could somehow bring her back.' His voice was wracked with anguish. 'After she was washed away in the flooded river, I searched for days, looking for her body. I needed to see her one last time, to say goodbye. But the gods did not even permit me that one small favour. Tell me who you are, how you come to be so like her?'

'Who exactly do you want me to be?' she asked gently.

Gerek sadly shook his head, staring at her in surprise as she began to unfasten his bonds. Gingerly he eased his stiff arms forward and rubbed his sore wrists. 'I want you to be Kitara,' he said pleadingly. 'But I know that's impossible.' He stared at her, trying to see behind the mask.

'Why not?' she asked. 'Why can't I be Kitara?'

'Because she's dead. My soldiers and I searched far and wide and never found her.' Tears spilled from his eyes and rolled down his cheeks. 'This is all in my imagination, some bizarre dream.' He touched the red lash marks on his thighs, and gave an uneasy laugh. 'But these still hurt, so I can't be dreaming. You look like her, smell like her, even feel like her. And you have her wild ways.'

'Gerek,' she said softly, as she tenderly kissed his lips.

'Are you real?'

'Yes.' She pulled off her mask, and he saw her beloved face once again. Feeling confused and totally bewildered, Gerek watched a lone tear slide slowly down her cheek. 'I'm told I was pulled from the river many miles downstream and cared for by peasants, but I have no memory of that time. A travelling warrior from Freygard came upon me and brought me home. When at last I did remember, I was led to believe that you'd deserted me, that you no longer wanted me as your wife. Many months had passed by then, and when you never came for me, I was forced to accept that what my sisters told me was true. Then I heard you were to remarry.'

'Remarry!' Gerek exclaimed. 'That was none of my doing. My advisors wanted me to marry again, but I rejected every woman they brought to me. All I wanted was you back, Kitara, but I thought you dead.' He held her face between his hands and looked deep into her eyes. 'I love you, Kitara, I always have.'

Gerek pulled her close, and kissed her with unrestrained passion. Gently, he eased the cruel clamp from her nipple and began to unlace the tight leather corset. As he drew it from her body, he tenderly stroked the livid red marks the restrictive garment left on her ivory skin.

'You are my life,' he murmured, kissing her again, wanting her forever imprinted on his mind.

They lay together, flesh to flesh. He pressed his hard shaft against the entrance to her soft sheath, and slid inside her, feeling a joy that knew no bounds. She twined her legs around his hips as he began to thrust into her, possessing her with such intensity that it left no doubt of his love for her. The scent of Kitara incited his senses; her beautiful flesh was made purely so that it could meld with his, and by doing so they could become as one. Now Gerek felt his life had purpose again.

Their pleasure peaked swiftly, as love and passion combined. Kitara's vagina contracted around his shaft and the rippling waves brought him to the ultimate peak of bliss. As Gerek's climax consumed him, he held Kitara close, never wanting to be parted from her again.

'Rianna,' Danara said, gently shaking Rianna awake. 'I've something to show you.'

Sleepily, Rianna rubbed her eyes. 'It's barely dawn,' she mumbled, climbing from the bed and shivering in the chill morning air.

'Here.' Danara wrapped a shawl around her shoulders and led her towards the window. 'You cannot miss this.'

Rianna felt incredibly weary. Last night, after Danara had entertained Lord Sarin and his men, she had come to Rianna's room and spent a long time talking to her.

Wanting to rid herself of the painful memories, Rianna had opened her heart to Danara. Everything had spilled from her mouth; the sensual demands Sarin had made on her flesh, the cruel ways he'd abused Tarn. Danara had appeared horrified, more by the way Sarin had treated Rianna than Tarn. She had promised Rianna she would have her revenge on Cador and Lord Sarin, although Rianna could not conceive how.

'Can you see which one he is?' Danara asked.

'Who do you mean?' Below her window was a wagon into which a number of number of slaves, chained hand and foot, were being loaded.

'Look closely at the brown-haired slave.' Danara smiled smugly.

'It is Cador!' Rianna gasped. She saw a frightened and confused Cador being pushed towards the wagon. When he tried to resist, he was beaten with a thin cane and bundled on to the floor of the wagon. 'Where are they taking him?' she asked, as the wagon moved slowly out of the gates.

'To a large town some distance from here, where a monthly slave auction is held. I've issued strict instructions. Cador is to be sold as a field hand. He will endure enforced hard labour for the rest of his miserable life.'

'What about the others?' Rianna asked. 'Lord Sarin and his soldiers?' She was still unaware that her father, Gerek, was also in the castle.

'I confess I couldn't resist taking hostage a number of the strongest and most well-favoured soldiers. They accompany Cador to the slave auction, although I think their fate will be kinder. Most will probably be purchased as coupling slaves. The rest of the soldiers left the castle some time before dawn. Believing they are under orders from Sarin, they are in pursuit of the fugitives. A number of my warriors accompanied them. They will endure a few uncomfortable days in the mountains before being led back to Percheron by a different route.'

'And Sarin?' Rianna pressed, realising uneasily that

she barely knew Danara at all. She had never expected any of this.

'I intend to keep him here as my personal slave, and give him a taste of the pain and misery he has dealt out to so many others,' Danara smiled cruelly. 'I'm looking forward to the challenge. He was so proud and arrogant last night. To see him cowering naked at my feet will be most invigorating.' She took Rianna's arm and led her back to the bed. 'Sleep a while longer, we can talk more later.'

'I cannot sleep now. If Sarin and his soldiers are no longer a threat, I'd like to see Tarn.'

Danara frowned and shook her head. 'That would not be convenient. Tarn is required elsewhere at present.'

'Doing what?' Rianna queried.

Danara smiled. 'You recall, you promised me that if I helped you escape Sarin's clutches, you would stay here with me. Tarn can never be anything but a slave in Freygard. So I've assigned him to the position he is best suited for. He will spend his days in the coupling chambers. At present he's most probably servicing one of my warriors.'

The colour drained from Rianna's face. 'You cannot do this . . .'

'I can, and I have,' Danara replied, unconcerned by Rianna's distress. 'Tarn's seed will provide my women with many fine offspring. The seed of our slaves has grown weak of late.'

'I will not remain here with you if you force Tarn to endure slavery. I'll leave,' Rianna threatened, suddenly realising that there was no sign of her clothes.

'I was not entirely sure you'd keep your promise.' Danara narrowed her eyes and stared at Rianna. 'So I took the precaution of removing all your garments to allow you time to consider your position. Remember, Rianna, I am the Queen and you will do as I say. You may be interested to know that Tarn does not appear unhappy with his new position. The warriors he has serviced so far seem very satisfied. He'll be in great demand.'

'How can you cause me so much pain, Danara?' Rianna asked unhappily. 'We are kin.'

'And you are too trusting of others, Rianna.' Danara moved to the door, but before she could leave, another woman entered the room. 'Cousin,' Danara said uneasily, 'I understood you were leaving.'

'I was,' Kitara said coldly. 'Until I discovered how much you'd deceived me.' She swept past Danara, then paused uncertainly as she caught sight of Rianna.

'Mother!' Rianna gasped in bewilderment. 'This cannot be!'

Sarin paced the room in frustrated fury, his only covering the sheet he'd pulled from the bed to wrap around himself. When he had awakened this morning he had found the door of his chamber locked and his clothing gone. Now he was hungry, thirsty and filled with so much anger he could scarcely contain himself.

As he heard the rattle of the latch, he turned to face the door. 'What is happening?' he blazed as he saw Danara enter, accompanied by three of her warriors.

'Have you not realised by now that you're a prisoner?' she mocked.

'Prisoner,' he hissed. 'How dare you. I'm the Lord of Percheron.'

'I dare,' Danara replied boldly. 'Your soldiers are gone. You're here alone and unprotected, Sarin.'

'Gone?' he grated, trying to hide his growing concern. 'That cannot be.'

'The main body of troops left here believing they were under your orders to continue in their pursuit of the fugitives,' she replied with a cold smile. 'While Cador and the rest of your men have been despatched to the slave markets of Freygard.'

'Do you want war?' he asked in disbelief. 'My army will attack Freygard, decimate your lands and rescue me.'

'Somehow I doubt that,' she said, appearing uncomfortably confident. 'Soon you and the rest of your men will be leaving for Percheron. Unfortunately you will be waylaid by bandits and brutally slaughtered. My warriors will find proof of the terrible tragedy. Everyone will believe you are dead, Sarin.'

'You will never get away with this,' Sarin flared, lunging at Danara. The warriors acted swiftly, restraining him, and pulling the sheet away to leave him naked.

'Chain him,' Danara ordered. 'Fit him with the slave collar.'

Sarin struggled to resist, but the women were far too strong. In a matter of moments he was kneeling in front of Danara, a thick leather collar fastened around his neck, his wrist chained behind his back. 'I'll never be a slave,' he yelled furiously.

'Perhaps a demonstration is in order.'

Danara nodded to the warriors, who dragged Sarin over to a heavy oak chest and pushed him forward so that he was half-lying across it. He went to move but gave a groan of anguish instead, as the sharp sting of the lash seared his shoulders. Another cruel blow followed, then another, criss-crossing his back. The lash moved lower as Danara began to concentrate the blows on his buttocks. Sarin felt as though his body was a mass of stinging agony; he had never known such pain.

The red lash marks stood out starkly against his olive skin. He shivered as Danara pulled back his head and stared into his eyes. 'Take your time, slave. I enjoying beating you into subservience,' she said with a cruel smile.

She pushed him down against the chest and resumed the beating. This time she used the lash more carefully. With each successive blow the fine leather strands curved around his hip to painfully caress the side of his stomach. Sarin drew in his breath, caging his groan of agony, fearing the whip would catch his sex. Sweat ran down his neck and pooled under his armpits. He pressed his thighs, slippery with perspiration, close together. For the first time in his life he recognised fear, but there was another emotion simmering inside him. The dark side of his personality, the part that revelled in causing others pain, recognised that same submissive need in himself. His fear consumed him, while he became more and more aroused.

Each stinging starburst of agony magnified the glowing heat in his buttocks. It spread like a creeping flame deep into the pit of his belly, increasing into a lustful inferno. The wanting, the dark need, grew in him. He felt his penis harden and his balls contract.

At the next stroke, he pressed his hips closer to the hard wooden chest, wanting to place pressure on his engorged cock. Sarin groaned, almost welcoming the pain of the blows now, as his arousal increased. His back and buttocks felt sore and abused, while his sex screamed for its release.

The lash curved round his buttocks again, the fine strands just stroking the soft skin of his balls. Sarin gave a harsh, sobbing groan, and moved his hips, trying to rub the stem of his manhood against the wooden chest. He strained for his release but the pleasure eluded him. Sarin moved his hips in a jerky, rocking movement, now agonisingly close to fulfilment. He awaited the next painful caress of the whip as he reached desperately for his climax. Instead, he felt hands grab hold of his abused shoulders and swing him around to face Danara.

She smiled derisively as she glanced down at his engorged member. It stood stiffly out from his belly, the swollen head moist and inviting. 'Leave,' she told her warriors. As they departed, she looked back at Sarin. 'So you crave pain, slave. It excites your senses.'

'No,' he denied, his eyes full of angry resentment. 'I will find a way to destroy you, Danara.'

'Will you?' she laughed throatily. 'I am willing to wager that I will destroy you first.'

She pulled open her loose robe. Sarin stared in surprise at her full breasts, their nipples imprisoned by decorative clamps. The desire in his loins surged excitedly into life again. He could smell her sweet, musky odour, see the thick pelt of auburn hair that covered her sex. He had desired her when he had first laid eyes on her, this warrior Queen who despised men, and took her pleasure only with her own sex.

'Now crawl forward and pleasure me with your mouth,' she ordered.

The fire in Sarin's belly increased, magnified by the sweet submissive lust her presence aroused in him. 'If I refuse?'

'Then I'll beat you again, this time without any mercy. You'll soon learn to obey me, slave.'

She parted her thighs as he crawled forward on his knees until he was crouching between her legs. As he looked up at her vulva she used her fingers to peel apart her labial lips. Her sex unfolded like the petals of a rose, pink, sweet-smelling and so inviting. Lifting his head, Sarin took the first tentative taste of her sex.

Tarn turned his head as he heard the door of the coupling chamber open. 'Come with me,' said the slave mistress sternly.

'Is Lord Sarin still in the castle?' Tarn asked anxiously, as she took hold of his arm and marched him out of the slave quarters and across the bailey. 'One of the other slaves told me he had arrived, along with a large troop of soldiers.'

'Matters such as that are not your concern, slave,' she replied curtly, then her manner softened. 'You perform your tasks well, Tarn. Most slaves only manage one coupling a night. If you carry on like this you will doubtless be rewarded.' She glanced towards him. 'Do you see any soldiers, here? No, you do not, because they departed early this morning. Queen Danara is not expecting them to return. Does that satisfy your curiosity, slave?'

'Thank you, mistress,' Tarn said politely, thinking that even the warriors of Freygard responded better to honeyed sweetness than to bitter aloes. 'Could I also enquire if Lady Rianna is still in the castle?

'You ask too many questions,' she said, her cold manner returning.

'So I cannot ask you where we are bound?' he pressed with caution.

She gave an irritated grunt and tightened her hold on his arm. 'Quiet,' she snapped.

The castle was almost deserted; just a few male slaves hurried along the wide corridors, too busy to even bother glancing at Tarn. They had just walked through the great hall when Tarn caught sight of a strikingly beautiful woman, who had a strong resemblance to Rianna. As he passed, she paused to stare thoughtfully at him, and when he glanced back at her she rewarded him with a warm smile. Wondering who she was, he accompanied the slave mistress up the stairs.

She led Tarn to a luxuriously appointed chamber. 'You are to wait here,' the slave mistress said. 'When your new mistress appears you are to do exactly as she orders.'

'New mistress!' Tarn exclaimed. 'How can that be?'

'So many questions,' she chided with a soft chuckle. 'Contain your curiosity, you will learn everything in the fullness of time.'

She left the room. Tarn waited for a few minutes. When no one put in an appearance, he stepped over to the window. He could just see over the battlements. Tarn stared at the thick forest, and high mountain peaks reaching up into the clear blue sky. Freedom beckoned him. Now that Sarin had departed, he must try to somehow see Rianna and plot their escape.

Hearing the soft rustle of silk, he turned. 'Rianna,' he gasped in surprise. 'They've not harmed you?' he added worriedly.

'I should ask you that question, my love.' She ran to him and flung herself into his arms. 'I was so concerned.'

Tarn held her close, never wanting to let her go. 'When I heard that Sarin had arrived at the castle, I feared the worst,' he said, pressing his face to her sweet-smelling hair.

'Sarin need never trouble us again,' she told him. 'So many things have happened, I have so much to tell you.'

'Later,' he whispered, capturing her lips with his. Tarn kissed her passionately, trying to convey the full depth of his emotion in that one kiss.

Breathlessly, she pulled away from him. 'We should talk.'

'In a moment,' he murmured.

Rianna gave a soft laugh as he lifted her into his arms and carried her towards the bed. 'So eager, my love.'

'I need you now,' he groaned, as he pushed aside the skirts of her pink silk gown and pressed his face to her pubis. He rubbed his cheek against the prickling softness where her red-gold curls were starting to grow again. 'Soon your glorious fleece will return. Promise me you'll never remove it again.'

'I promise,' she whispered, tensing her belly and pushing her hips towards him as he eased open her thighs. 'It seems so long since we lay together.'

'A lifetime.' Tarn kissed her sex, burying his lips deep in her vulva. It was hot, moist and wanting, eager to feel his hard, male flesh piercing its delicious folds.

Tarn pressed the tip of his tongue against her flesh hood, rubbing it backwards and forwards, further inflaming the bud beneath. He closed his lips around that sweet centre of existence, pulling it into his mouth and sucking on it gently until it grew into a firm, rosy pearl. She moaned with bliss as he slid his tongue into her vagina and caressed her silken sheath.

Tarn felt her flesh tremble beneath the merciless onslaught of his lips. 'Tarn,' Rianna gasped, as she meshed her hands in his hair. 'I need to feel you thrusting deep inside me.'

Lifting his head he smiled at her. 'How can I refuse you anything?' he teased.

With one swift movement, he grabbed hold of her hips and slid his engorged member deep inside her. Savouring the warm wetness as her silken valley embraced his penis, Tarn thrust into her, filled with an overwhelming need for the only woman he truly wanted. She was the most beautiful, the most desirable creature that ever walked the earth.

He drew the scent of her deep into his lungs, felt the smooth softness of her flesh beneath his roving fingertips, and knew without a doubt she meant more to him than life itself. Wanting to give her even more pleasure, he altered the angle and pace of his movements, ensuring that with each thrust his hard shaft tantalisingly caressed the bud of her clitoris. Shuddering with ecstasy, she pulled his face towards her and took possession of his lips. Rianna pushed her tongue into his mouth, employing the same seductive rhythm as the movement of his cock invading her vagina.

Tarn's pleasure peaked swiftly. He tried to hold back, but it was beyond his control.

'Forgive me,' he groaned, as his climax overwhelmed him. As he spilt his seed, he felt her vagina pulse, and saw her face tense in an expression of sublime anguish as her climax came.

After the strong pulsing had ebbed away, Tarn looked down at his beloved. Rianna smiled with serene contentment. He had never seen her look more glorious; her ivory limbs splayed across the coverlet, her red-gold curls surrounding her like a glowing halo, her green eyes looking lovingly up at him.

'Now, Tarn,' she said softly. 'We will be together forever.'

The group of travellers left the castle, descending into the valley on the road that eventually led to Harn. At the base of the steep slope, Rianna stopped her mount beside Tarn's and looked back at the castle.

'I almost pity Sarin,' she said thoughtfully.

'He deserves every wretched moment of his slavery,' Tarn said. 'You are too forgiving, my love.'

'Maybe so, but I feel magnanimous at this moment in

time. I have much to be thankful for.' She looked over at Gerek, who appeared happier than he had for years as he smiled at his wife, Kitara.

Kitara was returning with them to Harn. She could not forgive Danara for deceiving her, and failing to tell her of Rianna's presence in the castle. Kitara would never have known if it had not been for a close friend, who disobeyed Danara's orders and sent an urgent message to her. Kitara, as the Queen's cousin, had much influence in Freygard. When she had demanded that Danara release Gerek and Rianna, the Queen had been unable to refuse her request. After that it had been all too easy for Rianna to persuade her mother to use her influence to also obtain Tarn's release.

'So have I,' Tarn grinned. 'With Sarin no longer Lord of Percheron, and with your father's backing, it will prove easy for me to regain my rightful position in Kabra.'

'I cannot conceive how mother managed to persuade Danara to ally herself with my father. Once you are on the throne of Kabra, our lands can be at peace. Percheron will no longer be able to threaten yours or my father's sovereignty.' Rianna reached for Tarn's hand. 'So it is finished,' she said, turning her back on the castle and all those contained therein.

'No,' he smiled lovingly at her. 'It is only just beginning. Now we have the rest of our lives to be together.'

# BLACK LACE NEW BOOKS

*Published in April*

## PLEASURE'S DAUGHTER
### Sedalia Johnson
### £5.99

1750, England. After the death of her father, headstrong young Amelia goes to live with her wealthy relatives. During the journey she meets the cruel Marquess of Beechwood, who both excites and frightens her. She escapes from him only to discover later that he is a good friend of her aunt and uncle. The Marquess pursues her ruthlessly, and persuades her uncle to give him her hand – but Amelia escapes and runs away to London. She takes up residence in an establishment dedicated to the pleasure of the feminine senses, where she becomes expert in every manner of debauch, and is happy with her new life until the Marquess catches up with her and demands that they renew their marriage vows.

ISBN 0 352 33237 9

## AN ACT OF LOVE
### Ella Broussard
### £5.99

In order to be accepted at drama school, Gina has to be in a successful theatrical production. She joins the cast for a play which is being financed by kinky control freak, Charles Sarazan, who begins to pursue Gina. She is more attracted to Matt, one of the actors in the play, but finds it difficult to approach him, especially after she sees Persis, the provocative female lead, making explicit advances to him. Gina learns that Charles is planning to sabotage the production so that he can write it off as a tax loss. Can she manage to satisfy both her craving for success and her lust for the leading man?

ISBN 0 352 33240 9

*To be published in May*

## SAVAGE SURRENDER
### Deanna Ashford
### £5.99

In the kingdom of Harn, a marriage is arranged between the beautiful Rianna and Lord Sarin, ruler of the rival kingdom of Percheron, who is noted for his voracious sexual appetite. On her way to Percheron, Rianna meets a young nobleman who has been captured by Sarin's brutal guards. Their desire for each other is instant but can Rianna find a way to save her young lover without causing unrest between the kingdoms?

ISBN 0 352 33253 0

## THE SEVEN-YEAR LIST
### Zoe le Verdier
### £5.99

Julie – an ambitious young photographer – is invited to a college reunion just before she is due to be married. She cannot resist a final fling but finds herself playing a dangerous erotic game with a man who still harbours desires for her. She tries to escape a circle of betrayal and lust but her old flame will not let her go. Not until he has completed the final goal on his seven-year list.

ISBN 0 352 33254 9

*To be published in June*

## MASQUE OF PASSION
### Tesni Morgan
### £5.99

Lisa is a spirited fine-arts graduate who is due to marry her wealthy fiancé in a matter of weeks. As the day draws closer, she's having second thoughts, though, especially as her husband-to-be is dismissive of both her growing antiques business and her sexual needs. The rural English village where Lisa lives is home to some intriguing bohemian characters, including the gorgeous David Maccabene. When David introduces Lisa to kinky ways of loving, her life is set to change in more ways than she can imagine.

ISBN 0 352 33259 X

## CIRCO EROTICA
### Mercedes Kelly
£5.99

Flora is a beautiful lion-tamer in a Mexican circus. She inhabits a curious and colourful world of trapeze artists, snake charmers and hypnotists. But when her father dies, owing a large sum of money to the dastardly Lorenzo, the circus owner, Flora's routine is set to change. Lorenzo and his perverse female accomplice, Salome, share a powerful sexual hunger and a taste for bizarre adult fun. They lure Flora into their games of decadence. Can she escape? Will she even want to?

ISBN 0 352 33257 3

## COOKING UP A STORM
### Emma Holly
£7.99

Abby owns a restaurant in Cape Cod but business is not booming. Then, suddenly, someone new comes into her life: a handsome chef with a recipe for success. He puts together an aphrodisiac menu that the patrons won't be able to resist. But can this playboy-chef really save the day when Abby's body means more to him than her heart? He's charming the pants off her and she's behaving like a wild woman. Can Abby tear herself away from her object of desire long enough to see what's going on?

ISBN 0 352 33258 1

*Special announcement!*

## WOMEN, SEX & ASTROLOGY
### Sarah Bartlett
£5.99

Here's a first from Black Lace: an astrology book which is exclusively about sex and desire. You can draw up your own, unique erotic chart and check your compatibility with other signs and find out what turns you and your partner on. Sarah Bartlett uses a potent mixture of astrology, mythology and psychology to create an easy-to-use workbook which will reveal your deepest desires. If you have ever wanted to know how the planets affect your sexual psyche, look no further than this book.

ISBN 0 352 33262 X

If you would like a complete list of plot summaries of Black Lace titles, please fill out the questionnaire overleaf or send a stamped addressed envelope to:-

Black Lace, 332 Ladbroke Grove, London W10 5AH

## BLACK LACE BOOKLIST

All books are priced £4.99 unless another price is given.

**Black Lace books with a contemporary setting**

| | | |
|---|---|---|
| ODALISQUE | Fleur Reynolds<br>ISBN 0 352 32887 8 | ☐ |
| VIRTUOSO | Katrina Vincenzi<br>ISBN 0 352 32907 6 | ☐ |
| THE SILKEN CAGE | Sophie Danson<br>ISBN 0 352 32928 9 | ☐ |
| RIVER OF SECRETS | Saskia Hope &<br>  Georgia Angelis<br>ISBN 0 352 32925 4 | ☐ |
| SUMMER OF<br>  ENLIGHTENMENT | Cheryl Mildenhall<br>ISBN 0 352 32937 8 | ☐ |
| MOON OF DESIRE | Sophie Danson<br>ISBN 0 352 32911 4 | ☐ |
| A BOUQUET OF BLACK<br>  ORCHIDS | Roxanne Carr<br>ISBN 0 352 32939 4 | ☐ |
| THE TUTOR | Portia Da Costa<br>ISBN 0 352 32946 7 | ☐ |
| THE HOUSE IN NEW<br>  ORLEANS | Fleur Reynolds<br>ISBN 0 352 32951 3 | ☐ |
| WICKED WORK | Pamela Kyle<br>ISBN 0 352 32958 0 | ☐ |
| DREAM LOVER | Katrina Vincenzi<br>ISBN 0 352 32956 4 | ☐ |
| UNFINISHED BUSINESS | Sarah Hope-Walker<br>ISBN 0 352 32983 1 | ☐ |
| THE DEVIL INSIDE | Portia Da Costa<br>ISBN 0 352 32993 9 | ☐ |
| HEALING PASSION | Sylvie Ouellette<br>ISBN 0 352 32998 X | ☐ |
| THE STALLION | Georgina Brown<br>ISBN 0 352 33005 8 | ☐ |

- - - - - - ✂ - - - - - - - - - - - - - - - - - -

Please send me the books I have ticked above.

Name      ......................................................

Address   ......................................................

                 ......................................................

                 ......................................................

         ................... Post Code    ...................

Send to: **Cash Sales, Black Lace Books, 332 Ladbroke Grove, London W10 5AH, UK.**

US customers: for prices and details of how to order books for delivery by mail, call 1-800-805-1083.

Please enclose a cheque or postal order, made payable to **Virgin Publishing Ltd**, to the value of the books you have ordered plus postage and packing costs as follows:

UK and BFPO – £1.00 for the first book, 50p for each subsequent book.

Overseas (including Republic of Ireland) – £2.00 for the first book, £1.00 each subsequent book.

If you would prefer to pay by VISA or ACCESS/MASTERCARD, please write your card number and expiry date here:

..............................................................

Please allow up to 28 days for delivery.

**Signature**    ......................................................

- - - - - - ✂ - - - - - - - - - - - - - - - - - -

*WE NEED YOUR HELP . . .*
*to plan the future of women's erotic fiction –*

*– and no stamp required!*

Yours are the only opinions that matter.

Black Lace is the first series of books devoted to erotic fiction by women for women.

We intend to keep providing the best-written, sexiest books you can buy. And we'd appreciate your help and valued opinion of the books so far. Tell us what you want to read.

---

# THE BLACK LACE QUESTIONNAIRE

## SECTION ONE: ABOUT YOU

1.1  Sex (*we presume you are female, but so as not to discriminate*)
Are you?
Male                          ☐
Female                        ☐

1.2  Age
under 21        ☐        21–30          ☐
31–40           ☐        41–50          ☐
51–60           ☐        over 60        ☐

1.3  At what age did you leave full-time education?
still in education    ☐    16 or younger    ☐
17–19                 ☐    20 or older      ☐

1.4  Occupation _____

1.5 Annual household income _____

1.6 We are perfectly happy for you to remain anonymous;
but if you would like to receive information on other
publications available, please insert your name and
address

_____

_____

_____

_____

## SECTION TWO: ABOUT BUYING BLACK LACE BOOKS

2.1 Where did you get this copy of *Savage Surrender*?
    Bought at chain book shop ☐
    Bought at independent book shop ☐
    Bought at supermarket ☐
    Bought at book exchange or used book shop ☐
    I borrowed it/found it ☐
    My partner bought it ☐

2.2 How did you find out about Black Lace books?
    I saw them in a shop ☐
    I saw them advertised in a magazine ☐
    I read about them in _____
    Other _____

2.3 Please tick the following statements you agree with:
    I would be less embarrassed about buying Black
    Lace books if the cover pictures were less explicit ☐
    I think that in general the pictures on Black
    Lace books are about right ☐
    I think Black Lace cover pictures should be as
    explicit as possible ☐

2.4 Would you read a Black Lace book in a public place – on
a train for instance?
    Yes ☐    No ☐

## SECTION THREE: ABOUT THIS BLACK LACE BOOK

3.1  Do you think the sex content in this book is:
        Too much             ☐     About right         ☐
        Not enough       ☐

3.2  Do you think the writing style in this book is:
        Too unreal/escapist   ☐     About right         ☐
        Too down to earth    ☐

3.3  Do you think the story in this book is:
        Too complicated      ☐     About right         ☐
        Too boring/simple    ☐

3.4  Do you think the cover of this book is:
        Too explicit          ☐     About right         ☐
        Not explicit enough   ☐

Here's a space for any other comments:

___

## SECTION FOUR: ABOUT OTHER BLACK LACE BOOKS

4.1  How many Black Lace books have you read?       ☐

4.2  If more than one, which one did you prefer?

___

4.3  Why?

# SECTION FIVE: ABOUT YOUR IDEAL EROTIC NOVEL

We want to publish the books you want to read – so this is your chance to tell us exactly what your ideal erotic novel would be like.

5.1 Using a scale of 1 to 5 (1 = no interest at all, 5 = your ideal), please rate the following possible settings for an erotic novel:

Medieval/barbarian/sword 'n' sorcery ☐
Renaissance/Elizabethan/Restoration ☐
Victorian/Edwardian ☐
1920s & 1930s – the Jazz Age ☐
Present day ☐
Future/Science Fiction ☐

5.2 Using the same scale of 1 to 5, please rate the following themes you may find in an erotic novel:

Submissive male/dominant female ☐
Submissive female/dominant male ☐
Lesbianism ☐
Bondage/fetishism ☐
Romantic love ☐
Experimental sex e.g. anal/watersports/sex toys ☐
Gay male sex ☐
Group sex ☐

5.3 Using the same scale of 1 to 5, please rate the following styles in which an erotic novel could be written:

Realistic, down to earth, set in real life ☐
Escapist fantasy, but just about believable ☐
Completely unreal, impressionistic, dreamlike ☐

5.4 Would you prefer your ideal erotic novel to be written from the viewpoint of the main male characters or the main female characters?

Male ☐ Female ☐
Both ☐

5.5 What would your ideal Black Lace heroine be like? Tick as many as you like:

| | | | |
|---|---|---|---|
| Dominant | ☐ | Glamorous | ☐ |
| Extroverted | ☐ | Contemporary | ☐ |
| Independent | ☐ | Bisexual | ☐ |
| Adventurous | ☐ | Naïve | ☐ |
| Intellectual | ☐ | Introverted | ☐ |
| Professional | ☐ | Kinky | ☐ |
| Submissive | ☐ | Anything else? | ☐ |
| Ordinary | ☐ | _____ | |

5.6 What would your ideal male lead character be like? Again, tick as many as you like:

| | | | |
|---|---|---|---|
| Rugged | ☐ | | |
| Athletic | ☐ | Caring | ☐ |
| Sophisticated | ☐ | Cruel | ☐ |
| Retiring | ☐ | Debonair | ☐ |
| Outdoor-type | ☐ | Naïve | ☐ |
| Executive-type | ☐ | Intellectual | ☐ |
| Ordinary | ☐ | Professional | ☐ |
| Kinky | ☐ | Romantic | ☐ |
| Hunky | ☐ | | |
| Sexually dominant | ☐ | Anything else? | ☐ |
| Sexually submissive | ☐ | _____ | |

5.7 Is there one particular setting or subject matter that your ideal erotic novel would contain?

_____

## SECTION SIX: LAST WORDS

6.1 What do you like best about Black Lace books?

_____

6.2 What do you most dislike about Black Lace books?

_____

6.3 In what way, if any, would you like to change Black Lace covers?

_____

6.4   Here's a space for any other comments:

_____
_____
_____
_____

_____

*Thank you for completing this questionnaire. Now tear it out of the book – carefully! – put it in an envelope and send it to:*

> **Black Lace**
> **FREEPOST**
> **London**
> **W10 5BR**

*No stamp is required if you are resident in the U.K.*